"WHAT HAPPENS WHEN YOU GO TRAIPSING HALFWAY ACROSS THE CONTINENT ON ONE OF YOUR ASSIGNMENTS?"

"That's the hazard of my profession," he said with a shrug. "But I always return, my dear. And don't speak too soon...you may be sent off somewhere, as well. Godey often sends his writers to Paris, for fashion shows and the like."

She stiffened at the note of condescension in his voice. "Naturally, that is not as important as some war or other equally violent event!"

"Jemina..." He sighed heavily. "You are so infernally sensitive! You couldn't very well be sent off to cover a war, for two reasons. First, the *Lady Book* does not report on wars, or anything of a violent nature. Secondly, you are a woman."

Jemina's temper was still running, and for the moment, she was tempted to ask him why a woman could not report on a war, but then she decided it would be a mistake.

"All right, Mr. Thursday, you report on your battles, and I shall content myself with less violent matters."

Thursday and the Lady

PATRICIA MATTHEWS

Thursday and the Lady

WORLDWIDE®

TORONTO • NEW YORK • LONDON • PARIS
AMSTERDAM • STOCKHOLM • HAMBURG
ATHENS • MILAN • TOKYO • SYDNEY

THURSDAY AND THE LADY

A Worldwide Library book/November 1987

ISBN 0-373-97047-3

With love and affection to Jay Garon, friend and agent *extraordinaire*, who suggested the background of *Godey's Lady's Book* for *Thursday and the Lady*.

"It has been our constant aim to guide our...readers aright in their choice of literary amusement. That we do not condemn novel-reading as utterly useless, if not utterly bad, is true; but we truly hold that this 'delight' or amusement should be guided by wise principles of selection, and regulated by the sense of duty which, as accountable beings, should govern all our doings."

—*Godey's Lady's Book*

Prologue

THE AIR IN THE basement room on Hester Street was stifling, and a blazing grate of glowing flatirons added to the sultry summer heat.

Although the air was still, tiny bits of recently snipped cloth and thread floated into every nook and cranny; and these almost invisible particles clogged Jemina Benedict's nostrils. Some of the women claimed they'd become accustomed to it, but Jemina, who had been working in the shirt-making factory for a week, was convinced that she would never grow used to it; just as she knew she would never adjust to the long hours bent over the worktable in the weak light, plying needle and thread until her eyes burned and her fingers grew raw and sore. Even at night, in her tiny, airless room in the shabby lodging house, she could still see the flashing needles behind her closed eyelids.

Finishing the man's shirt she was working on, Jemina straightened up to wipe the perspiration from her forehead as she gazed around the huge, gloomy room. Her glance was furtive, since it was not deemed productive for a girl to look up from her work; and production was all, at least in the shop owned by Lester Gilroy.

Bundles of cloth, to be made into men's shirts, littered the floor. The narrow basement windows were dirty, letting in little light. They were never opened, having long since been painted shut.

Gilroy's factory was called a task shop. The seamstresses were paid by the garment—twenty-five cents per shirt—and even the best seamstress among them was doing well to make a dozen shirts a week. The children who carried the bundles of cloth and finished shirts along the streets were paid even less.

The East Side of New York City was filled with task shops that manufactured various items of clothing. Gilroy alone had a half-dozen shops along Hester Street. Jemina understood that some of the other shops paid better for the piecework, but the women here were desperate enough to accept the low pay and bad working conditions. Gilroy often proclaimed that any of his seamstresses could quit anytime they wished; there were dozens eagerly waiting to take their place.

Jemina wasn't familiar with the working conditions of the other task shops, but she doubted any could be worse than Gilroy's. Lester Gilroy hired brutal overseers and employed children and less skilled women; and the working conditions were abysmal. The women grumbled privately, and many complained openly to Jemina, but only when they were away from the shop for fear they would be overheard and reported.

Truly, Lester Gilroy had earned his sobriquet of America's premier exploiter of the working woman.

"Ida!"

For a moment Jemina did not respond to the summons. She had forgotten that she was using the name Ida Morgan.

"Ida! You'd better get back to work. Bully's coming."

It was May Carter, the seamstress at the table next to Jemina's. Bully was Bert Conroe, the overseer, who delighted in catching a girl "idling" so he could chastise her severely or discharge her if he considered the infraction sufficiently grave.

Jemina turned hastily back to her work.

Just as she bent to her task, a voice called out harshly, "You, there! I want a word with you."

Jemina turned about to see who was being hailed and saw Lester Gilroy and Bert Conroe hurrying toward her.

His face set in a fierce scowl, Gilroy halted before her worktable. "I've finally remembered where I've seen you before. Your name ain't Ida Morgan, it's Jemina something or other!"

Jemina faced the shop owner with a sinking heart. She had been warned that Gilroy was dangerous and that she was putting herself in jeopardy by coming here.

"You're here under false pretenses, girl," Gilroy growled, "and I aim to find out the reason why."

Jemina glanced around the room and immediately realized that she would receive no help from the others. They were staring at her with frightened, white faces.

"You come along with me," Gilroy said with a curt gesture. "Now!"

BOOK I

"In the last 'Table' we gave an excellent
'letter,' setting forth the benefits of
'Household Work.' It will, we are sure, be
approved by thoughtful men as well as our
constant readers—the best and kindest
women in the land. There is need of keeping
this subject before public sympathy till it
shall become the universal heart-feeling that
women, who are obliged to support
themselves, shall have the opportunity of
finding employment."

—*Godey's Lady's Book*

Chapter One

"THAT BLASTED WOMAN!" Henry Benedict said angrily.

A little startled at this unusual outburst from her father, Jemina glanced up from her book.

Across from her, Beth Benedict looked up from her sewing to stare at her husband. "What woman is that, dear?"

"Sarah Josepha Hale," Henry Benedict growled. Spectacles sliding down his rather prominent nose, he waved the magazine he had been reading. "And this publication, *Godey's Lady's Book*. It should not be allowed in decent, Christian households! Some of the things she publishes are downright seditious!"

"But, Henry, that magazine is very popular. I understand it has a very large circulation. All the best people read it."

"All the more reason it should be banned. Publishing scandalous articles, corrupting the minds of innocent women! I read that Sarah Hale once said husbands may rest assured that nothing found in the pages of her magazine would cause the wife 'to be less assiduous in preparing for his reception or cause her to usurp station or encroach on the prerogatives of men.' Hah! The woman is a liar. If she were a man, she would be called out!"

"But it *is* published for women, dear," his wife said mildly. "Why are you reading it?"

"Because I have a duty both as a husband and a father to be aware of the contents of publications read in my household."

Jemina felt compelled to speak up, even though she knew it would annoy her father. "I think Mrs. Hale is a fine woman, Father, an example to us all. She is intelligent, a good editor, and she expounds causes that should be supported by all women."

Her father's florid face reddened even further as he glared at her. "You think that, do you? I suppose you've been reading this penny-dreadful trash?"

"I have," Jemina said composedly. "And it is not trash, Father. The articles and stories Mrs. Hale publishes are well written and thought provoking, not at all like those published in some magazines and newspapers that strive for sensationalism."

"I suppose you don't consider screaming for women to be admitted to medical school scandalous? And I suppose that her insidious campaign to woo women away from wearing corsets is not sensationalism?"

"Why shouldn't women be allowed to practice medicine, Father? At least half of a doctor's patients are women. As for Mrs. Hale advocating that women cease wearing corsets, I fully agree with her that the tight waist lacing is injurious to one's health, leading to the vapors and frequent swooning in the female. In my opinion, corsets are not only uncomfortable and hateful, they are unnecessary."

"Unnecessary, are they?" Henry Benedict appealed to his wife. "You see, Beth, what thoughts this magazine puts into our daughter's head?" His voice rose. "I'll tell you why they are necessary, young lady! Corsets preserve the female decorum. I forbid you to read this publication again!'' He slapped the magazine against the arm of his chair.

Jemina's head went back. ''You cannot forbid me, Father. I am twenty-two and shall read anything I wish.''

''You are my daughter, and so long as you live in my house, you will do as I say!'' her father said explosively. ''As for this damnable magazine, I shall cancel the subscription at once!''

''That won't stop me from reading it, Father,'' she said serenely. ''All newsdealers have copies for sale.''

''I forbid you to buy it, do you hear? I forbid you!''

Jemina rose. ''I shall retire to my room now. Good night, Father. Good night, Mother.''

As she started out of the parlor, Henry Benedict called after her, ''I forbid you, Jemina!''

Jemina walked on, mounting the stairs to the second floor and her room. Although she had managed to maintain an unruffled exterior, she was quaking inside. Henry Benedict was afflicted with the common male intolerance toward the place of women in the world, but he was normally an even-tempered, reasonable man. Jemina could not remember seeing him quite so incensed. His fit of anger a few moments ago was not what was really bothering her; that would pass, but what would he think if he knew about the letter she had written to Sarah Josepha Hale a few days ago? He would have an apoplectic fit!

Once in her room, she walked to the window and stood looking out unseeingly at the streets of Boston's Beacon Hill. It was July 1848, and the streets swarmed with people seeking escape from the heat.

Jemina was a tall, well-developed girl, with a fine figure accentuated by the tight construction of the corset she so despised. Her long hair—so black that it seemed almost blue under certain lights—was parted in the middle, drawn down to conceal her ears and coiled in the back. Her blue eyes were intelligent and lively, set wide apart over her mother's short, slightly uptilted nose. Jemina also had her mother's rather large mouth. Her full lips were naturally red and well-defined.

There was nothing of her father in her face. In fact, Aunt Hester, her mother's sister, had once remarked, "I swear, Henry, there's nothing of you in that girl! If I didn't know my sister so well, I would have doubts about the girl's paternity."

Jemina's mouth curved in amusement at the memory. Henry Benedict had been shocked and outraged and had refused to speak to his sister-in-law for months afterward.

Of course, one had to make allowances for Hester McFee, for she was given to outrageous statements. She was pretty, bright and a trifle scatterbrained—apt to say anything that came into her head. Aunt Hester was a widow, living alone in Philadelphia, and— worst of all, as far as Henry Benedict was concerned—she *worked* for a living. She owned a millinery shop on Chestnut Street.

"Who knows what she does down there in Philadelphia?" Henry Benedict was wont to say darkly. "And working!"

But of all the many aunts and uncles on both sides of the family—some ten in all—Aunt Hester was Jemina's favorite.

Although Jemina might not have inherited any of her father's physical characteristics, she had inherited his stubbornness and inflexible will. After graduating from a finishing school in Boston last year, she had not been content to sit prettily in the front parlor to be wooed by the many suitors paraded past her by her parents. She had wanted to experience life first; perhaps get a job and work for a few years before settling down to domesticity.

"What, and be like Hester?" her father had snorted. "A woman's place is not in the working world, daughter, but in the home. It is the man's place to provide for his family, and the woman's rightful duty to stay in that home and tend to the needs of the family."

Jemina had known the futility of debating the issue with her father, but she could resist in one way—she spurned every suitor provided. Thank goodness, she thought, the world had advanced far enough that a daughter could no longer be married off against her wishes!

Henry Benedict had been baffled. "What's wrong with you, Jemina? Those young men are from Boston's finest families, all highly eligible. Most young women would be delighted at the thought of marrying any one of them."

"Then let those young women marry them, Father," she had retorted.

The other thing that she knew baffled her father was her obsession with literature. To his way of thinking, Jemina's constant reading was unhealthy. He could never understand why she would rather be by herself with a book than doing the social rounds with her peers. Jemina knew that she would never be able to explain to him the fact that she found better company in books than in the daughters and sons of

her parents' friends, most of whom she considered
shallow and vapid.

She had never cared much for social chitchat or for
the game playing that appeared to be a necessary part
of the social scene. She often dreamed of meeting
people she could really talk with, people who were
thoughtful and intelligent, writers, artists—people
who created, who did interesting things.

Also, although she had never spoken of this to a
soul, she harbored the secret dream that she might
someday become a writer herself.

Then, about six months ago, her mother had
started subscribing to *Godey's Lady's Book*. At the
window, Jemina laughed quietly to herself; it had
taken her father quite a while to discover what had
been right under his nose all the time.

Jemina had read every issue of the magazine from
cover to cover, and she had been particularly struck
by the fact that the editor was a woman, Sarah Josepha Hale. She became very curious about Mrs. Hale
and longed to know how a woman had come to hold
such an important post.

Frustrated at every turn, she had finally written to
Hester McFee in Philadelphia, and Aunt Hester had
replied by return post, telling Jemina what she knew
of Sarah Hale. Jemina found the information fascinating, and she saw many parallels between her own
life and Sarah Hale's. Mrs. Hale was also a New
Englander, born and raised in New Hampshire, and
she had waited until she was twenty-five before she
had married. After her husband's sudden death,
which left her destitute with five children to raise, she
had tried various means to earn her livelihood. Finally she had tried her hand at writing, progressing

from sentimental poetry to a novel, *Northwood*, which was well received when it was published.

The reception of her novel had led to Sarah's being offered the editorship of the *Ladies' Magazine*, a new publication exclusively for women. She accepted the post and was very successful at it; so successful, in fact, that Louis Godey, publisher of a rival magazine, tried to woo her away. Sarah refused; the *Ladies' Magazine* had given her an opportunity granted to few women, and she was fiercely loyal. In the end, Godey went so far as to buy out the *Ladies' Magazine*, merging it with *Godey's Lady's Book*; and thus Sarah had attained her present position.

"And that, dear Jemina, is about the extent of my knowledge," Aunt Hester had written. "I did meet Mrs. Hale at a social function here. I may tell you that I find her an intelligent, energetic, well-spoken woman.

"You did not tell me the reason for your interest in Mrs. Hale, and I must admit to a burning curiosity. So much so that I shall journey to Boston a week hence and learn firsthand what you have in that lively mind of yours. It is, I strongly suspect, something that your sterling father would very much disapprove of. Do not be concerned, I shall be the soul of discretion. Your loving aunt, Hester."

HESTER MCFEE HAD ARRIVED like a force of nature, moving like a fresh breeze through the Benedict household in her outrageous chapeau, gaiter boots and kid gloves and flourishing a fashionable parasol like a banner. As soon as he could, Henry Benedict retreated to his study and locked himself in.

Hester grinned at Jemina and winked. She puffed out rosy cheeks. "We can always depend on dear Henry to burrow himself away when I make a sudden appearance, can't we?"

"Now, Hester," Beth said, hiding a smile behind her hand. "That is unjust of you. Henry has work to do."

"Well, no matter. I came to visit with Jemina."

"You did?" Beth said in astonishment. "Whatever for?"

"Do not concern yourself, sister mine," Hester said airily. "After all, she is my precious niece, and we see little enough of one another, heaven knows."

She linked arms with Jemina. "Up the stairs with you, young lady."

Jemina, flustered but pleased, allowed herself to be hustled up the stairs and into her room.

Knowing how impetuous her aunt was and that it would do little good to chide her, Jemina nonetheless said, "Speaking of curiosity, you've really aroused Mother's."

"Piffle!" Hester said, waving her furled parasol. "I daresay I'm allowed to share secrets with my niece. Now! What is this about Sarah Hale?"

Jemina had given the matter considerable thought since receiving Hester's letter and had decided what she must do. "You must read something first." She went to her clothes chest and retrieved a manuscript. Silently, she held it out to her aunt.

Hester raised an eyebrow. "And what is this, pray?"

"Read it first," Jemina urged. "Then we shall talk."

Hester accepted the manuscript and seated herself on the window seat, reading quickly; but in a moment, after a surprised glance at Jemina, she read more slowly.

Finished, she rearranged the manuscript pages in her lap and stared at Jemina thoughtfully. "Well!" she said. "It appears that my niece has talent!"

Jemina felt herself flush. "Do you really think so?"

"I do indeed. I'm certainly not an editor, but I do read a great deal, and I believe that your writing is good. Good as, if not better than, much that I see published." Hester bent a thoughtful look on Jemina. "Why have you kept this a secret from me?"

"Oh, no one knew," Jemina said with a flustered gesture.

"Is this all you've written?"

"Oh, no, I have a number of other pieces in my drawer."

"Why haven't you submitted them for possible publication? Women may be barred from most professions, but there are any number of publications nowadays publishing pieces by women."

"I was afraid they wouldn't be good enough," Jemina said simply.

"That hardly sounds like the girl I thought I knew. You've never seemed lacking in confidence."

"This is different, Aunt Hester. Writing is so . . . well, so personal. It would be something like submitting a small part of myself to the world, and to be spurned would be painful."

Hester made a sound of exasperation. "My dear girl, pain is a part of life. Anytime we attempt to accomplish anything out of the ordinary, we risk being hurt."

"You're right, Aunt Hester. I know you are." Jemina began to smile. "Then perhaps you'll agree with what I've done."

Hester gazed at her suspiciously. "And what is that, pray?"

"The piece you've just read. I *have* submitted that one."

Hester broke into a grin. "You've sent it to *Godey's Lady's Book*! That's the reason you wrote to me inquiring about Sarah Hale."

"Yes, I sent the article to Mrs. Hale."

"Good for you, girl!" Hester struck the window seat a good thump with her parasol. "Good for you! Have you heard anything yet?"

"Not yet. But that's not all." Jemina reached into the drawer again. "Along with the article I sent this accompanying letter."

She handed her aunt another sheet of paper. Hester read aloud. "'Dear Mrs. Hale: I enclose the accompanying manuscript for your consideration, hoping that you will find it suitable for publication in *Godey's Lady's Book*.

"'Even if you do not find the accompanying piece suitable, I submit myself for employment by your publication. I know of your valiant efforts for the plight of womankind, and I applaud your endeavors.

"'Hopefully, you may judge my abilities from this sample of my work. I very much desire to make writing my profession and would be quite willing to serve an apprenticeship on your worthy publication, no matter how humble the position. Sincerely yrs., Jemina Benedict.'"

Hester glanced up. "Well!"

"Was it too forward?" Jemina asked anxiously.

"No, no, not at all. If a woman of our time doesn't extol her own virtues, who will do it for her? But are you really serious about seeking employment with *Godey's Lady's Book*? I admire your writing, what I've seen of it, but are you prepared to live away from home?"

"I have to get away, Aunt Hester. I am stifled here." In her agitation, Jemina began to pace. "All I am allowed to do is sit in the parlor with my hands folded, while Father marches suitors past me for inspection!"

"I know, dear girl. You think my parents didn't do the same thing?" Hester was smiling. "It makes one feel like a slave on the auction block. But there is *one* way of escaping. Marry one of them, as I did."

"I don't want that! It would be leaving one prison for another. Besides, when I do marry, I wish to do so for love, and so far I have met no man who arouses that emotion in me."

Hester nodded gravely. "I was fortunate. I was quite content and happy with my Thomas until his early death."

"Aunt Hester..." Jemina stopped pacing. "I thought that if, by some miracle, Mrs. Hale does see fit to employ me, I might live with you in Philadelphia. Or perhaps that would be too much of an imposition?"

"Not at all, Jemina." Hester got to her feet to take Jemina's hand in hers. "I would dearly love to have you. Ofttimes I am a lonely old lady. But have you thought of Henry?"

"He won't approve; I know that."

"That is putting a mild face on it," Hester said in a dry voice. "Living away from home, and with me, will be bad enough, but working! His own daughter working!''

"I am a grown woman." Jemina stood straight. "I have reached my majority.''

"In Henry's mind, if I am any judge of the man, I doubt that any woman *ever* attains her majority.''

"He can't stop me, Aunt Hester, short of imprisoning me in my room. I am fully prepared to defy him.''

"I can see that you are." Hester regarded her approvingly. "You are indeed a grown woman." She kissed Jemina on the cheek. "And you have my wholehearted support.''

"But this may all be for nothing," Jemina said, suddenly dejected. "Mrs. Hale may think that I have no talent at all!''

THE LETTER from Sarah Hale arrived in the next day's post. "Dear Miss Benedict: I have read your submission with much interest and accept it for publication in the *Book*. If the terms are agreeable to you, a bank draft for thirty dollars will be posted to you within a few days.

"It does so happen that I have need of a new assistant; however, I will need to know more of your qualifications, and I would need to meet you in person. Would you be willing to journey to Philadelphia and submit yourself to a personal interview? Would you let me know as soon as possible. Sincerely yrs., Sarah Hale.''

Chapter Two

SARAH HALE, hands folded neatly on her desk, looked gravely at the man seated across from her.

Louis A. Godey was absorbed in reading the letter Sarah had just given him. As he read, he fingered the watch chain dangling from the pocket of his vest, which stretched tightly across the ample expanse of his chest.

Godey had a high forehead where his hair had begun to recede, and his face was plump cheeked, with lines running down to his round chin, bracketing his mouth. He was somewhat vain of his appearance, and Sarah was always amused at one sign of that vanity—the curlicue of hair at the crest of his brow. His features gave an appearance of good nature and blandness, yet Sarah well knew that there was a shrewd brain behind that open countenance.

Now Godey glanced up, his lips pursed. "I don't know, Sarah. This letter doesn't tell us much about the girl. You say that her piece was good?"

"Excellent, Louis. She has a talent, I am positive. It just needs nurturing and shaping."

"Well, far be it from me to disagree with you on that. I well know your editorial acumen. You have discovered many fine writers for the *Book*. But what does the piece tell us about her editorial ability?"

"You know my opinion on that subject, Louis. To be able to recognize fine writing, an editor should also have writing ability. I am well aware that many do not agree with me, but that is my position. I am thinking of something along the line of contributing editor for her. *If* I employ her, of course. I will not make that decision until I have talked to her at length.''

"She is coming to Philadelphia, then?''

Sarah nodded. ''Yes, today. She should be arriving shortly.''

"Then I shall leave it in your capable hands. Now...'' Godey hitched forward in his chair. ''About your article for the next issue, about this Elizabeth Blackwell person . . .''

"Person?'' Sarah made a gesture, smiling slightly. ''Come now, Louis, Miss Blackwell is a woman. Why not say so?''

"All right,'' Godey said irritably. ''This woman, then.''

"What is wrong with the article, Louis?'' Sarah asked artlessly.

"Blast it, Sarah, you know what's wrong!'' Godey grumbled. ''This business of her getting admitted to a medical college goes against all tradition, and you well know it.''

Sarah smiled gently. ''I was, in part, responsible for her being admitted.''

"I know that, also,'' Godey grumbled. ''And I was not pleased about your using the *Book* as a forum for that purpose. You know my policy against involving the *Book* in politics and controversy.''

"Yes, Louis, I am aware of your position.''

Sarah got up and turned her back on him to stare out the window onto Chestnut Street. Although she was in her sixtieth year, she had the appearance of a woman ten years or more her junior. Dressed neatly

and conservatively—except for the lack of a corset—
hers was a commanding presence. Black hair, only
lightly touched with gray, fell in ringlets almost to her
shoulders. Her face was full and round, and her dark
eyes were gentle and intelligent, yet could flash with
fire when her crusading zeal was aroused.

Now she faced about, arms crossed over her
bosom. "I fail to see how this issue involves politics
in any way."

"But it *is* an issue, you must admit. And if not
concerned with politics per se, it is most certainly
controversial. And you know my policy regarding
offending the husbands of our readers...."

"Oh, yes, Louis," she said dryly. She looked up at
the ceiling. "I wrote the editorial for you, remember? 'Husbands may rest assured that nothing found
in these pages shall cause her (the wife) to be less assiduous in preparing for his reception or cause her to
usurp station or encroach on the prerogatives of
men.'"

"Many men will interpret Miss Blackwell's admittance to a medical college as an encroachment
upon the prerogatives of the male."

"But I also wrote in that same editorial, if you will
recall, 'In this age of innovation perhaps no experi-
ment will have an influence more important on the
character and happiness of our society than the
granting to females of the advantages of a systematic
and thorough education. The honor of this triumph,
in favor of intellect over long-established prejudice,
belongs to the men of America!'"

Godey was smiling. "I well remember. That last
line was a classic example of the Sarah Hale combi-
nation of tact and flattery and helped soothe many

ruffled feathers." He became grave. "But that does not address the issue here, Sarah."

"But you have often told me that you are strongly in favor of all possible education for women!" She flung the words at him in a challenge.

"That is correct, Sarah. I do hold that personal view, but you have accomplished your purpose. Why use the *Book* to rub salt in raw wounds?"

"The *Book*, Louis, has become a powerful voice in our nation, due both to your leadership and mine."

"Again, that is correct, but not by espousing unpopular causes."

Sarah smiled faintly. "Surely you know what happens to fence straddlers, Louis, especially of the male gender."

"Sarah, that is hardly the remark of a lady." Godey got to his feet. "Now, may I assume that the issue is settled?"

"May I assume that I am free to continue supporting Elizabeth Blackwell on my own?"

"So long as it does not directly concern the *Book*, you are free to espouse any cause you desire." Now it was his turn to smile. "Besides, I well know how futile it would be for me to lay down an edict against your doing so." He dipped his large head. "I bid you good morning, Sarah."

Sarah stood smiling after her employer as he made his ponderous way out of her office. She was inordinately fond of Louis Godey and not unaware that she owed him a great debt of gratitude. In giving her editorship of such a prestigious publication and in granting her free rein most of the time, he had demonstrated his confidence in her and given her a great boon. Although she had earned that prestige and influence, Sarah knew she was the envy of many women, and she would be forever grateful to Louis Godey.

As she started back to her desk, there was a rap on the door and before she could speak, it popped open and a man's face appeared around the jamb. "Top of the morning to you, my dear. I was walking past the building and thought I'd stop in to say good-day to my one and only love."

Sarah laughed fondly. "Owen, you are such a liar and a reprobate."

"Of course I am, my dear. Have I ever denied it?"

"The last I heard you were out west somewhere, reporting on some Indian war."

Owen Thursday came into the office and perched on the edge of Sarah's desk, one elegant leg swinging. "At the moment, the Sioux have gone to ground, so I hurried back to Philadelphia. Do you realize how boring it is on the frontier when things are quiet?"

"You mean there are no young ladies to whom you may pay court?"

He made a face. "The few young ladies on the frontier not married to army officers are hardly worth a man's time."

"I didn't know you were so particular, Owen."

"Oh, but I am. Besides, I missed you, Sarah."

"I'm sure you did, you rascal," she said dryly. She studied him intently.

Owen Thursday was only in his late twenties, but he was one of the most esteemed journalists in America. He had a flair for writing, with an ability to make even a dull event sound dramatic and exciting. He was also a remarkably handsome man. Tall and slim, he had flaming red hair, with sideburns framing a rather long face. Above a noble nose were piercing blue eyes that peered out at the world with intelligence and a sardonic humor. Or rather, Sarah amended, *one* blue eye. His left eye was covered with an eye patch, which gave him a rakish air. She had heard several stories about how Owen had come to lose the eye and was never sure which tale to believe. Each time she asked Owen, he had given her a different version, so she had finally given up.

She had no idea how Owen dressed when out on an assignment, but in the city he was always nattily attired and could even, she supposed, be classified as a dandy. At the moment, he wore highly polished boots, oxblood in color, dove-colored breeches, a bull broadcloth coat and a white silken cravat. He also carried a pearl-handled walking stick, which was rumored to contain a steel blade that sprang forth from the tip at the touch of a button.

Owen noted her observation of him with an amused smile. "My dear, you're studying me as if you'd never seen me before."

"I'm always curious about current fashions, and since the *Book* specializes only in ladies' fashions, I know that I can always rely on you to be wearing the latest male attire."

"Since I have no wife or children to support and relatively few vices, I can indulge myself."

"The fact that the clothes help you to preen like a peacock has naught to do with it, I suppose?" she said in a dry voice.

"You wrong me, dear Sarah," he said airily. "And speaking of the *Book*, how does it fare?"

"Very well, thank you. According to Louis, our subscribers are rapidly approaching the one-hundred-thousand mark."

Owen raised his walking stick. "I salute you, Sarah! And your precious causes, how are they faring?"

"Also doing quite well. In April of this year, the Married Women's Property Bill was passed in New York State, which enables married women to own real estate. I take some measure of pride in that, since it was dear to my heart, and I editorialized in support of it."

Owen shook his head. "I have always admired your intelligence, courage and persistence, Sarah, so much so that it often frightens me. If you had your way, women would soon be running the world."

"That might not be as terrible as you think. It might even improve matters. I'm sure that even you will agree that the world has fared badly in the hands of men."

"If I read my history correctly, some monarchies in the past ruled by queens have been equally disastrous. I can cite you numerous examples."

"True, but a monarchy cannot be truly compared to a democratic form of government such as ours. A monarch rules supreme, with no checks and balances such as our system offers."

"Ah, dear Sarah, how well do I know the futility of debating with you." Owen stood up, smiling crookedly down at her. "I suppose next you will be endeavoring to gain women the right to vote."

"That will come," she said with a smile of her own. "Perhaps not in my time or even yours, but it will come. We deserve the same right to select our leaders as do men. Besides, as you very well know, my young friend, I have never advocated that women should have more rights than men, and I do not press for *equal* rights, as some women today are doing. I happen to think that unfeminine of them, but I do believe there are many things denied us that should be our birthright.''

''Ah, well, as I have told you, dear Sarah, I enjoy playing devil's advocate for you. Now I bid you good-day.'' With a jaunty wave of his cane, Owen Thursday strolled out of her office.

Sarah stared at the closed door with a musing smile. Devil's advocate indeed! She was fond of Owen Thursday, and she enjoyed debating with him, yet he was a man of his time. Like most males she knew, Owen believed that the rightful place for a woman was in the home, or in a man's bed, and any attempt by women to encroach in the least way upon a man's prerogatives was viewed with disapproval and often outright hostility.

Sarah sighed, shook her head to clear it of all thoughts of the journalist and returned to her work.

JEMINA WAS A FEW minutes late for her appointment with Sarah Hale. Hurrying through the door to the building housing *Godey's Lady's Book*, head down in her haste, she collided violently with a tall figure.

Knocked aside, she probably would have fallen if strong hands had not caught her. Indignantly, she knocked the hands aside and straightened her bonnet, which had been knocked askew. ''Why don't you watch where you are going . . . ?''

She broke off as she found herself staring into the deeply bronzed face of a young man. One eye was hidden by a black eye patch, and the other, a bright, light blue, blazed at her with perhaps more intensity than would have been the case had he had the use of both eyes.

The blaze *had* been of anger but was now subtly softening as he studied her features. Jemina found herself transfixed by the force of his gaze as he swept off his hat and bowed. "My most abject apologies, ma'am. I was woolgathering and failed to watch where I was going."

Jemina flushed and averted her gaze. She stammered, "No, no, I was in far too great a haste. It was my fault." Now why did I say that, she wondered; it is always the man's responsibility to avoid colliding with a lady. She hurried on, ignoring the voice calling after her.

Jemina was quickly ushered into Sarah Hale's office and introductions were made. But she was still distracted, and it must have been readily apparent, for Sarah said, "My dear, you look flushed and flustered. Surely it is not because of me? I am no ogre, I promise you. There is no need to feel intimidated."

"Oh, it's not that, Mrs. Hale," Jemina said hastily. "It's just that coming into the building I collided with some oaf and was almost knocked down. Of course, I suppose..." She was struck by a thought. "I suppose it's possible he really didn't see me, since he had only one eye."

"One eye?" Sarah leaned forward. "He wore an eye patch over his left eye?"

"Well, yes. Do you know the man?"

"Oh, yes, I know him. That was Owen Thursday, and be assured that he saw you very well indeed.

Even with one eye, Owen can spot a handsome woman quicker than most men with two.''

"Who is he?" Jemina inquired.

"Owen is a journalist for one of the largest newspapers in Philadelphia, the *Ledger*. He's quite famous, and deservedly so. He is probably one of the best journalists I know. He is honest, a fine writer and less inclined toward sensationalism than most of his brethren. He is always dashing off somewhere. He gained his greatest fame during the war with Mexico two years ago. He accompanied General Zachary Taylor, and Owen's dispatches were masterpieces."

Jemina said cautiously, "He seems to be quite a fellow."

"Oh, he is, child, he is," Sarah said with a laugh. "But be warned. He is an incorrigible womanizer. I am quite fond of the young rascal, but I would be instantly alarmed should he start paying undue attention to any young lady of my acquaintance." She broke off to study Jemina intently. "You are very lovely, my dear."

Jemina felt herself flushing. "Why, thank you, Mrs. Hale."

"It is nothing but the truth. But enough of Owen Thursday." She made a dismissive gesture. "Let us discuss the matter at hand. You are here, of course, to discuss the possibility of your employment?"

Jemina leaned forward eagerly. "Yes, Mrs. Hale."

Sarah studied the girl again. She liked what she saw. Jemina Benedict was personable, she seemed intelligent, and the sample of her writing showed great talent.

"I liked the sample of your work, but that says little of your ability as an editor," Sarah said, then smiled to take the sting from her words. "I well realize that it is only recently that women have been afforded the opportunity to take on editorial positions, which means that very few women have prior experience. But why do *you* wish to become an editor, Jemina? More specifically, why do you wish to work for our publication?"

"Because of you, Mrs. Hale, because of the things you believe in and work so diligently for. I think that *Godey's Lady's Book* does a great amount of good for the rights of women."

"I may not be here forever, Jemina, and any editor replacing me could have a different outlook on the world of women."

"You're not thinking of leaving, are you?" Jemina said in alarm.

Sarah laughed. "I have no present plans, no, but I *am* almost sixty years of age. Also, Louis Godey and I get along well together, but we do not always agree, and we're both stubborn in our ways, in our beliefs. There may well come a day when we cannot reconcile our views, and I may be forced to resign."

"I cannot believe that will ever happen. From all I have learned, it is you who are responsible for the magazine's great popularity."

Sarah nodded gravely. "I refuse to indulge in false modesty. I do credit myself with much of the *Book*'s success." She laughed suddenly. "How can I not employ someone who holds me in such high regard?" She folded her hands on the desk and became brisk. "All right, Jemina. I have already discussed your employment with Mr. Godey. I can offer you a position as contributing editor, at five hundred dollars a year. I have two assistants, full-time editors. You will work with them for a part of each week, learning the editorial trade. In addition, you will be expected to contribute to the *Book* regularly; articles assigned to you, or perhaps the development of some ideas of your own. Is that satisfactory?''

It was more than Jemina had hoped for. She said in a rush, ''Oh, yes, Mrs. Hale! And thank you!''

''Since you are to work with me, I would prefer that you call me Sarah. We are not formal here, and being called by my first name makes me feel younger. A vanity, perhaps, yet it pleases me.''

''All right . . . Sarah,'' Jemina said hesitantly. ''When shall I start?''

''Have you found quarters here in Philadelphia as yet? And is everything settled at home, in Boston?''

''I shall be living with my aunt here. As for matters at home . . .''

Sarah peered at her shrewdly. ''There was some difficulty with your parents, I imagine?''

''Yes.''

Sarah nodded. ''I think I understand. The parents of a young woman of a family of standing— which I am sure is the case, judging by the breeding and education you display—would find it difficult to comprehend why you would want to venture out into the working world.

''You may start at the beginning of next week, Jemina. We have no empty offices at this time, but you shall have your own desk. . . .''

Sarah was interrupted by a soft knock on the door. She raised her voice. ''Come in!''

A slender man with quick, graceful movements and serious brown eyes came into the office.

"Warren! I'm glad to see you," Sarah said, smiling. "You're just in time to meet the newest member of our staff, Jemina Benedict. She is to be a contributing editor. Jemina, this young man is Warren Barricone."

The newcomer bowed slightly and said in a warm voice, "I am pleased to make your acquaintance, Miss Benedict."

His face was fine boned, with a generous mouth, and he was clean shaven. Jemina thought that he had the kindest, most sensitive face of any man she had ever met. His brown eyes seemed to harbor some deep, secret sorrow.

"Warren is the head of our fashion art department," Sarah said. "We like to think here at the *Book* that we set the fashion for the ladies in the country. And if we succeed in that, most of the credit must go to Warren."

With a shy smile, Warren Barricone raked slender fingers through his long brown hair. "You flatter me, Sarah. Actually, the ladies in my department are responsible. I consider myself mostly a peacemaker. Our fashion artists are rather on the temperamental side and tend to sharp disagreements."

"Don't you believe him for an instant, Jemina," Sarah said dryly. "Many of our best ideas originate with Warren—what he doesn't filch from the designers of Paris and the other fashion centers of the world. Actually, I think one reason Warren is still with us is he gets to make yearly trips to those centers, with all expenses paid."

"Wait until you are forced to make one of those treks to Paris, Miss Benedict," Warren said. "The first time, you'll no doubt be awed. Paris, the City of

Light! But soon the trips become tedious. At any rate, welcome to the *Book*, Miss Benedict.''

He took Jemina's hand in his and raised it to his lips. Jemina was flustered by such attention. ''Th-thank you, Mr. Barricone,'' she stammered, angry at herself for her lack of professionalism. ''I've long dreamed of working here.''

''Never say that in front of Sarah. Or Mr. Godey,'' he said in mock horror. ''If they think you like working here, they'll also think that you will be willing to work from year to year without a raise in salary.''

''Of course I know you are joking, Mr. Barricone,'' Jemina said, regaining some of her composure. ''Sarah has already promised me more than I was expecting.''

Warren threw up his hands. ''You see, Sarah? You've already woven your spell. The poor girl thinks it is an honor to work here.''

''For a woman today, it is not only an honor but a rare privilege,'' Jemina retorted.

Warren bowed slightly. ''My apologies, ma'am. I see that our dear Sarah has another recruit in her camp. Get this one behind one of your causes for the fair sex, Sarah, and you've got an advantage right away.''

''I intend to do just that, Warren,'' Sarah said complacently. ''And since you seem so taken with her, why don't you show her around and introduce her to the staff?''

OWEN THURSDAY STRODE down the dark corridors of the *Philadelphia Ledger* and into the office of his editor, without knocking.

Thomas Carruthers glanced up with a scowl, which didn't fade when he saw who it was. The air in the cramped office was fouled by the smoke from the cheroot smoldering between his thick lips.

Owen said breezily, "Good day to you, Thomas."

"What the devil are you doing back from the Dakotas, Thursday? And can't you see I'm busy? We're about to put the paper to bed."

"I see your disposition hasn't improved one whit, Thomas." Owen perched on the edge of the editor's desk, swinging his cane jauntily. "And the reason I am back is that there's nothing going on out there, not a damned thing."

"Even so, I don't recollect writing you to come back," Carruthers said grumpily.

"I figured it had just slipped your mind."

"And so you took it upon yourself to return."

"That's right."

"You're our field correspondent. That's what you're paid to do, not come in here and perch on my desk like a blasted buzzard."

"But you pay me to report events. Out there, there's nothing to report. Isn't there something going on somewhere around the country?"

"Not that I know about, but give me some time. I'll think of something, you can be sure."

"Well, while you think, Thomas, I believe I'll take a holiday." Owen stood up, grinning down at the older man.

Carruthers reared back, his scowl darkening. "Just like that, *you* decide to take a holiday?"

"Why not? I'm entitled to one. It's been at least two years since I've taken time off."

Carruthers snorted softly. "You'll be bored without something happening around you. To you, excitement is like a drug."

Owen twirled his cane and said softly, "Not this time. I have something in mind." He smiled to himself. What he had in mind was the girl he'd bumped into at *Godey's Lady's Book*, the girl with the black hair and sky-blue eyes. It had been a long while since he had met a woman who so stirred his blood. He didn't know who she was, but he figured it would not be too difficult to find out; he was positive she worked for Sarah Hale.

"Then go on your holiday, and let me get back to work," Carruthers said with a flip of his hand as he bent over his desk.

Chapter Three

"AS I IMAGINE you have already gathered, Miss Benedict," Warren Barricone continued, "we have an unusually large staff."

"I have observed that, yes. And please call me Jemina."

"It shall be my pleasure, Jemina," he responded with an inclination of his head. "I like your name. But in exchange, you must call me Warren, since we shall be working together."

Warren had taken her to the editorial offices and introduced her to the staff. They were all warm and friendly, and Jemina was sure it was going to be a pleasure working with them. She had even been ushered into Louis Godey's office and introduced to the famous publisher. She found him to be a bluff but friendly man. He welcomed her to the *Book* graciously enough, but she sensed a certain reticence about him.

Now, the tour completed, they were on their way back to Sarah Hale's office when Jemina saw a man coming along the corridor from the opposite direction. He wore a slouch hat and a black cape and was skeletally thin. The skin was drawn tightly over his cheekbones, and Jemina thought that his dark eyes had a haunted look.

He paused with his hand on the doorknob to Sarah's office as they approached.

Warren said, "Mr. Poe! Is Sarah expecting you today?"

"Probably not," the man said in a tired voice, "but I do hope she can see me briefly."

"Oh, I'm sure she will," Warren said heartily. "Mr. Poe, I'd like you to meet the newest member of our staff. Jemina Benedict, meet Mr. Edgar Allan Poe."

"It is indeed my pleasure, Miss Benedict," Poe said with a dip of his head.

Jemina was thrilled and flustered. "Oh, Mr. Poe! I am an ardent reader of yours. I have read all of your novels, and I vividly recall reading 'The Cask of Amontillado' in *Godey's Lady's Book*. It was a marvelous story."

"You are most kind, ma'am."

"I think you are one of our greatest authors."

"There are some who would debate with you on that point, I fear. Now, if you will pardon me, I must show Sarah my latest effort. She remains one of the few persons still receptive to my work."

As Poe opened the door and entered Sarah's office, Warren gazed after him pensively. "Poor fellow. He's in rather bad straits. His wife, Virginia, died last year. Since then his health has deteriorated badly. If the rumors are true, he uses drugs and drinks to excess. Whatever the truth of that, he hardly earns enough from his writing nowadays to support himself."

Jemina was shocked. "But he is a well-respected author!"

"By some, perhaps." Warren turned his gaze on her. "Unfortunately, much of his writing is too dark and gloomy for many readers. In my opinion, Mr.

Poe is before his time. Perhaps his great talent will be fully appreciated one day, but not now. And in addition, as you may know, he is a very controversial figure. He has attacked many of our prominent literary lights in print; vitriolic attacks, I am afraid. They have never forgiven him. He has even had bad relations with Mr. Godey and Sarah, but at least they are on amicable terms at the moment. In fact, I would venture to say that Sarah and Louis Godey are the only true friends he has left.''

"That's sad," Jemina said. "To think that such a talented man should go unappreciated."

"It is sad, I agree. But Mr. Poe has brought much of his misfortune down upon his own head. He has a tongue that burns like acid. Or perhaps I should say he writes with a pen dipped in acid." Warren took a watch out of his vest pocket and looked at it. "Duty calls, Jemina. Do you need to see Sarah again? I'm sure Mr. Poe won't be with her too long, if you'd care to wait."

"No, not really. I only arrived yesterday, and I haven't even unpacked as yet. I do wish to thank you, Warren, for taking time from your busy schedule to show me the premises."

"You are most welcome, Jemina," Warren said, smiling. "I think you'll be a lovely addition to the *Book*, and I'm looking forward to working with you."

HESTER MCFEE RESIDED in a flat not too far from her millinery shop on Chestnut Street.

Jemina had not unpacked last night, since she hadn't been too sure of her reception from Sarah Hale. But now, as she got out of the hansom cab before Aunt Hester's building, it was all she could do to restrain herself. She wanted to dance up the steps to the brownstone and sing at the top of her voice. She was on her way! Best of all, she was on her own.

There had been a great uproar at home in Boston when Jemina had announced her intentions. Her mother had wept and wrung her hands, and Henry Benedict had raged and roared.

"I forbid this. I absolutely forbid you to leave this house!" he had thundered.

"Father, I am of age," Jemina pointed out in a reasonable tone. "I don't know how you can keep me here, short of chaining me to the bedpost."

"You see, Mother!" Henry wheeled on his wife. "That's what comes of her reading that *Godey's Lady's Book*. Now she thinks she no longer has to listen to her elders!"

In response, Beth Benedict only wailed louder.

"Quiet, woman!" Henry roared. "You're no help at all. Talk some sense into her; she's your daughter."

Jemina said calmly, "Mother can't change my mind. Nothing either of you can say will change my mind."

Her mother raised a tearstained face. "If you go off like this, no man will marry you. A man doesn't want a working woman for a wife."

"Mother, you never listen to me. I don't know how many times I have told you that I'm not interested in getting married now. I'm sure I will someday, but not now."

Henry Benedict said, "And what about our friends, my business associates? They'll think I can't support you, that I sent you out to work."

Jemina stared at him steadily, and he had the grace to flush and look away. She laughed softly. "I hardly think anyone will believe that Henry Benedict of Beacon Hill is destitute."

In a last desperate ploy, her father said, "If you leave here against my wishes, I shall disinherit you!"

"I was wondering if you would get to that. You'd never do it, Father. I know you too well. And even if you did, do you really think that would stop me?"

That seemed the turning point. After that, they appeared resigned to her leaving. Her father still growled and blustered, but the steam had gone out of his opposition.

Her mother, in a moment of candor, even whispered that she felt a certain envy. "I've never lived anywhere but with my parents and your father. I have often wondered what it would be like to be free and independent, at least for a bit."

Free and independent, that's what she was, Jemina thought as she entered the brownstone. Her aunt wasn't home yet, for she often worked long hours at the shop. Jemina began unpacking her trunk and arranging her things in the spare bedroom that was to be hers for as long as she cared to stay.

By the time Aunt Hester arrived home, after six, Jemina was finished unpacking and had dinner prepared.

Hester McFee looked at the table set in the tiny kitchen and sniffed appreciatively at the good odors of food cooking. "Girl, you didn't have to go to all this trouble. I didn't agree to have you live with me just to get a cook and a housekeeper."

Jemina embraced her. "I intend to do my share, Aunt Hester."

One look at her niece's beaming face and Hester began to grin. "I gather that everything went well with you at *Godey's Lady's Book*?"

"It went splendidly! Sarah Hale employed me as a contributing editor. I'm to spend part of the time learning editorial duties, and the rest of my time is to be devoted to writing pieces of my own for publication in the *Book*."

"The *Book*?" Hester asked quizzically.

"That's what everybody who works there calls the magazine."

"Well!" Hester removed her hat and sat down at the kitchen table. "Now tell me all about it, every little detail."

FOR THE NEXT TWO WEEKS, Jemina was busier than she had ever been in her entire life, learning everything she could about the operation of the magazine. All of it was new and exciting, and she absorbed the knowledge like a sponge. Everyone was very helpful and friendly, the staff seemed happy and most of them worshiped Sarah Hale. And with good reason, Jemina soon realized. It was not that Sarah was an "easy" employer; she was a difficult taskmaster, demanding perfection. When she didn't approve, she took pains to point out what had been done wrong. Jemina noticed that a mistake was rarely repeated. However, to balance this, Sarah was unstinting in her praise for a job well done. As busy as she was, she went out of her way to give Jemina all the advice and help that she could.

Even Louis Godey occasionally deigned to give Jemina a word of advice and a rare nod of praise. Jemina was still intimidated by the publisher, but she soon realized that his gruff exterior was a shield behind which he hid a kind and rather shy nature. She soon concluded that his shyness was caused by the fact that most of his employees were female. Because of this, he had to tread a little gingerly, and there was no opportunity to display the male camaraderie that might have existed under different circumstances. Jemina worked long hours, both at the magazine and at home, where she worked hard at improving her writing. She took back issues of the magazine home with her and studied them assiduously. She wrote poems and short stories and was satisfied with none of them. She didn't think they were worthy of showing to Sarah.

Within a few days, she had made one fast friend on the magazine. Clara Dalhart was a few years older than Jemina; a handsome woman, with long, red-brown hair, sparkling green eyes and a generous figure—rather daringly displayed, Jemina thought.

Clara was one of Sarah's two personal assistants. She handled Sarah's voluminous correspondence and sometimes read pieces submitted to the magazine when Sarah wished a second opinion.

One of the first things Jemina had learned was that Sarah Hale personally read every piece of material submitted, and she was surprised to learn that Clara was sometimes required to do second reads. She said, "Sarah doesn't strike me as a person who would want a second opinion on anything."

Clara laughed. "She isn't really seeking my opinion. It's more of a confirmation, and that only on borderline material."

"I don't believe I understand."

"Well, we receive an enormous number of submissions, as I'm sure you know by now. Usually Sarah makes a decision instantly, on the first reading. But sometimes she may have doubts or questions about a piece, and in these cases she sometimes gives the article to me to read before returning the piece to the author."

"Do you ever disagree with her opinion?"

"Frequently."

"And does this change her mind?"

Clara laughed again. "Rarely."

"Then why does she bother?"

"She says it's good training for me, that she won't be here forever and someone will eventually have to take her place. In my opinion, I'll be old and gray before Sarah retires from the *Book*."

They were in Clara's small office, and Jemina had been sitting for a long while. Her corset was restricting her, and out of habit, she stood and gave it a pull, making herself a bit more comfortable.

"What's wrong, Jemina?"

"This corset I'm wearing. It's a new one, and it pinches," Jemina said in annoyance.

"Then why do you wear it? I never wear one. It's much more comfortable without. Besides, don't you know that Sarah disapproves of women wearing corsets? She's even written about it. She believes that corsets restrict the flow of blood, that wearing one is bad for a woman's health. What's good enough for her is certainly good enough for me."

Jemina flushed. "Well, yes, I know Sarah's views on the subject, and I heartily agree. I guess I just have not had the courage of my convictions."

THE NEXT DAY, when Jemina came to work, she was not wearing a corset. She did feel much more comfortable; yet she was certain that everyone noticed and was whispering behind her back.

She also brought along a short story she had written, one that she had polished again and again and yet was far from happy with. However, she didn't feel that she was objective enough to judge it fairly.

She carried it into Clara's office. "Would you do me a favor, Clara? Would you read this and give me an opinion?"

Clara took the story with a dubious expression. She looked at the first page. "'Autumn Sweethearts.' By Jemina Benedict. Is this for the *Book*?"

"Well, I hope so, but I'm not sure if it's good enough. That's why I wanted you to read it first."

"This should go to Sarah. She has a firm rule that all submissions must be read first by her."

"But I'd rather she didn't see it at all, if it isn't right."

"Well . . . all right, Jemina. But you must promise never to let her know that I saw it first."

"I promise."

"Then I'll read it right away, and we'll talk about it over luncheon."

"Oh, it's not urgent!"

Clara grinned. "You really are nervous about it, aren't you? Don't fret, Jemina, it's not the end of the world, good or bad."

THE TWO WOMEN had developed a habit of having their noon meals together in a small restaurant two blocks from their building.

Jemina was already seated at a table when Clara entered, carrying the manuscript under her arm. She sat down and handed the manuscript across the table.

Looking Jemina directly in the eye, she said, "I had made up my mind before I even read it to tell you to submit it to Sarah. I was sure it couldn't be too awful, but . . . it won't do, Jemina. I'm sorry."

Jemina's heart plummeted. "Then it *is* awful!"

Clara was shaking her head. "Not at all. For what it is, the story's fine. You're a good writer, Jemina. But the stories published by the *Book* are for genteel women readers. The stories are romantic, sentimental. Your story, unfortunately, has too many touches of realism."

"But many of the articles published deal with the stark realities of life."

Clara nodded. "True. But those are articles, not stories. I read your first piece, the one you sent to Sarah. It was an article, and very good. Would you care for a word of advice?"

"Of course," Jemina said instantly.

"First, I want to say something in confidence. I don't much care for many of the tales and poems we publish in the *Book*, but the pieces are popular with the readership, and ours has a subscription list equal to, if not better than, any other magazine of its kind in the country. I do like *some* of the stories, of course, like those written by Mr. Poe, but they are the exception.

"It is the articles that I chiefly enjoy. As I'm sure you know by now, Sarah is something of a crusader for the rights of women, as is Mr. Godey, in a more cautious manner. Sarah crusades for women's suffrage, for instance. She's in favor of public playgrounds for children, better sanitation and better working conditions for women. She strongly supports child-labor laws and many other unpopular causes. Do you know about Elizabeth Blackwell?''

Jemina nodded. ''Yes, I've heard of her. Isn't she the woman who wants to become a doctor?''

''That's right.'' Clara smiled. ''She had the devil's own time getting admitted to college and probably never would have but for Sarah. Sarah fought for her all the way and finally managed to get her into Geneva College in New York State. She's going to receive her medical degree this year.''

Jemina clapped her hands. ''I think that's wonderful.''

''So do I. And I also think it would be wonderful to publish an interview with Elizabeth Blackwell in the *Book*. How it feels to be the first woman medical student in this country. The prejudices she encountered, the difficulties she had to overcome.''

''Are you suggesting that *I* do the interview?'' Jemina said in dismay.

''I am.''

''But I have never done an interview.''

''There has to be a first time, Jemina. And I happen to think that it's your forte. You see, Mr. Godey is gradually changing the scope of the magazine. The word 'magazine,' you know, originally meant 'storehouse.' That's what Mr. Godey aimed for originally, a miscellany of pieces he thought women would like.

''But women are becoming more literate than they were when he started the magazine, more sophisticated. So Sarah has been pressuring him to publish more material that will appeal to the newly literate, the middle- and upper-class woman, something more than the usual articles on fashion, cooking, architecture, and the romantic stories and poems. She wants to add pieces to stimulate women's thinking, and to do that, we're going to have to be more daring, even controversial, from time to time. She's gradually winning Mr. Godey over to her way of thinking.''

Despite her reservations, Jemina experienced a throb of excitement. ''But why should she trust me, a mere neophyte, to do such an important interview?''

''Well...'' Clara hesitated. ''I happen to know that she has one article about Elizabeth Blackwell that she was considering publishing, but Mr. Godey balked and she backed down. Sarah told me that she didn't fight too hard because she wasn't totally pleased with the article. The man who penned it isn't on the staff here, and Sarah didn't care for his viewpoint. But if you, a woman, give her what she wants, I think she will stand up to Mr. Godey over it.''

''I'll talk to her right away about it.''

''No, don't be too hasty,'' Clara said slowly. ''Do you mind another suggestion?''

''I'd welcome it.''

''Why don't you do the interview on your own?''

''You mean without talking to Sarah first?'' Jemina was horrified. ''I couldn't do that!''

''Why not? Sarah likes initiative. She might be a little upset at first, but not if the article is good.''

''But what if it isn't?''

''It will be; I'm confident of that. And if it isn't...'' Clara shrugged. ''We all have to take risks, Jemina.''

"But will Elizabeth Blackwell consent to an interview with a writer she's never heard of?"

"Tell her you work for Sarah. She owes Sarah a great debt. I'm sure she would be most happy to cooperate."

"But that would be playing her false!"

"How so? You do work for her." Clara leaned forward. "Go ahead, Jemina, do it! Go to Geneva. It should take you only a few days to make the trip and do the interview."

"What will I tell Sarah?"

Clara shrugged. "Tell her you suddenly had to go to Boston. Something happened in the family."

"I could never lie to her."

Clara sighed. "You *are* an innocent, aren't you? Well, leave it to me. I'll handle matters with Sarah."

Jemina gazed down at her plate, thinking. She took a bite of food. Despite Clara's reassurances, she knew that she would be risking a great deal. She had already changed her life drastically by coming here. Now she had the job she wanted more than anything in the world; and after working on the *Book* for only a month, she was seriously considering something that could cost her her position.

Still, the thought of interviewing such a person as Elizabeth Blackwell, soon to be the first woman doctor in the United States, was terribly exciting. And if she could carry it off, if she could write an article that met with Sarah's approval and have the piece published under her own name...!

She knew that Clara was right about one thing—authoring stories and poems was not her strong suit.

She glanced up. "I'll do it!"

Clara smiled brilliantly. "Good for you, Jemina!" Then she looked wistful. "You know, I envy you. You have a talent I'd gladly kill for. I have always wanted to be a writer, but I know I never will. I am a good editor, but an author I will never be."

Embarrassed, at a loss as to what to say, Jemina looked away. Then her glance fell on a familiar figure in a distant corner of the room. It was Warren Barricone, eating alone. His head was bent over his food, and his tall figure had a disconsolate droop.

She said, "There's Warren over there."

Clara turned to look.

Jemina said, "He seems so lonely. Maybe we should attract his attention, ask him to join us."

Clara shook her head. "No, it wouldn't be wise. Maybe you haven't noticed, but Warren usually prefers to be alone."

"Why is that? He seems friendly enough."

"Oh, he's friendly around the magazine. He never lets his private life intrude there."

"His private life? What do you mean by that?"

"Don't ever tell him that I mentioned this to you, Jemina." Clara lowered her voice. "It's his wife. She's ailing, bedridden for some time. I understand that the doctors say it is unlikely she will ever recover."

"Oh, the poor man!" Jemina glanced again at Warren, remembering the sadness she had glimpsed in his eyes. Now she could understand the reason. "What's wrong with her?"

"I don't know. Nobody seems to know, not even the doctors. That's what is so sad about it. If they knew what was wrong with her, she might be cured."

"Do they have any children?"

"No, which is probably a blessing. If they had children, the burden might be too heavy for poor Warren to bear."

WARREN BARRICONE was thinking just the opposite that evening as he stepped off the horsecar a block from his home, a small brick house on the outskirts of Philadelphia. His footsteps dragged as he walked down the block and mounted the steps.

He loved Alice with all his heart and soul, but despite himself, he had recently begun to dread coming home to her. She had been sickly for over a year now, steadily wasting away. She never complained, never whined about her plight, and she always greeted him with a smile, yet he knew she was in constant pain.

There would be no one else in the house in the evening because Mrs. Wright, who came in daily to tend Alice and keep the house, was always eager to leave the minute Warren stepped through the front door.

If only they had children! True, children would cause problems, and he might have to hire extra help, but they would be worth it. Bright, smiling faces, happy laughter ringing through the house and tiny feet racing to meet him at the door! Ah, how much cheer it would bring to a house hushed and shadowed by illness. Children might be somewhat of a burden to Alice, yet Warren was certain that she would welcome the distraction, as long as there was someone to care for them.

But during the three years of their marriage, Alice had borne him no children. She had always been frail, but soon after they were married, her condition worsened and the doctors had advised that she might not live through childbirth. Now it was too late.

Warren paused, his door key in his hand.

Against his will, his thoughts leaped back to the lunch hour. He had seen Jemina Benedict across the restaurant and had studied her when she wasn't looking. He had been drawn to her from the very first moment, and she certainly looked robust enough to bear a man children. . . .

With a forcible wrench he tore his thoughts away from Jemina. With a sigh he turned his key in the door and, pushing it open, went in.

Mrs. Wright, a middle-aged, plump woman, greeted him in the foyer. She had her cloak on, her reticule in her hand, ready to depart.

He nodded. "Mrs. Wright."

"Your supper is made and warming on the stove. I made a nice stew. Please urge Mrs. Barricone to eat heartily. She needs her strength."

"I shall try, Mrs. Wright, but she . . ." He hesitated. "How is she today?"

"About the same. I bid you good-day, Mr. Barricone."

"Good day, Mrs. Wright."

When the door had closed behind her, Warren squared his shoulders and started down the hall toward the back bedroom, calling out in a hearty voice, "Alice! Darling, I'm home!"

Chapter Four

THE TRAIN had scarcely left Philadelphia before Jemina was immersed in the story of Elizabeth Blackwell. The *Book* had an extensive collection of back issues of newspapers and magazines, and with Clara's help, Jemina had found a great deal of material on Elizabeth Blackwell.

Now she began studying the notes she had written in her neat, slanting hand.

"Well, hello!"

Jemina glanced up with a start, instinctively covering her notes. Owen Thursday stood looking down at her, his hat in one hand, a cane in the other.

"Mr. Thursday! What a surprise."

"Yes, isn't it?" His smile was intimate and warm. "I thought I recognized you from my seat in the back of the car, but I wasn't sure. I simply had to make certain. May I sit down?" With the cane he indicated the empty seat beside her.

Jemina hesitated for an instant, resentful at being interrupted in the perusal of her notes. Yet such was the charm and magnetism of this man that she did not want to spurn him. She moved over against the window. "Of course, Mr. Thursday. Please do."

He said, "You have the advantage of me."

"In what way is that, sir?"

"You seem to know my name, while I am completely in the dark as to yours."

"Oh! I'm Jemina Benedict."

"Jemina," he said musingly. "I like that name. But tell me, how did you learn mine?"

"Sarah Hale told me."

"Ah, the light dawns. You are employed at *Godey's Lady's Book*, then?"

"I am."

"Odd. I often pop in and out when I am in the city—Sarah and I are old friends—yet I've never encountered you there, except for that unfortunate meeting at the door." His smile flickered, his gaze briefly appraising her. "I fail to understand how I have missed you. I have an eye for a pretty woman."

"So Sarah informed me," Jemina said in a dry voice. "I've only recently become employed there."

"That explains it, then. What exactly did Sarah tell you about me?"

"She warned me against you, very strongly." Jemina smiled to take the sting from her words.

He made a rueful face. "Trust Sarah for that. And did her warning frighten you, Jemina?"

"Of course not. Why should it?" She looked at him in challenge.

He shrugged negligently. "No reason, of course. I'm no monster." His glance dropped to the sheets of notes in her lap. "Are you writing something for the *Lady's Book*? Since you're working there, I assume you're an author."

"Yes, I'm a contributing editor," she said, without directly answering his question.

"I've always considered that a contradictory phrase, contributing editor. It's always been my opinion that editors and writers are natural enemies. Editing is the exact opposite of writing."

"I think that's a rather arbitrary view, and certainly Sarah doesn't agree with you."

"Perhaps a magazine is different from a newspaper. Writing for a newspaper, as I do, means writing what's newsworthy, and I'm always at loggerheads with editors who change my copy."

Jemina's temper stirred. "The *Book* also publishes articles and stories about people and events that are newsworthy."

"It publishes nothing current. News is what happened today, certainly no later than yesterday." His contempt was barely concealed.

"Newspapers publish feature articles about people and past events."

"I don't write that kind of thing. There's nothing more exciting than writing about what's happening at the moment. Anything else is stale."

"I don't agree with you. I happen to think that readers like a thoughtful piece on personalities, something that the writer has taken time and effort to pen, something where the writer has a viewpoint on the subject in question."

He dismissed this with a gesture. "My business is reporting the news, not delivering a message. That's the job of the editor. But then, of course, that's what you are, isn't it? An editor?"

Stung, she retorted, "Take your eye, for instance."

His one good eye glared at her, flashing. "My eye?"

"The one with the patch." Despite all her efforts, she had caught herself staring at the eye patch from time to time. "In straight news reporting, whatever happened to it would be reported, if at all, in just a few lines. How it happened and when. Perhaps why it happened, but again perhaps not. But if I was reading about it, I would like to know not only why it happened, but how you felt about it, how the loss affected you afterward. As a writer, that would be of paramount interest to me.''

Owen had gone pale, and for a moment Jemina feared that she had gone too far. He looked ready to lash out at her. Then, to her astonishment, he threw back his head and roared with laughter.

"You have brass, girl, I must say that for you," he gasped out. "Very few men, much less women, would dare comment on my eye patch."

"I shouldn't have said what I said. I'm sorry," she said quickly. "It was a cruel thing to say."

He motioned with one hand. "I'm not offended, don't fret. I suppose Sarah made some comment about it?''

"She mentioned it in passing," Jemina said diffidently. "She said nobody knows how you lost the eye, that you tell different stories to different people."

"Suppose I told you that it happened in a duel with an editor, over a difference of opinion about something I had written. Would you believe that?''

"Should I believe it?" she said coolly.

He gave an indifferent shrug, looking away. "I don't really care what you believe, Miss Benedict."

There was an undertone of bitterness in his voice, and Jemina decided that he was sensitive on the subject; if not over the loss of the eye, at least over the reason for it.

They rode in silence for a few moments. The faint swaying motion of the train, the clicking sounds of the wheels, were almost hypnotic.

"At any rate, our debate is pointless," Owen finally said. "I doubt that you will ever edit any copy of mine. Our fields are worlds apart."

"Have you ever conducted an interview?"

His gaze swung back to her. "Of course."

"Then I fail to see that we're so far apart. I'm presently on my way to conduct an interview, with a . . . a person very much in the news." It was a rash statement, and Jemina regretted it almost at once.

"Are you actually comparing the *Book* with my newspaper?" he said incredulously.

"Well, yes, in some ways. There are differences, but the aim of both is to tell the truth."

"*Truth!*" He gave a bark of laughter. "Do you know what Edgar Allan Poe called *Godey's Lady's Book* in a survey he made titled 'Our Magazine Literature' several years ago? 'A clever magazine for the entertainment of ladies'!"

"Yet he publishes in the *Book.*"

"Only because the poor sod needs the money. I consider Poe a genius, but unfortunately, his genius goes unappreciated. Therefore, he has to sell his work where he can."

"Well, at least we agree about something," she said heatedly. "About the talent of Mr. Poe."

Angry enough to spit, she turned her face aside to stare unseeingly out the window at the scenery gliding past. The man was insufferable! Arrogant, opinionated, blind to the possibility of a woman's being able to compete with him!

"Jemina . . ." He touched her arm. "You're angry with me. I apologize."

Reluctantly, she turned her face to him. He was smiling warmly.

He went on, "I know I sometimes get carried away. I do admit that I'm somewhat old-fashioned. I've yet to become accustomed to the way women are leaving home and entering into professions heretofore reserved for men." His smile took on a touch of rue. "Do you suppose it's because I'm afraid they might offer too much competition? Some men have that fear, I know."

His manner completely disarmed her. "There's no reason that you should feel threatened." She smiled suddenly. "Certainly not from me, Mr. Thursday."

"Jemina . . ."

He touched the back of her hand with his fingers. His touch burned, and she was abruptly all too aware of his nearness. His thigh touched hers, and she could smell the bay rum he used.

"To atone for having upset you, I would very much like to take you to supper while we're both in New York. Perhaps to the theater."

"I'm afraid I can't accept your invitation. I shall be leaving as soon as possible after I detrain."

"Where are you going?"

"To . . ." She broke off. "I'm sorry, I can't tell you that."

"Why not?" Then his curious look turned knowing. "By God, you're afraid to tell me, afraid that I'll learn who your subject is and do the interview first!"

Jemina felt herself flushing. "Would you tell me, if you were on your way to conduct an interview?"

"It's not the same thing, and no, I certainly wouldn't be afraid to tell you. By God, I don't believe this!" He laughed, thumping his cane on the floor. Then, at her set expression, he sobered. "There I go, doing it again. I'm sorry. But you needn't worry, this isn't a working trip. I'm on holiday." He adopted a wheedling tone. "Surely you can manage to stay overnight in the city and have supper with me?"

"I cannot, Mr. Thursday," she said coolly. "Certainly, with your wide range of female acquaintances, you can find someone to sup with."

He looked at her appraisingly. "None as pretty as you, Jemina. Of that you may be sure."

JEMINA WAS EXHAUSTED by the time she arrived in the little town of Geneva, located on the northwest corner of Seneca Lake. She was also somewhat out of sorts, for it had been a long and tiresome journey.

She was cheered a little by the sight of the town with its neat, green square and the mellow hues of the fine brick houses. It was early afternoon and Jemina knew that Elizabeth Blackwell would be in class at the college. She had written to Miss Blackwell telling her that she would come to her boardinghouse on the evening of her arrival.

Jemina took a room in a hotel. As she washed her face and hands and changed out of her traveling clothes, she reviewed what she knew about Geneva College. It had been established in 1822 and had evinced a fine pioneering spirit from its very beginning without the rigid, conventional thinking of many colleges. An example of this independent spirit was the addition of a medical department in 1827, after a number of eminent physicians had been refused the opportunity to give medical instruction in New York State. Geneva College opened its doors to them.

It must, Jemina concluded, be a liberal college in other ways, aside from being the first medical school in the country, since it had accepted a female student.

As the evening shadows began to lengthen, Jemina set out for a Miss Waller's boardinghouse, where Elizabeth Blackwell resided. The leaves had begun to turn, and the air was crisp; it was much cooler than it had been in Philadelphia.

The boardinghouse was well kept, with a fresh coat of paint, and the interior was neat and clean. Jemina was ushered into the parlor, where Miss Blackwell awaited her. Jemina knew that the woman was twenty-six years old, although she appeared somewhat older. After a little while, Jemina decided that it was because of her serious mien. She wasn't a beautiful woman—her cheeks were too thin, her chin too square, and her eyes were deep set, under low, heavy brows. But there was a strength and intelligence in her face; and her eyes, a bluish-gray in color, studied Jemina in a cool, unwavering appraisal. Her straw-colored hair hung straight.

She was cordial enough, certainly. "Welcome, Miss Benedict. How is dear Sarah?"

"Sarah is fine, busy as always."

Miss Blackwell nodded. "Without Sarah's support, I doubt that I would ever have been admitted to Geneva College. But I must admit to some puzzlement. Although I was not interviewed, it is my understanding that *Godey's Lady's Book* is publishing a piece on me already."

"They've decided not to publish it. It was unsuitable, in Sarah's view," Jemina said, rather too quickly. In an attempt to change the subject, she glanced around. "You have a pleasant place to live while you're attending college. I suppose most of the boardinghouses are filled during school term. You were fortunate to find such a comfortable place."

"Fortunate is hardly the word," Miss Blackwell said in a dry voice. "It was almost as difficult to find a boardinghouse as it was to get into Geneva College."

Jemina had her notebook and pen out. "You mean there *was* a shortage of rooms?"

"Oh, there were rooms available. I went to five boardinghouses. All had signs announcing rooms for rent. But as one landlady so kindly informed me, she didn't have a room for the kind of woman who would want to be a doctor. I finally found a kindred spirit in Miss Waller."

"Well, at least you finally found a college that would accept you. I was thinking earlier today how liberal the faculty must be to go against tradition."

"Liberal? Oh, my dear!" This time Miss Blackwell laughed aloud. "Didn't Sarah tell you the story of how I got into Geneva College?"

"I'm afraid not."

"I had tried for some time to get admitted to a medical school. Sarah helped whenever she could, but all doors were closed to me. Then she convinced a reputable Philadelphia physician to write a letter to Geneva College recommending me as a student. I had been studying medicine in his office, but of course that would never have qualified me as a doctor of medicine. Well, Dr. Warrington wrote the letter. Upon receipt of it, the faculty was at a loss as to what to do. They didn't wish to offend the good doctor. So they finally decided on a ruse that they calculated

would take the onus of refusal off them. They decided to submit the matter to the students of Geneva
College, and if they reached a unanimous decision to
accept me, I could attend. Of course, the faculty
members never dreamed that such a student decision would be made.''

Jemina, busily taking notes, glanced up. ''Why
was that?''

''Because of the students themselves. The medical
class, about a hundred and fifty students, is com-
posed of young men from nearby towns. They are the
sons of farmers, tradespeople and the like. They hold
no abiding interest in medicine. They love fun more
than learning. There is a saying among the townspeople: 'A boy who proves unfit for anything else can
always be a doctor.' In fact so rowdy are the students
that the townspeople, on numerous occasions, have
demanded that they be expelled or that the college be
closed.''

''But the students did vote to admit you, obviously.''

''Yes, as a joke.''

Jemina glanced up again. ''A joke?''

''Yes. They are unruly, as I mentioned, and they
knew that the faculty expected them to vote against
my admittance. So, in effect, they thumbed their
collective nose at the faculty and voted to accept me.
They also thought it would be great sport to have a
lone woman in the class. I have since learned that
many of them thought I would never enroll, and even
if I did, I would never complete a full term.''

''Have they given you a difficult time? The students, I mean?''

"Oddly enough, not as much as I expected. Oh, there have been a few instances of bad behavior, but the majority of the students have shown remarkable decorum. In fact—" Miss Blackwell smiled "—one doctor, a Dr. Lee, told me that my presence in the classroom seems to have a salubrious effect on the rowdies. They behave like perfect little gentlemen." She sobered. "Actually, I have experienced more hostility from the townspeople than from the students."

"In what way do you mean?"

"Well, when I first arrived, every time I walked down the street, people would gather to stare at me, as though I were some sort of strange animal. It took me a while to discover that the townspeople sincerely believe that I'm either a scarlet woman or that I am insane and will eventually do violence to someone. So, I seldom venture onto the streets nowadays." Miss Blackwell shrugged. "I spend my time either at the boardinghouse or at the college. It's no hardship, since study takes up all my time."

"Speaking of your studies..." Jemina was hesitant. "Don't you find it difficult to observe some of the things required of you?"

"Yes, some things are difficult, especially the anatomy class when we did our first dissection of a cadaver, and when we began to study the reproductive organs." Miss Blackwell smiled grimly. "When we reached that point, Dr. Webster told me privately that I could be excused, but I was determined to go through with everything any would-be doctor would experience. It was just about all I could bear. It certainly shocked my sense of delicacy. Some of the students blushed, others giggled, and many of them kept sending me furtive glances to see if I was shocked. I managed, with great effort, to maintain my composure.''

"Tell me, Miss Blackwell, since it has obviously been very difficult for you, what made you decide to become a doctor in the first place?"

"There were many factors involved." Miss Blackwell looked pensive. "My father died a horrible death, as did a dear aunt, and I always felt that their deaths would not have happened so prematurely if they had received proper medical care. But what finally decided me was a close family friend, Mary Donaldson.

"The poor thing was dying, horribly, of cancer. The disease had ravaged her. She told me, in all frankness, that it was a terrible thing to die such a death, but one thing would have made her suffering much more bearable. If only she didn't have to be examined and treated by a man! And she asked me why I didn't try to become a doctor. It was a startling idea, but she made me promise that I would at least think about it.

"And from that day forward, I couldn't *stop* thinking about it. Of course, I thought it was impossible. It was unheard-of, a female physician. I had heard of only one, a Madame Restell in New York, who *called* herself a physician. It had been in all the newspapers. But she wasn't actually a doctor, she was a noted abortionist, made famous and wealthy by her infamous practice...."

ON HER RETURN to Philadelphia, Jemina worked very hard on her article. When it was finally done to her satisfaction, she approached Sarah Hale with some trepidation. From Clara, Jemina had learned that Sarah had not questioned her absence.

When Jemina was admitted to Sarah's office, the editor leaned back and smiled at her. "Is everything all right at home, Jemina? I'm not that hard a taskmaster, you know. If you had urgent business at home, you could have asked my permission, without going through Clara. I know, Clara said it came up rather suddenly, but even so . . ."

Trembling inside, Jemina stood straight before her editor's desk, clutching her manuscript to her bosom. "That was an untruth, Sarah, and I shouldn't have involved Clara. That was cowardly of me."

Sarah began to frown. "An untruth? I don't understand."

"I went to Geneva, New York. I conducted an interview with Elizabeth Blackwell and wrote an article," Jemina said in a rush. She placed the manuscript before Sarah. "And here it is."

Sarah leaned forward, eyes flashing. "You took time off for something like that, and without asking me? I told you that such articles were done on assignment!"

"I was afraid that if I came to you, you would . . ."

Sarah glared. "Afraid! It seems to me that you have a *lot* of gall, girl! You've worked here . . . what? Three months? And you just take off like that?"

"That was the reason I didn't come to you," Jemina said in a whisper. "I was afraid that you wouldn't agree to my doing the interview."

"And you would certainly have been correct about that." Sarah slapped the desk with her palm. "I should . . ."

"Please, Sarah," Jemina broke in. "Don't do anything until you've read the article. Then I'll abide by whatever decision you reach."

"Such effrontery! In all my years as an editor, I have *never*..." She stared at the manuscript, and as if of its own volition, one hand crept across the desk to finger the pages.

Finally, she glanced up. Some of her outrage had dissipated. "I suppose I can at least do that. Now you'd better leave me, girl, while I have my temper under control."

With a sigh of relief, Jemina turned to leave.

"Jemina?"

She turned back with a look of inquiry.

"Elizabeth, how did she take to all this? You didn't...?" Sarah's eyes narrowed dangerously. "You didn't tell her I'd sent you?"

"Oh, no, I wouldn't do that! I told her that I worked for *Godey's Lady's Book*, and she was more than cooperative."

Sarah nodded in dismissal. She waited until the door had closed behind Jemina before she leaned back, her gaze fastened to the door. Most of her initial anger had abated, yet she was still upset. It would have been bad enough for someone who had been working on the magazine for some time, but it was unthinkable that a person as new as Jemina Benedict should dare to do such a thing without asking her permission.

Abruptly, she laughed softly. How many times had she told Louis that she wanted editors and writers with initiative and drive, as well as ability? Well, this one certainly had initiative and drive!

IT WAS LATE AFTERNOON when Jemina received the summons to Sarah's office. She went, feeling as though she was on her way to the guillotine. And her first glance at Sarah's face was far from reassuring. Sarah was stern and reserved.

Sarah gestured. "Sit, Jemina." When Jemina was perched on the edge of her seat, Sarah continued, "I've been debating with myself as to what I should do with you. You have impressed me enormously the short time you have been with us. You are diligent and hardworking and appear to be a good learner. Yet, should I let such impudence go unpunished?"

Jemina sat tensely, not daring to speak.

"Clara came to me a bit ago and confessed that she was largely instrumental in this brash undertaking of yours."

Jemina finally felt compelled to speak. "I wish she hadn't done that. It might have been her suggestion, but the responsibility is all mine, not hers."

"Loyalty to a friend is a cardinal virtue. I approve of that. However..."

Jemina could wait no longer. "The article, Sarah, how is it? Is it too awful?"

Sarah stared, then began to laugh. "That's really all you're concerned about, isn't it? Not your position here, not if I may discharge you, but the article."

Jemina held her breath.

"In fact..." Sarah relaxed even more. "For someone who is little more than a beginner, it is a fine piece of writing. You caught the essence of Elizabeth Blackwell, as I know her. You have painted a portrait in pen and ink, Jemina."

Jemina felt herself begin to glow. "Oh, thank you, Sarah!"

"No need for that. I don't stint praise when it is due," Sarah said somewhat tartly. "Now, the question is, what to do with it."

Surprised, Jemina said, "Why, publish it, of course, if you think it's good enough."

"If it was only that simple," Sarah said with a sigh.

"I'm afraid I don't understand."

"Well, maybe you don't know it, but I already have an article on Elizabeth on hand."

"Clara mentioned that, but it was her understanding that it wasn't good enough to use."

"It was below standard, true enough, but I would have used it. However, Louis takes the position that a piece on Elizabeth is—well, 'political' is the way he puts it. And since it wasn't quite good enough, I didn't fight too hard for it."

Jemina leaned forward. "And mine is?"

Sarah gave her a wry look. "Are you willing to do battle with Louis to get it published?"

"Fight Mr. Godey? I don't know, I . . ." Then she straightened up. "Yes, if you deem it necessary."

"Oh, it's necessary. But if we present a united front, perhaps we shall prevail. I have asked Louis to come to my office at four." She glanced at the grandfather clock in the corner. It showed five minutes of the hour, "He is usually quite prompt."

As if on cue, a knock sounded on the door. Sarah leaned back, an anticipatory smile on her face, and Jemina realized that she was relishing the prospect of a fight.

"Come in, Louis," Sarah called out.

Louis Godey entered, stopping short at the presence of Jemina.

"Louis," Sarah said, "you remember Jemina Benedict?"

"Of course. How are you, Miss Benedict?" he said stiffly, then turned to Sarah. "What is this all about, Sarah? You said it was important."

"I happen to think so. But first—" she picked up Jemina's manuscript and held it across the desk "—I think you should read this."

Godey took it gingerly and, sitting down in the chair next to Jemina, began reading. Before he had finished the first page, he glanced up, glowering. "Why, this is about the Blackwell woman."

"Please, Louis, read it first," Sarah urged.

With a shrug, he resumed reading. Jemina sat very still, but her mind was racing, marshaling arguments to throw at him.

Finally, the publisher looked up, first at Sarah, then at Jemina. "Since your name is on this, Miss Benedict, I assume you wrote it. Well, it is a fine piece of work."

Jemina's hopes soared, then plummeted again, as Godey said to Sarah, "I thought we had settled this."

"First, Louis, do you agree that this is a far better piece than the other one?"

"That is clearly evident. However, it's not the quality of the work that concerns me, but the subject matter."

To her horror, Jemina heard herself saying, "And what is wrong with the subject matter, sir?"

Godey glared at her. "Young lady, it is not your province to decide what is a proper subject for my publication!"

"Who better to argue the subject matter of the piece than the author?" Sarah asked. "Go ahead, Jemina," she added with an encouraging nod.

And suddenly, it seemed that the discussion was between Louis Godey and Jemina. He said, "My policy is to steer away from political controversy, Miss Benedict."

"I fail to see how this subject is political," she said. "Miss Blackwell is not running for public office. She is merely trying to become a doctor."

"But many men with political power opposed her admission to a medical college."

"I'm sure that many men did," she retorted, giving special emphasis to *men*. "However, as I recollect, you were not one of them, Mr. Godey. You permitted Sarah to support her, and according to Miss Blackwell, and I so quote in my article, she would not have been admitted but for the support of the *Book*."

"That is true, but she is soon to gain her degree. She has attained what she wanted, so why stir the whole matter up again by publishing this article? Let sleeping dogs lie."

"'It has long seemed to us an imperative duty to train every female in the art of attending the sick.'"

Godey blinked. "That sounds very familiar to me."

"It should," Jemina said. "I'm quoting from something Sarah wrote in the *Book*."

Sarah snorted indelicately. "She has you there, Louis."

"But that only supports my position. That was published before Elizabeth Blackwell attained her goal."

Jemina said, "Sarah also wrote that for centuries it has been the duty of women to care for the sick in the home, and for nothing. Why not give them the medical training they need, so they can not only perform the better for it but be allowed to become doctors and be paid for it? Why, even such a personage as Dr. Oliver Wendell Holmes agreed that women of serious purpose should at least be allowed to attend lectures on medicine."

"Young lady, you are telling me things that I already know," Godey said impatiently. "That still does not argue for the publication of your article."

"How about other women?"

"What about them?"

"The article would give those who wish to emulate Miss Blackwell some encouragement. It will show them that it is possible for a woman of determination to attain her goal."

"It is not my purpose to offer such encouragement," Godey growled. "My purpose is primarily entertainment."

"And to inform and to educate. I can quote your own words to that effect...."

"Never mind." Godey held up his hands, stopping her. His face had reddened. "I have no wish to listen to my own words from the mouth of an impudent young woman!"

"Impudent, Louis? I would call her spirited and determined," Sarah said, ignoring the fact that she herself had labeled Jemina impudent a short time ago. "How many times have you told me those are the kind of people you want working here, not sycophants?"

"You are also impudent, Sarah. But then, you always have been." Godey smiled slightly, then threw up his hands in defeat. "All right! Publish the double-damned piece! It will arouse a storm of protest, in all likelihood, but I have weathered those in the past." He got to his feet. "You will make of me an old man before my time, Sarah. As for you, young lady—" he rounded on Jemina "—the next time you decide to pen a piece which is controversial in nature, I would very much appreciate being consulted first."

Shaking his head dolefully, the publisher strode from the office.

Jemina was astonished by his abrupt capitulation, and she looked across the desk at Sarah.

Sarah was smiling. As always, she felt stimulated after winning an argument with Louis. "Did I not say that together we stood a good chance of winning?"

"Thank you for supporting me, Sarah," Jemina said fervently.

"I shall always support you, if you are in the right. But I must repeat Louis's warning. The next time you embark upon a project such as this, discuss it with me first."

Jemina nodded quickly. "I will, Sarah."

"I am of the opinion that your future lies with pieces of this nature, instead of fiction and poetry."

"Clara said the same thing."

Sarah nodded. "Clara is a fine editor. So, I think you should concentrate your efforts in that direction. And in that regard, I have an assignment for you."

Jemina leaned forward eagerly.

"For some time now, I have been contemplating organizing a ladies' medical missionary society here in Philadelphia,'' Sarah continued. ''It is going to be a difficult undertaking and will take some time, since it's a new, radical concept. Just as with doctors, people think that missionary work is the exclusive province of men. The purpose of the society, as I see it, will be to disseminate medical knowledge to the wives of missionaries, or to single female missionaries, so that hygiene and other matters of health may be spread to the natives in foreign countries.''

''I was unaware there are women missionaries. Single women, that is.''

''There aren't. Not yet.'' Sarah smiled tightly. ''I hope to remedy that oversight. And it is going to require a great amount of groundwork. I want you to write an article about this, perhaps even a series of them, articles that will give me a basis for my organizing efforts. . . .''

Jemina was so overjoyed that she was light-headed. Not only was her Blackwell article going to be published, but she had received her first assignment!

Chapter Five

JEMINA FOUND that she was constantly surprised by Sarah Hale, for there were many facets to this amazing woman. Jemina was astounded to learn that Sarah, who seemed so austere and businesslike in the office, loved lavish parties and would give one on almost any occasion.

In October, only a few days after Jemina's Blackwell article was accepted, she received a note to drop into Sarah's office.

As she entered the editor's office, Sarah glanced up from editing a manuscript. "Ah, there you are, my dear!" She leaned back, smiling. "I wanted to invite you to a party this coming Saturday night. It will be given by Louis at his residence. There will be many literary lights in attendance; Edgar Allan Poe, for one."

"I shall be more than happy to attend, Sarah. May I ask what the occasion is?"

"A celebration, Jemina. This year the Married Women's Property Bill was passed in New York State. The bill will enable women to finally own real estate in this country of ours."

"And Mr. Godey is giving a party in celebration of that?" Jemina said in astonishment. "I didn't know he was such an ardent supporter of rights for women."

Sarah's smile sparkled with mischief. "I talked him into giving the party. And Louis is not so much opposed as he may often sound. It is only when his magazine is involved that he becomes cautious. And by the way—" Sarah sobered "—I do not much care for that phrase, 'rights of women.' I have an almost constitutional aversion to it."

Jemina stared, wondering anew at the contradictions of this remarkable woman.

Sarah smiled at her look of bewilderment. "Of course I am strongly in favor of women's greater freedom through greater education. I believe that professions now closed to them should be open. I deplore the working conditions many have to endure. Yet, at the same time, I fear they may become too demanding and domineering. I would never advocate that women sacrifice their femininity. It is my fervent hope that men will eventually become convinced that knowledge, equality and freedom need not add merely to a woman's usefulness, but also to her powers of pleasing; and that intellectual cultivation gives new charms to beauty, and loveliness to grace.

"In some ways, I equate our present status with slavery, which I abhor with a passion." She made a face. "But as a slave owner has almost the power of life and death over his slaves, so do men have power over us. If we tried to eradicate slavery overnight, we would have civil war in this country. And so, if we women try to throw off our shackles too rapidly, we would cause a battle of the sexes we couldn't possibly win at this time...." She broke off, flushing. "Good heavens, I had no intention of lecturing, but that's what I'm doing, isn't it, my dear? Anyway, we may expect you at our little soiree, Jemina?''

''I'll be delighted to attend. But, Sarah...'' Jemina hesitated, not sure how to put what was in her mind.

Sarah arched an eyebrow. ''Yes, Jemina?''

''Nothing, nothing important.'' Jemina got to her feet. ''And thank you for inviting me, Sarah.''

On leaving Sarah's office, Jemina went in search of Warren Barricone. She found him in the fashion department, supervising the selection of fashion engravings to be used in the next issue of the magazine.

''Warren, may I talk to you for a few minutes?''

''Of course, Jemina.'' He turned to the women standing beside him and indicated the engraving they had been studying. ''That one should do excellently. We'll select the others a bit later.'' He turned to Jemina. ''Would you like to talk in my office?''

She nodded, and he led the way out of the large fashion room to an office next door. It was the first time she had been inside his office. It was small and contained only a desk, two chairs and several file cabinets.

Warren smiled somewhat abashedly. ''I must apologize for the untidiness. I know my office looks like a rat's nest, but I entertain anyone so rarely that I give little thought to tidying it. Would you care for a cup of tea?''

''I'd love a cup of tea.''

He nodded and crossed to one of the cabinets. On top was a serving tray, a teapot and a small alcohol stove, which Warren proceeded to light. There was something touchingly domestic about him, Jemina thought; and she realized that he must prepare tea, and perhaps meals, for his ailing wife at home.

As Warren busied himself making the tea, she scrutinized his office more closely. Back issues of the magazine filled every available space, and the top of his rolltop desk was piled high with fashion engravings, manuscripts and other items she could not identify. She sensed that this was the office of an extremely busy man. Perhaps an excessively busy man, one who immersed himself in work in an attempt to temporarily forget a painful existence elsewhere.

"Sugar and lemon?" he asked.

"Both, please."

In a moment, he came toward her with saucers and teacups on the tray. "This tea is Nuwara Eliya, from Ceylon. I buy only the best. I fear that tea is something of an expensive fancy of mine."

Jemina took a sip of the fragrant tea, which was delicious, while Warren settled down at his desk with a sigh, sitting sideways. He took a sip of tea and set the cup down in the saucer with a clatter. His warm brown eyes regarded her curiously. "Now, what do you want to talk about, Jemina? Nothing dire, I hope?"

"No, nothing like that." She laughed nervously. "I assume you are going to Mr. Godey's party this Saturday night?"

"Well, I've been invited, naturally." He seemed to withdraw slightly, a veil dropping over his eyes. "I doubt if I will attend, however."

"I'm going, and that's what I wanted to talk to you about." She paused, searching for the right words. "This is a little embarrassing, but I am seeking your advice about what to wear," she said in a rush.

"My advice?" He gave her a look of amusement. "Surely a young lady of your upbringing needs no such advice from a man, Jemina!"

"My mother taught me about clothes, of course, but we were never very social, and this soiree... Well, Sarah said that many important people would be present. I need more . . . well, sophisticated clothes."

"In my opinion, Jemina," he said warmly, "you would be the belle of the ball, no matter what you wore." He stopped short, as if suddenly realizing what he had said, and the veil dropped over his eyes again.

Jemina was flattered by the compliment, yet she deemed it wise to ignore it. "In view of the fact that you are the head of the fashion department of the *Book*, I thought you could advise me as to what would be suitable, the latest fashions to buy."

"Of course, Jemina, I'll do what I can. Actually, the shops aren't likely to have the newest fashions yet; certainly not the ones we're running in this month's issue. They're the latest styles from Paris, and there's always a time lapse before the shops in Philadelphia stock them. However, I'll be more than happy to browse through earlier issues with you. I'm sure that we can find something to please you."

He fell silent, taking a sip of tea, gazing down into the cup. Finally, he glanced up. "Jemina . . . I said I wasn't sure I would go to the party, but I will if you will do me the honor of letting me escort you."

Jemina made a sound of surprise, her eyes going wide.

He flushed slightly. "I know, I'm a married man. But that does not present a problem. Alice, my wife, is always urging me to attend more social gatherings." His features darkened with melancholy. "Although I haven't mentioned it to you, I'm sure you have heard that my wife is bedridden."

"Yes, Warren, I was told so, and you have my deepest sympathy. What is wrong with her? No one seems to know."

"Nor do the doctors," he said gloomily. "We have consulted with doctor after doctor, and to no avail. All confess to being completely baffled."

"I *am* sorry.... I would be most happy, Warren, to have you as my escort."

He smiled, banishing the gloom, and got to his feet briskly. "Then shall we look through the books?"

He rummaged among the stack of magazines in one corner and separated two from the pile. "Here are the May and June issues. You should be able to get an idea from these as to what is fashionable for evening."

He sat down again and opened one of the magazines. Jemina arose, to stand leaning over his shoulder as he leafed through the beautifully drawn fashion plates, many of which folded out to double-page width and were protected by sheets of tissue.

"As you can see," Warren said, pointing to color plates that showed a group of women in evening dress, "sleeves are short, and the, er—" he blushed slightly "—the necklines are being worn quite low. Skirts are being worn very full, with deep points, for it makes the waist look small without the discomfort of tight lacing." He flushed again and hurried on, as if to reach safer territory. "This new wrap is called the 'Cornelia' and is quite versatile. It has no seam on the shoulder and can be gathered on the arms like a shawl. White shawls are also very popular this year.

"As to fabrics, chameleon silk is very lovely. It has two or three colors, which change with the light. This dress, with the Marie Stuart cap, might be a good style for you, Jemina. Or perhaps this."

He pointed, and Jemina leaned over his shoulder to admire the illustration of a crepe robe of pale rose color, embroidered up the front of the skirt. The gown was girdled with a band of wide, brocaded ribbon in the same shade. The model's hair was arranged in plain bands with a wreath of mingled sweetbrier and lily of the valley.

"They all look so beautiful," she said, touching the plate delicately with her fingers.

Warren glanced at her and then down at the plate. He murmured, "No more beautiful than you, I think."

At her startled look, he became flustered. "I shouldn't have said that. Pray, forgive me."

Jemina felt her own face growing warm. It *was* a very personal remark, and not a proper one, coming as it did from a married man. Still, he seemed so contrite that she could not take umbrage.

"Well, I think I've seen enough to have some idea of what would be suitable. Thank you so much for your time, Warren. I really appreciate it."

"I am delighted to have been of assistance," he said rather awkwardly. "I wish you luck in finding what you want."

IT WAS DARK when Warren and Jemina got out of a carriage at 489 Chestnut Street, the residence of Louis Godey. The hum of voices could be heard through the open front door, and warm light spilled out through the narrow windows.

Jemina had found, in a little dress shop near her aunt's store, a gown of lovely brown barege, or gauze, over light blue satin. The dress had been so close a fit that only slight alterations had been necessary. Her hair was dressed in flat bandeaux and circled with a wreath of brown velvet leaves and blue forget-me-nots. She felt beautiful and special in the gown, which was the most elegant she had ever owned.

Warren took her arm, smiling down at her. Jemina had noticed that while he was rather careless of his dress at work, tonight he was well turned out in a black broadcloth cutaway coat over a white satin vest, ruffled shirt, high stock and narrow black trousers. The ensemble was capped by a tall black silk hat.

Warren patted her hand. "Ready for your first Philadelphia soiree, my dear?"

"Ready as I'll ever be."

Just before they went in, Warren said, "Alice asked me if the girl I was escorting tonight was pretty, and I told her that she was the prettiest woman I had seen since I married her."

"And what was her response?"

Warren's glowing eyes met hers. "She congratulated me, of course."

Jemina felt heat burn her face, and her eyes dropped away. Warren's comments were disconcerting. And she had to wonder just what her father would think should he learn that she was attending a social function with a married man.

They went up the short flight of steps, and Warren thumped the large knocker. A liveried black servant appeared and ushered them into a large parlor. The sound of voices rose and fell around them. Overhead a great crystal chandelier glittered, holding an amazing number of candles.

With his mouth close to her ear, Warren said, "Have you ever met George Graham, the publisher of *Graham's Magazine*?"

"Not yet, but I have heard much of him."

Warren chuckled. "Well, aside from being business rivals, Graham and Louis Godey are also somewhat social rivals, vying with one another to give the most lavish parties. Graham has an enormous chandelier, said by some to be the largest in America. That one up there—" he nodded his head "—is Godey's attempt to emulate his closest rival."

A voice said, "There you are! Welcome, Jemina. And you, too, Warren. I don't know how you managed to lure him out, but I'm glad you did. It will be good for him." Sarah Hale stood smiling broadly at them.

Jemina flushed. "I didn't lure him, Sarah...he..." She stammered to a halt, at a loss for words.

Warren touched her elbow and said easily, "It's true. She didn't lure me, Sarah. She sought my advice on the latest fashions. In exchange, I demanded the privilege of being her escort. After all, it would hardly do for her to come alone, now, would it?"

"Oh, I think Jemina could manage quite well alone," Sarah said dryly.

Sarah was elegant tonight in a black silk gown. Her dark hair fell in ringlets around her full face. The gown had a deep V neckline, and at the throat she wore a bit of lace, held together by a ruby brooch.

In that moment, Edgar Allan Poe ranged alongside Sarah. His curling hair was untidy, and his deep-set eyes gazed with melancholy languor. In one hand, he held a wineglass.

"Oh, Edgar," Sarah said, "have you met our newest addition to the staff, Jemina Benedict?"

"I believe so," Poe said, stroking his full mustache.

"Yes, I met Mr. Poe at the magazine on my first day there. I am an ardent admirer of his work. How do you do, Mr. Poe?"

"As well as can be expected, Miss Benedict. I am in excellent company, with good wine and good food. What more could a poor author demand of the world?"

His words were slurred, and Jemina realized that he had been imbibing rather heavily of the wine.

Sarah moved to take her arm. "Let's get you a glass of wine, Jemina, and I shall introduce you to some of our guests."

A few minutes later, a glass of port in her hand, Jemina moved around the room with Sarah. She met their host, and his wife, who seemed shy and retiring. Godey's rather plump face was flushed with high spirits, and he welcomed Jemina effusively.

In the next half hour, Jemina met a bewildering assortment of people, including the acclaimed novelist Nathaniel Hawthorne, who was in Philadelphia to lecture on his latest work; Lydia Sigourney, who had once been an editor at *Godey's Lady's Book* and who still contributed to the magazine; Nathaniel Parker Willis, who wrote light fiction and travel pieces; and many others whose names were unfamiliar to Jemina. There were also a number of artists present who did artwork for Godey's publication, as well as for other magazines and books.

Jemina was dazzled by it all and slightly out of breath by the time Sarah left her alone as she went to greet some new arrivals.

Clutching her glass of port, Jemina looked about for Warren. She spotted him across the room deep in conversation with Mr. Poe. Jemina didn't feel quite up to working her way across the room at the moment, so she backed into a corner out of the way of the crowd.

"So you're working on Godey's magazine, eh?"

With a start, she glanced around to see Nathaniel Willis smiling at her. She said, "Yes, Mr. Willis, but I've only worked there for a short time."

"Do you enjoy it?"

"Oh, yes, very much."

Willis nodded, pursing his thick lips thoughtfully. "I've often thought that if I was ever forced to work as an editor—God forbid it should ever happen—I would choose Godey's publication."

"Why?"

"Probably for the same reason that I *write* for the magazine. Godey is liberal with his rates. Did you know that he once paid me fifty dollars for an article that ran only four printed pages? An unheard-of sum. Many rival publications do not pay anything at all. In addition, Godey sees to it that the pieces are copyrighted in the author's name, something that few other publications bother to do. Yes." Willis nodded in satisfaction. "Yes, Godey's liberal rates are like a sunrise in the magazinist's world. And Sarah Hale is an excellent editor, most excellent."

"It seems to me those are all good reasons to remain an author," Jemina observed, "instead of becoming an editor."

"True, dear lady, true. And an author I shall remain. You may note that I said *forced* to work as an editor."

"Of course, few men work on the magazine," Jemina said with a touch of mischief. "A large number of the staff are female."

"True, true. But that might not be so bad." Willis preened, staring at her boldly. "Especially if all the women are single, young and pretty, like you, my dear."

Thinking to fend the compliment aside with a light air, Jemina said, "Thank you, kind sir." As she did so, her glance was drawn toward the spot where Warren and Mr. Poe were conversing. Several men had been attracted to the pair, and voices were rising in contention. Curiosity drew Jemina in that direction. Excusing herself to Willis, she went across the room.

As she drew near, she heard Poe's voice grow heated. She stepped behind Warren and touched him on the shoulder. He glanced around with a smile.

Jemina focused her attention on the group gathered around Poe. She had been introduced to most of them, but the only one she could put a name to was Nathaniel Hawthorne, an imposing figure with a high forehead, deep-set eyes and a thick mustache. She soon realized that the discussion involved Poe's "Literati" articles, published in *Godey's Lady's Book* some years earlier. The articles had been controversial at the time and, from the tenor of the conversation, remained so.

"My views concerning Henry Wadsworth Longfellow remain unchanged," Poe was saying. He stroked his mustache with his finger; his words were even more slurred than they had been earlier. "In my articles, I named him a determined imitator and a dextrous adapter of the ideas of other people. The fellow plagiarized my own 'Haunted Palace.'"

"It's a puzzlement to me that Longfellow didn't sue you for libel," one man remarked with a grin.

"That is because he had no grounds," Poe said triumphantly. "He well knew that I penned the truth."

"How about Thomas Dunn English? That created quite an uproar, as I recall."

"Perhaps I may have been overly vigorous there," Poe admitted. He drained his wineglass with a toss of his head. "I did offer the man an apology, and I was answered by blows. I then sued the *New York Mirror* for printing his libelous reply. And if you recall, I won, receiving damages and costs."

"You gained very little," his tormentor said with a shrug. "In my opinion, you lost much more in damage to your reputation."

"You go too far, sir!" Poe said angrily.

"Sir, I do believe that you do Mr. Poe a grave injustice." This from Nathaniel Hawthorne. "After all, he is surely entitled to his opinion, and can he be blamed if his opinion doesn't always coincide with that of others?"

Poe's tormentor laughed derisively. "That's all very well for you to say. He called you an 'extraordinary genius.'"

"Gentlemen, I believe you are all overlooking one thing here," said a voice from behind Jemina.

She turned her head to see Owen Thursday, immaculately attired as usual, standing behind her. He grinned lazily at her.

"And what is that, Thursday?" asked one of the men.

"Why, the undeniable fact that the pieces were very popular. The first installment of Mr. Poe's 'Literati' published in the *Lady Book* caused the magazine to completely sell out that particular issue immediately, and it had to be reprinted quickly."

One man scoffed, "The popularity of a piece of writing is no criterion of its worth."

"And pray, why not?" Owen Thursday said with a wicked grin. "Any writer worth his salt aspires to a wide readership, to fame and fortune."

"Fame, perhaps, but hardly fortune," Poe said in a grumbling voice.

"It is scarcely your fault, Mr. Poe, that your talent is ill paid." Owen clapped the author on the back.

"Ill fame is more like it," another man said. "It is my understanding that Louis received a great many letters complaining about the inclusion of the 'Literati' pieces, many threatening to cancel their subscriptions."

"That is true, but I refused to honor the complaints." Louis Godey had strolled up in time to overhear the last remark. "If you, by chance, happened to read the June issue of that year, in which I reprinted the first 'Literati' article, you will recall that I also added a lengthy statement in rebuttal. In essence, I said that we were publishing Mr. Poe's opinions, not our own, and whether or not we agreed with Mr. Poe was immaterial. I firmly stated that we were not to be intimidated by the threat of a loss of friends. . . ."

Owen touched Jemina on the elbow and led her aside. In a low voice, he said, "I was hoping you would be here, Jemina. I wish to tender an apology."

"An apology? From you, sir?"

"Yes, about that article you wrote on Elizabeth Blackwell. It is a fine piece of work. I must confess that I was pleasantly surprised, and I feel that I owe you an apology for any disparaging remarks I may have made on the train that day."

"But how did you see the article? It hasn't been published yet!"

He waved a hand airily. "Oh, I have my ways!"

"Did Sarah show it to you?" she demanded.

"A good newspaperman never reveals his sources," he said with a grin.

"I can't believe Sarah would do such a thing!"

"What does it matter?" He thumped his cane on the floor. "I'm simply trying to pay you a compliment, blast it!"

"I have not coveted a compliment from you, Mr. Thursday."

"Never mind, you have it. And now..." His smile was beguiling. "Since you couldn't see your way clear to taking supper with me in New York, how about tonight?"

"I did not come unescorted, sir," she said stiffly.

"You didn't?" he said, taken aback.

"You find it hard to believe that I could find an escort?" she asked, suddenly enjoying herself.

He said hastily, "No, no, on the contrary. But it didn't occur to me...."

"I came with Mr. Barricone."

"Warren Barricone?" His eyebrows climbed. "But Warren has a wife."

"A bedridden wife," she said tartly. "And we had her blessing." Even as she spoke the words, Jemina

wondered if they were true. "And now, if you will
excuse me, Mr. Thursday, I must speak to Sarah."

She moved quickly away before he could respond.

Owen gazed after her bemusedly. She looked very
beautiful tonight, and he had to admit that he was a
little piqued by the way she spurned his advances. On
the other hand, he supposed he was somewhat
spoiled. It was rare indeed that his attentions were
scorned by any woman.

He was surprised that she had been escorted by
Warren Barricone. He knew Barricone only to speak
to and knew that he had a wife who was ailing. Beyond that, he knew very little of the man.

He turned slowly and found Barricone looking at
him with an expression of displeasure. Then Barricone's gaze left him to follow Jemina's progress across
the room. In a moment, he glanced back at Owen,
frowning now, and he took a step in Owen's direction.

The man feels more toward Jemina than just
friendship, no matter what she might think, Owen
thought. Not in the mood for a confrontation, which
he feared was about to take place, Owen nodded
coolly to Barricone and sauntered away, losing himself in the crowd.

Chapter Six

EARLY ON THE MORNING following the party at Louis Godey's, Jemina sought an audience with Sarah Hale.

Sarah greeted her with sparkling eyes. "Did you enjoy the party, my dear? I had a grand time, in spite of the fact that Mr. Poe was in his cups and became rather... disputatious before the evening was past." Her expression saddened. "But then, poor Edgar has his burdens to bear, so I suppose he must be forgiven, as much as I dislike intemperance in anyone."

"Yes, Sarah, I enjoyed the party. Again, thank you for inviting me. Did you know that Owen Thursday was there?"

"Of course. I invited him. However, I must admit I was a little surprised that he attended. Owen usually disdains such gatherings." She studied Jemina curiously. "Why do you ask?"

"Because I . . ." Jemina hesitated, then blurted, "Did you let him read my Blackwell article, Sarah?"

Sarah's lips thinned, and she folded her hands on top of the desk. "I could point out that such matters are not your concern, Jemina, but I shall answer your question. Yes, he asked to see it, and I let him read it."

"But why, Sarah?"

"Why? Because Owen is an old friend, and I deeply value his judgment on such matters," Sarah said evenly.

"But it doesn't seem ethical, to let an outsider read something before it's in print."

"Not ethical? Jemina, when you finish a piece and it's on it's way to being published, it's no longer your property. You are an employee of the magazine, and what you write belongs to us." Sarah's expression was severe, and she was tapping a pen on the desk. "Even if you were an independent author and I accepted a manuscript from you, it would no longer belong to you. Certainly, it would be copyrighted in your name, but if it belongs to us, and if I see fit to let someone peruse it, that is my prerogative. Of course, I don't let just *anyone* read it, but Owen is not just anyone."

Jemina was not appeased. "I fail to see how Owen Thursday is different from any other outsider."

"He is different in that he is a good news reporter—in my opinion the best I know—and your article is news, Jemina. He told me that he had met you on the train to New York and you told him you were on your way to conduct an interview. Is that true?"

"Yes, that's true enough."

"He said he was simply curious as to what kind of a writer you were. If it's any consolation, he agreed with me that it is a fine piece of work."

Jemina realized from Sarah's manner that it would be risky to push the matter forth, especially in view of the fact that she was fortunate to have escaped unscathed thus far. She got to her feet and said reluctantly, "I suppose you do have the right to do as you wish."

"I most certainly do."

Jemina started toward the door.

"Jemina . . ."

Jemina turned back.

"A manuscript is not a baby, my dear, although I realize that an author feels as protective toward it as she would a child." Sarah's smile took the sting from her words.

DESPITE HAVING BEEN in Philadelphia for well over three months, Jemina had seen little of the city. So far, her time had been spent either at the magazine or at home with her aunt.

That afternoon, after leaving work late, she felt restless and still resentful over Sarah's letting Owen Thursday see her manuscript prior to its publication. She decided to explore a bit before going home. She didn't feel that in her present mood she would respond properly to her aunt's lively chatter.

She was well aware that Philadelphia was steeped in history. There was the Carpenter's Hall, where Thomas Jefferson, John Adams, Patrick Henry and many other fiery, loyal Americans had met and debated the Continental and Constitutional congresses; and it was the city in which the Declaration of Independence had been conceived and signed.

A city of twenty-two thousand people, Philadelphia was considered by many to be "the Athens of America." It had one of the finest libraries in the United States, the country's first science museum and a renowned academy for artists, founded by the painter Charles Willson Peale. For ten years the national capital, it was now the magazine capital of the country.

Jemina strolled along Chestnut Street, peering into the windows of the many fashionable shops. Just as the gaslights came on in the street, she entered Roussel's, the country's first soda fountain, and lingered awhile over a flavored ice.

After leaving Roussel's, she wandered up and down the side streets. Philadelphia streets, except for a few main thoroughfares, were narrower than those of her native Boston. Most of the brick town houses were built close to the sidewalks and had wrought-iron railings and narrow, white marble steps. On the whole, many of these streets were similar to those found in Beacon Hill, near Jemina's own home.

Suddenly, Jemina was assailed by a wave of homesickness. She had promised her parents that she would be home for the Christmas holidays, yet that date was some distance off.

Lost in melancholy and remembrance, Jemina walked on, paying no attention to which turns she took. Suddenly, she became aware of wheels behind her on the cobblestones, and with a start she took notice of her surroundings. She looked about, realizing belatedly that she had wandered far afield. She was out of the residential district and on a narrow street lined with large buildings that appeared to be factories of some sort, and she could see the Delaware River up ahead. She was in the waterfront area, and she had been warned that it was unsafe for a woman to be alone here.

It was very dark; streetlights were situated only at the end of each block. Jemina was in the middle of a block and all alone. Instead of residential windows warm with light, the few windows she saw were dark and grimy.

Then she realized that she could no longer hear the sound of wheels, and she turned toward the street, her heart hammering with sudden fear. A buggy, the top down, had stopped beside her, only two feet away. Its lone occupant was a man. He stared at her out of deep-socketed eyes. For a fleeting moment, in the shadows, his face took on the appearance of a skull.

Under his bold appraisal, Jemina shrank back.

"Well, what a pretty you are," he said in a growling voice. "And out here all alone, too."

He tied the reins off and stepped down in a fluid movement. He was tall, bulky, with broad shoulders and black, coarse hair, worn long. His narrow, bony face looked incongruous perched atop such a bulky body. He was carelessly dressed; and as he moved toward her, Jemina saw that his deep-set eyes were black as ebony and equally expressionless. He looked to be in his mid-fifties.

Jemina stepped away until her back was against the wall of the building behind her. For such a big man, he moved easily, quickly; he was close to her now. Without taking her gaze from his face, Jemina began to slide along the wall.

He moved again, and then he had both hands flat against the wall on either side of her, caging her. She pushed frantically against one arm and found it as unyielding as an iron bar.

"Why the hurry, pretty? Why not get acquainted?"

AT APPROXIMATELY the same time that Jemina had been in Sarah Hale's office, Owen Thursday was in the office of his own editor, Thomas Carruthers.

"I have an assignment for you, Thursday," Carruthers announced in his usual brusque manner.

Owen sprawled in the office's one visitor's chair and tried to see the editor's face through a haze of cigar smoke. "Where am I going this time?"

"You're not going anywhere," Carruthers said with a touch of malice. "The assignment is right here, in the city."

Owen sat up in dismay. "In Philadelphia? I'm a field correspondent, Thomas. I don't work in the city. Haven't for years, not since my beginning on the *Ledger*."

"Might do you good to go back to your beginnings, Thursday." Carruthers waved the smoke away from his face. "Ever think of that? Or have you come to believe you're too high-and-mighty for a city assignment?"

"No, of course not. But it *has* been a long time."

"Well, there's nothing else, no place to send you right now, and you *are* on salary. We're not a charitable institution, you know. You have to do something to earn your keep."

Owen heaved a sigh. "All right, Thomas, what's the assignment?"

"You ever hear of a man named Lester Gilroy?"

Owen considered for a moment. "Can't say that I have."

"He's not local; he's from New York City. He's big in the garment industry, coat making, shirt making and shoe factories. We've learned that he is in Philadelphia, and the rumor is that he's looking for a building to buy."

"You think he's considering opening a garment factory here?"

"That's what the fear is. Gilroy has the reputation of being a shoddy operator, and we don't want such a fellow to set up shop here."

"*We?*" Owen said with an edge of sarcasm. "You're all heart, Thomas."

"Well, the publisher and the city fathers want him kept out," Carruthers said righteously. "The thinking is that a strong article, exposing Gilroy for what he is, might cause him to change his mind about opening a factory here. What I want is for you to dig into his background, then interview him, see if you can get him to admit what he's doing in Philadelphia. Perhaps follow him around, see what he's up to. You know the procedure."

"Follow him around? Damn it, I'm no detective!"

"Try it anyway, Thursday. You might even learn a new profession, one you can get into when you foul up on the paper; which you will do sooner or later, I'm quite confident."

"I'm sure you would love to see that happen," Owen said without rancor, getting to his feet. "But don't hold your breath. I'll still be here when you're gone, Thomas."

Owen spent the rest of the morning and much of the afternoon going through the back files of the *Ledger* and the New York papers for what information he could glean on Lester Gilroy. When he was finished, he decided that Gilroy was indeed a slimy character. The man had grown wealthy off the cheap labor of women and children. As a rule, Owen paid little attention to civic matters; he had learned early on that the world was filled with injustices and he could do little about them. But what he learned about Gilroy filled him with disgust; something should be done about the man. For the first time, he felt some interest in this assignment. If he could in some way be instrumental in keeping the bastard out of Philadelphia, well and good.

He decided to drop by Gilroy's hotel. If he was lucky, he might be able to catch the fellow in. Owen doubted that Gilroy would even talk to him, much less reveal his purpose in the city; but at least it might bother him to learn that his presence was known and that someone was keeping an eye on him.

On his way into the hotel, Owen passed a heavyset man with a bony, unsmiling countenance, dressed all in black. At the desk, Owen inquired after Lester Gilroy.

"Oh, Mr. Gilroy just this minute left the hotel," the desk clerk informed him.

"The fellow in black?"

The clerk nodded, and Owen wheeled, legging it out through the entrance doors. He was just in time to see the bulky man getting into an open buggy. Owen started toward the buggy, then stopped as Gilroy flicked the reins and the buggy started away. Owen looked quickly about. In front of the hotel was a hackney for hire.

He hurried to the hack and told the driver, "I want you to follow that buggy." He pointed to Gilroy's buggy, which was just rounding a corner up the street. "Don't stay too close to him. I don't want him to get the wind up."

The driver eyed him distrustfully. "You a copper?"

"Never mind who I am," Owen snapped. He extracted several coins from his pocket and gave them to the driver. "Just follow that buggy. There's more for you if you don't lose him."

"Yes, sir!" The driver touched his cap, and Owen hopped into the hackney.

Gilroy's buggy was easy enough to keep in view, and there was enough traffic on the streets so that Owen's hackney could remain back discreetly without losing sight of the buggy.

Before long, the buggy was off the main-traveled streets, however, and into a less busy, industrial section of town. Owen leaned forward to speak to the driver. "Keep well back. I don't want him to catch on that he's being followed. There's scarcely any traffic now, so it isn't likely we'll lose him. Stay at least two blocks behind him."

"Whatever you say, governor."

Shortly thereafter, Owen saw the buggy stopping on a side street, which was ill lit and completely deserted. "Stop here," he told the driver.

The driver stopped the hackney two blocks back. Owen saw Gilroy get out of the buggy and go into one of the commercial buildings. He was tempted to get out and stroll along the street in order to see what kind of a building Gilroy had entered; but since he had no way of knowing how long the man would stay inside, he decided to curb his impatience and wait.

Owen leaned back at an angle so that he could keep an eye on Gilroy's buggy and thought again of what he had read about Lester Gilroy.

And then, for some strange reason, the thought of Jemina Benedict entered his mind. Jemina was a fine writer and would be even better with more experience. She reminded Owen of himself ten years ago, when he had started on the *Ledger* as a brash, young reporter. He, too, had been filled with fire and zeal, determined to make a mark for himself. And he had succeeded. His rise had been rapid; first as a reporter and then, beginning four years ago, as a field correspondent.

His first field assignment had been to cover James K. Polk's presidential campaign in 1844, and his coverage had been so impressive that he was given other top assignments. He had been in Texas when that state had ratified its annexation to the United States in 1845; he had been with Colonel Stephen Kearny at the beginning of the war with Mexico, when Kearny was sent on an expedition to New Mexico to occupy its capital, Santa Fe; he had been with General Winfield Scott through most of the campaign in Mexico, up to the time Scott had captured Mexico City last September, effectively ending the war with Mexico; and Owen had only recently returned from reporting cavalry and Indian skirmishes on the Great Plains.

In fact, Owen thought with a wry grin, the past months had been the longest he'd been home in three years. But it had been a satisfying life, full of adventure and excitement, and it had given him the feeling of being privy to great events.

He sat up suddenly as he saw Gilroy come out of the building and get into his buggy. To the driver, Owen said, "There he is. Wait until he gets to the end of the block, then start after him."

Owen was debating whether he should continue to follow Gilroy or let him go on and attempt to learn whom he had seen in the building and what his purpose was there; but as the hackney began to move after the buggy, he made up his mind to follow Gilroy

for a while yet. He could return to the building another time. As the hackney rattled past the entrance
to the building, Owen made a mental note of the address for future reference.

It soon became clear that Gilroy was headed in the
general direction of his hotel, although they were still
in the ill-lighted factory section near the river. Now
the buggy turned down a street that Owen knew led
to a busy boulevard.

He spoke to the driver. "You can disregard caution now. It's no matter if he knows he's being followed."

The driver urged his horse to a greater speed, but
before the distance between the hackney and the
buggy had narrowed to any great extent, Owen was
surprised to see the buggy halt. He was even more
surprised to see that the buggy had stopped alongside a fashionably dressed woman.

What, Owen wondered, was a lone woman doing
in the waterfront area? She didn't appear to be a
woman of the streets. And even if she were a street
woman, why was she in this area? There was no
business to solicit here.

Owen saw Gilroy begin to climb down from the
buggy and saw the woman shrink back from him.
There was something naggingly familiar about
her. . . .

"Stop here, driver, and wait for me."

Before the hackney had come to a full stop, Owen
had swung down and was striding along the narrow
sidewalk, twirling his cane. He saw that Gilroy had
now pinned the woman against the building, with an
arm on each side of her, and his step quickened.

He reached the pair in time to hear Gilroy say, "Why the hurry, pretty? Why not get acquainted?"

Owen reached out his cane and tapped Gilroy on the shoulder. "Perhaps the lady doesn't care to make your acquaintance, Mr. Gilroy."

Gilroy's head whipped around, and dead eyes stared into Owen's. Past him, Owen looked into Jemina's frightened face.

Gilroy snapped, "Do I know you, sir?"

"Not to my knowledge," Owen said lightly. "But it is possible that you may soon become acquainted with my name. I'm Owen Thursday."

"That name means nothing to me. I would suggest that you move along and leave us."

"Suppose we ask the lady about that. The lady, by the way, is Jemina Benedict. Jemina, meet Lester Gilroy. Do you wish me to move along, Jemina?"

"No, Owen. Please stay," she said in a tense voice.

"There, you see?"

"Well, if you know the lady," Gilroy said sullenly. He stepped back. "I saw her all alone. I thought I would offer her a ride in my buggy. A woman alone in this neighborhood isn't safe."

"Obviously you are correct about that."

Gilroy flushed and said indignantly, "Do you mean to infer that she was in danger of being molested by me?"

"That's the way it struck me, to be truthful."

Gilroy's thin lips tightened. "I resent that, sir!"

"Resent all you like." Owen twirled his cane.

Eyeing the cane, Gilroy muttered, "I suppose the circumstances might give that impression." His eyes narrowed. "What did you mean by remarking that I may soon become acquainted with your name?"

"I am a newspaperman, with the *Philadelphia Ledger*, and you, Mr. Gilroy, should be pleased to know that you are my present assignment."

Gilroy stepped back, his breath hissing in quick inhalation. "Of what possible interest could I be to your newspaper?"

"Don't be modest, Gilroy. Your reputation has preceded you. My editor is curious as to the reason for your presence here." Owen grinned. "That is why I have been following you."

"Following me? What impudence!" Gilroy said angrily. "I am in Philadelphia on business, sir!"

"But on what business? Would you care to enlighten me?"

"I will do no such thing! It is a sad day when a man cannot go about his business without interference."

"That depends upon the business."

Gilroy gave him a murderous look, turned about, climbed into his buggy and whipped the reins. The startled horse bolted, and the buggy clattered away at a fast clip.

"Owen . . ."

He turned to look down into Jemina's pale face.

"Thank you for rescuing me. I'm not sure that I really needed rescuing, but—" she laughed shakily "—but he did give me rather a fright."

"He has a bad reputation, that one, and it just may be fortunate that I happened along when I did."

"Are you really assigned to do a story on that man?" she asked curiously.

"I am indeed, but first let's get you out of this district." He took her arm and steered her toward the hackney. "What in the world were you doing around here, anyway?"

"I'm not really sure," she said, flushing. "I was out walking and I had an attack of homesickness. I wandered rather far afield before I realized it."

Owen gave her a hand up and got in beside her. Before speaking to the driver, he said, "Have you supped yet?"

"Well, no. I had an ice at Roussel's."

"That is hardly sufficient to sustain a healthy girl like you. Would you have supper with me? Now, wait before you refuse." He held up his hand. "I think you owe me that privilege for rescuing you."

"*Owe* you that privilege?" She stared at him, and at his artless look she began to laugh. He was such a charming rogue, how could she stay angry with him? "You know, I was very upset with you today. I talked to Sarah, and she *did* let you read my piece on Elizabeth Blackwell."

"Why should you be so upset? I complimented you on the piece, didn't I?"

"I still feel it's an invasion of my privacy."

Owen threw back his head and roared with laughter. "I'm sorry," he finally gasped out. "You have done an article that will be read by thousands of people. I only read it a bit early! Now—" he sobered "—you haven't answered my question."

"Oh, all right, Mr. Thursday," she said, also laughing. "I suppose if I don't have supper with you sometime, you will devil me until I do."

"That's exactly right," he said cheerfully. "I'm a very determined fellow." He leaned forward to give the driver an address.

"Now, are you going to satisfy my curiosity about that man?"

"Lester Gilroy?" Owen made himself comfortable, stretching his long legs out as far as the confines of the hackney would permit. "Our Mr. Gilroy is a shady character. He is from New York's garment district. He owns spinning mills and clothing factories. He employs women and children, working them long hours and paying them a mere pittance. From this, he has grown quite wealthy."

Jemina said indignantly, "But how can he get away with that? Are there no laws governing working conditions for women and children?"

"Laws? Hardly." Owen smiled grimly. "There has been some agitation for having legislation passed governing the employment of children. But always such men as Gilroy say they are merely providing employment for improvident widows, young unmarried women and poor children. Without their generosity, they maintain, the poorhouses of the country would be filled to overflowing."

"He seems like a dreadful man. Is he planning on opening such a factory here in Philadelphia?"

"That's what my editor wishes me to find out. If I find it to be true and expose his intentions in the paper, perhaps he will have second thoughts and change his plans."

"But why you, Owen?" she asked, a note of slyness creeping into her voice. "You've reported wars and rumors of wars all over the continent, and now you're given a picayune assignment such as this? Isn't that somewhat demeaning?"

His face darkened, and for a moment Jemina thought she had gone too far. Then he grinned and wagged a finger at her. "Touché! I know you're trying to ruffle my feathers, but I'm feeling too good

right now to lose my temper. Besides, is it my fault
that there are no great events anywhere in the world
right now worthy of my attention?''

ALTHOUGH SHE WAS dressed well enough, Jemina felt
a little uncomfortable in the restaurant, which she
knew was one of the finest in Philadelphia. She hadn't
really considered that when she had accepted his invitation; she would have much preferred to have gone
home first, to bathe and change into other clothing,
but it was too late now.

Owen Thursday seemed perfectly at home in the
restaurant, clearly a regular of the place, for the
maître d' addressed him respectfully and by name.
They were escorted to a corner table, covered with
snowy-white linen, polished silver and sparkling
crystal.

Owen ordered a bottle of champagne and also their
food: squab, venison and an array of side dishes.

The waiter poured champagne for them, and after
he left, Owen raised his glass in a toast. ''Here's to
us!''

Jemina had picked up her glass, but instead of
touching it to his, she stared across the table. For
some strange reason, she felt warm and flushed. She
said tartly, ''To us? That strikes me as rather pre-
sumptuous, Mr. Thursday!''

''How so?'' he said airily. ''Oh, I didn't quite
mean it the way you evidently infer. But here we are,
a successful newspaperman and a lovely lady who
strikes me as being well on her way to making her
mark as an author. But perhaps I should rephrase the
toast. How about to you, Jemina Benedict, and to
your future success?''

"I could hardly refuse to drink to that, now, could I?"

They clicked glasses and drank. The champagne was dry and tickled Jemina's throat. At the moment, Owen was looking off, waving to someone across the room, and she took advantage of the opportunity to study him. He *was* handsome, no gainsaying that. The patch over his eye, instead of detracting from his looks, lent him a piratical air.

Without warning, as though he felt her gaze, he turned his head and looked at her. Usually he was smiling, wearing a careless manner, but now his expression was grave.

A charged feeling seemed to emanate from him, coming across the table in waves, and it aroused a strange emotion in her, one both frightening and exciting.

Hurriedly, she said, "I'm surprised at your toasting my future success. You strike me as the sort of man who disapproves of a woman working, a man who believes a woman's only rightful career is marriage and children."

"I have no great objection to a woman working." He toyed with his glass, his gaze riveted on hers. "Until marriage, that is. *Then* I think it is only fitting and proper for her to devote her time to those things you mentioned."

"I see." She lowered her gaze to her glass. "But what happens if a woman does not wish to get married?"

He looked at her in astonishment. "I thought all women wanted to get married."

"I didn't say that I did not want to marry. I probably will someday, when I find the right man and fall in love. How about you?'' she asked. ''Aren't you going to marry? Most men your age are already married.''

''Oh, I'm sure I'll marry someday, also.'' He smiled slightly. ''Also, when I find the right woman. So far, at least as of this moment, I haven't found her.''

She found his look disconcerting and had to look away; and to her consternation, she felt herself flushing.

THREE DAYS LATER, an article appeared under Owen Thursday's byline in the *Philadelphia Ledger*. The article concerned Lester Gilroy. Carefully skirting libel, it detailed Gilroy's background, his shoddy operations in New York, and hinted at the possibility that he was considering opening a factory in Philadelphia.

In his hotel room, Gilroy read the article with mounting rage. Afterward, he paced the room in angry strides, contemplating what his next move should be. Newspaper articles of such nature had been published about him in the past, but he had generally laughed them off. This case was different; all the other stories had been about factories already open and thriving, while this article concerned one still in the planning stages. He could still open his factory; nothing in the article could prevent that. Yet the story would create an unfavorable climate, placing obstacles in his path.

Abruptly, he crumpled up the newspaper and threw it into the corner of the room.

To hell with it, to hell with Philadelphia! He didn't need the kind of problems the newspaper article would generate. There were other cities aside from this one where he could locate, cities that would be delighted to have him open a factory. Fortunately, he had not yet signed a lease on the proposed factory building, so he was out of pocket only his hotel bill and travel expenses.

But he determined to remember the two people who had caused his trouble. The reporter, Owen Thursday, and the woman . . . what was her name? Jemina Benedict, that was it. Gilroy never forgot or forgave a slight, never forgot anyone who balked him.

He would remember those two names; and if either one ever crossed his path again, giving him the opportunity to do them harm, he would most certainly do it!

Chapter Seven

JEMINA AND CLARA were taking a brief stroll along Chestnut Street during the noon hour, idling before the shops and chatting. The area along Chestnut between Fourth and Tenth streets was the town's fashion center, called by many the "Broadway" of Philadelphia. The fashion editor of the *Book* once called Chestnut the street where fashion, folly, pleasure and business reigned in turn.

During her brief time of employment at the *Book*, Jemina had become very conscious of fashions. Today, she was attired stylishly in a moiré dress of pearly gray, with immaculate gaiter boots and kid gloves. She carried a white parasol against the sun. It was a hot day, made much warmer by the brick buildings that walled the narrow streets.

Clara was well dressed, although not as fashionably. Early on, she had told Jemina, "I spend no more on clothes than necessary for good taste. I have an ailing mother to support, and the doctor fees are alarming. Besides, I've decided that if I'm ever to catch a beau, it will be because of the inner woman, not because of some frippery I'm wearing."

As they quickened their steps, a newsboy came down the street, hawking that day's edition of the *Bulletin*. Clara said, "Jemina, did you read Owen Thursday's story in yesterday's *Ledger* about Lester Gilroy?"

Jemina nodded. "Oh, yes, I read it. It was a strong story. It should serve Owen's purpose and discourage Mr. Gilroy from opening a factory here in Philadelphia."

"Owen, is it?" Clara looked at her curiously. "I didn't realize you knew him that well."

Jemina felt heat rise to her face. "I didn't, until four days ago, when he rescued me from Mr. Gilroy's obnoxious attentions."

"What?" Clara came to a momentary stop, staring at her. "How did you happen to come across that man?"

Quickly, Jemina told her what had happened.

"Well, Mr. Gilroy sounds like a proper villain."

"He is, believe me. I was fortunate that Mr. Thursday came along when he did."

"I almost envy you," Clara said wistfully. "Owen is a handsome devil."

"Why, Clara! I thought you weren't all that interested in men."

Now it was Clara's turn to flush. "That wasn't exactly what I said. Besides, there are always exceptions. Not that it matters; Owen would never look at me twice. He can probably have any woman in Philadelphia with a snap of his fingers."

"A heartbreaker, is he?" Jemina said with a sinking feeling.

"Oh, yes. Even Sarah is taken with him."

"I wonder why Sarah has never married again. Her husband has been dead for a long time."

Clara shrugged. "She told me once that she has been too busy with her career to think of marriage. You know the way many men look upon a woman who insists on working. Sarah says she wouldn't give up her career for any man.'' Clara looked at the watch pinned to the waist of her dress. ''We've been gone for some time. We had better get back.''

''All right.'' They turned and started back down Chestnut. ''How about you, Clara? If you had a choice, would you choose marriage over a career?''

Clara laughed somewhat self-consciously. ''Fortunately, or unfortunately, that is a choice I haven't had to make as yet. But I think that if I found a man I loved, I'd settle for marriage, if I had to make a choice.''

''It would be a difficult decision, wouldn't it?'' Jemina said thoughtfully. ''I will never understand why most men are so opposed to their wives working.''

''At your age, Jemina, I wouldn't worry too much about it. There will be time enough for that later.'' She glanced over slyly. ''You're not thinking about Owen Thursday and marriage, are you?''

''Of course not!'' Jemina said heatedly.

''Because if you are, you had best forget about it. Mr. Thursday is hardly the marrying kind.''

''You need not worry. If and when I decide to get married, Owen Thursday would hardly be my choice!''

THE DOOR TO Sarah Hale's office swung open, and Owen breezed in.

Sarah, occupied with copyediting the issue of the *Lady's Book* soon to go to press, looked up in annoyance. ''Owen, doesn't it ever occur to you to knock?''

He grinned lazily. ''My dear Sarah, if I announced myself, you might turn me away, and I wouldn't take kindly to that.''

She leaned back, smiling in spite of her annoyance. "I don't suppose you would. Imagine, the great Owen Thursday spurned by a mere woman."

He sprawled in the chair before her desk, long legs stretched out before him. "I thought I was always welcome here, Sarah."

"There are times and there are times. Right now, I'm quite busy, as you can see. Sometimes I think you might as well work here, the way you come and go at liberty."

"There is no use trying to recruit me, Sarah," he said solemnly. "You know it would never do, my working here. Writing about recipes and ladies' fashions is not my métier."

"That's not all we write about, and you well know it!" Then, at his grin, she sighed in exasperation. "What is it you want, Owen?"

"Why, I thought you were always delighted to have me visit, Sarah, for our usual exchange of views."

"Owen!" she warned.

"All right! Lord, it must be difficult working for you. I just wondered . . ." He made his voice casual. "I wondered if you had read my piece on Lester Gilroy?"

"Well, now." She began to smile. "The great Owen Thursday soliciting my opinion of his work."

"Well, it does involve the welfare of the city we both love, Sarah," he said somewhat defensively.

"My first reaction was surprise that you, of all people, would be doing a story of such insignificance. No far-off wars, no exciting battles."

"I was here, it was a story that badly needed doing, and I was bored sitting around doing nothing. And it was *not* insignificant!"

"I thought it was a fine piece, Owen," she said, suddenly serious. "And I agree, it was certainly a piece that badly needed doing. We have no need of such trash operating in Philadelphia."

He was smiling broadly at her praise, and Sarah had to wonder at such a renowned journalist as Owen Thursday seeking accolades from her; yet, at the same time, she was flattered.

He leaned forward. "You'll be happy to know that the article served its purpose. Mr. Gilroy departed our fair city this morning, as if his tail feathers were on fire. And I'm willing to wager that he'll not be back anytime soon."

"Then I suppose congratulations are in order for a job well done, Owen."

Before he could respond, a light knock sounded on the door. Sarah called, "Come in!"

The door opened, and Jemina entered. "Sarah, I wanted to talk to you about . . ." She broke off at the sight of Owen.

Owen got to his feet and bowed slightly. "Miss Benedict, I was hoping I would see you today."

Sarah, watching Jemina's face flush and seeing the bright smile on Owen's face, suddenly knew the real reason for Owen's unannounced visit.

Now Jemina darted a glance at Sarah.

Owen was going on, "I have theater tickets for tomorrow evening, Miss Benedict. Edwin Forrest is starring in *Macbeth*. I would be most honored if you would accompany me."

"Oh, I've never seen Mr. Forrest, and I've read so much about him. . . ." Jemina broke off to look again at Sarah, who gave a slight shrug.

Owen said, "Then you will accompany me? We can have a late supper after the theater, if you like."

Jemina stared at him, her face still slightly flushed, and Sarah noticed that the attraction between these two was glaringly apparent. She remembered the warning she had given Jemina the day she came to the magazine. Owen was a womanizer, true, but he was also handsome as sin, and good company. However, Jemina had given every evidence that she could take care of herself. Besides, Sarah reflected, it's none of my business. Although she felt protective of the girl, Jemina was an employee, not one of her children.

Jemina was saying, "Yes, Owen, I will go with you to the theater."

"Good!" Owen flashed his beguiling smile, winked at Sarah and bounced his cane on the floor. "Then if you would be so kind as to give me your address, I will call for you at seven sharp tomorrow evening."

Jemina gave him her aunt's address, and Owen bid them both good-day and took his departure.

Still flushed, Jemina sat down in the chair he had vacated. "I hope you don't mind, Sarah."

"Mind? Why should I mind, child? I am not your social arbiter. I am fond of Owen, but I will warn you again . . . do not become enamored of him. If you do, it will likely be to your sorrow."

Jemina's head went back. "That will never occur."

Won't it? Sarah thought; that is something only time will tell. She said, "What did you wish to see me about, Jemina?"

"Oh." Jemina had to pause for a moment to get her thoughts in order. Why was it she always became so flustered around Owen Thursday? "About the ladies' medical missionary society you wish to organize. Remember, you assigned me to write some articles about the project? Sarah, there just aren't that many ladies qualified. Although I have found a few women with nursing training, all but two of those are married."

"You've just told me the basis for your articles. Why *aren't* there more women qualified for such duties? Inform the reader just how few women receive medical training, even something as rudimentary as nurse's training. You can mention Elizabeth Blackwell. Talk to the women who have gotten married. Did they choose marriage over careers as nurses? Use your imagination, Jemina!"

Jemina was nodding. "All those things have occurred to me. There is sufficient material for the articles, I agree. But you also wanted me to find women around whom you could form the missionary society."

"You said there were two who aren't married?"

"Yes, but one of the two is ill, much too ill to participate in what you have in mind."

"And the other?"

"Martha Sanders. Yes, she is young, healthy, with three years of nursing experience, and she seems quite interested in the project. At least, she said she would volunteer her services, go anywhere in the world she might be needed."

"Then begin with her." Sarah leaned forward, her expression intense. "Any journey must begin with the first step, Jemina. Let this Martha Sanders be the first step in this project. Let her be the first step toward a bright tomorrow, to all our bright tomorrows.''

Jemina felt a stir of excitement. ''I can build the first article around her, making the point that she is the only person presently available for the project you have in mind.''

Sarah nodded approvingly. ''Excellent thinking! Be sure to stress the ultimate goals of the society as I outlined them for you. I do not expect overnight results. Past experience has taught me that these things build slowly. It took me years of work to form the Seamen's Aid Society in Boston and twelve years to see the Bunker Hill Monument finally completed. . . .''

THE WALNUT STREET Theater was the oldest theater building in Philadelphia and one of the oldest in the United States.

The front of the building sported six Doric columns, each topped with beautifully cast iron wreaths. A crowd of well-dressed people milled about under the flickering gaslights as Owen helped Jemina out of the carriage.

Owen looked as dashing as ever, perhaps even more so in evening dress, Jemina thought. Tall, smiling, urbane, he gave a small bow, held out his arm and escorted her into the theater.

The lobby was spacious, with recesses for confectionery alcoves. Owen escorted her through the lobby and up a stairway to one of the upper boxes.

''A box!'' she exclaimed. ''However did you manage?''

Owen arched an eyebrow. "A newspaperman develops a wide acquaintance among the swells, and often favors are granted."

After they had settled in their comfortable seats in the spacious box, Owen said, "Edwin Forrest is rather eccentric, you know."

"No, I didn't know." She had to raise her voice slightly to be heard above the precurtain buzz of the crowd. "I know that he has a worldwide reputation."

"He has that, in more ways than one. He has a violent temperament and is outspoken in support of American actors. He made his stage debut at the age of fourteen, made his New York debut as Othello in 1826 and is now regarded as the greatest tragedian in the world. He almost caused a riot in England three years ago, in this very same play. The audience favored one of their own, William Charles Macready, and were hostile to Forrest. He was equally hostile and spoke forcefully to the theatergoers."

"You mean, he actually talked back to the audience?"

"I told you he was eccentric," Owen said with a laugh. "I've seen Forrest act once before, and as you'll soon see, he has a rather... well, shall we say, a bravura style of acting?"

When the play began and Macbeth met the three witches on the dark moor, Jemina saw the truth of Owen's statement. Forrest's acting style was very florid; but he had a rich, eloquent voice, a forceful stage presence, and from the moment of his entrance, she was caught up in the play. She actually believed that he was the thane of Glamis.

When Lady Macbeth finally prevailed upon her husband to murder Duncan, king of Scotland, and Macbeth crept into the king's bedchamber to plunge a knife into the king's heart, Jemina grasped Owen's hand tightly. She allowed it to remain in his grip throughout the rest of the play.

At the climax, during the battle, when Macduff severed Macbeth's head, Jemina wept unashamedly. Perhaps Edwin Forrest's performance at that point was overly melodramatic, but Jemina thought it was very powerful.

In the carriage leaving the theater, Owen said, "How did you like the play?"

"Oh, I loved it!" she said enthusiastically. "Did you?"

"I must confess that I missed quite a bit of it," he said, smiling. "I was more interested in watching you."

"Watching *me*? Why on earth would you do that?"

"I was intrigued by the play of emotions across your face. Everything you feel is revealed in your face. I would advise you never to play poker, my dear."

Jemina knew that she was blushing furiously. She was not aware of that facet of her personality.

"But at least there is one advantage to that, as far as I am concerned," he went on. "I'll always know when you're angry with me, pleased with me or whatever."

"Aren't you assuming a great deal, Mr. Thursday? Assuming that we are going to become such close acquaintances?" She recognized that she was playing the coquette, but for the moment, at least, it fitted her mood.

Owen was smiling again. "I will admit that I hope we will be seeing a good deal of one another in the future. I think we make a handsome couple. . . ."

"Well! There is certainly nothing modest about you."

"I have never laid claim to modesty," he said, unabashed. "But it seems to me that we have a lot in common, and we enjoy ourselves together."

"And what happens when you go traipsing halfway across the continent on one of your assignments?"

"That's the hazard of my profession," he said with a shrug. "But I always return, my dear. And don't speak too soon. You may be sent off somewhere, as well. Godey often sends his writers to Paris, for fashion shows and the like."

She stiffened at the note of condescension in his voice. "Naturally, that is not as important as some war or other equally violent event!"

"Jemina . . ." He sighed heavily. "You are so infernally sensitive! You couldn't very well be sent off to cover a war, for two reasons. First, the *Lady Book* does not report on wars or anything of a violent nature. Second, you are a woman."

Jemina's temper was still running, and for a moment she was tempted to ask him why a woman could not report on a war, but then she decided it would be a mistake. Owen would think her daft for even thinking such a thing; and she had to confess that she had no interest in covering a war, so why create a scene?

"All right, Mr. Thursday, you report on your battles, and I shall content myself with less violent matters."

Owen took her to supper in another fine restaurant. As before, a tuxedoed maître d' greeted Owen and escorted them to a quiet table in the back. All the diners were obviously well-to-do, and the hum of conversation was muted, broken only by the occasional clink of heavy silver striking fine china.

Owen ordered a bottle of French champagne, and when their glasses were filled, he raised his toast. "Here's to a fine evening, even if Edwin Forrest's performance was a little ripe for my tastes."

"I will drink to that." They touched glasses, and Jemina sipped cautiously at the wine. "I'm not quite sure what you mean by ripe, since I thoroughly enjoyed his performance. However, I will be candid enough to admit that my experience of theatergoing has been rather limited. My father is quite rigid in that respect, holding the opinion that all theater people are sinful."

"That's a rather provincial attitude," he said with a raised eyebrow. "True, down through the ages theatrical people have not enjoyed enviable reputations, but certainly a performance of Shakespeare should be respectable enough."

"Not for my father. He claims that the works of William Shakespeare are vulgar, not fit for a young girl to see or hear."

Owen laughed. "Well, often old William's subject matter is lurid enough, I grant you...."

He was interrupted by the arrival of a waiter with a menu, which he handed to Owen. After the waiter left, Owen glanced across the table. "I suppose you disapprove of not being given a menu. I can't say that I approve, either. So, if you'd like to see it..." He held it out.

After a moment's hesitation, Jemina said dryly, "No, you order for both of us. It's plain that you have had a good deal of practice."

"If that's supposed to put me in my place, it falls short of the mark," he said cheerfully. "Why don't you tell me of your life in . . . Boston, is it?"

She was startled. "Whatever for? It's certainly not very interesting."

"To a good newspaperman, almost everything is interesting. Besides, I'd like to know everything about you, Jemina."

"There's not that much to know. I am twenty-two years old. I was born and raised in Boston. I went to school there. And I had never traveled more than a hundred miles from Beacon Hill until this summer."

"Beacon Hill, is it?" That eyebrow again. "That's a high-toned neighborhood."

"My father is a banker," she said with a shrug. "The typical proper, staid Boston banker. He would not be considered extremely wealthy, I suppose, but he has always provided well for us."

The waiter returned, and Owen ordered turtle soup, breast of veal with vegetables, and ices to come afterward. Turning back to Jemina, he said, "And your mother?"

"Married my father before she was the age I am now and lived happily ever after. . . . Well, I may be wrong there. To my surprise, when I told her about getting the position on the *Lady's Book*, *and* while Father raved and ranted, she confided in me that she envied me."

"How about siblings?"

"None. I'm an only child."

"Not totally spoiled, as is often the case of an only child." He smiled. "Except for a certain streak of mulishness."

"I could say that you bring it out in me."

"I suppose you could." He regarded her intently. "Now for the important question... How about beaux?"

"You are impertinent, sir!"

"Perhaps." He shrugged. "I didn't mean now, here. I meant back in Boston."

Despite her annoyance, Jemina found herself answering, "There were a few men—boys, rather. My father was always marching them past me."

"But none suited, I take it?"

"When I am ready to marry, I shall do my own choosing."

"I applaud you, ma'am." He clapped his hands together softly. "Most girls your age are wed and with family by this time." He fell silent, his attention on his food for the moment.

Jemina leaned forward. "And you, Owen?"

His gaze came up. "Me? You mean as regards women?"

"Oh, I know your reputation in that regard, having been warned from several quarters. No, I mean about this... the way you live." She waved a hand around the restaurant. "Nothing but the very finest dining establishments. Expensive clothes. I know the recompense for our profession. It would scarcely support such a way of life."

"Now who is being impertinent?" He laughed softly. "But I will gladly answer your question. When I am in Philadelphia, I live the life of a gentleman. But, you see, Jemina, I am here only a part of each year, often a very small part. When I am on assignment, the *Ledger* pays all of my expenses, so I am thus able to save the bulk of my salary.''

''My father, being a banker, would certainly not approve. He would inquire as to what arrangements you are making for your old age.''

''Old age?'' Owen grimaced. ''How depressing! Besides, there is ample time for consideration of my old age.'' He grinned lazily. ''And, in any event, mine is a rather precarious profession. I may never live to reach my dotage.''

It was on the tip of her tongue to ask him if it wasn't time he was saving money toward marriage, a wife and family, but she stayed herself in time. This near disaster kept her silent for the rest of the meal.

It wasn't until they were ready to leave the restaurant that something occurred to her. While he knew a great deal about her, Jemina still knew almost nothing about Owen Thursday; and most of what she did know had come from others. Owen was a good conversationalist—almost glib, in fact—but he somehow managed to reveal very little of himself.

''How did you enjoy the theater last night, Jemina?'' Sarah asked her the next morning.

''I enjoyed it very much, even if Owen did scorn Mr. Forrest's performance as being too flowery.''

''Owen likes to consider himself an expert on the theater.''

Jemina leaned forward. ''I find something very strange about him, Sarah. I've been in his company for supper twice now, and he's a great talker, as I'm sure you know, but he says very little about himself.''

"That's true," Sarah said with a smile. "Owen is something of a mystery man. I met him several years ago, when he went to work at the *Ledger*. Since that time, we have become good friends, but he has revealed very little of his past to me. I have never inquired too deeply, but whenever a question does come up, he is quite vague. No one even seems to know where he came from originally."

"But why all the mystery? Is it possible that he has a dark past, that he is concealing something bad, perhaps even criminal?"

Sarah frowned in thought. "I must confess that has never occurred to me. Owen has certainly never given any reason for me to think so, and he doesn't strike me as a man with a criminal past. Some men, you know, deliberately cultivate an aura of mystery, in the belief that it makes them more attractive to women."

Jemina said doubtfully, "From what you've said of him and from what I have observed, Owen surely doesn't need something like that to add to his appeal to the opposite sex."

Sarah gazed at her through narrowed eyes. "Jemina, why all this sudden interest in Owen, in his past?"

"I'm just curious, is all."

"You're positive it is nothing more than curiosity?"

"I'm positive. What else could it be?"

"I certainly hope it is nothing more than that. At the risk of repeating myself, I warned you not to become romantically involved with Owen Thursday. I have observed many a girl marrying a sot, a scoundrel, a gambler, even a criminal, in the hope of reforming him. There is an appeal there that I have never understood. In each instance, it has ended in disaster. I am not saying that Owen fits any of those categories, but if you are attracted to him because of a mysterious past, be very, very cautious, my dear.''

''That is not the case at all, Sarah! I told you, I am simply curious.''

Jemina jumped up and hurried from the office, leaving Sarah staring after her solemnly.

Chapter Eight

IN HIS OWN ESTIMATION, Owen had a very good reason to keep his past a secret.

He was a bastard. He did not even know his father's name; nor, from all he could gather, did his mother. Owen was the result of her brief sexual congress with a man whom she could identify only as a seaman or a canaller; all she knew was that her lover had some connection with boats.

His mother had always been a frail woman. A dressmaker by trade, she was never strong enough after Owen's birth to work full-time; and Owen had known nothing but dire poverty from the time he was old enough to remember. They never seemed to have enough to eat, and what clothes he had owned were either made by his mother or bought secondhand. His earliest memories were of his tubercular mother lying in bed as still as death, or struggling off to work, leaving Owen in the care of their neighbor in the tenement building, a widow lady with three children of her own.

Owen was seven or eight when he learned what little there was to know about his father. At supper one evening he asked, "Mama, is my daddy dead?"

His mother gazed at him sorrowfully. "No, sonny, your father is not dead. Not so far as I know, but then, I haven't seen him in a long time. I could lie to you and tell you that he is dead, but you're sure to find out the truth eventually.''

''Then is he sailing around the world on a ship? You said he was a sailor.''

''I said I believed he was, sonny. Either a sailor or a canal boatman. I was never sure. I only knew your father for one week. He was the first, and only, man I ever knew. He took me by storm, and I succumbed to his charm, much to my great regret.''

''But will he be back? When his voyage is over?'' asked Owen, who had no idea how long a sea voyage around the world would take.

''No, Owen, your father will not be back. I thought he would be, but not long after you were born I realized that he never would return.'' She said wistfully, ''You know what I remember about him? On the biceps of his right arm was the tattoo of a ship. When he flexed his muscles the ship seemed to be sailing. Isn't that a queer thing to remember about a man?''

''But he must come back!'' Owen said desperately. ''He is my daddy!''

His mother focused her gaze on him, her face suffused with an ineffable sadness. ''He doesn't even know you exist, sonny. You were born out of wedlock. You do not know what that means now, but you will someday. Once I had hoped to keep it from you, but now I know that it cannot be. Other people know, and they would see that you know, too.''

As the years passed, Owen's mother's illness ravaged her, until she was little more than a skeleton. Yet she clung obstinately to life and continued to work when and where she could. By the time he was ten, Owen was also working, at what poor jobs he could find—selling newspapers on street corners; washing dishes and scrubbing floors; delivering pails of beer from the corner saloon. What little he earned augmented their income so that they could pay the rent and keep scraps of food on the table. Owen became fleet of foot and crafty enough to steal fruit and vegetables from the produce stalls and to snatch lumps of coal from the delivery wagons.

Two things saved him—he was born with an insatiable yearning for knowledge, and his mother, who had some education, taught him how to read and write. There was no time or money for schooling, but he read every word in the newspapers he sold, and he discovered used bookstores, where he could browse to his heart's content among dusty bookshelves and where he could buy books for mere pennies. Every penny he could spare was spent on books. He read indiscriminately—the classics; history and literature; and any recently published novels he could afford.

His was a self-education in every sense of the phrase. By the age of twelve he recognized that his reading would never completely teach him to speak correctly, so he started hawking his papers before the clubs of the proper and wealthy Manhattan males. Also, he put together a bootblack box and lingered around the club entrances after his papers were sold, offering shoeshines for a penny. In this way he managed to listen as the swells conversed among themselves.

Later in life, Owen came to believe that he would have made a good actor; certainly he had a talent for mimicry. His fine ear for dialogue allowed him to pick up the sounds and nuances of proper grammar, and by the time he was full grown, he could speak as well as any college graduate. Also, he learned something that was to prove valuable to him later—he learned the finer points of male attire, which enabled him to dress as well as any man.

He was thirteen years old when he found out what it truly meant to be a bastard. He seldom had time to play with the other lads in the neighborhood. In fact, he had only two friends, Tod and George Reardon, the sons of the widow next door, both near his own age.

One Sunday afternoon, when he had a half day free, he was playing with the Reardon boys in an empty, weed-grown lot next to the tenement building, roughhousing, wrestling one another to the ground as boys will. Due to the life he had led for the past few years, Owen felt years older than the Reardon boys; yet he experienced a certain release in the rough, boyish play. He certainly had had few moments of enjoyment in his life.

Tod Reardon, a year older than Owen, was heavier by some twenty pounds and taller, but Owen was lithe and quick, and the long, hard hours of physical labor had developed his muscles. He pinned Tod's shoulder to the ground after a few minutes' tussle. Laughing, he released the older boy and sprang to his feet.

Tod Reardon, Owen well knew, hated to lose at anything. The other boy got slowly to his feet, scowling. "You didn't whup me fair and square. You took advantage."

"What advantage?" Owen laughed scornfully. "You wanted to wrestle, so we wrestled, and I pinned you."

Tod turned aside, picking up a sharpened stick from the weeds. He drew a line in the dirt, then said tauntingly, "I dare you to cross that line, Owen."

"Dare?" Owen laughed again. "Tod, we're too old for that sort of thing."

"You're scared, that's what."

"All right, so I'm scared." He started to turn away. "I have to go. Mamma may be needing me."

"Mamma's boy, hiding behind her skirts! Could be you even lift them. From what I hear, it ain't all that hard to lift her skirts."

Owen tensed, turning back. "What do you mean?"

"You're a bastard, that's what, Owen Thursday," Tod said in a jeering voice. "Everybody knows your ma ain't married, and you ain't got no daddy. Bastard, bastard!"

Fury exploded in Owen, propelling him across the line drawn in the dirt and full tilt into the other boy. They went down onto the ground, with Owen on top. His world focused on that hateful face inches from his. Burying his fingers in Tod's long, lank hair, he raised the other's head and pounded it savagely against the hard earth.

Tod yelled and tried to roll away, but Owen was astraddle him now, his fingers still locked in the long hair. Again, he raised Tod's head and thumped it hard against the ground. And yet again.

Dimly, he saw George dancing around him, yelling, "You're hurting Tod! Let him up!"

Owen ignored him and bounced Tod's head off the ground again.

Now George began beating Owen about the head and shoulders with the stick Tod had used to draw the line in the dirt. Goaded, Owen turned his head to warn George off, and George rammed the sharp end of the stick into his left eye.

The pain was immediate and unbelievable, far beyond anything Owen had ever experienced. He let go of Tod and reared back, his hand going to his eye. He could feel hot blood gushing out, and then he fell into unconsciousness.

If he had received proper medical care, it was possible that the eye might have been saved; but there was no money. Only one visit was made to a doctor, during which the eye was removed, leaving an empty socket.

Owen was in pain for months, until the empty socket finally healed; but there was no healing the canker of bitterness in him over the loss. In time, he learned to conceal the bitterness with jokes about how he lost the eye, yet it was always there, under the surface. The fact that he was a bastard and the loss of his eye were ever after linked together in his mind. He was determined that the world would never know about his bastard birth.

From the time Owen lost the eye, he began to hate the unknown man who was his father. He lived with a recurring fantasy that he would one day find the man from whose careless seed he had sprung and would gain vengeance and retribution against him.

After the accident to his eye, his mother's health began to deteriorate badly. She died only a few months after the incident, and he had one more debit to add to the column against the man who had fathered him.

Left alone now, Owen began to look around for a better means to advance himself. Within a month, he heard that there was an opening for a copyboy at the office of the newspaper he had been hawking from street corners for so long. He applied for the job, and to his great delight the job was his. The wages were low, but the money was a good deal more than he was accustomed to; and he was able to move out of the squalid area where he had lived with his mother. He rented a small, clean room for himself close to the newspaper and moved in.

Owen had long been fascinated by the idea of working on a newspaper. Newspapers had been his early means of learning to read and had served as his window to the world. Once he was actually employed by the *New York Post*, he became even more intrigued. The pace, the pulse-pounding excitement of a daily deadline—it was meant to be his life! He was convinced of it. It promised an escape from poverty, it promised glamour and excitement, and he soon learned that it meant molding public opinion. People's lives revolved around what they read in their daily papers. They received not only the news but their concepts of fashions and information on the theater and on books from the reviews. Their views of the world's public figures and events as they happened were shaped by newspaper editorials.

From the very first day that he went to work, Owen set about learning everything he could about the newspaper. Life outside the office consisted only of eating and sleeping. His job toting copy back and forth from reporter to editor gave him a good overview of the workings of the paper. And since he was always willing to run errands for the reporters and the editors—fetching cheroots, food or whatever else was required—he soon became a favorite among them.

Finally, Owen dared to reveal his ambition to Jack Stephens, a cynical twenty-year veteran of the profession.

Stephens leaned back from his desk and studied him with faded blue eyes. "So you want to become a newspaper reporter, do you?"

Owen said eagerly, "More than anything else in the world!"

"Now how many copyboys have I heard say that?" Stephens sighed. "How old are you, laddie?"

"Fifteen, sir."

"Are you, now? More likely fourteen at the outside. You have a number of years to go before you can become a reporter. That is what discourages most of the lads, the long, hard wait."

"I can wait. I intend to wait, no matter how long it takes."

Stephens squinted at him. "Do you, now? Well, you seem determined, and bright enough. Although, God knows, intelligence is hardly a necessity. Otherwise, who would choose newspaper reporting as a lifelong work?"

"But *you* did, Mr. Stephens."

"All too true, laddie, which doesn't say much for my intelligence. But far be it from me to discourage a fine lad like yourself. But be prepared for a hard road. If you do remain long enough and you are finally promoted, you'll start your apprenticeship by joining the casket brigade."

"Casket brigade, sir?"

"That's what I call the obit department. Writing the obituary column. Most of us started that way. I know I did. If you turn out to be good at that, they may eventually trust you to write about live people."

Stephens's prophecy became true. At eighteen, Owen started writing the obituary column. Since he had lasted much longer than the average copyboy, and since he continually harried the managing editor for a job, it seemed perfectly natural that he be given the column when the former writer moved up.

Writing obituaries was a dull, boring routine, consisting of collecting pertinent facts about the lives of the people who died. Usually, Owen could make two lines suffice; but when the deceased was an important personage, more research had to be done, and the obituary expanded to a paragraph or more.

At least he was writing, seeing *his* words in print, even if they were uninspiring words and he received no credit. The latter, of course, was the norm; bylines were unheard-of, although more and more newspapermen were beginning to agitate for their names to be put on the more important stories.

He remained with the obituary column for over two years, always trying to advance to writing the news. He studied the work of the other men, word for word, line for line, and he was confident that he could do as good a job as they, if not better. He was turned down time after time.

Finally, he reached a decision that had been fermenting in his mind for some time. He had to get out of New York; he had the strange feeling that he would never attain his ambitions here.

Although New York was gaining ground as a publishing center—of newspapers, magazines and books—Philadelphia was considered the publishing center of the United States. That city published a large number of newspapers, and many of them were well-thought-of.

Owen was fortunate in two respects—he looked much older than his twenty years, and he had absorbed enough newspaper lore so that he could talk like a seasoned newspaperman.

So he quit his job and left for Philadelphia, where he first became associated with Thomas Carruthers. The two-penny *Philadelphia Ledger*, was the most popular of the some dozen newspapers printed in the city, with a circulation comparable to the *London Standard*. The *Ledger* was printed and published in the Philadelphia Arcade, not far from the location of *Godey's Lady's Book*. The marble mall contained some eighty shops along two skylighted aisles stretching back from the Chestnut Street entrance.

Dressed nattily, Owen strode confidently into Carruthers's office. He had been informed that Thomas Carruthers had approval of any newspaperman employed.

"I'm Owen Thursday," he announced. "I'm a newspaperman, looking for a job with your fine paper. I was told that you were the man to see."

Carruthers leaned back, his dark face set in a scowl that Owen was soon to learn was habitual, his cigar fuming. "'Fine paper,' is it? I suppose you figure that flattery will help you?"

"It doesn't hurt, I've found," Owen said with a grin.

"And I suppose you have had some 'fine' experience?"

"The very best. I've worked several years for the *New York Post*."

Carruthers nodded skeptically. "If I employed everyone who strolled in here claiming to be good newspapermen, I'd soon be chin-deep in reporters."

But he did not dismiss Owen out of hand; he quizzed him extensively on newspaper work, and Owen answered all the questions without hesitation.

Finally, Carruthers nodded. "All right, you're employed. Conditionally. It will all depend on the caliber of work you can turn out." He shuffled some papers on his desk. "I have an assignment for you. The *Ledger* is running a series of articles on some of the leading citizens of Philadelphia. Have you heard of Sarah Hale? Or Louis Godey?"

"The editor and publisher of *Godey's Lady's Book*, respectively?"

Carruthers smiled marginally. "At least you know something about what is being published today. Interview both Mrs. Hale and Godey, write your article, and we shall see."

And that was the way Owen met Sarah Hale. He immediately liked the prickly, independent-minded woman, and something about his brashness must have appealed to her.

Owen wrote the article very quickly and turned it in to Carruthers, hoping that the editor would read it and like it before he heard from the *New York Post*.

Two days later, Carruthers summoned Owen into his office. "I have an interesting message here from the *New York Post*." He held up a letter. "It appears that one Owen Thursday did indeed work there." He bent a malevolent glare on Owen. "As a copyboy and obit writer!"

Damnation, Owen thought; I was hoping for a little more time.

He shrugged. "Well, I thought it was worth trying. And I didn't lie to you. I just didn't tell you what work I did on the *Post*."

Carruthers stared hard at him for a moment, then dropped the letter onto his desk. He lit up a cheroot, batted smoke away from his face and glared at Owen again. "That piece of yours on Godey and Mrs. Hale. It will be in tomorrow's issue."

Owen leaned forward, holding his breath. "You mean you liked it?"

"Let's just say it will do," Carruthers said grudgingly.

Owen's pulse picked up. He was already familiar enough with Carruthers to know that such words were about the only praise he gave out. "Then I'm not going to be discharged?"

"I'll let you stay around for a while. Again, conditionally, depending on how you do. Just don't lie to me again. I know—" he held up a hand "—you weren't lying, but as far as I am concerned, a lie of omission is still a lie. Now I'll tell you something, Thursday. I usually don't employ any man who just walks into my office, not without a thorough check into his background. But the day you came in here, I was short two men and was desperate for a replacement. So consider yourself damned fortunate, my lad!"

Over the next few years, an affectionate bond grew between the two men, editor and reporter. As Owen's work steadily improved, Carruthers gave him more assignments, until he was considered the top newspaperman on the *Ledger*. In return, Owen's respect for the older man increased apace, especially when he learned that Carruthers's tough exterior hid a heart with a soft center. In time, their relationship became that of a gruff father and a brash son.

The *Ledger* was a relatively new paper, having been established in 1836, and had never used a field correspondent. It took several years of badgering from Owen before Carruthers finally made him a correspondent, covering Polk's presidential campaign. Even then, this job probably would not have been granted to him, except for something that had happened in New York City. In April 1841, Horace Greeley started publishing the *New York Daily Tribune*, which was an immediate success. Greeley brought a number of radical innovations to newspaper publishing: he published two editions daily, morning and evening, six days a week; he began using field correspondents; and he started giving bylines to his top reporters.

Owen used Greeley's actions as pressure on Carruthers, and that was the chief reason he became the *Ledger*'s first field correspondent. It took him longer to get his own byline. He finally threatened to quit and seek employment with the *Tribune*, which was something he half-seriously considered. Carruthers growled and grumbled, claiming that Owen's threat wounded him deeply; but by the time Owen went with Kearny's expedition into Mexico, he had his own byline.

So, by the year 1848, he was reasonably content. He had the life he had long dreamed of, and most of his ambitions were now realized.

However, one thing still gnawed at him. Often, in the small hours of the night, he would start awake from a dream, a nightmare, in which he was pursuing a faceless man with a ship tattooed on his arm.

Owen was still determined, one way or another, to track down the man who had so carelessly fathered him, and gain some measure of revenge.

Chapter Nine

JEMINA WAS DUBIOUS about her latest assignment. She was a city girl, and what little she knew about the country came from what she had observed of it from trains and carriages. Of farming, she knew nothing.

When she told Sarah this, the editor had waved her objections aside, saying, "That doesn't matter. You should bring a fresh perspective to matters of agriculture. You see, Jemina, a great many of our subscribers come from farm families, and we have tended to ignore farm families in the *Lady's Book*. Most of our stories and articles are aimed at city dwellers. I think an article about farm life would be timely and would be welcomed by women of farm communities. In a survey taken at the beginning of the decade, it was found that there were five and a half million workers in the United States, over three and a half million of those are employed in agriculture. What really brought all this to mind is a letter I recently received from one of our subscribers."

Sarah had picked up an open letter from her desk. "It is from a Mrs. David Monroe. In her letter, she says that she is a longtime subscriber to the *Lady's Book* and she adores it. But she also says that she cannot understand why we publish so few pieces about farm families. I wrote her in response, mentioning that I would be most happy to publish pieces of such a nature, if it would be possible to send one of our

authors to her area to do research. She answered by
return post, stating that it was not only possible but
that she would be happy to welcome an author into
her home, to stay as long as is necessary, and that she
and her family would be eager to provide any assistance possible. Well, the gist of the matter is, I wrote
her that one of our authors would be visiting her
shortly.''

"Where is the farm located?''

"Just this side of Allentown. She said someone
would meet your stage.''

"I seem to recall reading that many of the people
in that area are Quakers. Are the Monroes Quakers?''

Sarah gave her a hard look. "I have no idea, but
their religion is of no concern. Religion is one of the
subjects we tend to avoid in the *Book*, except in
general terms, writing of Our Savior, without referring to a specific religion. Louis says it is too controversial, and I tend to agree with him.''

"Then basically, what I should write about is the
life of farm women?''

"That is what Mrs. Monroe wants to see in the
Book, and I assume, hopefully, that is what our other
readers will be interested in.''

JEMINA WAS IN a rather apprehensive frame of mind
when she got off at the designated stage stop a few
miles south of Allentown proper, not having the least
idea as to what to expect.

She was met by Carter Monroe, a strapping youth
in his early twenties who was shy in her presence. He
was driving a shining black buggy, drawn by a
prancing gray horse. Carter introduced himself,

stowed her traveling bag in the buggy and helped her up onto the seat.

As they drove away, Jemina asked, "How large is your family, Mr. Monroe?"

"Seven of us, ma'am," he said with his bashful grin. "Five of us young 'uns; three boys and two girls. I'm the oldest."

"A good-sized family," she commented.

"Yes, ma'am. Pa says we have to raise our own help so we won't have to pay hired hands." Then he blushed scarlet and refused to look at her again.

They traveled down the dirt road at a good clip, dust rising behind them. The houses they passed were neat and well cared for, and the fields on each side of the road were all in cultivation. Corn, in long rows, stood shoulder-high. The scent of something fragrant reached Jemina's nostrils.

"What is that I smell?"

Carter finally looked at her. "That's freshly cut alfalfa, ma'am."

"Is that one of your main crops?"

"That and corn, potatoes and other vegetables we can sell to the townspeople up in Allentown."

He was turning the buggy now, off the main road onto a narrow lane leading toward a two-story white house about a hundred yards away. Behind the house loomed a large barn.

In a few minutes, Jemina was being helped down from the buggy in the yard before the house and being introduced to Ellen Monroe and her two daughters, buxom, giggling girls glowing with good health.

Mrs. Monroe, a plump, beaming woman of perhaps forty years, was profuse in her welcome. "My husband, David, and my other two sons are out working in the fields. You'll meet them at supper-time.''

''I think it is exceedingly generous of you, Mrs. Monroe, to offer your hospitality.''

''It is an honor to have someone from your publication as our guest. *Godey's Lady's Book* is my favorite publication. I really didn't expect Mrs. Hale to answer my letter.''

''Sarah always tries to personally answer as many letters as she can.''

In a moment, Jemina was ushered upstairs to a nice corner bedroom, done in pleasing colors, with curtains stirring in the faint breeze that made the room pleasant in spite of the early autumn heat.

Unpacking the few belongings she had brought with her, she began to feel more relaxed. She had been received so warmly, how could she feel alien?

Weary from her trip, she stretched out across the comfortable four-poster bed and dozed. She woke to the mouth-watering odors of food cooking, just as the evening shadows were creeping across the land. She quickly made her toilet and went downstairs, where she met David Monroe and his other two sons.

Their chores done, they were on the front gallery, waiting for their supper. David Monroe was a taciturn, spare man who took his pipe out of his mouth to greet her shyly.

With some amusement, Jemina noted that, as the daughters resembled their mother, the sons resembled their father—tall, spare, shy and quiet.

''What can I do to help?'' Jemina asked Mrs. Monroe.

The older woman fluttered her hands. "Good heavens, child, you are our guest! I wouldn't think of you helping."

Jemina said firmly, "No, I insist. I must confess that I have never been on a farm before, and how can I write about your life if I don't participate in what you do?"

"Some hard work involved, Miss Benedict," Mr. Monroe said solemnly. "Milking the cows, gathering eggs, slopping the pigs. Think you're up to all that?"

"Now, David!" Mrs. Monroe batted a hand at her husband. "You'll be scaring the poor girl away."

"If you and your daughters can do it, so can I," Jemina said stoutly. "At least I can try."

"Well," said Mrs. Monroe, "I suppose you can help set the table, Jemina. We'll be eating in a few minutes."

Jemina helped carry platters of food to the dining-room table—late sweet corn on the cob, mounds of snowy mashed potatoes, a huge beef roast nicely browned, a platter of fried chicken, fresh garden peas, loaves of freshly baked bread and at least half a dozen side dishes and relishes. She had never seen so much food at one time.

Mrs. Monroe chatted as she bustled about the kitchen. "You came at a good time, Jemina. My eldest girl, Martha, is getting married two days hence." Beaming, she indicated one of the girls, a tall girl with long blond hair. Blushing furiously, the girl hung her head.

"Oh, I am sorry, Mrs. Monroe," Jemina said in dismay. "The last thing you need is a stranger in your midst during your preparations for a wedding."

"Nonsense, child," Mrs. Monroe said briskly. "We'll have so many guests, what will one more matter? We're more than happy to have you." She added shyly, "Maybe you can write a line or two about the wedding."

At supper they all bowed their heads as David Monroe, at the head of the table, gave the blessing in his rumbling voice. At a gesture from him, the platters began their rounds, and Jemina soon saw why there was so much food. They all ate with hearty appetites, especially the boys and their father. But even Jemina ate more than she usually did; the country air had given her a good appetite, and the food was good and wholesome.

THE NEXT MORNING she regretted her decision to share the work of a farm woman. She was awakened long before dawn by the sounds of activity on the first floor. Quickly, she got dressed and hurried down the stairs. The family was around the table, just finishing breakfast.

Mrs. Monroe fluttered her hands in distress. "Oh, I was hoping we wouldn't disturb you, Jemina! I know you said you wanted to help us with the chores, but I thought at least this first morning we should let you stay abed."

Jemina took a deep breath and smiled. "Since I shall only be here for a few days, I believe that I should start immediately."

Mrs. Monroe appeared pleased. "Well, if you really want to."

By the time Jemina had finished a quick breakfast, the men had already gone to work in the fields and Mrs. Monroe and her daughters were preparing for the milking. Jemina accompanied them to the barn.

"We have a dozen milk cows," Mrs. Monroe explained. "Much more than we need for our own use, but we sell milk and butter in the city; also several dozen eggs a week, since we have almost a hundred laying hens."

Jemina watched as Mrs. Monroe and the girls positioned themselves under the cows on little three-legged stools, milk pails gripped between their legs. She observed with interest as the girls and their mother gripped a cow teat in each hand and expertly directed a stream of milk into the pails.

After a bit, she urged Mrs. Monroe, "Show me how to do it and let me try."

Jemina took the stool vacated by Mrs. Monroe, and the woman watched as Jemina squeezed and released the milk-swollen teats; but try as she would, Jemina could get only a few drops of milk out. Soon, the two girls, who had gathered around to watch, were giggling, and even Mrs. Monroe was smiling.

"I can't do it!" Jemina cried in exasperation. "What's wrong with me?"

"Never mind, child," Mrs. Monroe said. "It takes practice, and I have seen many people who just never seem to get the knack of it."

After the milking was done, Jemina helped the girls slop the pigs—there were a good dozen of them—and then gather the eggs. At least in that, she thought wryly, she could help, since neither required any particular skills.

After the morning chores were done, the housecleaning followed, and then it was time to prepare the noon meal for the boys and their father. The afternoon was spent mending and sewing. During this time, Mrs. Monroe suggested that Jemina might like a nap; and Jemina was happy enough to accept the suggestion.

She slept for at least an hour and awoke feeling guilty. No doubt while she had been napping, Mrs. Monroe and her daughters had been working on.

Hurriedly, she straightened her clothing and hair and returned downstairs. As she made her way toward the kitchen, whence she heard the sound of the women's voices, she passed the downstairs sitting room. Glancing in, she saw that the sitting room was filled with books and magazines.

As she began helping Mrs. Monroe and the girls prepare supper, Jemina asked the older woman, "I noticed that you have many books and periodicals about the house. Does your family read a great deal?"

"I do, and the girls do, also." Mrs. Monroe nodded vigorously. "David and the boys . . . well, not so much. But David and I insisted that all the children learn to read and write and do their numbers, although they've little formal schooling. I have always been a great reader myself."

"You all seem so busy, I don't see how you find the time."

Mrs. Monroe laughed. "That's just now, child. Spring planting, summer and fall harvesting, those are the busy times. But in the winter months there's not so much work. We spend a great deal of our time around the fire, reading."

"Do other farm women read as much?"

"I can't speak for other families. Some of the ladies I know read quite a bit, others do not. But I can tell you this . . . many of the farm women I know are sub-scribers to *Godey's Lady's Book*!''

Adroit questioning of Mrs. Monroe and her daughters revealed to Jemina that they were surprisingly well-informed about many things other than recipes and current fashions. For instance, they were aware of current events.

Jemina was also surprised by one other thing she learned. As she followed Mrs. Monroe on her round of chores the next morning, Jemina said facetiously, ''Seeing how much physical labor you do, I think I can understand the reasoning behind the slavery advocates in the South.''

''Don't speak of such things, child,'' the older woman said, bristling. ''I detest slavery. It is an abomination in the eyes of God. No man should enslave another!''

Although, to be truthful, Jemina had never given much thought to the issue of slavery, she said, ''I agree, Mrs. Monroe. It was a thoughtless remark, spoken carelessly.''

Mollified, Mrs. Monroe nodded. ''And I should not be so easy to take offense. It's just that folks hereabouts are becoming more and more upset about the subject of slavery. It is going to tear this country apart, my David says.'' She lowered her voice. ''I will tell you something, though perhaps I shouldn't, seeing you work for a magazine and all.''

''You have no fear. The *Lady's Book* does not publish articles on such controversial matters as slavery.''

''And you are a Northern girl, against keeping the slaves?'' Mrs. Monroe said with a questioning glance.

Jemina nodded. "Yes, I am from Boston, and my family is opposed to slavery, although it is a subject rarely mentioned at home."

"Well, Quakertown, not too far from where we are, has started what is called an 'underground railroad.' They are involved in smuggling slaves out of the South to a new life of freedom. They are receiving a great deal of support from the people hereabouts."

That evening after supper, in her room, humming to herself, Jemina began her article: "Agriculture is the cornerstone, the very foundation of our country. Not only does it feed our people, our cities and towns, it promotes a moral manner of living not customarily found in our cities, large or small.

"Agriculture is considered by many to be the father of all arts; not only was it the first art practiced by man, but all other arts are the legitimate offspring of agriculture and could not long exist without it. The prosperity of a country is always dependent upon its agricultural industry. And certainly no one can deny that a nation not only cannot prosper but cannot survive without food.

"If, then, agriculture is the foundation of our nation, the farm wife is the very bedrock of that foundation. The farm wife will be the focus of this article, and others to follow, in this series of pieces about the farming communities of our great country...."

THE THREE ARTICLES, published in three consecutive issues, were an immediate success.

The last half of the third article had to do with the wedding of Martha Monroe: "Births, weddings and funerals are the hallmarks of all our lives, but these events, perhaps, have the most impact on farm families—especially weddings, since they hail a new beginning for two people.

"Your correspondent was witness to just such a wedding at the home of David and Ellen Monroe, on the occasion of the wedding of their eldest daughter, Martha, to Jed Lakes, the son of a neighboring farmer.

"The time of farm weddings is either after spring planting or following the harvest, and this wedding followed the harvest; it was, in a manner of speaking, a double celebration. It was a time of frolic; yet a prodigious amount of labor went into the preparations, in which your correspondent participated to the best of her poor ability. Incredible amounts of flour and sugar, milk and eggs, were converted into delicacies to delight the palate. It was a feast!

"All day people came from far and near. The dresses and decorations were surely such as not to shame the court of Louis XIV. Not a silk gown at the gathering but shone; not a Sunday suit but had new buttons. Every damsel wore the greatest number of curls and braids. Every matron's head carried all the bows and border that her cap would support.

"But none of the later merriment was evident in the beginning, for all present were hushed and subdued, awaiting the ceremony.

"It was not until the minister spoke his final solemn words, 'I now pronounce you man and wife,' that the mood changed.

"Congratulations were exchanged, the bride was properly bussed by all, and the groom's hand was shaken until it must have ached. Then the celebrants fell to with gusto, demolishing the food-laden tables;

the fiddles struck up, and the dancing began. The dancing went on, and the hilarity continued unbroken, until eleven o'clock, when the company dropped off a wagonload at a time, 'til at length all was quiet. No sign of life was left about the premises, except for a light or two burning dimly in the Monroe house.

"Thus we end on a happy note, as a new farm wife is joined with her husband. Soon, they will begin a new life as a farmer and his wife. Martha Lakes will join the legions of happy farm wives, as did her mother before her, and as will her friends in time to come. These women, dear readers, form the very core to the heartland of America, and we can only be grateful that they exist."

Sarah Hale praised the articles; even Louis Godey unbent enough to offer a compliment. Yet Jemina was not really sure about the quality of what she had done until letters began to come in from subscribers, not only from farm wives but from city subscribers, as well.

There was an air of respect now from the other *Book* employees, and Clara said with some envy, "Your future is assured, Jemina."

"Oh, I think it is much too early to tell that." Nonetheless, Jemina felt herself flush with pleasure.

"Perhaps not everything you write will be as good or garner as much attention. But you have the touch. It's a talent you have to be born with," Clara said. "God knows I don't have it, nor will I ever."

Even Owen had some kind words. "It's damned fine writing, my dear. Insightful, interesting and colorful. One would think you had been born and raised on a farm, instead of Boston bred. You not only have the ability to write well, but you have the ability to enter a strange environment, or milieu, and absorb what you need quickly. Many people can put the words together, but all too many are never able to inhabit the skins of their subjects or grasp the true essence of their daily lives, professions or environments.''

She gazed at him with some astonishment. ''I never expected to hear such words from you.''

''Why not?'' he said with a shrug. ''I complimented you on the Blackwell piece, didn't I? I never turn away from praising a colleague.''

''Not even if the colleague is a woman?'' she said teasingly.

He grinned. ''I must admit that you are the first woman author I've *felt* like complimenting.''

Owen Thursday was still capable of surprising Jemina. In the beginning she had thought him handsome, charming and good company—all of which was still true—but she had also thought him vain, arrogant and condescending, *none* of which was true.

They saw each other once or twice a week on the average, for a concert, a play or at least for supper, and never once had he overstepped the bounds of decorum. In the carriage he might hold her hand; occasionally he would kiss her good-night, but only with a light brushing of the lips. It had never gone beyond that.

Where was the womanizer, the dangerous roué, she had been warned about?

SHORTLY AFTER the first of the three articles was published, Owen had taken Jemina to a late supper.

He appeared subdued, even melancholy, which was unusual for him.

She felt prompted to say, "Is something wrong, Owen?"

He gave her a startled look. "Does it show that much? It's just that I'm growing a little restless. This is the longest I've been in Philadelphia since I became a field correspondent, but Carruthers, my editor, says that there's nothing of import going on anywhere, nothing of news value."

"You mean no wars, no one being killed anywhere?"

He frowned at her. "It doesn't have to be a war. For instance, there's been word of a fabulous gold discovery out in California. I asked Carruthers to send me out there, but he wants to wait and see if it's just a rumor and just how important a discovery it is."

"California! Good heavens, that means you'd be gone forever!" she said in dismay.

"It would be a lengthy trip. I'd probably be gone for at least a year." He smiled slightly. "Would you miss me, my dear?"

She flushed in annoyance. "Such conceit!"

"That doesn't answer my question. Would you miss me, Jemina?"

Retreating behind flippancy, she said, "You're amusing, Owen. I'm sure I would miss that."

"That remark is unworthy of you," he said dourly.

Nothing more was spoken about the matter during their meal, and Jemina was regretting her flippant remark, for the truth of the matter was she *would* miss Owen. On the other hand, she deemed it unwise to let him know this.

As their carriage clattered away from the restaurant, Owen said unexpectedly, "You've never been to my quarters, have you?"

Taken aback, Jemina wasn't sure whether she should be offended or pleased. "You know I haven't."

"Would you do me the honor? I have a bottle of excellent Napoleon brandy, and although mine are a bachelor's digs, I manage to keep a pleasant abode, especially considering the little time that I spend there."

Jemina found herself suddenly breathless and pleasantly flushed. She had not been unaware of the sensuality of her nature, unexpectedly deep and powerful, stirring in Owen's presence.

She was under no illusion as to why he had invited her—he was finally making an overture. Searching her feelings, she found that she was not really offended. She felt that she was now far more sophisticated than the girl who had come from Boston not too long ago; and she knew her own mind. If she was ready for sexual initiation, it was her decision, without consideration of what her parents might think, or Sarah Hale, or even Aunt Hester.

Realizing that a considerable amount of time had lapsed since Owen's question, she said, "Yes, Owen, I would like to see where you live."

He gave a small grunt, which could have indicated astonishment or pleasure, and tapped his cane against the roof of the hackney. When the driver leaned his face down inquiringly, Owen gave him their new destination.

Jemina was a little surprised to learn that the address was in the Society Hill district as the carriage stopped before a two-story, narrow brick house on Delancey Street opposite the park, which was lined with feathery honey-locust trees. The district was rich in history and in the main was now occupied by Philadelphia's more well-to-do citizens.

Owen had spoken very little on the way but sat slumped in a reflective silence that puzzled Jemina.

Actually, Owen was puzzled himself, puzzled as to his motives. The invitation had come unbidden to his lips, surprising him almost as much as it had Jemina. True, he had long desired her, and it was also true that many times he had considered inviting her to his quarters. Much of his reputation was deserved—he had a strong appetite for women. Yet he was particular; he had never patronized prostitutes, for instance. When he once confided this fact to a close friend, the man had commented dryly, ''That's because you don't need their services.''

This was also true, and Owen certainly was not above taking advantage of his attractiveness to women. But something about Jemina had made him wary. In the first place, to his mystification, he felt differently about her than any woman he had known before; and despite her growing worldliness, at times a vulnerability peeped through the thin layer of sophistication. He sensed that she could easily be wounded, and he did not want to hurt her.

Also, for the first time in his life, he had found a woman who, just possibly, might have more than an impermanent hold on his affections, and Owen was not sure if he was ready for that; and if he was not, it would be unfair to Jemina to trifle with her feelings.

But now, to his further surprise, she had accepted his impulsive invitation, and he could not really back out without appearing an utter ass.

As they got down from the hackney before his building, Owen smiled at her look of surprise. "I suppose you think this is a rather posh neighborhood for a journalist, eh?"

"Well, yes, I am rather surprised."

"I like it here, and I can afford it. The woman who lives downstairs owns the building. She's a widow and likes to have a man on the premises, so she lets the second floor rather cheaply.

"Some famous people have lived in this area, you know. Up on Fourth and Walnut, for instance, is the Todd house, where Dolley Payne Todd, who married James Madison after her husband's death in the yellow-fever epidemic in 1793, once resided. When Madison was elected president, Dolley became our most celebrated White House hostess. And many other famous people have lived in the area over the years...."

He was talking too much, too rapidly, and Jemina realized that he was nervous. She hid a smile behind her hand. It struck her as incongruous that this usually self-assured man could be nervous about taking a woman to his flat!

Owen occupied the entire upper floor of the building. Jemina was surprised by several things: the spaciousness of the rooms, considering his single status; the tasteful, even expensive, furnishings; and the accumulation of books.

After he had taken her cloak and gone to fetch the brandy, she wandered around the book-walled parlor, examining the titles. His reading tastes were catholic: biographies, history, learned volumes on many varied subjects and, most surprisingly of all, a great many novels, both classic and current.

She found a number of books recently reviewed by Sarah in her monthly column, "Editor's Book Table"; books that Jemina had wanted to read but had yet to find the time to do so. She was not at all surprised to discover such recent books as *Our Army at Monterey*, by T. B. Thorpe, Esq., and *Campaign Sketches of the War with Mexico*, by Captain W. S. Henry, since she had learned that Owen had covered much of that war.

But *The Beautiful French Girl*? The author of the novel was anonymous. Jemina had read it and found it well written, with beautifully drawn characters, yet she was amazed that Owen should find it of interest. She could easily understand why he had *The Crater; or, Vulcan's Peak*, by J. Fenimore Cooper, since it was an adventure tale of the Pacific, more a man's book than a woman's.

The more she knew of Owen, the more complex she found him, she thought, as he returned carrying balloon glasses with an inch of brandy in each.

"You read a great deal," she commented.

"Yes, I do. I always take along a pack of books when I'm in the field somewhere. No matter how exciting the event I am reporting, there are always long periods of boredom. With a book in hand I can always while away the time."

"There are no women available?" she asked with a twist of malice.

"Very few," he said with a straight face. "On military posts, only army wives and a few camp followers. Despite what you may have heard about me, I do maintain certain standards.''

''I'm sorry, Owen. My remark was uncalled-for.''

Without comment he gave her a brandy glass, then raised his in a silent toast.

Jemina took a sip, feeling the fiery brandy like an explosion in her gullet. Drinking brandy, alone with a man in his quarters, she reflected wryly; how shocked Father would be!

Setting his brandy glass down, Owen studied her intently. Jemina felt herself growing warm and flushed under the impact of his gaze; and for a panic-filled moment, she considered leaving immediately.

Then she forced herself to relax, ready to accept whatever was to happen. She had recognized the possibilities when she agreed to come here; and she was no longer a child but a full-grown woman, with a mature woman's keen desires. And with that thought, she found herself yearning toward him.

Owen must have read some of what she was thinking in her face, for he took the necessary steps to reach her. His hands came up to cup her face, and he stood thus for just a moment, without speaking. There was something tentative about his touch, about his expression, and she realized anew that he was unsure of himself.

This thought brought a smile to her lips, and then he lowered his face to hers, kissing her smiling lips. The kiss was soft, undemanding; and yet the touch of his mouth set her heart to pounding, and heat raced through her with the speed of wildfire.

Abruptly, he let her go and took a step back, his gaze searching. She had the feeling that if she so much as demurred, he would desist. Instead, she felt bereft, and she took an involuntary step toward him, aching for his touch again.

"Jemina..." he said haltingly. "I've wanted you for a long time, probably from the first moment I saw you. But are you sure you want...?"

"I want ... something. I'm not sure what."

Now that she had irrevocably committed herself, she experienced another spurt of panic. What was she to do now? What was expected of her? She knew almost nothing of physical relations between a man and a woman. Not a single word of advice about sexual matters had come from her mother; what little she did know had come from Aunt Hester.

The few times her aunt had been confronted by Jemina's tentative questions, the woman had never completely answered her. "I'm sorry, girl, it's just too embarrassing. Women are brought up never to discuss such delicate matters, and no matter how much I might consider myself a modern woman, I just can't bring myself to do it. But there is one consolation, Jemina ... it's a natural function between men and women, and when the time comes, if you love the man, you will get through it all right. *If* the man is decent and kind, and not a brute, you won't have to *do* anything."

In short order, Jemina found this to be pretty much true. Owen led her into the bedroom, sat her on the bed and began to undress her, stopping now and then to kiss her lips, then her neck and shoulders as they became exposed, and then touching her tenderly but intimately as he removed more of her clothing.

Her emotions ran riot, the blood roared in her head, and she was in such a daze of desire and sensation that she was scarcely aware of what he was doing. Yet a small part of her mind made note of the fact that Owen *knew* what he was doing; even in her inexperience she realized that he was a skillful lover.

When Jemina was finally naked and stretched out upon the bed, Owen stood back and began removing his own clothing, his gaze never leaving her. There was a small lamp burning on a table in the corner, enough light for Jemina to see her first man in the natural state. She wanted to tear her gaze away, knowing that her face was burning with embarrassment; yet she could not. When he was finally exposed in all his manhood, she drew in her breath sharply. He was at once beautiful and frightening.

He came to her then, lying beside her on the bed. He touched her here and there, his fingers feather light, as he murmured endearments. Her body began to respond to the strokings of his fingers, the touch of his mouth, on her lips, her neck and then her breasts as her nipples grew tumescent.

He seemed to know when it was time to take her. She tensed herself for the pain she knew enough to expect; and yet so gentle and knowing was he that the brief pain had come and gone almost before she realized it. She was lost in the intimacy of the moment.

And so it was that Jemina experienced her first pleasure of physical love, her first sexual ecstasy.

It was not until they lay side by side, heartbeats and breathing slowly returning to normal, that Jemina had time to sort out her feelings. If she was supposed to feel guilt, then she must not be normal, she concluded. Besides, what could be so wrong with anything that gave so much pleasure? Why should she feel guilt over something that had brought such

closeness between two human beings, an intimacy
that melded two people into one?

She glanced at Owen. His face looked serene,
peaceful. Yet, even in repose, there was an air of
danger about him. But how could a man who had just
been so gentle and loving pose any kind of a threat to
her? Or to anyone?

She reached out a hand to touch his chest, then let
it fall away. But the movement of air, or some animal sense, must have warned him that she had
moved; for suddenly he was looking at her. A faint
smile curved his lips.

"Owen...if it's not too personal, I'd like to ask you
a question."

"Ask away," he said with a shrug. "There's no
guarantee that I will answer it."

"About your eye...I asked you once, but you never
really told me how you lost it. I've heard several
stories about it. One story has it that you lost the eye
during a duel over a woman, another that you lost it
during the war with Mexico."

"Those are the only versions you've heard?" He
laughed softly. "There are others. I know, because I
fostered them. I thought, why not make it sound
glamorous and romantic? Actually, the truth is not
romantic at all."

He told her then how he had lost the eye. But he
couldn't bring himself to tell her that he was a bastard; he said only that the boyhood fight had been
brought about because of a derogatory remark about
his mother. He lied about his father, telling her that
the man had been a sailor lost at sea when Owen was
very small. "The only thing I remember about him
is that he had the tattoo of a ship on his right arm.

When he flexed his muscles, the ship appeared to set sail.''

"I am sorry, Owen, about your father." Then she smiled. "At least you lost the eye for the honor of a lady."

He looked at her strangely. "You know, you're the first person I've ever told the truth to about my eye. I wonder..." He sat up abruptly. "It's late. I had better see you home." He got out of bed and began dressing.

A short time later, they went down the narrow stairs, Jemina going first. Just as she stepped into the vestibule, the door opened and a woman in a dressing gown stood framed in the doorway. Her eyes widened and she gasped as she saw Jemina, and she took a half step back.

Then Owen spoke from behind Jemina. "Mrs. Logan, how are you this evening? Jemina, this is my landlady, Etta Logan. Mrs. Logan, this is a friend, Jemina Benedict."

The woman said in a low voice, "How do you do, Miss Benedict?"

Jemina knew that her face was scarlet. She endeavored to keep the quaver out of her voice. "I am pleased to meet you, Mrs. Logan."

The woman nodded, stepped back inside and began to close the door. As Jemina went down the front steps with Owen, she was certain that she had seen the shadowy figure of a man standing behind Owen's landlady.

BOOK II

"A philosopher, being asked what was the first thing necessary towards winning the love of a woman, answered, 'An opportunity.'"

—*Godey's Lady's Book*

Chapter Ten

JEMINA HAD ALWAYS possessed a sunny disposition, but as her affair with Owen progressed, she began to take on that special glow that only being in love can bring to a woman.

Her aunt was the first to notice; at least, the first to comment. One morning as they dawdled over Sunday breakfast, Hester looked across the table at Jemina. "What's come over you of late, girl?"

Startled into stillness, Jemina said warily, "Nothing that I know of. I'm just delighted with the way things are going at the *Book*."

Hester shook her head. "No, it's more than that. Are you in love, Jemina?"

Jemina was at a loss as to how to respond. She had confided in no one about Owen. If word got out about their affair, her reputation would be ruined; and undoubtedly her position at the *Book* would be forfeit. She knew that Sarah was liberal of mind; but she was also very religious, with a strict moral code, and sexual congress outside of wedlock would be beyond the pale.

Was she in love with Owen? Astonishingly enough, she now realized, she had given the matter little consideration; for the moment she was simply content with the delights of their lovemaking.

She looked at her aunt directly. "Aunt Hester, that is a personal question!"

"Piffle!" Hester waved a hand. "But never mind, I have my answer, and I am not particularly surprised. After all, you are twenty-two years old and a beautiful young woman. But heed me closely, girl." She leaned forward. "I beg of you to be careful. You are not quite the woman of the world that you imagine yourself to be. You could easily be hurt. But it had to happen sometime. Who is the fortunate man?"

Jemina was shaking her head, deeply disturbed that she had inadvertently revealed as much as she had. "I can't tell you his name."

Hester shrugged. "Actually, I have no wish to know the man's name, Jemina. But do heed me, pray. Be careful."

FOR A FEW DAYS after her conversation with her aunt, Jemina tried to act more subdued, but her newfound happiness refused to be held in check. She concluded that if any other people had noticed her happiness, they probably credited it to her success at the magazine; for there was no longer any doubt—she had exceeded her expectations. With the success of her Blackwell article and the first of her farm pieces, she was drawing top writing assignments.

She had learned that the magazine articles generally fell into two categories—"event" pieces and "people" pieces. She could handle both, but she much preferred stories dealing with people. She also realized just how fortunate she was. Most new people on the *Book* were assigned articles on fashions, cooking or sewing; she had escaped that and was glad of it.

She continued to see Owen at least once a week, and their affair grew ever more satisfying. There was

no mention of love, for although Jemina now realized that she loved him with all her heart, she sensed
that it would be a mistake to mention it. With the ancient instinct of womankind, she was sure that Owen
cared deeply for her. However, she recognized that he
was a free spirit, accustomed to going his own way,
and that he undoubtedly feared making any kind of
commitment.

This did not concern her unduly, since she was far
from sure that she was ready for marriage herself,
even to a man she loved. She was quite content with
her life as it was; and marriage would almost certainly bring about changes. Most women, she knew,
would be busily contriving some way to get a proposal of marriage out of Owen. But she wasn't like
other women, and she was smugly proud of that fact.

Once, quite late, as they were getting out of a
hackney before Owen's building, they met a man just
coming out of the ground-floor flat. He was a tall,
middle-aged swell, but Jemina didn't get a good look
at his face—he ducked his head aside and scurried
past them without a greeting.

Upstairs, Jemina said, "Does Mrs. Logan have a
friend? The man we just saw?"

"I have no idea," Owen said curtly. "She has that
right, doesn't she? And anyway, it's none of our affair."

A week later, on the day of an evening they had
arranged to meet, Owen sent a message around to the
Book, informing her that he would be delayed and
asking if she would mind meeting him in the vestibule of his building at seven sharp. She did not have
a key to his quarters and had not asked for one; it

seemed to her that that would really place her in the scarlet-woman category.

She left the magazine, hailed a hackney without any difficulty and arrived at Owen's building a half hour early. After a moment's indecision, she knocked on Mrs. Logan's door. She did not relish the idea of waiting for thirty minutes in the uncomfortable vestibule; and she had been introduced to the woman, after all.

There was an immediate scurrying sound from the inside, and the door opened. Mrs. Logan stood in the doorway, a smile beginning to form on her lips; but when she saw Jemina, the smile quickly died. Jemina noticed the signs of recent tears on the woman's face, and she regretted knocking on the door.

She said quickly, "Mrs. Logan, I'm Jemina Benedict, remember? Owen introduced us a few days ago."

"Yes, I remember you," Mrs. Logan said dully. "You're Owen's . . ."

She broke off, and Jemina wondered, Owen's what? She said, "I was supposed to meet him here at seven. But I'm early, and I thought . . ."

"I was just making tea," Etta Logan said. She stepped back, opening the door wider. "Would you like to come in and wait?"

"Are you sure I'm not imposing?"

"No, not at all," the woman said in the same dreary voice. "I would welcome the company."

Jemina followed her inside. All the curtains in the flat were drawn, and the interior was dim and warm. The small parlor was cluttered with comfortable furniture and many knickknacks. A grandfather clock ticked loudly in one corner.

Etta gestured to the divan. "Please take a seat. I'll just fetch the tea. It should be ready."

Jemina sat down gingerly as the woman left the room. She regretted more than ever the impulse that had prompted her to knock on the door. There was an unhappiness about Etta Logan, hovering about her like a sour miasma; and Jemina suspected that it had to do with the mysterious man she had seen coming out of the woman's apartment.

For a moment, she felt a stab of apprehension. Was this to be her fate? Would her affair with Owen leave her sour, bitter and disillusioned?

She shook her head sharply, dismissing such gloomy thoughts, as Etta came back carrying a laden tray. Jemina noticed that the woman had washed her face, eradicating all traces of the tears, and she seemed in a more cheerful mood.

As Etta busied herself pouring the tea, Jemina studied her covertly. She judged the woman to be in her early forties. Her face was not beautiful, but it was not unattractive, and her figure was full, almost buxom. There was more than a hint of sexuality about her, and Jemina could easily see why a mature man might be attracted to her.

The tea was a trifle bitter for Jemina's palate, but the sugar cakes were delicious. She noticed that Etta ate the little cakes greedily, as though feeding an unhappiness.

Jemina was caught staring at her and quickly looked away.

"Have you known Owen long?" Etta asked.

"For several months, since I first came to Philadelphia."

"Oh? You're not from here, then?"

''No, I'm from Boston. I work at *Godey's Lady's Book*,'' Jemina said with a touch of pride.

The first flicker of real interest showed on the other woman's face. ''Do you, indeed? That must be interesting work. I must confess that I don't read the magazine regularly, but I do read it from time to time.''

''It *is* interesting work. I love it.''

''What do you do there?''

''I'm a contributing editor.'' At Etta's uncomprehending look, Jemina continued, ''I should say that I am learning to be an editor. An editor reads articles, stories and the like and decides if they are suitable for consideration for publication in the magazine. Editors also correct and polish manuscripts. As a contributing editor, I also write pieces for the *Book*.''

''Oh, yes, I thought your name was familiar! You wrote about that woman doctor, Elizabeth Blackwell, didn't you?''

Jemina nodded, suddenly realizing that Etta was the first person who had mentioned having read anything of hers. There had been numerous letters from readers, but it was different, somehow, speaking to a reader face-to-face. Of course, Etta's words weren't exactly praise, but Jemina was absurdly pleased, nonetheless.

''I've often thought that I would like to work, but I know no trade,'' Etta was saying. ''I got married very young, you see, and when my Daniel died, there was no job I could do. I was fortunate that he left me well-off.''

''You *are* fortunate, then,'' Jemina said brightly.

"But sometimes it gets so lonely." The woman gestured vaguely. "We had no children, and I have no relatives, you see. I'm all alone."

For a moment, Jemina feared that Etta might break into tears as her face worked convulsively, but the woman quickly swallowed some tea and regained her composure.

"You're the fortunate one, Miss . . . may I call you Jemina?"

"Please do, Etta."

"Owen is such a charming, handsome fellow."

Etta's look was sly, somehow conspiratorial, and Jemina felt suddenly warm. Was the woman equating her own situation with Jemina's? But of course the parallel existed, Jemina thought, as much as she might wish to deny it. She regretted deeply the impulse that had brought her in here. She sneaked a glance at the ticking clock and felt a sense of relief—Owen should be arriving any minute.

Etta was saying wistfully, "Many times I have seen the pair of you going off at night, dressed to the nines, probably on your way to a fine dinner or a good time at the theater, and I so envy you, Jemina. . . ."

Jemina heard the vestibule door open, and footsteps. She got quickly to her feet. "There's Owen now. Thank you very much for the tea, Etta."

She hastened to the door, opened it and stepped into the vestibule.

Owen was just starting up the stairs. He glanced over his shoulder with a startled look. "Jemina! What . . . ?"

She closed the door and hurried to take his arm. "I was early, and Etta invited me in for tea."

He glanced at the door to Etta Logan's flat. "I didn't realize you knew her well enough to socialize."

"Well, I didn't want to wait out here for you, and she seemed quite happy to have the company. Poor woman, I think she gets lonely."

"Lonely?" He raised an eyebrow in sardonic amusement. "How about that friend of hers we were talking about a few days ago?"

He gestured her ahead of him up the stairs.

"That's just it," she said back over her shoulder. "I don't think she is too happy with the situation. In fact, in my judgment, Etta Logan is a very unhappy woman."

At the top of the stairs she stood aside so Owen could open the door with his key. As they stepped inside and the door closed behind them, Owen said casually, "Probably trying to lead him to the altar and he's balking."

His casual manner struck a spark of irritation in her. "So what if she is? I fail to see anything wrong in that."

"Well, there's an old saying," he said with a faint leer. "If you're getting free milk, why. . ." He broke off, flushing darkly.

It took her a moment to comprehend his meaning. In a rush of anger, she snapped, "What a terrible thing to say, Owen Thursday! I thought better of you!"

"I'm sorry, it was just a joke. A bad one, I will admit," he muttered. "But some men *do* think that way. Perhaps that's the way her friend thinks."

She glared at him, unappeased. "And you, Owen? Do you think that way?"

He recoiled. "Now wait, Jemina. How did I get drawn into this?"

"Because of us. Do you think that way about me?"

"Of course not, Jemina! How could you think such a thing? You know me better than that."

"Do I? I thought I did, but then, I would never have thought you would make such a vulgar, unkind remark about Etta, either!"

He winced. "I spoke without thinking. I said I was sorry, didn't I?"

"What would you think, or say, if I tried to drag *you* to the altar?" she said challengingly.

He grew still, staring at her in speculation. "You once told me you didn't wish to get married."

"I don't, not now. But how about in the future? I will want to get married eventually."

"Jemina . . ." He sighed, half-turning away. "I'm in no position to get married. I'm gone most of the time. This is the longest I've been in Philadelphia in years. What would you do while I'm away?"

"Why, just what I'm doing now," she said, her anger receding. "Working for the *Lady's Book.*"

"I don't approve of wives working," he said stiffly. "It's all right for you now, unmarried. But it's not a married woman's place to work. It's not proper."

"Not proper! Why, Owen, I thought you were more modern than most other men." Somehow, she was amused now, and she had to laugh.

Still not looking at her, he said, "When a wife works, people always think the man can't support her."

"You sound just like my father," she said, still smiling.

"Did it ever occur to you that perhaps he might be right?" he said gruffly. Then he gestured. "Anyway, is this the time to talk about it?"

She went to him, reaching up to turn his face toward her. "I think we've just had our first quarrel. And don't worry, darling, I'm not trying to maneuver you into a proposal of marriage. You're right, this is certainly not the time."

She stood on tiptoe, kissing him warmly. She put her arms around him, pressing her lower body against him.

His response was instant and fierce. Just before she gave herself up to passion, Jemina had to wonder at her boldness. This was the first time she had made the advances, but instead of feeling shame, she was secretly delighted with herself.

A short time later, as they lay side by side, Owen murmured in her ear, "I am sorry, Jemina, about the remark I made earlier. It was a damned nasty thing to say, and I swear to you that I have no such thoughts concerning you."

"JEMINA," SARAH SAID, "I have a project in mind for you, one I've been thinking about for some time. We recently published a series of articles on heroines of the American Revolution, and they were well received. Now I am considering a series of pieces on important women of Philadelphia, women who have also figured prominently in the history of our country: Betsy Ross, Dolley Payne Todd, who later became Dolley Madison; Mrs. Read; Lydia Darrah; and numerous others."

"I have heard rumors that Betsy Ross didn't really have a thing to do with making our first flag," Jemina said.

"I've heard the stories, as well, but I do not know how much truth there is in them. It will be your job to find out."

Jemina was silent in thought for a few moments. "This is something entirely new to me, Sarah. I've never written about people or events from the past."

"I realize that," Sarah said with a crisp nod. "But it'll be a good exercise for you. I gather you've had little experience with historical research?"

"None whatsoever."

"That's why I am assigning the project to you, Jemina. At one time or another, any good author should learn how to research. I have enough faith in you to know that the writing will pose no problem."

"Of course, I *did* do some research on the Elizabeth Blackwell piece, but only as background for the interview."

"This will be much the same, except you will have to go back much farther into history. Peruse old newspapers, books on American history and the like."

"It might be interesting to do, at that," Jemina said slowly.

She suddenly remembered the collection of books Owen had; she hadn't examined them too closely, yet she knew that quite a few of them dealt with history. Perhaps somewhere in them she could uncover valuable information.

When she mentioned the project and her thought that his books might be of help, Owen nodded. "I don't recall any specifics, but I know there is quite a bit scattered through the books about the women you have mentioned. You're more than welcome to use any of the books you wish."

Jemina had noticed a change in Owen's attitude toward her work of late, especially since the first piece about farm women had been published. She sensed in him a growing respect for her work.

"Of course, if you're going to be using my books," he said with a grin, "I suppose I'll have to give you a key to my place."

She laughed softly. "Do you suppose you can trust me with it?"

"It seems I'll have to."

"You know, one of the women Sarah mentioned was Betsy Ross. I've heard from some source or other that she actually had nothing to do with making the first American flag."

He nodded. "I've heard the same thing. But the original story makes for a beautiful myth, you must agree." His gaze became intent. "How will you handle it if you find out it *is* a myth?"

She gave him a startled look. "I don't know. I haven't given it any thought. I suppose I'll make that decision when the time comes."

JEMINA BEGAN GOING to Owen's flat during the day and delving into his books. She also, as Sarah had suggested, consulted old newspaper files, old letters written about her subject matter—and she slowly learned how to research. She had supposed it would be dry, not nearly as interesting as dealing with living people and events; yet she became fascinated, as she learned much she had never known before about the history of her country.

She soon had much of the material she needed, except for information on Betsy Ross. There was an aura of mystery about the purported maker of the country's first flag. Betsy Ross had been dead for only twelve years, and members of her family still lived in the house on Arch Street between Second and Third, where Betsy Ross had supposedly sewed the flag; they were still in the flag-making business.

They stoutly maintained that the rumors were ridiculous—of course Betsy had made the flag! Yet others Jemina talked to stated firmly that someone else had made the flag. However, when questioned closely, they were vague about who actually had produced the country's proud banner.

Jemina remembered Owen's remark that if it was a myth, it was a beautiful myth; and she interpreted that to mean that the country needed its heroes and heroines, whether mythical or not. And so, since she had no firm evidence to the contrary, she decided that she would include Betsy Ross in her articles as the maker of the first Stars and Stripes.

Now she was ready to start work on the pieces, and she decided to do most of the writing in Owen's quarters. It was quiet there in the daytime, and she would have ready access to his books. She had seen Etta Logan several times in her comings and goings and was on friendly terms with the woman. But she hadn't seen Etta's man friend and had to wonder if the relationship had been broken off.

Jemina began to write the first article one chilly autumn afternoon. Humming under her breath, she picked up her pen: "There have been a large number of Philadelphia women prominent in our country's history, including a number of heroines of the

American Revolution. Our pieces, dear reader, will deal with these noble women and with others who have distinguished themselves in some manner. Perhaps it would be fitting here to quote an excerpt from a speech given by one of the heroines of the revolution here in Philadelphia. The address was given in June of 1780 and was published in all the Philadelphia newspapers.

"Speaking of the brave men who were then engaged in the death struggle with the British, she said, 'And shall we hesitate to evidence our gratitude? Shall we hesitate to wear clothing more simple, and dress less elegant, while at the price of this small privation, we shall deserve your benedictions? Who, among us, will not renounce, with the highest pleasure, those vain ornaments, when she shall consider that the valiant defenders of America will be able to draw more advantages from the money she may have laid out for these? that they may be better defended from the rigors of the seasons? that, after their painful toils, they will receive some extraordinary and unexpected relief?—that these presents will be valued by them at a greater price, when they will have it in their power to say—this is the offering of the ladies.'

"These fine sentiments were present to a degree in all the ladies we shall write about in the ensuing pieces...."

She was suddenly interrupted by the sound of loud, quarreling voices from the flat below. She could not make out the words, but there was no doubt of the gender of the voices—male and female.

She glanced out the window. It was a cold, blustery day, with snow clouds hovering low, and it was almost dark outside.

The sound of voices ceased, and she had picked up her pen to resume writing when the sound of a gunshot froze her in midmotion. The shot had come from downstairs, no doubt of that....

After a moment of indecision, Jemina jumped up and ran for the door, then hastened down the narrow stairs, with no thought of possible danger to herself.

She knocked on the door, calling out frantically, "Etta! Etta, open the door!"

It was a few moments before she heard the sound of dragging footsteps inside, and the door opened slowly. Etta Logan, a pistol in her hand, faced her. Etta's face was chalk white, her eyes wide and staring.

"Etta, are you all right? What has happened?"

Without answering, Etta stepped back, and Jemina followed her inside. There, lying on his back on the floor, was the man Jemina had seen coming out of Etta's apartment. His eyes stared sightlessly up at the ceiling, and blood covered his chest.

"My God!" Jemina's hand flew to her mouth. "What happened here?"

"He promised," Etta said in a dull voice. "He promised. He promised!"

Jemina stared at the woman in shock.

"He promised, and then today he told me that he would never marry me. I couldn't endure any more!"

Chapter Eleven

THE MURDER CAUSED a sensation in Philadelphia.

The victim was Homer Murdock, a widower who owned a dry-goods store in the city. He was well-thought-of, and he had two children—two married sons—who soon added their voices to the general clamor demanding that Etta Logan be quickly tried, convicted and hanged.

On the afternoon of the shooting, a neighbor had heard the shot and immediately summoned the police. Owen had come home just before they arrived, to find Jemina with Etta, attempting to comfort her.

Etta, in a state of shock and nearly inarticulate, kept repeating the same phrase over and over. "He made me a solemn promise!"

She said the same thing to the police and did not deny that she had killed her paramour.

After the police had carted Etta away, Owen took Jemina upstairs. Jemina, very upset, was close to tears.

"That poor woman! What will happen to her, Owen?"

"There seems little doubt but that she will be convicted of murder and likely hanged. They don't often hang women, but this seems such a blatant case that I'm afraid she'll get little sympathy."

"Will you be reporting the story for the *Ledger*?"

"No, I'm sure Carruthers has already assigned the story." He looked at her curiously. "Why do you ask?"

"I thought you might write a story favorable to Etta."

"How could I do that?" he said with a trace of annoyance. "She killed the man. She doesn't even bother to deny it."

"But he had promised to marry her!"

"That's hardly an excuse for murder. Besides, we have only her word for that."

"But why should she lie about such a thing?"

"Jemina, when you've been in the newspaper business as long as I have, you'll learn that people will lie about anything, especially when they are in a bad situation."

"That's a cynical attitude!"

"Perhaps," he said with a shrug. "But unfortunately it's true more often than not. You're going to acquire a little cynicism of your own somewhere along the line."

"There should be *something* we can do for Etta."

"I can't think of anything. Why should you be so upset, Jemina? You scarcely know the woman."

"That has no bearing on the matter. It is not right that a man should promise to marry a woman, take advantage of her repeatedly and then go back on his word."

"There is such a thing as a breach-of-promise suit, but such suits are only effective when filed by a woman of unimpeachable reputation. You could hardly call Etta Logan that."

"I fail to see what Etta's character has to do with it. A promise is a promise!"

"Public opinion will have it otherwise, my dear. Within days Etta will be known throughout Philadelphia as a fallen woman who killed her paramour."

"Even if she was a harlot, she should have *some* rights!"

"Society doesn't view it that way...."

Jemina was no longer listening. She was thinking ahead, trying to figure out something that she could do. Owen wasn't going to help; that was abundantly clear. He was on the side of the man, as she supposed all other males would be.

She said, "I'll discuss it with Sarah. Perhaps she will let me do an article about Etta."

"The *Lady Book* publishing an article defending a wanton and a murderess!" He laughed scornfully. "Louis Godey would have apoplexy if such a thing was even mentioned to him."

"I'm going to try, anyway," she said stubbornly. "What harm can it do?"

"For one thing, it could lead to your being discharged from the *Lady Book*."

"SARAH, I PROMISED I would consult with you before I wrote another article on my own," Jemina said.

Sarah looked across the desk at her. "What do you have in mind?"

"Have you heard about Etta Logan?"

"No, I don't believe..." Sarah's eyes widened. "Isn't that the woman who killed her lover the other day?"

"Yes, that's the one."

"And you want to write a piece about her? Why?"

"Well, I happen to think that what has happened to her is unjust. She was driven to kill that man."

"Driven?" Sarah's eyes narrowed. "You speak as if you know the woman."

"Well, I do. Slightly. Etta Logan is Owen's landlady."

"Owen Thursday?" Sarah studied her thoughtfully.

Belatedly, Jemina realized that she had made a mistake. Without thinking, she had revealed a closeness to Owen that Sarah was unlikely to approve of.

However, Sarah made no comment as to that. Instead, she said, "I am afraid that I cannot see this woman as the subject for an article."

Jemina plunged into the story. "Etta was in love with this man, Homer Murdock, and he not only claimed to be in love with her but had promised repeatedly to marry her. And then, on this particular day, he finally told her that he had no intention of marrying her at all!"

"A sad story, undoubtedly, but one that has been repeated down through the ages."

"But you see, that's why she killed him!" Jemina said intensely. "She saw her whole future shattered. She saw that he had intended to betray her all along. She was *driven* into killing him!"

Sarah was looking puzzled. "Jemina, I repeat, a tragic story, and I feel some sympathy for the woman; but I still cannot excuse her for killing him. But all that aside, how can you possibly see a piece for the *Lady's Book* in all this?"

"I thought I could write it so that it would reveal how unfair such a situation is to a woman. A woman who is used, under the promise of being wed, then tossed aside like a broken doll when the man tires of her. If done properly, such a piece might save Etta's life.''

"My dear Jemina..." Sarah sighed. "Forgetting everything else for the moment, by the time we could print such a piece, your friend would already be tried and convicted.''

"But even if it would be too late for Etta, it might help other women in the future!" Jemina urged passionately.

"In effect, condone immoral conduct in the *Lady's Book*?''

Jemina was silent, groping for a response.

"For that is what it would amount to. Jemina, you're young yet; you have much to learn," Sarah said kindly. She leaned forward, her hands palms down on the desk. "You must see that this is the sort of material we would never publish in the *Book*. I happen to agree that Etta Logan is suffering because of the mores of our society, yet it cannot be denied that not only is she a woman of loose morals, she committed murder, no matter what her motives were. This is the kind of thing that the scandal sheets thrive on, not the *Lady's Book*.'' She smiled grimly. "I can just imagine what kind of reaction Louis would have should even a hint of this reach him.''

Jemina could only stare back, defeated; yet she knew, in her heart, that Sarah was correct—a story of this sort was not for the *Book*. Owen had been right, also; it had been a mistake even to mention the subject.

Apparently reading her reaction, Sarah said, "You have ideals, passion and compassion. I admire that, my dear; yet there are times when you mustn't let your feelings interfere with your professional life.

Now run along and—'' she smiled gently ''—and perhaps have a good cry.''

Jemina left the office, numb with a feeling of hopelessness, but she did not resort to tears. Instead, she went to visit Etta Logan. Etta's trial was to start within the week.

Etta was the only woman in confinement, and she had a small cell to herself. Jemina felt a pang of dismay when she had her first look at the other woman. Her dress was shapeless and badly wrinkled, as though she had slept in it. Her hair was a wild tangle, and her face was gray and lifeless, her eyes as dull as slate. She looked as if she had shrunk since her confinement.

Jemina tried to force some cheer into her voice. ''How are you, Etta?''

''I'm all right,'' Etta said drearily.

''You look so . . . so thin. Aren't you eating well? Is the food that bad? Perhaps if I said something to whoever is in charge . . . ?''

''The food is all right. I have no appetite.''

''Etta . . . I'm sorry for all that has happened.'' Jemina took the other woman's hand and found it cold as ice. ''I've tried everything, but . . . I wanted to publish something in the *Book* about your plight, but they won't allow it.''

A spark glowed briefly in Etta's eyes. ''I'm going to die, aren't I?''

''Oh, Etta, don't say that! You can't give up hope.''

The spark died, the eyes becoming lifeless again. ''Oh, it's all right,'' Etta said indifferently. ''I want to die. I have nothing left to live for.''

They talked a bit more, but Jemina made her escape as soon as decently possible. Talking to Etta was a depressing experience.

And yet, as Jemina left the jail, she was still wondering what she could do to help the woman. It had become almost an obsession, and for the first time, she began to wonder as to the reason.

Was it because her own situation somewhat paralleled Etta's? Certainly Owen hadn't made any promises to marry her, yet she was sleeping with him without benefit of wedlock; and there might come a time when she would feel betrayed, badly used, by him.

If she was to be strictly honest with herself, she supposed that was a small part of her motive; and yet that was not the real reason—at least, so she told herself. Etta had been treated shabbily by Homer Murdock; and while that was certainly no excuse for murder, it could be said that she had been goaded into it. Murdock had smirched her reputation under the promise of marriage; and when he ended the affair, which he no doubt had intended doing all along, Etta had only one way to go—down.

Should Etta have to die for what she had done? Surely she had been mad with despair when she had committed the crime. She should be punished, no gainsaying that; but put to death?

Jemina knew there was nothing more she could do for the woman. She had tried and, she now realized, had risked losing her position. What more could she do?

And yet, two weeks later, she made another effort.

Etta Logan had been brought to trial. The trial lasted only two days, and Etta was found guilty of murder. The judge, who had presided over the proceedings, postponed the sentencing for a week, but there was no doubt in anyone's mind that the sentence would be death.

Jemina heard the news at the magazine. Without even giving much thought to the matter, she sat down at her desk, took up pen and paper and wrote an impassioned letter: "Honorable Sir: I pen this letter in the hope that you, in your infinite wisdom, will see fit to find leniency in your heart toward Etta Logan.

"Do not sentence her to death, I beg of you.

"Homer Murdock used Etta badly and lied to her, promising to marry her. When he was finally revealed for the villain he was, Etta, in a moment of passion, killed him. She was not herself and would not have committed her crime had she been in her right mind.

"Surely she does not deserve to die. In such a situation a woman is defenseless, at the mercy of the man, and should be shown some leniency.

"I pray that you, Most Honored Sir, will not send this long-suffering woman to her death. Yrs. sincerely, Jemina Benedict."

Folding the single sheet of paper, she sealed it in an envelope and wrote across the face of the envelope: "Judge Phineas Ruteledge: Personal." Then she summoned Timmie, the lad who ran errands around the magazine, and asked him to hand deliver the letter to the judge's chambers.

TWO DAYS LATER Jemina was summoned to Sarah's office.

When she was admitted, she found Louis Godey present, pacing nervously. At Jemina's entrance, he wheeled on her with a thunderous scowl. Sarah sat rigidly behind her desk, her face grave.

"What is the meaning of this, young lady?"

Godey thrust a sheet of paper at her. Recognizing it with a sinking heart, Jemina took it with trembling fingers.

"Since your name is attached to it, I assume you wrote that damnable letter?" Godey demanded.

"Yes, of course I wrote it," Jemina whispered. Then she glanced up in outrage. "This was personal! He had no right to show this to you!"

"No right? No *right*! Young lady, you are the one who had no right, no right at all, to write this in the first place." In his agitation, Godey began to pace again. "What you did was highly improper, even unethical. Phineas Ruteledge is a good friend of mine. He was deeply offended that my magazine should resort to such tactics."

"My sending this letter has nothing to do with the *Book*. I sent it on my own initiative."

He stopped short and thrust his angry face at her. "You had the letter delivered by Timmie. Naturally, Phineas thought it had come from the magazine, with my approval. He thinks we are trying to influence his sentencing of the Logan woman. What you have done, young lady, is unconscionable! It took all my powers of persuasion to convince him not only that I was ignorant of this letter but that I did not agree with the sentiments expressed in any way whatsoever! This woman is a harlot and a murderess, and you have the gall to beg mercy for her!"

Jemina quailed before his rage; she had never imagined him capable of such anger. "I am sorry, Mr. Godey. I never thought . . ."

"Never thought! It strikes me that you are incapable of thought!"

"I see now that it was a mistake having Timmie deliver the letter." She rallied herself. "But the contents of that letter were my own thoughts, and I am entitled to my personal opinion!"

"Not when it affects my magazine, you're not!" He glowered at her. "What you have done is more than reason enough for me to dispense with your services."

Sarah spoke for the first time. "Now wait, Louis, don't be hasty. I fully agree with you; it was a rash thing for Jemina to do. But she is a young woman with strong convictions, no matter that we don't agree with them. We need people of that caliber on the publication. How many times have you told me that what *I* do outside the magazine is my own affair?"

"But you would never do such a thing as this, Sarah."

Jemina said, "At the soiree at your house, Mr. Godey, I heard you defend Mr. Poe. You mentioned that you even wrote an editorial stating that although your magazine did not necessarily agree with his views, you declared that you would not be intimidated by reader complaints."

His stare was baleful. "There is a vast difference between you and Mr. Poe, young lady. First, he does not work for me, and more important, he is a famous author."

"But even so . . ."

"No more." He cut her off with a curt gesture. "I have stated my position. I will take into consideration your youth and zeal and Sarah's defense of you. I will take no further action."

He started for the door. Opening it, he paused to turn back. "But I will leave you with this warning. Do not try my patience further. One more such incident as this, and you face dismissal, Miss Benedict."

After the door closed behind him, Jemina turned to Sarah. In a trembling voice she said, "I'm sorry for getting you into trouble, Sarah."

"I am not in trouble, my dear, although I must confess that I have never seen Louis quite so enraged," she said with a slight smile. She leaned forward. "Writing that letter was a foolish thing to do, Jemina. What did you hope to accomplish?"

Jemina made a helpless gesture. "I don't really know. But I felt that I had to do something!"

"Jemina, unfortunately the world is filled with injustices," Sarah said gently. "I don't happen to agree with you that the case of Etta Logan is one of them, but that isn't important. There are certain things we can do nothing about, my dear. We can only trust in God's judgment for the ultimate justice and do what we can in our small way...."

THAT NIGHT in Owen's flat, after Jemina had told him everything, he sighed heavily. "I agree with Sarah, Jemina. It was a damned foolish thing to do. Damn it, you don't even *like* Etta!"

Startled, Jemina realized that he was correct—she didn't particularly like the woman. She said obstinately, "My liking or not liking her has nothing to do with it. She should not have to die for what she's done. If she does, I will always feel that I didn't do enough. And so should you, Owen."

"Don't place any responsibility on me!" he said harshly. "Just because you've taken leave of your senses, don't . . ." He broke off, turning away, running his fingers through his hair. He said something Jemina could not hear.

"What did you say, Owen?"

He faced around. "I said . . . I'm getting out of it anyway." He took a deep breath. "I'm leaving tomorrow, for California."

"California!" Stunned, she sank down into the nearest chair. "Tomorrow?"

"Carruthers finally recognized that the gold strike at Sutter's Mill is a news story of major importance, and he agreed that I should cover it." Jubilant, Owen strode back and forth. "You must remember, I mentioned that I wanted to go."

"Yes, but that was some time ago. How long will you be gone?"

"Quite a while. Perhaps a year." He shrugged. "What the hell, it takes forever to get there, this time of the year, anyway." At her stricken look he stopped pacing and squatted before her chair, taking her lifeless hands in his. "Don't look so shocked, Jemina. I told you this was the way it always would be, that this is the reason it would be unfair for me to get married. I'll always be running off somewhere."

"Unfair to whom?" she murmured.

"Why, to you, of course," he said with a raised eyebrow.

All at once, her surprise was gone, and she was swept by anger. "You didn't just learn about it today, did you? When did you find out you're going?"

"Last week," he said with averted gaze.

"Why didn't you tell me? Why did you wait until the last minute?"

"Well, you've been so caught up in this thing with Etta.... No, I won't lie to you." He looked directly into her eyes. "I didn't know exactly how to tell you. I was afraid you'd be hurt...."

"You bastard!" She surged to her feet, blind fury riding her. "You don't care if I'm hurt. You don't care about anything but Owen Thursday!"

He winced. "That's not true, and you know it. It's just that you have your work, and I have mine. It won't really be all that long, sweet." He reached out and pulled her into his arms. "You'll be busy at the *Lady's Book*. The time will pass quickly...."

"Don't try to sweet-talk me!" She beat on his chest with her fists. "You deliberately waited until the last day to tell me!"

She tore out of his grasp and stumbled toward the door, hot tears blinding her. At the door she turned back. "Don't expect me to be waiting for you, pining away for you, like some simpering little chit of a girl. I'll be busy, all right. You can be sure of that, Owen Thursday!"

THE DAY AFTER Owen left Philadelphia, Etta Logan hanged herself in her jail cell, before her sentence had been passed. She had torn her dress into strips, made a noose out of the pieces and hanged herself from the jail bars.

From the *Ledger*, Owen's own newspaper, Jemina scissored the story out, sealed it into an envelope and mailed it to Owen, by way of the *Ledger*.

BOOK III

"Commentators have imputed weakness of the mind to the woman, because the Tempter first assailed her. Does it not rather show that she was the spiritual leader, the most difficult to be won where *duty* was the question, and the Serpent knew that if he could gain her, the result was sure?"

—*Godey's Lady's Book*

Chapter Twelve

"Then blow, ye breezes, blow!
We're off to Californi-o
There's plenty of gold,
So we've been told,
On the banks of the Sacramento."

Owen watched and listened amusedly as two young men pushed their way down the crowded waterfront street, singing lustily.

The New York waterfront was literally crawling with would-be gold seekers, thousands of them, all attempting to find passage on the ships leaving for San Francisco. Each day brought more of them, until there was hardly a place to sit, stand or walk, all of them with that hopeful look in their eyes.

It was amusing, Owen thought, and yet tragic. How many of these men would actually find their hoped-for fortune? And how many would find only bitter hard work and failure?

Again, Owen smiled to himself. Well, whatever these men found, it was dramatic as hell and would make a great story.

Although gold had actually been discovered near Sutter's Mill in early 1848, few people had then believed the reports trickling back to the East Coast.

It had all truly begun when President James Polk made his opening address to the second session of the

Thirtieth Congress on December 5. In his message
the President said, "At the time of California's ac-
quisition it was known that mines of precious metals
existed to a considerable extent. Recent discoveries
render it probable that these mines are more extensive and valuable than was anticipated. The accounts of the abundance of gold in that territory are
of such an extraordinary character as would scarcely
command belief were they not corroborated by au-
thentic reports."

This made it official, and all at once gold fever became an international epidemic. But even this presidential confirmation had not convinced Thomas
Carruthers that the gold discovery in California
merited sending a correspondent there. Thinking
about Carruthers, Owen grinned to himself. Carruthers had always considered the *Ledger* a worthy rival of Horace Greeley's *New York Daily Tribune*, and on
December 9, four days after the president's speech,
Greeley's newspaper had trumpeted: "We are on the
brink of the Age of Gold! We look for an addition
within the next four years equal of at least One
Thousand Million Dollars to the general aggregate of
gold in circulation."

This finally moved Carruthers off his fat rump,
and he agreed that Owen should go to California.
Once committed, Carruthers got behind the project
with enthusiasm.

Owen's grin turned into a frown. If Carruthers had
only acted sooner, he would already *be* in California.
Of course, in that case he might never have met
Jemina.... But now was not the time to think of
Jemina.

If Carruthers had given him permission to go to the goldfields in early summer, Owen would have been able to take the fastest route to California, which was overland, across the continent. A traveler encountered many hardships overland, but it was the most direct route. However, overland was out of the question in the middle of winter, for the mountain passes would be closed now until spring.

The other two choices were by water; the first, the all-water route, down the coasts of both Americas, around Cape Horn and then up the Pacific to San Francisco. This was a long and hazardous journey, taking at least four months and often much longer. In winter the trip around the cape was treacherous, and stories had drifted back of many ships that had ended their journey at the bottom of the sea.

The third route, the way Owen had chosen, was by sea and land—down the Atlantic coast to the mouth of the Chagres River at Panama, across the isthmus to Panama City on the Pacific side, then up the coast to San Francisco.

It was an expensive trip—it would cost the paper approximately two thousand dollars to transport Owen to California—and, Owen knew, from the stories he had heard, it would be uncomfortable. The ships were badly crowded, now that the rush had started, and most people had to wait days or weeks for passage. But since Owen was a newspaperman, he had been given priority, and he was waiting now to board his ship.

Adjusting his cap, Owen brushed a spot of soot from his coat sleeve. People in Philadelphia who knew him would likely not have recognized him at first glance. He was far from the nattily dressed man he was at home. He had long since learned that it was not wise to wear fine clothes when he was in the field. Not only was it impractical, but a dandy, among the type of men he would encounter on the journey and in the goldfields, would be the object of ridicule. He was wearing rough clothes, serviceable boots, a wool cap and a heavy coat. The only item he carried that was unusual was the cane, and he carried that because of the steel blade that could slide out at the press of a button. He also had a small pistol in his carpetbag. He well knew that the kind of people he would be mingling with would rob a man without compunction if they believed it worth their while.

Unlike most of those waiting for passage, Owen was traveling light. He had only his carpetbag with him, in which he had packed two changes of clothing, his toilet necessities, his writing materials and a bedroll. Most of the forty-niners—as the gold seekers had recently been labeled by the press—toted all the baggage they could carry; and Owen was sure that most of their possessions would be either lost or stolen before they reached their destination.

Now, he saw the barrier being removed at the top of the gangplank, and he joined the jostle of men crowding up the plank. He had a cabin of his own for the first leg of the journey, but he doubted he would be so fortunate from Panama City onward.

OWEN WAS MET by a depressing sight when he and the other passengers disembarked at Chagres, a village consisting of little more than a cluster of huts. The terrain was swampy and, Owen knew, would be a breeding place for fevers.

The distance across the isthmus to Panama City was seventy-five miles, and the first fifty miles were made in long dugout canoes, which the natives called *bungos*. They were paddled and poled by native boatmen who were either Spanish or Indian. They stopped for frequent siestas and stoked themselves with a local rum, which Owen found almost undrinkable.

Most of the Americans hiring passage on the canoes were a blustery lot, armed with bowie knives and pistols, with which they frequently threatened the boatmen, urging them on to more speed—all to no avail. The boatmen became sullen and rebellious and only slowed their pace.

Owen kept himself aloof from his fellow passengers, reflecting on how gold lust could quickly change a man for the worse. He made copious notes, when it wasn't raining, which was most of the time. The heat was almost unbearable, settling on them like a wet, smothering blanket. The moist air swarmed with mosquitoes and other bothersome insects. Parrots screeched at them from the trees, and iguanas sunned themselves on the rocks.

But it was the muddy water of the river that hid the real danger, for it was alive with alligators. Owen saw one forty-niner, drunk on brandy, poke at an alligator with a stick. The reptile seized the stick between cruel jaws and jerked the man out of the canoe. Before anyone could come to his aid, the alligator had the screaming man clamped between his jaws and had disappeared with him under the water.

A number of the passengers came down with cholera or malaria, and many of them died and were buried on the muddy banks of the river. Owen was careful of what he drank and ate and was still in good health when they reached the village of Cruces. From there to Panama City they would be at higher altitudes, and conditions would be better.

There were only two ways to travel the twenty-some miles to Panama City—on foot or by mule. Owen was able to purchase a mule, and the remainder of the trip was a bit more pleasant. At least he was able to travel alone, away from the drunken rabble.

Panama City proved to be a town of shacks and tumbledown buildings, with grass growing in the streets. There were no hotel accommodations. The town dated from the seventeenth century, when it had been a major seat of Spanish power in the New World, but little of its former grandeur remained.

The most discouraging fact of all was the number of gold seekers thronging the town, seeking transportation to San Francisco. There were hundreds of them swarming the city, all futilely trying to get passage. The small number of ships plying the Panama-California sea route was woefully inadequate. Despite the fact Owen was a journalist and despite his willingness to pay an outrageous price, he was unable to book passage.

Owen observed men fighting for berths on the few available ships; they fought with fists, knives and even pistols. He saw several duels end in death.

Owen had reached Panama City the first week of January, 1849, and he was still there two weeks later, when his fortune finally changed.

On January 17, he was on the waterfront when a wondrous sight came into view. It was a steamship, flying the flag of the United States and coming from the south! As it steamed into the bay, spewing black smoke, he could read the name painted in bold letters on the side—*California*.

Before leaving Philadelphia he had learned the Congress, under the urging of the president, had voted mail subsidies of more than half a million dollars to give incentives to private companies to build steamships for regular service between New York and Chagres, and between Panama City and San Francisco and other ports on the West Coast; five mail steamers were to service the Atlantic side and three the Pacific coast. At the time Owen sailed, one steamer had been placed into service.

This steamship, a one-thousand-ton side-wheeler, had sailed from New York on October 6, 1848, to steam around South America to Panama City, which would henceforth be her home port. The ship was built to hold sixty saloon passengers and one hundred and fifty steerage. Since the sailing date had been before President Polk's address to Congress officially confirming the gold strike, the *California* had sailed virtually empty. She had been scheduled to arrive in Panama City on January 5, but a stormy voyage through the Straits of Magellan had delayed her.

Owen was exuberant. Now he could finally finish the remainder of his journey!

He soon learned that it wasn't going to be that simple. There were now some fifteen hundred gold seekers clamoring for transportation. Although the *California* had left New York practically empty, she had stopped at Callao and taken on board seventy Peruvians also bound for the goldfields.

When this fact became known, there was a near riot. It was only when an American military official, Major General Persifor F. Smith, also in Panama

City, on his way to become the ranking military official in California, read a letter of protest to a gathering of the American forty-niners that the tension eased somewhat. The letter was addressed to the U.S. consul in Panama, maintaining that United States citizens should receive priority as regards passage on the steamer.

After the meeting Owen managed a few minutes with Major General Smith. ''General, my name is Owen Thursday. I am a correspondent for the *Philadelphia Ledger*, on my way to report on the gold strike. I have been here since the first of the month, and it is urgent that I continue on to California as soon as possible. Do you think you can help me?''

''I accept your priority, Mr. Thursday,'' the general said briskly. ''Your business is certainly more urgent than these gold seekers'.'' His lip curled. ''A scurvy lot, on the whole. I shall demand that the commander of the *California* provide you with passage on his departure.''

''I would be most appreciative, General. Thank you.''

THE *CALIFORNIA* STEAMED out of Panama City on February first. The commander had acceded to General Smith's wishes and had granted accommodations for two hundred and fifty Americans; he had forced the seventy Peruvians to sleep on deck, which meant that the ship carried almost twice as many passengers as she had been built for.

Owen had to share a cabin with others, but at least he was on his way. He sat on deck as they departed, writing the beginning of a new article, in which he intended to chronicle the voyage to San Francisco. He wrote: "Just short of nine in the morning of February 1, we steamed on our way, to the accompaniment of rousing cheers from all on board. The noise was tremendous, since the cocks, hens, sheep, goats, cattle and pigs on board ship joined in the chorus.

"Eating clubs have been formed on deck, with captains appointed to portion out the food. It will be a giant task to feed us all, since the ship is not appointed to provide food for so many. . . ."

The *California* arrived in San Francisco on February 28. Owen wrote: "Today, we dropped anchor in the bay at San Francisco. Your correspondent counted some thirty ships already at anchor. Most of them are rotting, some laden with cargo that was never unloaded. I was informed that the moment a ship drops anchor in the bay, all aboard flee the ship, including the ship's crew, all bound for the goldfields.

"Often, it is impossible to hire men to unload the cargoes. All are after gold, gold! Gold is on everyone's mind; it is the subject of all conversations. Many ship's captains put their seamen in irons the instant the ships drop anchor, so that they cannot run off to the goldfields.

"In conversation with Captain Cleveland Forbes, the commander of the *California*, I was informed that he has promised his chief engineer and cook five hundred dollars a month, and the ordinary seamen two hundred dollars a month, to remain with the ship. The captain himself receives only a monthly stipend of two hundred dollars!

"As for San Francisco itself, its population has increased greatly within the past two years. In 1847 the city went by the name of Yerba Buena, which was changed to San Francisco later that same year. At the time it contained three hundred inhabitants. Today, it is much larger, but most of the buildings are hastily erected tents serving as saloons, restaurants and brothels, whose only purpose is to fleece the gold seekers as they arrive and depart. Some gold hunters make a strike in the fields, come here to seek transportation back home, spend all their gold before they can buy passage and thus have to return to again seek their fortune. A dreary cycle indeed!''

Before he left the *California*, Owen handed his dispatches over to Captain Forbes to carry to Panama City, the first leg of the journey back to Philadelphia. Owen knew that many weeks would elapse before his articles reached Thomas Carruthers, but at least he had the pleasure of knowing that he was one of the very few field correspondents in California.

Owen lingered in San Francisco only overnight, just long enough to buy a horse and saddle and outfit himself with necessities, including as much food as he could carry; for he knew that, as dear as supplies were in San Francisco, they would be even more expensive in the gold camps.

Then he rode north and east out of San Francisco, generally following the Sacramento River. He could have gotten transportation on one of the boats busily plying their trade on the river, which would have been more comfortable; but he knew he would need a means of getting around when he reached the goldfields.

He was in no particular hurry, so he set a leisurely pace, observing the countryside as he rode. He couldn't help thinking of the contrast in the weather between California and Philadelphia. Although the nights here were quite chilly, the days were pleasant.

At this time of year, Philadelphia would be locked in with snow and ice. Of course, fog rose off the Sacramento River on wet days, but on the clear days the sun shone warmly out of a brilliant blue sky.

Before Owen reached the junction of the American River and the Sacramento, he struck off in an easterly direction. After several days' travel, he rode up to the edge of a flat plain, and there below, in a meandering, shallow valley, stretched the American River. In a bend of the river he saw what he knew was Sutter's Mill.

He dismounted and stepped closer to the edge of the slope, gazing down at the river. Shacks and adobe huts were clustered around the sawmill, and tents sprouted like mushrooms.

"Can you believe that a year ago there were less than a hundred people living down there?" said a drawling voice from his right. "Now Coloma sports close to ten thousand souls."

Owen spun about. Sitting with his back against the trunk of a large oak tree was a thin, gangling man with a narrow, bony face topped with rust-colored hair that fell to his shoulders.

Owen started toward him. "Coloma? I thought that was Sutter's Mill?"

"Was, friend. Now it's called Coloma," said the stranger. There was more than a touch of the South in the man's soft voice.

As he stepped closer, Owen noticed that the man had a huge sketch pad propped against his knees, and he had a pencil in his right hand; a box of paints and pencils was open beside him.

Owen stopped before the seated man. "I'm Owen Thursday."

"John Riley. Pardon me for a moment here." Squinting out over the valley, he drew a couple of quick, broad strokes with the pencil.

Moving around to the side, Owen looked down at the sketch pad. Riley was drawing the amber and brown hills rising beyond the river. Owen realized that the man was good, damned good.

Now Riley put his sketch pad down and stood, uncoiling his great length. He held out a hand. "Welcome to El Dorado, Owen."

Owen shook the proffered hand. "Why are you up here sketching, instead of down there with the others?"

"Because it's what I do, sketch and paint for a living. It's a poor living, most times, but I like it nonetheless. As for joining those poor sods down there, it's not all it's made out to be. The lucky strikes are the only ones you hear about. Most of them scratch and work their tails off for just a few ounces of gold." His gray eyes studied Owen curiously. "Are you here to hunt for the yellow stuff, Owen?"

Owen shook his head, smiling slightly. "No, I'm here to write about it. I'm a field correspondent for the *Philadelphia Ledger*."

"Aha, that explains it, then! You looked too intelligent to be a gold hunter." Riley's eyes twinkled slyly. "You'll hear many tales here to send back to your paper, some true, some mythical. For instance, one story goes that a certain gold hunter had looked and looked, and nary a trace of yellow did he find. Then one morning, while he sat on a rock, discouraged and homesick, he kicked the rock to vent his anger and broke two toes. But his kick dislodged the rock, and he found a seven-pound nugget under it. Truth or myth?

"There is another story that I do know to be true, because I was there when it happened. It was over on Carson Creek. A miner died, and since he was a popular fellow, his fellow miners decided to give him a decent funeral, instead of the usual quick burial. First, of course, the miners had to have a few drinks, to get in the proper mood. That is how I learned about it; I was in the same saloon.

"When they left for the graveyard, carrying the dead miner, I went along to sketch it. One of the miners had been a preacher before the gold fever got him. He preached and prayed while the miners knelt by the open grave. The preaching went on at some length, and the miners sobered up and became restless.

"Now, miners cannot resist running their fingers through dirt, and several of them gathered handfuls of the loose dirt at the grave's edge, letting it sift through their fingers. Suddenly, one shouted out, 'Color!' He had found traces of gold, you see.

"The preacher thundered, 'Congregation dismissed!' " Riley began to laugh. "The body was quickly taken out of the hole, set aside and forgotten, at least for a time, while the preacher and the mourners began digging. And you know, they found enough gold there to make it profitable for all concerned.

"You think that will amuse your readers back in Philadelphia?"

Owen was grinning. He had a sudden idea. "You said you were at the graveside, sketching. Do you happen to still have the sketch in your possession?"

"Why, I believe so." The man reached into a pack propped against the tree and took out a rolled sheet of paper.

Owen took it, unrolled it and studied it intently. It was a comic sketch, almost a caricature. The dead man lay to one side of the open grave, hands folded peacefully across his chest, while the miners, including the preacher dressed all in black, dug furiously at the sides of the grave, their faces frozen in grimaces of intense greed.

"This is good, Riley. Do you happen to have any more you can show me?"

"Naturally. Not many chances to sell anything out here."

Riley dug into his pack and gave Owen several more rolled-up sheets. Owen unrolled them one at a time. Most were sketches done in pencil or charcoal, but there were a number of paintings done in water-colors. One of them depicted a river running like a silver thread through dark lines of timber. Another was of a plain dotted with autumnal flowers and a grove of evergreen oak. And yet another showed a herd of black-tailed deer and a second herd, this one of antelope, grazing along the lower slopes of a mountainside, with the snow-capped peak of Mount Shasta in the distance thrusting up into a bright blue sky.

Owen returned the paintings to Riley. "You're damned good, Riley."

"I know that I'm good," the painter said without modesty, adding with a wry grin, "not that it brings me much money out here. But I'm hoping to have enough for a profitable showing when I finally return to the East.''

''How much longer do you intend to remain?''

''Until my money runs out,'' Riley said with a shrug, ''and that won't be much longer. I've been here since last July, and I'd like to stay out here a full year. But soon I may be eating wild berries or digging for gold, and I don't know which would be worse.''

''I may have a way out for you, if you're agreeable.''

Riley studied him keenly. ''Well, I'm certainly willing to listen.''

''Well, I think that I can convince my editor to use many of your sketches. The one at the grave site, for instance, would be great. You can do one for every story I send in. I can't pay you much at the present, but I have enough money to keep us both eating until arrangements are made with my paper, and additional funds can be sent. But you know how slow mail is between here and the East, even sending all my dispatches by military packet, which I have made arrangements to do.''

''That sounds fine,'' the painter said cautiously. ''That will mean we have to travel together much of the time.''

''That's true enough. I will need your guidance, in any event, since this is all new to me, and you've been here for a spell.'' Owen cocked his head, grinning. ''Do you think we can bear each other's company?''

''I'm pretty much a loner, always have been. But you seem like a genial enough fellow. I must warn you, however. I've been known to take more than a drop on occasion.''

"I'm not averse to taking a drink myself. Shall we shake on it then, John Riley?''

"I think we have a bargain, friend.''

Riley held out his hand, and they shook solemnly.

Chapter Thirteen

IT WAS A DISMAL WINTER for Jemina. Since Etta Logan's suicide and what she thought of as Owen's defection, the world had taken on a dreary cast. She still performed her work well enough, but some of the joy had gone out of it, a fact she soon discovered when she started a new piece and realized that she wasn't humming to herself.

She had been given permission to take a week off over the Christmas holidays, and she spent the time with her family in Boston.

When Jemina arrived, Beth Benedict began to fuss over her at once. "Jemina, you're thinner, and you're pale as can be. Are you ill?"

"Mother, I've always been pale, you know that," Jemina said lightly. "And I may have lost a pound or two, but it's all to the good, in my opinion."

"You're probably not eating well," her father said in his best grumbling voice. "That Hester always was a terrible cook."

"Father, I do most of the cooking. And I'm a good cook. Mother taught me well," Jemina said, kissing her mother on the cheek.

"Hester is making you cook the meals?" Henry Benedict said in outrage. "She's probably making a slave out of you, cooking and keeping the house. And you working long hours!"

"Father," she said with a sigh, "Aunt Hester works, too, running her shop. We share the house-keeping duties, which is only fair."

"I thought by this time you would have had your fill of that magazine and be ready to move back home, where you belong," he said with a scowl.

"That is not likely to happen. I love what I'm doing. It is absorbing work and exciting."

She had to somewhat force enthusiasm into her voice, but despite her present malaise, she still loved working on the *Book*, and she was sure that her moodiness would soon pass and she would be her old self again.

She had thought that she might relax, regain some of her old high spirits, with her family; but she had not been home three days before she knew this was not going to happen. Everything appeared dull and gray in comparison to her life in Philadelphia, and she soon realized that she had changed drastically in the few months she had been there. However, she had promised to spend a week at home, and she knew that her parents would be sorely hurt if she did not stay out the time.

On the day after Christmas, Henry Benedict invited James Worthington and his family for dinner. Worthington was her father's closest friend and associate at the bank. He was as stodgy as bankers are supposed to be, and his wife, a plump, friendly woman, had only one interest in life—her son, William Worthington, who was attending Harvard and was home for the holidays.

Willie Worthington was a good-looking young man, a year older than Jemina, good-natured and with a certain stiff charm. He was one of the boys her father had marched through the Benedict parlor for Jemina's inspection.

After the usual heavy Boston dinner, Willie asked Jemina if she would like to take a walk. Glad of an excuse to escape the stultifying atmosphere of the house, Jemina agreed readily, feeling amused as she noticed the smug glances exchanged by both sets of parents.

It was frigid outside. It had snowed heavily on Christmas Day, and snow lay like a thick blanket of white on the ground; but the night was clear, with little wind, and stars glittered coldly in the dark sky.

Jemina stopped on the walk in front of the house. The clear, cold air seemed to energize her, and she felt her spirits lift. "Willie, let's go sledding!" she said, her breath puffing like smoke in the icy air.

He gave her a startled look, then slowly began to grin. "All right." Then he paused, frowning. "But we don't have a sled."

"There's one in the carriage house out back, a sled I used when I was a girl."

At his nod she led him around to the back of the house, being very quiet. She had the feeling that her father wouldn't approve of such frivolity. They found the sled buried under a pile of debris in one corner of the carriage house. It was covered with dust and cobwebs, but it was still usable.

Pulling the sled behind them, they made their way down the hill to the common. Apparently, others had the same idea, for several young people were sledding on the snow. Jemina arranged herself in the sled, and Willie started to pull her across the snow, which was already packed hard. Laughing like children, they went back and forth across the common.

After a bit she insisted that it was her turn to pull the sled. Willie looked dubious. "It's a heavy pull, Jemina."

"Nonsense," she said. "I'm strong for a woman, Willie. You'll see."

By now the sled runners were sufficiently iced, and the snow had hardened enough so that she could pull him easily once she got the sled underway. It was great sport; and for the first time in weeks Jemina laughed joyously, forgetting her problems and enjoying the moment.

When they finally left the common and started back, their faces were pink and stinging from the cold.

"That was fun, wasn't it?" Willie said, a note of surprise in his voice.

"It was marvelous fun, Willie." She laughed, throwing her head back.

Willie changed the sled pull from his right to his left hand and groped for her hand. Jemina went tense, started to pull away, then relaxed.

As they came in sight of the Benedict house, Willie slowed his step. "They're probably all wondering where we've been for so long. Perhaps we shouldn't tell them we have been sledding."

She laughed again. "I won't, if you won't."

"Jemina..." He stopped, turning toward her, her hand still in his grasp. "You're going back to Philadelphia to work on your magazine?"

"Of course."

"During the spring recess..." He drew a deep breath, his hand tightening on hers. "Philadelphia is not all that far. If I came over for a few days, could I see you?"

Involuntarily, she withdrew her hand from his grasp. "Ah, Willie, that is sweet of you. But no, don't do that. I'm..." She took a deep breath. "I'm involved with someone in Philadelphia. You're a nice man, Willie, and I'm flattered that you would want to go to so much trouble, but it would be to no purpose."

The expression of disappointment upon his face caused her to turn away.

ONCE BACK IN PHILADELPHIA and at work, Jemina found her enthusiasm again flagging. She believed that she was performing her work well enough, but apparently that was not so.

She turned in her last article about the important women who had figured in Philadelphia history and two days later was called into Sarah's office. It was now well into February and Jemina had caught a cold; so not only was she low in spirit, but she was physically miserable.

Sarah leaned back in her chair, tapping her fingers gently on the desk top, and studied Jemina closely.

Finally, she said, "You do not look too well, my dear."

"I have a severe cold," Jemina said, and sneezed violently.

"I'm sorry to hear that. Perhaps you had better go home and get into bed after we're through here. Get under thick covers and perspire." Sarah smiled faintly. "I know that ladies aren't supposed to perspire, but I have found that to be the best remedy for your condition. But first we must discuss this...."

Sarah tapped her fingers again, and for the first time Jemina noticed that a manuscript was on the desk. With a feeling of dismay she recognized it as hers.

"I do apologize for bringing this up when you aren't feeling well, my dear," Sarah continued, "but it must be done." Again she tapped her fingers. "This latest piece of yours will not do."

"What is wrong with it, Sarah? I researched this woman's life thoroughly." Jemina had worked hard on the article; since Owen's departure she no longer had access to his books, and she had had to scour the libraries and even private book collections for the material she needed.

"Oh, the facts are all there, but the piece is merely a recital of cold, hard facts. Although I always wish the pieces of this nature to be factual, we are not publishing history in the *Lady's Book*." Sarah leaned across her desk. "In your Blackwell article, Elizabeth came alive. And in the pieces on the farm women, you caught the very essence of them. In my many years as an editor, I have recognized that some authors can write well about living people but somehow fail when it comes to figures of history, people long dead. I would think this the case with you, had it not been for the first piece in this series, the one on Betsy Ross. She came alive, right off the pages. You managed to convince me that, contrary to some rumors, she really *did* make the first American flag.

"But this, Jemina..." Sarah picked up the manuscript pages and waved them at her. "I must say that I am disappointed in you. I realize that I set high standards, but I expect nothing but the best from my people."

Jemina wondered if she was going to be discharged, and the possibility bothered her, but on the surface only; deep down she wasn't sure that she really cared.

She was aroused from her bleak thoughts by Sarah's voice. "Often, in instances such as this, Jemina, I would assign the article to another author. But since I do have faith in you, would you like to try again?"

She was holding the manuscript pages out, and Jemina leaned across the desk to take them. "I will try, Sarah," she said in a dull voice. "I'm sorry, I just haven't been myself of late." She gestured helplessly.

"That, my dear, is quite obvious," Sarah said in a dry voice.

Jemina got to her feet and went out. As she opened the door, she discovered Warren Barricone with his fist raised to knock.

"Why, hello, Jemina," he said with a startled look.

"Hello, Warren," she said, and passed by him.

Still looking after Jemina, Warren slowly closed the door and took the seat Jemina had vacated. "I wanted to talk to you about the plate illustrating a story, Sarah, but..." With a frown he looked at the closed door. "I've noticed that Jemina isn't herself of late, since sometime before Christmas."

Sarah leaned back. "Yes, it dates back to around the time Etta Logan hanged herself."

"Was Jemina involved in that?"

"In a way. At least, she concerned herself with the affair, and the woman's tragic death depressed her. But I do believe there is more to it than that. I think Jemina became romantically involved with Owen Thursday...."

"That scoundrel!" Warren sat forward, his fists knotted. "If he has hurt her . . . !"

"Warren, I am surprised at you," Sarah said in amusement. "What would you do, challenge him to a duel? You're hardly the sort of person for that. Besides, it's a little late. Owen is in the goldfields in California. He left back in December, and Jemina's malaise dates from that time."

"But doesn't she know what he is?"

"Exactly what *is* he, Warren? He is everything that would appeal to a young woman like Jemina. I warned her about him, but I suppose I never expected her to take much heed. Besides, I really don't know what occurred, and it is none of my affair. Nor yours, Warren. Except that I despair to see the child like this."

"It is affecting her work, I gather?"

Sarah simply nodded.

Warren pondered for a moment, then looked up with a beginning smile. "I have a suggestion, Sarah. You may think it drastic, but a change of scenery often works wonders. . . ."

SHORTLY BEFORE time to go home that afternoon, Jemina received word that Sarah wanted to see her. Jemina had not gone home as Sarah had suggested but had been struggling to rewrite that offending article, without a great deal of success. Thinking the piece was what Sarah wanted to discuss, Jemina was in a rebellious mood as she trudged down the hall. How could the editor expect her to have finished redoing the article so soon? By the time she reached Sarah's office she was boiling.

Once inside, she burst out, "Sarah, I have hardly started to rewrite yet! How can you possibly expect me to be finished this soon?"

Sarah stared at her in astonishment. "My dear child, of course I do not expect that. I wanted to talk to you about something else entirely. Now, sit down and listen."

Deflated, Jemina sat down.

Sarah folded her hands on her desk. "As you know, we usually send two or three people to Paris every spring, for a preview of the new fashions."

Jemina stared at her, her heart beginning to beat wildly.

"This year we have decided to send you, Jemina. I have just discussed it with Mr. Godey, and he has agreed."

Paris? Jemina was both thrilled and frightened. She, who had never been out of the country, going to Paris on assignment?

She said hesitatingly, "But I know nothing of fashion, Sarah."

"That might be all to the good, a fresh viewpoint. You knew nothing about farming, yet you wrote some fine pieces. But there is more." Sarah paused for a moment, gathering her thoughts and gazing into the wide eyes of the young woman across from her. Should she tell Jemina that the suggestion came from Warren Barricone? For a moment a doubt nudged her mind. Did Warren have some ulterior motive in mind? Then she dismissed the thought out of hand; Warren Barricone was one of the most moral, upright men she had ever known.

"You will be going over early, if that's agreeable to you," she went on. "Warren will not be going until late March so he can arrive in time for the spring fashion shows. But I would like you to go fairly soon. I have in mind a series of articles from you, Jemina. Impressions of Paris and its people. We occasionally publish pieces of such nature. 'Impressions of Rome' was a recent piece, even 'An Impression of Russia.'

"And I would wish you to also do a series of pieces about women important in the history of France, something in the nature of the recent ones about Philadelphia women. Before you leave, we will structure a formal agenda." She was beaming now. "How does that strike you?"

Jemina was breathless. "I don't know what to think, Sarah. It is a marvelous opportunity, and I had hoped someday to be sent to Paris, but this is so unexpected."

"I fully realize that, but if you are to go, time is of the essence. We have plans to make, an agenda to outline, your passage to book." She paused, studying Jemina keenly. "One thing gives me some trepidation. You are young, not accustomed to travel. A woman of your years and inexperience alone in a foreign city..."

It was not a challenge, but Jemina took it as such. In that moment all her reservations were swept away. She sat up, eyes flashing. "I am now twenty-three years old and fully capable of fending for myself!"

"Are you indeed?" Sarah said, a smile curving her lips. "Well, perhaps you are. We shall see. I take it, then, that this meets with your full approval?"

"Oh, yes!" Jemina cried. Then a sudden thought sobered her. "But what about this last article I am working on?"

"Perhaps you will find time to finish it before you leave. If not, there is not that much urgency. You can finish it when you return." Sarah smiled. "Perhaps by then you will be in a better mood to work on it."

Jemina stared intently at the editor. "Sarah...are you doing this just for me? I mean, after the way I have been acting of late..."

"That may have something to do with it, yes." Sarah felt obscurely embarrassed and glanced away for a moment. Then she looked again at Jemina and said sternly, "But, do not mistake me, my dear. If I did not believe you could handle this assignment, I would not send you. But I also firmly believe that a change of environment will do you a world of good."

Jemina had to wonder how much Sarah knew or suspected about her affair with Owen. Certainly Sarah was not stupid; she had to have made the connection between Owen's departure and Jemina's despondency. Yet, if she knew about the affair, wouldn't she be censorious? Jemina well knew the older woman's deep religious convictions and her strong feelings about morality.

Getting to her feet, she said, "Whatever your reason, Sarah, I want you to know how grateful I am for this opportunity. I promise that you will never regret it."

"I'm sure that I shan't, Jemina," Sarah said warmly.

Back at her desk, Jemina picked up the manuscript that Sarah had turned back and quickly read through it again. Now she seemed to have a new insight into it, and she quickly grasped what Sarah had been getting at. The piece was dull, little more than a compilation of dry statistics.

Although it was past time to go home, she began to work on it, her brain swarming with fresh ideas. Even her cold symptoms had receded. After a bit she stopped writing, holding her pen poised. Slowly, she began to smile. She had been humming to herself!

NEW YORK TEEMED, reared and clattered. The pace of life in Philadelphia, in Jemina's opinion, was much more sedate. The only other time she had been in New York City was when she had been on her way to Geneva to interview Elizabeth Blackwell, and that had been only long enough to change trains.

Sarah had allowed her to leave ten days before her ship was to sail for France, so she would have some time to spend with her parents in Boston. But Jemina found that four days was all she could bear at home.

Her parents had been horrified that she was going off to France by herself.

"It is bad enough that you're going to Paris at all, such a sinful city," her father had roared. "But to go off alone, a girl of your years. I will not permit it, Jemina!"

Jemina had had to laugh. "Father, you should realize by now that you cannot forbid me anything. I am my own woman now. For heaven's sake, I have recently celebrated my twenty-third birthday!"

Undeterred, he had thundered, "And that is another thing! Twenty-three and not yet married. You are long past the age when you should be wed. You are an old maid, Jemina. Men will begin to think that something is wrong with you, unwed at your age!"

The thought of Owen had crossed her mind and caused her temper to rise. "I shall marry in my own good time, and nothing you can say will rush me into it.''

Two days later, she had left Beacon Hill and traveled to New York, although there was almost a week left before her ship sailed for France.

Now, as she walked the streets of New York, Jemina was glad that she had this extra time in the city. New York pulsed with vitality and movement. Horse cars, carriages, hackneys and pedestrians thronged the streets. Within the space of a dozen blocks she heard as many languages spoken. Her brain teemed with ideas for articles, and she had to laugh at herself—perhaps she should remain here instead of going to Paris. Of course, all she knew of Paris was what she had read, but she doubted that any city could be as exciting as this one.

She walked the busy streets until she was exhausted before going back to her hotel for a good night's sleep.

Every day she walked through the city, each day finding something new to marvel at, from the fine clothing shops on Fifth Avenue to the depths of the Bowery.

On her next-to-the-last day, she found herself on the Lower East Side of Manhattan Island. It was a while before she realized that she was in the heart of the garment district. The pace here was frenzied, but the traffic was mostly foot traffic. It took her a few minutes to figure out why the pace was so hurried; and then, as she saw figures bent under heavy loads of garments, she realized that the garment industry was preparing for the change of seasons—spring fashions would soon be in all the shops.

As she looked more closely at the figures loaded down with piles of clothing on their backs, Jemina was appalled. Most of the carriers were little more than children, not only boys but girls, as well. They were so heavily laden she did not understand how they could endure their burdens. Their faces were dulled with weariness and apathy, and the muscles of their arms and legs strained under the piles of fabric across their heads and shoulders. She noticed that they walked as if permanently bowlegged, with their feet wide apart and wobbling. In spite of the chill March wind coming off the East River, their thin faces were pallid and sweating. They all looked badly undernourished; many staggered under the heavy loads, as if they might collapse at any moment.

Jemina was so moved by pity that she felt tears sting her eyes, and she hastened onward, her head down. She turned a corner and looked up to see that she was on Hester Street. She started walking along the street, hurrying faster to get out of the neighborhood. Halfway down the block, something caught her eye.

She stopped short, staring intently to her left. Short steps led down to a narrow door, and over the door was a sign: L. Gilroy, Fine Cloaks.

Could it be the same man who had tried to molest her that day in Philadelphia? Gilroy certainly was not a common name. . . .

Suddenly, the narrow door opened wide, filled with two struggling figures. Without thinking, Jemina moved closer to the head of the steps. In the dimness she could make out a man and a woman. The woman was struggling wildly, held firmly in the man's grip.

Jemina heard her say in a sobbing voice, ''Please, sir! Do not do this! I sorely need the work. I have two young ones to support.''

"You should have thought of that before," the man said roughly. "I have no place for laggards in my shop. Now take your leave, woman—you are finished here!"

The man's face turned up, and Jemina shrank back. It *was* the same man. He didn't appear to recognize her, and at that moment he gave the woman a hard shove. She clutched at his arm and in so doing tore the sleeve of his shirt. He muttered a curse and shoved the woman again, knocking her back against the steps. He stood watching as the woman began to crawl up the steps on her hands and knees.

As the woman reached the street level, Jemina instinctively leaned down to give her a hand up. Putting a supporting arm around her, she said soothingly, "Come along with me, my dear," and led her up the street.

ANGER STILL RIDING him hard, Lester Gilroy stood glaring up as the well-dressed woman helped his recent employee out of his sight. He wondered briefly who the other woman was. Probably some swell down here trying to help out what she thought of as the downtrodden. People like that seemed to be too stupid to realize that many women and children would go begging in the streets but for his largess in giving them gainful employment.

He glanced down at his torn sleeve. Damn the infernal woman, anyway! She had managed to ruin a perfectly good shirt.

In an angry gesture he seized the sleeve and tore it all the way up to the shoulder, exposing the tattoo of a ship on his upper arm. He tensed his biceps, and the ship rolled across a tattooed sea.

Chapter Fourteen

COMING INTO THE OFFICE at her usual early hour, Sarah Hale found a letter from Jemina awaiting her.

"Dear Sarah: I shall be embarking for France early in the morning, but I wanted to get this into the post to you before I left.

"You once told me that I was never to start on a project without first discussing it with you. Of course, what I have in mind cannot be done until I return from Paris, yet I would like you to consider it in my absence.

"I had some time here before leaving, so I set out to explore the city of New York. I found it to be a fascinating city, but I discovered that it has its dark, depressing side. I also discovered a rank injustice that cries out to be rectified!

"While walking through the East Side one afternoon, I found myself in the garment-manufacturing district. Sarah, the things that take place there are unbelievable! Mere children, both boys and girls, some ten or less in years, labor in the streets carrying bundles of clothing so heavy they can scarcely walk!

"Even more cruel, they are employed in the factories, under abysmal conditions, and are forced to work up to fourteen hours a day. The places they work in are little better than pestholes, with dim light and poor ventilation. And for this the children are paid only a few pennies a day. The women are fortunate to earn a dollar a day.

"No, I did not learn these bitter facts by going into the garment factories myself but received my information from a reliable source.

"I am sure that you recall a reprehensible man by the name of Lester Gilroy, who came to Philadelphia with the purpose of starting one of his garment factories but was discouraged when the *Ledger* published a piece about his evil practices. Well, during a walk along Hester Street, I came across his name on a building! As I stood there, struck dumb by the coincidence, he came to the door and threw a woman out into the street.

"I acquainted myself with the poor woman and took her along to my hotel for a decent meal. Marigold Tyler; what a lovely name for someone who must endure such a miserable existence! Marigold has two small children, and she is their only means of support. Her husband deserted her, and the only skill she has is in the use of needle and thread. She got a job with Lester Gilroy, sewing buttons on the women's cloaks he manufactures.

"You may find this hard to believe, Sarah; I know I most certainly did. She worked fourteen, sometimes sixteen hours a day, and for wages of less than a dollar a day! She told me that the material for a cloak, plus the labor cost, is less than a dollar per garment, and it is then sold to the retail shops for three dollars and often more. This means that Mr. Gilroy reaps a two-hundred-percent profit on every garment he produces and yet pays his workers starvation wages! This is a crime not only against women but against all humanity, since he also employs children, both girls and boys.

"Marigold told me that Mr. Gilroy discharged her because she fell asleep at the worktable. She had worked sixteen hours the day before and then had been forced to sit up all night tending her youngest child, who had become violently ill with a stomach ailment. The dastardly Gilroy would not heed her pleas and discharged her.

"I wept when I heard her sorrowful tale. There was little that I could do for the poor creature beyond buying her a decent meal and giving her what few dollars I could spare.

"Sarah, this evil should be exposed to the light of day! What better forum for exposing these nefarious practices than *Godey's Lady's Book*? For Marigold told me that Lester Gilroy is only one of a large number of garment manufacturers who exploit women and children for their own ungodly profit.

"I realize that I cannot write anything about them until I have thoroughly researched the garment industry, but I wanted to write my thoughts to you, so that you may ponder the subject during my absence. I would like to take on this assignment immediately upon my return to America.

"On a more personal note, I am eagerly looking forward to my sojourn in Paris. I fully realize that recently I have allowed my personal problems to affect my work. I have high hopes that I am well past that now and will endeavor to write some exciting pieces while in Paris. Affectionately yrs., Jemina."

Sarah leaned back, letting the letter fall to the desk. She had not failed to take note of the fact that Jemina had carefully avoided mentioning Owen's name when referring to the piece he had penned about Lester Gilroy.

She sighed, rubbing her eyes. Was I ever that young, she thought, filled with such crusading zeal? Yes, she had to admit that she had once possessed the same zeal and still did to some extent; but she had learned to temper it. The world was full of compromises, and that was a lesson that Jemina had to learn. Sarah could only hope that Jemina would not be hurt too badly in the process.

As she pondered the letter, a knock sounded on her door. At her invitation, Warren Barricone came in.

"Ah, Warren. What can I do for you?"

"These fashion plates for the May issue are ready. I thought you might like to have a look at them."

He gave her the plates and sat down as Sarah studied them one by one. Finally, she glanced up with a pleased nod. "They're fine, Warren. The best I've seen in some time. Hopefully, you'll come back from Paris with ideas for even better ones. And speaking of Paris . . . I received this from Jemina in this morning's post."

She held up Jemina's letter, and Warren reached out for it. As he began to read, he started to smile, and then he laughed aloud as he finished it. "She is a firebrand, isn't she?"

"Too much so for her own good, I'm afraid. We could never publish this sort of thing in the *Lady's Book*."

He nodded soberly. "Yes, I realize that."

"Not that I don't admire her spunk and crusading zeal. And heaven knows, she's right. Something should be done to unveil the practices of these scoundrels to the public eye. I had some experience with their work when I was still in Boston. I don't know if you've heard the expression 'slop shops'?''

"I don't believe I have, Sarah."

"Well, I was instrumental in organizing the Seaman's Aid Society. Seamen have a hard life and are a poor lot. They are away at sea for months at a time, and while they are gone, their wives and families suffer, for a seaman's wages are very low and their families must struggle to keep alive.

"And then there are the times when he does *not* come home at all. A ship sinks or runs aground, and dozens of families are left fatherless.''

Sarah shook her head. "Yes, it was the widows and orphans that touched me the most. Some of the women had come from affluent homes and had known a better life, and then one day they are left alone and virtually penniless.

"But to get back to the point of my story. Most seamen and their families were forced to buy their clothing from the 'slop shops' at outrageous prices, and they were usually poorly made. 'Slop shops' was a term coined for the stores selling these shoddy goods.

"I soon realized that the women needed employment, not charity. This was back in the last decade, and a woman's lot was even more severe than it is today. There were then only three ways for a decent woman to support herself and her children. Domestic service, washing and needlework. So we supplied the women with instructions in sewing and other forms of needlework, and we opened a well-supplied clothing store, catering to the seamen. Within two years we were receiving upward of five thousand a year for garments sold, mostly to the seamen, of course.

"We paid the women we employed a living wage, a just wage, and this immediately aroused the ire of the slop-shop owners, who paid their seamstresses only enough to keep them in grinding poverty."

Sarah smiled grimly. "I did not let their opposition deter me but continued to do whatever I could. So, you see, I know whereof Jemina speaks, and while it is true that I used the *Ladies' Magazine* as a forum for organizing the Seaman's Aid Society, I did *not* use it to do battle with the slop-shop operators.

"Can you imagine Louis's reaction should I propose such a project? His heart would probably stop beating."

"Well, Jemina should be in Paris soon. Perhaps she will be so caught up in the life there, and the spring fashions showing, that she will forget all about this."

"I would pray that were so, but I have come to know Jemina too well to hope for that. She will return all prepared to charge ahead. Speaking of the fashion showings . . ." She studied Warren intently. "It will be time for you to depart for Paris before long. Are you sure you want to go this year, Warren? Is your wife well enough for you to leave? I can always send someone else."

"Oh, we have discussed the matter at length. Alice wants me to go. Strangely enough, she has been feeling better these past weeks. She perks up during the cooler months. Hot weather seems to affect her adversely. Mrs. Wright will stay with her during the day while I am gone, and I have arranged for another woman to spend the nights at our house, so Alice will not be alone at any time. In fact, they can tend to her needs better than I can."

Sarah nodded. "Well, as usual, we will reimburse you for the extra expense while you are away."

Despite his reassurances to Sarah, Warren was laden with guilt as he walked home from the horse-car that evening. The thing was, he wanted to get away from Alice; the time in Paris would be a welcome reprieve from the sickroom atmosphere that so depressed him at home. And of course, Jemina would be there....

The thought of Jemina was what made him feel so guilty—the thought of being in Paris with her, in effect being alone with her, in the City of Light, the city of lovers! Normal marital relations between Warren and his wife had ceased to exist after Alice took ill; it was not Alice's idea, but the doctors had advised that it would be bad for her already frail health. And if she were to become pregnant, it would be fatal. Not once had Warren seriously considered being unfaithful to his wife—until he had met Jemina. Now he found carnal thoughts of Jemina intruding into his mind increasingly often, no matter how hard he fought against them.

He sighed as he opened the door. Mrs. Wright greeted him in her usual brusque manner and was out the front door two minutes after his arrival.

Warren made his way down the hall, calling out, "I'm home, darling!"

Alice was sitting propped up in bed, her black hair combed and brushed. She was very thin, almost ethereal looking, except for the unnatural brightness of her grey eyes and the fever spots, like hothouse roses, blooming on her cheeks.

He stooped to kiss her lightly, and her arms went around him, clutching him desperately to her for a moment.

After a moment she loosened her hold, and he pulled up a chair beside the bed. "How was your day, sweetheart?"

"Fine," she said brightly. "I even felt good enough to get up and sit in the parlor with my needlework for a time, and I hardly coughed all day."

"That *is* good. First thing you know, you'll be wanting me to take you out to supper."

"Any day now." She looked at him intently, and Warren was made uneasy. Alice had an uncanny knack for reading his feelings and thoughts. "How was your day, dear?"

"Oh . . . about as usual." He glanced away, then blurted, "Sarah talked to me today about going to Paris next month. She wanted to know if you were up to my being away for such an extended period."

"Warren . . ." Alice moved up higher against the headboard. "We have discussed this before. I would feel terrible if you allowed my condition to interfere with your work."

"Sarah would understand. In fact, she stated that it wasn't all that necessary for me to go to Paris. She could send someone else."

Alice was shaking her head from side to side. "No, I won't hear of it. I am no worse than I have been for years. I couldn't bear it if I thought I was in any way responsible for keeping you away from the work you love. After all, you have nothing else, no children, no wife. . . ." Tears came to her eyes, and she said in a choked voice, "I am not even half a woman, Warren. You deserve more out of life."

"Now don't talk like that!" he said severely. "We agreed that we would never have that sort of talk between us. After all, I married you for..." He had started to say "for better or for worse," but fortunately he had caught himself in time. He reached over with his forefinger to rub the tears from her eyes. "I married you because I love you, and nothing has changed that."

"I don't know how you can love me the way I am now," she said disconsolately.

"Well, I do. You are my life, Alice. Now," he said firmly, getting to his feet, "Mrs. Wright left a nice roast in the oven. I will prepare the trays, with a bottle of good wine, and we'll have our supper in here."

He walked jauntily from the bedroom, but as he moved out of her sight, his footsteps dragged. He had loved Alice, and he still loved her, yet it was not the same. He could not deny that to himself, and he was certain that Alice fully realized that fact.

As he prepared their trays, his thoughts once again jumped to Jemina. In the fullness of her youth and health, she was undoubtedly enjoying herself in Paris. On Warren's own first trip to Paris, Alice had still been well enough to accompany him; and they had had a marvelous time, a memory to cherish forever.

FOR THE FIRST TWO DAYS in Paris, Jemina did not enjoy herself in the least. The Atlantic crossing had been rough; they had run into foul weather about halfway across, and she had been seasick, so ill and miserable that she would have welcomed death.

In fact, she had still felt so unwell during the carriage ride into Paris that the things she had read about so often—the Cathedral of Notre Dame, the Seine, the splendid boulevards of the city and the magnificent shops—hardly received her notice.

Sarah had given her instructions and a letter of introduction to a Madame Blanc, who operated a small pension on the Right Bank; a room awaited her there.

"It is where our people usually stay during their time in Paris," Sarah had explained, "and Madame speaks excellent English. I have already written her to expect you."

Jemina saw Madame Blanc, a bustling, bright-eyed little woman, through a blur. When Jemina explained that she was still ill from the voyage, the woman became instantly solicitous.

She bobbed her small head, her brown eyes concerned. "*Oui*, Mademoiselle Benedict. The *mal de mer*, I know. So many suffer from the sea voyage."

She hustled Jemina upstairs and down a short hallway to a suite of two rooms. "Remove your clothing and into bed," Madame Blanc said. "I shall be right back."

Jemina hastily disrobed and crawled into the bed without even thinking of washing. Shortly, Madame Blanc reappeared with a bowl of steaming turtle soup, a cup of hot tea and a washbasin.

As the odors of the soup reached her nostrils, Jemina turned her head away, her stomach roiling. "No food, please! I beg of you!"

"*Mon Dieu*, but you must, little one. But first, the tea."

She sat on the bed, raised Jemina's head slightly and held the cup to her lips. Jemina sipped and almost gagged. She spluttered, "What did you put in this? It tastes awful!"

"*Naturellement*, little one," Madame Blanc said with a sly smile. "It is my own remedy. All good cures taste awful. But drink," she urged.

With great difficulty, Jemina managed to get most of the bitter tea down, and Madame Blanc let her head back down. At that moment Jemina felt the bed move and opened her eyes to see an enormous gray tiger-striped cat gazing at her with expressive gray eyes. It was the largest cat Jemina had ever seen; but despite its muscular bulk, its soft white chin and long whiskers set off a face with a gentle and curious expression.

Madame Blanc, clucking, reached for the animal. "*Non, non*, Monsieur Avide, you must not bother our guest!"

The cat allowed himself to be placed on the floor, and Madame Blanc straightened the bedclothes. "I keep several cats. I hope you like animals. I try to keep them in my rooms, but cats are..." She shrugged expressively. "Well, you know how cats are!"

Jemina managed a wan smile. "Monsieur Avide? I'm not sure what that means."

Madame Blanc laughed. "Mr. Greedy! He eats and eats."

Jemina realized, with a feeling of relief, that the tea had settled her stomach.

"Now some soup," Madame Blanc said briskly.

After much effort, Jemina also managed about half of the small bowl of soup. Nodding, clucking to herself, Madame Blanc helped her wash and tucked her under the covers, and Jemina drifted off to sleep—the first decent sleep she had enjoyed in days.

She slept the rest of the afternoon, rousing only long enough for Madame Blanc to give her more bitter tea and soup at dinnertime, then fell into a deep slumber.

She awoke to a cock crowing shortly after dawn the next morning. She felt much better but was still weak. Then she remembered. Here she was in Paris, and she could recall little of what she had seen.

She got out of bed and crept to the window, the smooth, wooden floor cold against her bare feet. She pushed aside the curtains and looked out. People were just beginning to stir on the street below. She looked farther out, and there was the broad flow of the fabled Seine. A mist hung over the river; but even as she looked the mist turned pearly pink in color as the sun peaked over the spires and towers of the buildings to the east.

It was a lovely view, and Jemina drew in her breath sharply as she felt the first faint stir of excitement. She was in Paris, and it was a sight to stir the soul. She could hardly wait to venture out and explore.

She turned at a light knock on the door and said, "Do come in."

The door opened and Madame Blanc peeked around the edge, her gaze going to the bed. Her eyes widened when she discovered it empty.

"Here I am, Madame Blanc. Over by the window."

The woman came into the room and began fluttering her hands. "*Mon Dieu*, little one, you have on almost no clothes, and the room is chill." She clapped her hands. "Now back into the bed with you!"

Jemina obeyed, getting back into bed, pulling the covers up to her chin. Her feet, she realized, were like ice. It was all she could do to keep her teeth from chattering.

"And how do you feel?"

"I think I am better this morning, but I still feel weak."

"*Naturellement*, you have eaten no solid food. Do you have hunger this morning?"

Jemina realized that she was famished. She nodded quickly.

Madame Blanc beamed. "That is good! The food is already being prepared."

Jemina said tentatively, "Perhaps I should come down...."

"*Non*! Little one, you will stay in bed," the woman said emphatically.

"But I came here to work, not to stay in bed. I have already lost a full day."

"To work well, you must feel well." Madame Blanc wagged a finger. "You Americans! Run, run, all the time. You shall remain in bed today. Tomorrow, we shall see."

Jemina smiled in amusement as the little woman bustled out of the room. Much later, she would learn from Sarah that Madame Blanc always fussed over her charges, especially those from the *Lady's Book* who came to Paris once a year; Madame Blanc was convinced that whatever they eventually published in the *Book* was to the ultimate good not only of Paris but of all France.

Shortly, a maid came into the room with an omelet, a crusty roll and coffee with milk. Jemina ate with a good appetite. Despite her determination to be up and about, she found herself drifting off to sleep again. She awoke sometime later to find Monsieur

Avide curled up beside her. She tentatively stroked the cat and was rewarded by a contented purr.

Jemina napped off and on all day, but when she was awake she managed to get her unpacking done, all her things stored away, and found time to jot down a few impressions of Paris. These were necessarily few, since she doubted very much that her readers would be much interested in what Madame Blanc called her *mal de mer*.

The next morning she felt herself again, full of energy and eager to set out on an exploration of the streets of Paris.

When informed of her plans, Madame Blanc said, "Then you must dress correctly, little one." She smiled broadly. "We have a saying here in Paris. 'When going abroad in March or April, dress like an onion.' As the day warms, you may peel off outer garments. If the day turns chill again, you may replace as needed."

Soon after, Jemina ventured out into the streets, her little French phrase book clutched in her hand. Since learning of her trip to France, she had been studying the French language in every spare moment and could now converse in a rudimentary fashion; but fortunately she soon discovered that many of the shopkeepers spoke at least some English.

For much of the week she roamed Paris—the teeming, colorful streets; the shops; museums, especially the art museums including the Louvre; and the many cathedrals. She didn't even think about the articles she intended to write; she thought it behooved her to first absorb a certain amount of Paris herself.

Everywhere she saw artists at work, not only on the fabled Left Bank but in the rest of the city, as well.

She soon learned that the artists loved the streets and loved to paint Parisians at their daily chores. They seemed to have as avid an interest in the people and places of Paris as did she, a complete stranger to the city.

Another thing that intrigued her was her developing relationships with the shopkeepers along the street where she was staying—the owners of the small street cafés and other establishments she patronized. They soon grew familiar with her and became quite friendly and serious about her work; Madame Blanc had introduced her as a working journalist from America, not just another tourist. The shopkeepers treated her with a deference unlike the noisy greetings they gave their neighborhood customers or the familiar contempt they expressed toward the occasional prostitute who came into the shop.

Jemina was also struck by the reverence the typical shopkeeper displayed toward his work and toward others who were serious about their labors. From what she had read Jemina had received the impression that the people of Paris were frivolous, devoted more to the pursuit of pleasure than labor. This she soon found to be erroneous; the Parisians, at least the ones she met, took their jobs seriously; much more seriously, she decided, than did many of her fellow countrymen.

She took copious notes about the things she saw and the people she met, not knowing what portion of the material she would eventually use.

Finally, at the end of her first week in Paris, she decided that it was time she got down to work. In regard to this particular project, Sarah had offered no suggestions as to the subject of her pieces, leaving that decision up to Jemina. So Jemina decided to consult Madame Blanc.

Madame Blanc seldom ventured beyond the street where her pension was located. She had been born and raised on the street, and Jemina was astounded to learn that the woman had not been across the Seine since she was a young girl.

"Why should I go elsewhere?" Madame Blanc maintained. "I have everything I need here in my building. I have my cats, my lovely tenants and my books; and everything I require in the way of necessities I can purchase in the shops on my street. *Non*, I am quite content, little one."

She did indeed have her books. One whole room of her living quarters had been turned into a library, with so many books there was scarcely room enough for a chair and reading table.

"I am here to work," Jemina explained to her landlady. "And I have been here a whole week without doing anything of substance. I haven't even decided on the subjects for my pieces."

Madame Blanc nodded. "Yes, perhaps it is time now. What is this subject you speak of?"

"Mrs. Hale wishes me to write some articles about women who figured in the history of France, of Paris. Or perhaps some women who are important today."

"Today? *Mon Dieu*, little one, there are no important women in France today, in my opinion. Modern women have fallen into a low estate. But . . . !" Her eyes began to gleam, and she wagged a forefinger. "The history of France chronicles a number of women who were important. Jeanne d'Arc comes to mind." Madame Blanc's voice became reverent.

"The Maid of Orléans. A saint, little one, a true saint!"

"But so much has been written about Joan of Arc, I thought perhaps someone a little less known. At least in our country."

"Ah! Madame Roland!" Madame Blanc's eyes took on a zealot's fire. "And Marie Antoinette!"

"Madame Roland?" Jemina was puzzled. "Marie Antoinette I am familiar with, but I am afraid I have never heard of Madame Roland."

"Ah! She was the torch of the revolution! Jeanne Roland! The people rallied around Madame Roland and her husband, Jean Marie, and together they taught and lived the ideals and philosophy of the great Rousseau! Madame Roland should be of great interest to your countrymen, little one, since you also had your own American Revolution, throwing off the tyrant's yoke. Madame Roland gave her life for France, as did Jeanne d'Arc. On her way to the guillotine Madame Roland proclaimed, 'O Liberty, what crimes are committed in thy name!'"

Jemina nodded. "Yes, I remember reading those words somewhere. But something puzzles me, Madame Blanc.... Writing pieces about *both* of these women strikes me as a little . . . well, strange. If I understand correctly, they were on opposite sides. Madame Roland, as you say, was a revolutionary, while Marie Antoinette was royalty. In fact, to use another quote, one attributed to Marie Antoinette—'Let them eat cake'—many people believe that was the prime cause of the revolution, or at least that she was the focal point of the revolutionary ire."

Madame Blanc looked thoughtful, a finger at one corner of her mouth, her gaze directed at the ceiling.

Then she clapped her hands together excitedly. "But that would be the best way, do you not see? I am not an author, but I am a great reader. This way you could show both sides of our revolution, but the . . . how could one put it? The cause and the effect! If I had read only about Madame Roland, I would not know the other side. Would not your readers get what you call the broader picture?"

Jemina leaned forward. "Of course, you are right, Madame Blanc!" She smiled suddenly. "Perhaps you *could* make an author. The contrast between the two women would be made stronger if I write an article about each. It is a marvelous suggestion!"

Madame Blanc affected modesty. "Ah, little one, you give me too much credit. But perhaps I could be of some assistance, since I know both women well through my reading. I have a number of books about them, which you are free to use. And I can suggest other places for you to do your . . . research, is it? For instance, you must visit our Louvre. There you will find illustrations by Chardin of Madame Roland in her youth. There is much material on her in our National Library. I could guide you through the quarter where Madame Roland's father plied his trade as a goldsmith. There you will find the house where she was born, the church where she received her first communion, the prison where she spent her last days before she went to the guillotine. And of course you must journey to Le Clos."

"Le Clos? What is that?"

"Le Clos was the country estate of the Roland family. It had been in the Roland family for a hundred years before the revolution. It is thirty miles north of the city of Lyons, near a hamlet called

Theizé. Madame Roland spent four years there when her husband served as an inspector of manufacture at Lyons. There you may see the magnificent Swiss Alps, and you may, on clear days, see the crown of Mount Blanc against the skyline.''

''Mount Blanc? But that is your name!''

Madame Blanc threw back her head and laughed in delight. ''As much as I should like to claim a connection, there is none that I am aware of.''

Jemina began her project with enthusiasm. She was both amused and pleased when Madame Blanc threw herself into the project with an enthusiasm to equal her own. The woman, Jemina soon found, was an immense help. She accompanied Jemina on trips to the Louvre, to the National Library and to other places that contained valuable information on both Madame Roland and Marie Antoinette. Since Jemina did not read French, Madame Blanc acted as an interpreter, which naturally made things much less difficult.

One evening, as they walked through the quarter where Madame Roland had once lived, Jemina said, ''I can't express how grateful I am for your help. I could not have accomplished nearly so much without you. But I do feel that I am taking advantage of your good nature. When I first came, you told me that you seldom ventured out anymore. Now you're out almost every day!''

''I do believe it is good for me, little one. I was growing stuffy and dull. Now I feel like I have opened windows on a closed room. It is exhilarating! I am alive again!''

But Madame Blanc balked at accompanying Jemina to Le Clos. ''It is too far to travel,'' she said, ''and

I have my guests to oversee. *Mon Dieu*, if my guests knew I was to be away for a few days, they might destroy the place. I choose them carefully, yet I have discovered that people are much like cats. Leave them alone, unsupervised, and destruction follows. And there are my precious cats. How could I leave them in the care of another? *Non*, little one, to Le Clos you must go alone.''

The trip to Le Clos was a long, tiresome one, made by coach to Villefranche, and then another hour by horse cart to the estate. Jemina observed the countryside with great interest as the cart traveled up and down hills and across valleys. The land had many small farms, devoted in the main to orchards and vineyards, with splendid trees lining the narrow road. Spring growth was just beginning, with new leaves and some blossoms showing. All the farmhouses were constructed of yellow stone, which she learned was the stone of the country.

The hamlet, Theizé, was on high ground. The horse cart drove between the high walls of the village and stopped at the end of the lane before a large gate set in a yellow wall.

The cart driver turned his broad peasant face to her and spoke in atrocious English, ''Is Le Clos, *mademoiselle*.''

Beyond the gate was the white château of Le Clos, with a court to one side, a garden on the other. Beyond, to the east, lay the panorama that Madame Blanc had mentioned—a breathtaking vista of hills and valleys and vineyards. In the far distance, the Swiss Alps towered against the sky.

Jemina was admitted by a caretaker, who told her that the present owners were away. Jemina showed him the letter that Madame Blanc had written for her, explaining who she was and asking permission to explore the château. The caretaker was hesitant, but eventually he let her enter, after she had promised, in her few words of halting French, that she would harm nothing.

Jemina soon realized that the château had changed little from Madame Roland's time. She viewed the same great, dark kitchen, with the original stone floor; the kitchen had a huge fireplace, and the walls were hung with shining copper cooking vessels, which the caretaker told her went back a hundred years or more.

The billiard room held an ancient table, and the floor was made of aged brick. The walls were decorated with the guns and uniforms of successive generations of Rolands, denoting their periods of military service, some dating back long before the French Revolution.

The only room in the château that was very bright was the salon, done in yellow plush; the room had Roland family portraits on the walls, with a piano and many books.

It had been Jemina's intention to find a room in the village for her brief stay; but the caretaker, who had trailed her from room to room, seemed to trust her now; and he allowed her to take up quarters in the château—a room as bare and severe as a nun's cell, yet it filled Jemina's needs well enough.

She spent three days at the château. There were a great many books, including a full set of Voltaire's revolutionary writings. Since the books were all in French, she gleaned very little from them; but to her great delight she found notes and letters written by

Madame Roland hidden between the pages of the many books. She copied these down for Madame Blanc's interpretation when she returned to Paris.

The rest of the time she devoted to talking to the people who lived in the village and on the neighboring farms. To her astonishment she learned that the villagers and farmers had never been ardent revolutionaries; "La Marseillaise," the theme song of the revolution, was never played in Theizé; and the fourteenth of July, a date comparable to America's own Fourth of July, was never celebrated in the area.

Jemina also learned that Madame Roland, during the years she spent at Le Clos, had devoted her time to good works, much as any woman would. She had filled her days with the affairs of the estate, ministering to the ill, tending to the problems of the peasants, in general discharging the responsibilities of the family and the estate. Certainly, Jemina could find no evidence that she had in any way attempted to convert anyone to her revolutionary ideas.

It struck Jemina that Madame Roland had been, to a certain extent, a member of royalty herself, if without title.

JEMINA FOUND that in her absence spring had arrived in Paris. Trees were almost in full leaf; flowers were blooming everywhere she looked. The air was warm and perfumed, and the people on the streets appeared gay, as though happy to put winter behind them.

She took her paper and pencil down to a sidewalk café not far from the pension. She breakfasted on bread, jam and chocolate. Then, with a cup of chocolate at hand, she gazed down at the paper before her.

She had yet to arrange her notes in proper order for the articles, yet she had formed a few thoughts and impressions that she wanted to put to paper before they escaped her mind.

Humming contentedly, she wrote: "All of us are far more complex than we appear on the surface, particularly women.

"In your correspondent's opinion, dear reader, Madame Jeanne Roland was more complex than most. She was a devoted housewife; she was fully capable of doing the things required of her in running a large estate; yet at the same time, she was a fiery revolutionary, always able to instill her zeal and fervor in others.

"However, there is a paradox involved in Madame Roland's role in the French Revolution. She thirsted to bring down the king and queen, to eliminate all those of royal blood. She wanted France to become a republic, the first country to have a constitution through a revolution; yet she lost her head to her own followers, to those who were not content with eliminating the king and queen. As soon as Madame Roland and her admirers began to trumpet for order out of the chaos left by the revolution, she was marched to the guillotine for her efforts...."

A shadow fell across the page, and a voice said, "Madame Blanc said that I might find you here."

Jemina glanced up, blinking against the strong sunlight. Then she let out a glad cry. "Warren! I wasn't expecting you just yet."

Warren Barricone's smile was uncertain. "I thought I would surprise you, Jemina."

Chapter Fifteen

"THE CONFUSION in the goldfield is compounded by colorful and unusual place names," Owen wrote. "There are four towns named for the biblical city of Ophir. There are four gold camps named Poverty Bar, four called Missouri Bar and three named Long Bar. To list but a few of the others: Angel's Camp; Cuteye Foster's; Coyote Diggings and Old Dry Diggings; Drunkard's Bar; Dead Man's Bar; Gouge Eye; Slumgullion Gulch; Murderer's Bar; Rattlesnake Bar; Whiskytown.

"The list is diverting and endless and often misleading. Yankee Jim's, for instance, is named for an Australian gold seeker. There are no volcanoes in Volcano, and Dry Bar has, at last count, twenty saloons. . . ."

At the sound of angry voices, Owen glanced up from where he sat at a rickety table with pencil and paper. He was in one of the many tent saloons in Coloma, a glass of whiskey, untouched, by his elbow. It was a warm early-April afternoon, and the tent sidewalls were propped up to admit a hoped-for breeze. Unfortunately, what air did come in stank of offal, both human and animal. The sanitary conditions at the gold camps were not the best, resulting in much sickness.

The contents of the saloon consisted of a few jerry-built tables and chairs and a bar that was nothing more than a long plank laid across empty beer kegs. The whiskey served was vile stuff, made, Owen was sure, by the fat, sweating bartender.

Since it was some time before the evening rush, the tent held only a half-dozen men, all in various stages of drunkenness. One of the drunken men, unfortunately, was John Riley, and his was one of the voices raised in contention.

Riley's remark, the day they met, that he liked to take a drink now and then had proved to be quite an understatement. He drank whenever he had the opportunity and the money to pay for his liquor. Not only did he get drunk readily and often, but he became argumentative when in his cups, and the size and strength of his opponent mattered not a whit. Owen had commented once, "Riley, enough liquor in you and you'd take on a grizzly."

"Probably whup him, too," the Southerner had said cheerfully.

Owen had yet to see him win a fight; in fact, he had been forced, reluctantly, to come to Riley's rescue any number of times.

Riley's one saving grace was that he was a very talented artist and a great caricaturist. Owen had sent three dispatches back to the *Ledger* during his four-month sojourn in California and had included a number of Riley's sketches. Since mail was so infernally slow, he had yet to receive a response from Carruthers; but he was certain that the editor would use the sketches.

Owen hoped that he would receive mail from the East soon; his funds were dangerously low, since he now had to support both Riley and himself. Also, he was hoping for a letter from Jemina. He had written her twice, including nothing of a personal nature, just general comments on what he had seen and experienced in California.

Now he saw John Riley turn away from the argument and pound on the plank bar for another drink. With a relieved sigh, Owen turned his attention back to the pages and resumed writing: "Gold seekers be warned! All is not wine and roses, although wine is available if one has the wherewithal. But the work is very hard. Contrary to the tales current, gold cannot be picked up from the ground, except in rare instances. Where one miner might strike it rich, twenty others go wanting. In most instances it is a matter of hard labor and drudgery.

"The price of necessities in the goldfields is appalling. A mule may cost as much as $200.00. Eggs sell for $6.00 the dozen. Such items as suspenders and toothbrushes sell for ten times their original cost. One enterprising young man of your correspondent's acquaintance peddled his goods up and down the gold diggings. His stock, even at such outrageous prices, was soon depleted, except for 248 small packs of toothpicks, the kind that are given away in high-class restaurants and that he had brought along mainly for his own use; each small pack contained two dozen toothpicks. He was able to sell all of his toothpicks for two dollars a pack; pure profit, since he had paid nothing for them!

"In essence, this means that those fortunate enough to find gold are willing to spend it on anything that is for sale. That is, of course, if they have anything left after the saloons, the cardsharps and the brothels are finished with them...."

At the sound of raised voices at the bar, Owen glanced up again. Riley was at it once more. This time his opponent was a huge man, outweighing Riley by at least fifty pounds. They were standing toe to toe, faces red.

Even as Owen watched, Riley swung, a roundhouse right, which the big man blocked easily by ducking his right shoulder into the blow. Then he delivered a mighty blow of his own. The punch knocked Riley off his feet and sent him skidding halfway across the tent. The big man stormed after him.

Owen was already on his feet, cane in hand, crossing the tent in bounding strides. He reached the big man just as the stranger raised one foot to put the boots to the fallen Riley, a common practice in saloon brawls around the gold camps.

Owen prodded the man in the back with the tip of his cane. As the man whirled, bellowing in drunken rage, Owen said mildly, "I'd advise you to keep your feet on the ground, friend."

"What for you buttin' into what don't concern you?"

"But it does concern me, you see. The man on the ground is a friend of mine."

"You should be more careful about picking your friends." The big man grinned savagely. "Now I'll whomp on you, then put the boots to the pair of you." He took a step forward, beginning to raise his fist.

"I think not," Owen said softly. He pressed the button on the cane handle, and the blade slid out with a soft hiss. "You come any closer and I'll gut you like a fish ready for the skillet."

The big man skidded to a stop, his gaze fastened on the wickedly gleaming blade. "That ain't hardly fair."

"Fair?" Owen drawled. "You weigh almost as much as both Riley and I put together. I figure I need something to even the odds." He gestured with the cane. "Now why don't you just move along, find another place to do your drinking? God knows there are enough to choose from. And we'll just forget this ever happened."

The big man focused on Owen's face angrily, then turned on his heel and strode out. Sheathing the blade, Owen glanced around the saloon. The others in the place were bent over their drinks, as if they had noticed nothing untoward. Violence was such an everyday occurrence in the camps that it was no longer a novelty to them.

Owen turned toward John Riley. The Southerner was propped up on one elbow, looking around groggily.

Owen bent over him. "Come along, champ, you've won another one," he said dryly. "I think it's time you had a lie-down."

He gave Riley a hand up, supporting him, starting him toward the tent entrance.

The artist held back. He muttered, "I need another drink."

"A drink is just what you don't need. Besides, I only have enough money to feed us for a week or so. If the paper doesn't send me some funds soon, we'll have to start grubbing for the yellow stuff ourselves, or starve."

Outside, it was spring along the American. New shoots were showing on the trees, and wildflowers were beginning to bloom on the hillsides. The caps of snow on the distant mountains were beginning to shrink.

The fresh air seemed to sober Riley somewhat. After a moment he shook off Owen's supporting arm and walked by himself without too much difficulty.

"I don't know why you put up with me, Owen," he muttered.

"Sometimes I wonder myself," Owen said with a grin. "I don't suppose I would if you weren't such a talented bastard."

"I told you I drank a little."

"A little!" Owen hooted with laughter. "That's like saying there's only a little water in the Sacramento River!"

"Anyway, I am sorry, Owen, for all the trouble I have caused you."

Owen had lost count of the number of times he had received just such an apology, and of course the momentarily repentant Riley would likely repeat the incident before the week was out. Owen said, "Did you get into fracases like this back East?"

"I'm afraid so," said Riley sheepishly.

"Then I can't understand how you stayed out of jail! Out here, of course, there's very little law, and you can get away with such shenanigans."

"That's one reason I came out here. I wore out my welcome back East."

They were approaching the lean-to they had found on their arrival back in Coloma. The lean-to had been unoccupied, so they had appropriated it for their own use. Owen went in with Riley, saw to it that the man was rolled up in his blankets, then left him alone.

When Owen emerged from the lean-to, evening shadows were falling, and most of the miners had stopped work for the day. Some washed up in the river; others flocked to the town just as they were, prepared for another night of revelry—those that had found enough dust that day to afford it.

The street was lined with every kind of building imaginable: round tents, square tents, plank hovels, log cabins. There was even one structure made of pine boughs, covered with tattered calico skirts. Men pushed and shoved along the street, and every nationality could be seen: Negroes, Spanish, Orientals, Germans, Frenchmen and many Owen couldn't identify.

He stopped on the edge of a group of men gathered around a table set up in the street. A card dealer stood behind the table, calling out: "Bet on the jack, gents! The jack's the winner! Three ounces no man can turn up the jack!" Men jostled one another to get their gold dust down.

A little farther along, a man stood atop a box, a pair of boots in his hand. "A pair of brand-new boots, gents! Cowhide, double-soled, triple-pegged, waterproof boots! Fit your road smashers exactly! What am I bid? Four ounces and a half? Any more bids? Going, going for four ounces and a half! Sold! Step right up, sir, and weigh out your dust. Honest scales, God's word on it!"

Owen strolled on, making his way toward a structure at the end of the street. The building was part lean-to, dug back into the hillside; and the front sides were canvas, with a crude door hung on a crooked frame. A sign hanging over the front, the letters

branded in wood, stated: Miranda Kent, Miners'
Supplies.

A lamp was burning inside, throwing a yellow glow
on the sidewalls. Owen could see shadows flickering
against the canvas as figures moved about inside. He
paused for a bit, thinking back over the past months.

There was a paucity of women in the gold camps.
Owen had learned that only about five percent of the
California population was of the female gender, that
their number was far less in the gold camps and that
the vast majority of these were of questionable virtue. The few respectable women in the camps received courteous consideration and were seldom
accosted by the swarms of women-hungry men.
Miranda Kent, a comely widow, was this type of
woman.

Owen smiled, remembering the brawl from which
he had just rescued Riley. The tensions of an all-male
community were the excuse given for so much
drunken brawling. Owen recalled a sketch Riley had
drawn of just such a fight. In the sketch two men were
clawing and scratching at each other while miners
ringed them, urging them on. One man's shirt had
been ripped from his back, and the seat of his trousers had been torn to reveal a bare backside.

John Riley, especially when drunk, would lie with
any woman; to Riley, a woman was a woman, a
whore or not. Where, Owen often reflected, is the
sensitive soul of the artist?

Despite his strong sexual urges, Owen had not relaxed his own standards. He had been celibate during his time in California—until a few weeks ago,
when he had become acquainted with Miranda Kent.

Miranda and her husband had come to the gold-fields a year ago, but with no intention of searching for the elusive yellow stuff. Instead, they had hauled a wagonload of miners' supplies from San Francisco; their plan was to open a store in Coloma. On the day they arrived, Joseph Kent was stricken by peritonitis and died within twenty-four hours.

Although desolated by her husband's sudden death, Miranda, remaining true to their intentions, had opened the store alone.

"What else could I do?" she had told Owen shortly after they became intimate. "Joseph had been a merchant back in Pennsylvania, and I helped him in the store. We sold everything we had to come out here and had just enough left to buy the wagonload of goods. I couldn't have resold the goods wholesale for enough to buy passage back home, and I have no one back there. Besides, I like it out here. I fully intend to stay."

Owen had to admire her pluck, if not her good sense. And yet he soon saw that there was nothing wrong with her judgment. She was prospering. She gave good value for the money. She sold honest merchandise and for a fair price; the majority of the merchants in the gold camps doubled their prices over what they had paid for the goods in San Francisco. For this reason, Miranda had all the business she could handle.

The miners respected her for her fair dealing; and although she was a widow woman, she was never molested. Owen suspected that if she ever was, a lynch party would immediately be organized for the offender. Besides, she had a Colt Dragoon within easy reach below the counter and let it be known that she was not averse to using it. To the best of Owen's knowledge she had never fired it at another human being; but on occasion she had hauled it out when she felt threatened, and she had assured him that she would not hesitate to shoot if need be.

The door opened and two men exited the store. Owen waited until they were out of sight, then went in.

Miranda was alone in the store now. She stood with her back to him, arranging stacks of miners' clothing on the shelves behind the plank that served her for a counter.

She was a tall woman, with a slender and supple figure. Her lustrous brown hair was pinned up in a bun at the back of her head. She was wearing a calico dress, which she usually did when the store was open, but she often wore men's trousers when she was unloading a wagon or moving goods around. Strangely enough, although the wearing of men's clothing was frowned upon, even here in the goldfields, Owen had yet to hear a word of criticism.

Miranda looked delicate, yet Owen had seen her haul fifty-pound sacks of flour about. Fiercely independent, she refused to employ anyone to help her in the store. The wages, of course, would be exorbitant, since any male, man or boy, would rather be seeking his fortune in the hunt for gold; and Miranda claimed she could manage on her own, thank you very much.

Owen coughed politely, and Miranda spun around. Her narrow, delicate face began to glow when she saw who it was. "Owen! I wasn't expecting you yet."

"You invited me to supper, remember?"

"Of course I remember. The mulligatawny is on the stove, cooking away."

"Is that the best you can offer a gentleman of my refinement?" he said with a grin.

"Be happy with what you can get, my fine friend." She ran a hand over her brow. "I've been too busy to cook anything too complicated."

"I've been busy, too, nursemaiding John Riley. He had too much to drink again and almost got his head taken off by a rowdy. I herded Riley to the lean-to and tucked him in."

"That son of a sow!" she said explosively. "He's not worth your trouble!"

Owen smiled faintly. Miranda hadn't picked up many bad habits during her time in the gold camps, yet her language did tend toward the salty side when she became annoyed. Also, she did not care at all for Riley. Riley had once sketched an unflattering caricature of her working in men's clothing and had made the mistake of showing it to her. Miranda had never forgiven him for that.

Owen said, "You know why I put up with him. He has a talent that I can use. Anyway, he's a decent enough gent when not in his cups."

"When *isn't* he in his cups? Mind you, he's going to get into bad trouble someday," she said darkly. "And quite possibly involve you in it."

"I've yet to see him win one of the brawls he starts."

"But someday he might run across somebody who can't fight back. As for his being decent when sober, I think he has this vicious, mean streak in him all of the time, or else it wouldn't crop up when he's drinking. I've always believed that people tend to show their true nature when they are intoxicated."

"I'd rather not talk about John Riley, my dear. Not when there are pleasanter things we could be doing." He cupped her chin in his hand and bent to her lips. Miranda struggled briefly, then melted against him.

After a moment she tugged herself free. Flustered, she said, "Goodness! What if someone came in and caught us like this? Word would be all over the camp within hours. My reputation would be ruined."

"Then, to save your reputation, why don't you close up? I imagine you've been open since daylight, as usual?"

"Sunup, anyway," she said with her flashing smile. "I think I *will* close up."

She fastened the bolt on the door, and then, with Owen's help, she strung a clothesline across the bottom and the top of the canvas walls, across the front and down both sides. The clotheslines had cowbells fastened to them a few inches apart. Cases of thievery weren't too prevalent in the camp, yet there was always the chance that some miner, either drunk or improvident, would slit open the canvas and loot the store. The cowbells would give Miranda ample warning in her sleeping quarters in the rear, so that she could come charging out with her enormous Dragoon pistol in both hands.

When the lines of cowbells were in place, Miranda led Owen into the back, behind the canvas curtain separating the store from her living quarters. The living quarters had been dug back into the hillside and lined with logs on three sides. Another canvas partition divided the room into two sections, one for sitting and cooking, the other for sleeping. Dug into the hillside as it was, the room was cool in the summer heat and snug against the winter cold.

The sitting area was furnished simply—a crude table and two chairs, a wood-burning cookstove and a divan. Originally, the floor had been hard-packed dirt, but Miranda had added a plank floor by dint of her own labor.

The room smelled of cooking and of various fruits and vegetables, which Miranda stored on shelves in the comparative coolness to prevent them from spoiling too quickly.

"There is a bottle of wine cooling in the bucket on the table, Owen. Help yourself while I wash up and change into fresh clothing."

Owen nodded and watched her walk across to duck behind the fall of canvas, into the bedroom. He could tell by the slump of her shoulders that she was tired, yet she walked with a conscious and seductive grace, for she knew that he was watching her.

Grinning, he crossed to the table, uncorked the bottle of port and poured a glass for himself. He sat down on the divan, sipping the wine, listening to the sound of water splashing behind the curtain, followed by the rustle of clothing. It was an erotic sound and caused him to think of the fine evenings they had spent romping in Miranda's bed.

The thought of Jemina came into his mind and was quickly gone, as Miranda pushed aside the curtain and entered. She had changed into another calico dress, with a bright, flowered pattern, and she had loosened her long, wavy hair. Her face was scrubbed and shining, and her smile seemed, to Owen, as fresh and beguiling as a morning flower.

He was on his feet in an instant, pouring another glass of wine and holding it out toward her. She cocked her head at him. "Well, do I pass inspection, sir?"

"You always pass inspection, my dear Miranda," he said gravely. He held up his glass. "Here's to the Flower of Coloma!"

She did not blush under his compliment; he had never seen Miranda blush. She cocked her head again in that way she had and said roguishly, "You are a great flatterer, Owen Thursday, and I love it. You may have your wicked way with me anytime."

Two hours later they lay together in the big four-poster bed, after a rousing interlude of passion that had left Owen sated and Miranda drowsing on his shoulder. He smiled as he thought of the bed. Not only was it the most comfortable bed he had slept in in the camps, but to the best of his knowledge it was the only four-poster in the area. Miranda had brought it all the way across the country, determined that she should have at least one thing from her former home back in Pennsylvania.

He certainly had no need to worry about marriage with Miranda. She had made her thoughts on that subject abundantly clear in the beginning: "I loved Joseph with every fiber of my being, and I doubt that I shall ever love any man that much again. If I do re-marry, it will be to a man of wealth and standing, a man who will provide me with a fine home for my-self and any children I may bear him. I like you, Owen, or I would never have bedded down with you, but I certainly will never marry a man as footloose as you appear to be. But it is also in my nature to like what happens between a man and woman in bed, and that is the reason I took you for a lover. I expect nothing more from you than that." Then she had grinned. "And I'm sure that you are greatly relieved, hearing me say so."

Remembering, Owen smiled down at her sleeping face. It was time for him to depart. They had an agreement that he would never spend the night. If he left in full daylight, he would likely be seen, and the damage to her reputation could be serious.

He eased her head off his shoulder. Miranda murmured in protest but did not awaken. He kissed her lightly on the forehead and slipped out of bed to get dressed. In the store he looked outside to check if the street was deserted. Finding it so, he left, heading for the lean-to and his own bed.

OWEN AWOKE shortly after sunrise the next morning to find Riley still snoring in his blankets. Owen got dressed and went outside.

It was a fine April morning. Birds sang, and the grass rippled in the cool breeze. Men were already stirring. Although the section of the river here had long since been combed thoroughly for gold, still a few hopeful souls were at work with their pans, picks and shovels. Most of the men, Owen knew, were here for a few days of rest and recreation or were stopping overnight on their way to another diggings.

The main thrust of the search for gold was now either down the river or up beyond the Sacramento; and Sutter's Mill, now Coloma, where it had all begun, was now mainly a way station and supply depot for miners heading down the American or north to the Feather River, looking for new strikes.

Owen had a table in the shade of the lean-to that he used for a desk. He arranged paper, pen and ink and sat down. Shortly, either he or Riley would have to prepare breakfast—eating in the restaurants was too expensive, especially now that his funds were running low. The two men took turns cooking, but Owen suspected that Riley, hung over and repentant over yesterday's fracas, would volunteer to do the morning's chores, although it was Owen's turn.

Instead of writing, he sat, his mind empty of ideas, staring down toward the river. For some reason, this morning he had awakened thinking of Jemina, and he was puzzled as to why. Certainly it could not be guilt; last night had not been the first time he had slept with Miranda, and he had felt no qualms before. But even now images of Jemina filled his mind: the loveliness of her; the ivory whiteness of her skin; the mischief that sparkled in her dark blue eyes when she was delighted; the solemn look she wore when they made love; the way she hummed to herself when she was deeply absorbed in a piece of writing. . . .

His reverie was shattered by the sound of a horse's hooves, and he glanced up to see a horse reining in before the lean-to. The rider wore an Army uniform. With a creak of saddle leather, the man dismounted.

"Ah, Mr. Thursday! I was informed that I might find you here," said Major General Persifor F. Smith.

Owen got to his feet. "General Smith! It is a pleasure to see you, sir."

"I am on inspection tour of the gold camps. I hoped that I might find you in Coloma. I brought along a mail pouch directed to you. I thought I would deliver it personally."

General Smith removed a leather pouch from his saddle bags and handed it to Owen.

"Thank you, sir. I appreciate this. I have been waiting months for mail from Philadelphia."

The general nodded. "Mail has been collecting in San Francisco for some time, and it should have been sent along to you before this."

"If it would not be too much of an imposition, General, I have a number of dispatches to send back with you."

"I would be most pleased to be of service, Mr. Thursday."

Owen quickly emptied the contents of the pouch onto the table—a number of newspapers, a large envelope sealed with wax.

"My apologies, General, but I cannot offer you any refreshments. I just rose a bit ago. I could make you a cup of tea if you'd care to wait."

"No need, sir, but I do thank you for your kind offer. I rode out immediately after breakfast, and I have a hard day's inspection ahead of me. I must be on my way."

"Then I shall be just a minute."

Owen took the pouch into the lean-to. As he filled it with his latest dispatches, he puzzled as to the general's reason for delivering the pouch personally. When he returned outside, he immediately divined the reason—the general was staring wistfully at the stack of newspapers.

"Sir, if you have another moment," Owen said, "while I look through the newspapers, I'm sure I will find the issue containing my article about the arrival of the *California* in Panama City and your part in arranging passage for the gold seekers."

"If it would not be too much trouble, Mr. Thursday," the general said formally.

"No trouble at all, General." Owen was already going through the newspapers. In a moment he found the one he was seeking; he held it out. "Here you are, sir. Accept it with my compliments."

General Smith nodded stiffly. "My gratitude, sir."

"General, one more favor, if you please. It is likely that my mail will require a reply. I should like to send it back to San Francisco with you, by return post. How long will you be in Coloma?"

"I leave early in the morning, for Sacramento. But if you have your mail ready by this evening, you may drop it off at my tent. I am bivouacked near the fort. If I am not back at that time, you may leave it with my aide. I shall be most happy to be of service."

"Thank you, General. I appreciate it."

"You are most welcome. I bid you good-day, Mr. Thursday." The general inclined his head fractionally, mounted and rode off.

Owen sat down at the table and sorted through his mail. He did not bother reading his articles in the newspapers; he never liked to read anything of his own once it was printed.

The sealed envelope contained a letter from Thomas Carruthers, with two bank drafts included, one in Owen's name and the other made out to John Riley. There was a smaller, sealed envelope, with just his name printed across in a small, neat hand.

Owen read Carruthers's letter first, chuckling over portions of it. It was not a long letter; Thomas Carruthers was as sparing of words as he was of praise: "Thursday: The pieces are adequate. I must admit to having received much favorable mail from readers, but I believe that comes about through interest in the subject, not from the excellence of the writing. Interest in the gold strike is at a fever pitch back here.

"I must, however, congratulate you on your acumen in employing John Riley. His work is excellent! The sketches have received nothing but favorable comment. Sometimes, Thursday, you manage to surprise me.

"I have also enclosed two bank drafts. I think that you were overly generous in your promised recompense to Mr. Riley; but since he does such splendid work, I reluctantly made out the draft in the amount you promised him. The other draft is your salary and expenses. Do be sure to keep meticulous accounts of your expenses, Thursday. You have an unfortunate tendency to be lax in this regard.

"Also enclosed is a message from one of your young ladies, Jemina Benedict by name. I frown upon including personal correspondence such as this, but she did say it was rather urgent. Please see that this does not happen in the future. Yrs., Thomas Carruthers."

Owen picked up the envelope from Jemina, both anxious and hesitant to open it. He looked at the bank draft made out to Riley. If he turned that much money over to the artist, it would likely be spent in the saloons in a very short time; yet he couldn't do otherwise, since Riley had more than earned the money.

"Stop procrastinating, sport," he said aloud, and ripped open Jemina's envelope with fingers that trembled slightly.

His first feeling was that of disappointment—the only item enclosed was a paragraph clipped from the *Ledger*. Had Jemina forgotten to enclose her letter?

He read the item: "Etta Logan, 52, convicted of the murder of Homer Murdock, an esteemed merchant in Philadelphia, today hanged herself by the neck in her cell. The widow Logan was awaiting sentencing for the crime she committed. She leaves no known relatives."

Owen sat lost in thought for a long time, staring into the distance. Finally, he sighed heavily and prepared his pen for a letter: "My dear Jemina: Today I received, by delayed post, the clipping reporting the death of Etta Logan. Naturally, I am saddened by this tragic occurrence. However, if it is your intent to make me experience guilt, disabuse yourself of this notion. I feel no responsibility for her death. The woman was a murderess, Jemina, and she had to pay the penalty for her crime. If Etta had been a man in the same situation, he would have paid the same penalty.

"During the intervening months since we parted, I have been giving much thought to our situation. I know that you thought I was using the assignment in California as a convenient excuse to avoid a proposal of marriage. I have concluded that you may be right, at least in part. I must confess that I have some trepidation about marriage.

"In a relaxed moment I told you about my childhood, about my mother and father. I must confess that I did not tell you everything, my dear. In blunt terms, I am a bastard, and I lied to you about remembering my father and the tattoo. He knew my mother for only a week. After that she never heard from him again. I was born out of wedlock, and she told me about the tattoo. She was not even sure of his name. And my mother's maiden name was not Thursday. After her death, when I moved from my old neighborhood, I changed my name to Thursday. I did not want anyone to know that I was a bastard.

"For this reason I have reservations about getting married. What if I have inherited my unknown father's villainous traits? What if someday I decided to desert you, as my father did my mother? More importantly, what if we had a son, and by some mischance he were to someday learn that his father was a bastard? What would that do to him?

"Perhaps none of these concerns seem important to you, yet they are to me. Hopefully, someday I will be able to overcome these fears, but I cannot promise at this time.

"I care for you deeply, dear Jemina, and I miss you horribly. I have had occasion to regret our acrimonious parting, and while I have no right to ask you to wait for me, I beg of you not to forget me. Do not forget our times together. I know now that I will not. I have tried to put thoughts of you from my mind, and however much I may succeed during the day, I dream of you often at night. Sad, sweet dreams. Often, I waken and reach out for you, only to find you gone.

"I hope to return to Philadelphia during the summer months. Until that time, I remain, yours with love, Owen."

Chapter Sixteen

WARREN BARRICONE, Jemina discovered, was a different man in Paris. In Philadelphia, he had been warm and friendly enough but always somewhat reserved and melancholy. In Paris, the sad look was gone from his eyes, and he seemed to have shed both years and worries.

That morning, after greetings had been exchanged, he eagerly questioned Jemina about her stay. "Are you enjoying Paris?"

She smiled. "Why, yes, very much. But I must confess that I haven't seen as much of the city as I'd like. Some art museums and cathedrals. And Madame Blanc has shown me around and introduced me to people in this area."

"What? At your age and on your first trip to Paris, and that's all you've seen? My dear, you have been here... what, for six weeks?"

"Well, I *have* been busy. I came here to work, after all," she said somewhat defensively. She told him then about her project, about her articles on Madame Roland and Marie Antoinette, about the trip to Le Clos. "In fact, I was just beginning my first article when you walked up," she finished.

He shook his head. "I'm disappointed in you, Jemina. To be young in Paris is an experience to be forever treasured, but you must *experience* Paris. So, we must remedy that. Fortunately, I have been here before, a number of times. I know Paris and the surrounding countryside intimately, and I now volunteer to be your guide!''

''But do we have time?'' she asked dubiously. ''Aren't you here for the fashion showing?''

''We have some time. I came a week in advance. Knowing your penchant for work, I suspected that you might not be enjoying Paris to its fullest. Now, no argument.'' He held up a hand, smiling. ''I am your superior, and you are to take orders from me!''

Thus began a dizzy whirl that left Jemina breathless. She discovered that Warren did indeed know Paris intimately. He spoke the language well; he knew its restaurants, museums and theaters; and he seemed suddenly filled with an energy that equaled Jemina's own.

He was marvelous company, knowing just how to provoke laughter and enjoyment in her. Through his eyes, she saw a Paris that she realized she would never have seen without him.

She had always thought that Warren was a very serious person, perhaps *too* serious; but now she wondered if he had not been something of a gay blade in his youth. Perhaps his wife's illness had turned him toward the gray side of life.

The comparison was inevitable—Owen versus Warren. Warren did not possess Owen's physical attractiveness; and when he inadvertently touched her, Jemina did not go weak in the knees as she did with Owen. On the other hand, there was a gentler, more sensitive side to Warren, and he had none of Owen's male arrogance. When they did discuss their work during that whirlwind week, Warren listened to her with respect, not with thinly concealed scorn; he appeared to accept the fact that she was a good journalist, a fine author, even if she was a woman. Warren did not have Owen's dash and verve, and there was no sense of danger about him; yet she had the feeling that he was solid and dependable, not likely to go rushing halfway across the continent on a whim. Most of all, he was gentle and caring.

Not only did they explore Paris under Warren's guidance, but he rented a carriage and they visited Fontainebleau and some of the great cathedral and château towns. Jemina was to look back upon that gay, carefree week as one of the most exciting times of her young life.

Near the end of the week something suddenly became clear—Warren was courting her! At first she was scandalized and angry; Warren was a married man! And then she was intrigued and flattered. They were, after all, in Paris, the city of lovers, where it was not unusual for a married man to take a mistress, or a wife to take a lover. Somehow, it didn't seem so wicked here. Naturally, back in America, Warren's behavior would be considered reprehensible. But Jemina had to wonder if it had crossed Warren's mind back home or if it was all due to the influence of Paris.

Not that he did anything outrageous or even overt; but his feelings were clearly evident in the way he touched her, in the manner in which he helped her in and out of a carriage and the way he catered to her every wish. More than once she had caught his glance on her, when he thought she was not looking, and glimpsed the naked emotion in his eyes.

Ah, well, she thought again; Paris! And it was nice to be wanted, to be cherished, after Owen's almost brutal rejection. She had warned Owen that she had no intention of pining away for him.

Once or twice, a disturbing thought intruded into the magic tenor of the days and nights—was Warren going to demand her capitulation to his obvious desire? Each time, she pushed such concerns out of her mind, living for the moment. If she was asked to pay the piper, she would make that decision when the time came. She wasn't in love with Warren, not in the way she had been with Owen, but she did care for him.

Was her love for Owen really part of the past? She was still angry with him; of that there was no doubt. But had she stopped loving him? She was wise enough to realize that she would never know for certain until she was face-to-face with him again. However, whatever her feelings for Owen Thursday, she could see no future in a relationship with him. It would always be the same; he would never change. He was too content with his life the way it was, and she would only be hurt again and again.

Her feelings toward Warren were equally hard to define. She liked him immensely, and she felt a strong affection for him. But there was always his wife back in Philadelphia.

Warren finally declared himself on the night before they were to attend their first fashion showing.

They were taking a cruise on the Seine. It was a beautiful, moonlit evening, with the usual mist beginning to rise off the water. Very romantic, Jemina thought.

The boat wasn't particularly crowded. Warren ordered glasses of champagne from the bar, and they stood alone at the railing in the stern, sipping champagne and gazing at the banks of the river, as the boat was slowly poled along. Jemina was in a mellow mood from the champagne and the week's activities.

Impulsively, she turned her face to Warren's. "Warren, I wish to thank you for this past week. I feel some guilt, like a schoolgirl skipping classes, but it has been highly enjoyable, and I will remember it always."

He took her hand, and his gaze became intent. "I cannot remember when I have enjoyed myself so much, Jemina. You have made me feel young again, young and alive. I have been able to forget . . . everything."

His hand tightened around hers. Jemina let it remain in his grasp, not wishing to offend him. She said gently, "But it must end now. Tomorrow, we return to work."

"It doesn't have to end, not yet," he said with a burning gaze. "We still have a full week in Paris."

She laughed lightly, wondering how to head off what was coming, not sure she wanted to. "A week of work, no time for what has transpired these past few days."

"We shall have the nights," he said urgently. "Can't we accept what we have, as long as we're in Paris? I need you, Jemina; I need the days with you, no matter how few they may be. I love you, my dear Jemina. I have loved you since the moment I saw you."

She gently withdrew her hand from his grasp. "Warren, aren't you forgetting something? You have a wife back in Philadelphia."

"A wife who is ill, Jemina. I once loved her, and in a way I still do, but it's different now. It's like the affection a doctor must feel toward a patient who is dear to him. There has been nothing between us for a long time, for years. I swear that is true, Jemina!''

''But what will happen when we return? Will you leave your wife?''

For the first time in Paris, that sad look returned to his eyes. He turned to gaze moodily down at the Seine flowing beneath the boat. ''No, I could never do that. I won't lie to you,'' he said in a low voice. ''I will never desert Alice so long as she is alive. There has been too much love between us.''

''Well, I certainly admire you for that, Warren. But if I do what you're asking, what will happen back in Philadelphia? Will I be your mistress? Is that what you have in mind?'' Jemina was amazed at what she was saying. Paris was indeed an insidious influence. ''That could destroy our careers, perhaps even our very lives.''

''I fully realize that.'' He gazed at her now, his look solemn and intent. ''But I'm talking about *now*. We can face that when we . . . Alice does not have long to live, Jemina. My God, I can't believe I said that,'' he said miserably. ''I feel like such a cad!''

He turned away from her again, and Jemina reached out to touch his hand on the rail. ''I'm sorry, Warren. I know you didn't mean that the way it sounded.''

Her touch seemed to galvanize him, to break loose a torrent of emotion long dammed up inside of him. With a groan he whirled and took her into his arms.

At the touch of his lips on hers, Jemina felt herself go lax and pliant. She had not realized how much she had missed a man's touch. Her body responded without her willing it, and she returned his kiss with a rising passion.

After a moment he stepped back, saying triumphantly, "You see, you do love me!"

"I care for you, Warren. I care for you deeply. But I wish you wouldn't read anything more into it than that. It could only end with both of us being badly hurt."

"I am willing to take that chance."

"Perhaps *you* are, but I'm not so sure about myself."

"Jemina, I need you. I want you. Surely you cannot deny me, not after what we've shared this week."

Warren reached for her again, and the touch of his hands, his mouth on hers, set up a wanting in her, a wanting that swept away all thought.

The boat bumped against the dock, and they jumped apart guiltily.

"The boat is docking; the ride's over," Warren said unnecessarily.

They didn't speak as they disembarked, and they walked a few inches apart from each other. But when they reached the top of the bank and started the short walk to their pension, Warren found her hand and held it tightly. Jemina did not try to pull away, and they walked along in silence. Her thoughts were in great turmoil. She knew that Warren was going to ask her to come to his room. Thoughts of Owen and Warren's wife aside, why shouldn't she? She had no strong moral scruples about it. If nothing else, her relationship with Owen had taught her that there was nothing wrong when two people came together in love. True, she did not love Warren, certainly not in the way she had loved Owen; yet she did feel a strong affection for him. Who would be hurt, except perhaps themselves, in the end? Anyone else who might be hurt was across the Atlantic. Why should she be concerned about how Owen might feel? He had shown little concern for her feelings.

It was late when they reached the pension, and the only light showing was in the entryway, behind Madame Blanc's small reception desk.

Just inside the door, Warren turned to her, and as she had anticipated, he asked in a whisper, "Will you come to my room later, my dear?"

As she hesitated, he said quickly, "If you are thinking of Alice . . . I know this may sound strange, but I don't think she would really mind. Alice is a very understanding person."

Jemina reached a sudden decision; it was sometimes wrong to think *too* much. Perhaps this was one of those times. She said softly, "But what about Madame Blanc? What will she think if she finds out?"

He smiled quickly. "Madame Blanc is French. She is always on the side of lovers."

Suddenly, all resistance crumbled and she found herself nodding.

His face broke into a smile of delight, and he kissed her lightly on the lips. "You will not regret it, sweet Jemina."

He was gone then, bounding up the stairs ahead of her; Jemina followed more slowly. When she reached the top of the stairs, Warren had already disappeared behind the closed door of his bedroom at the far end of the hall. At least, Jemina thought, Madame Blanc's quarters are downstairs, so we likely won't disturb her. Despite Warren's reassurances of the woman's liberal outlook on lovers, Jemina would much rather Madame Blanc remain unaware of their tryst. There was always the possibility that she might divulge the secret to Sarah inadvertently.

With a last, lingering look at the door to Warren's room, Jemina entered her own room. She could still feel the touch of his mouth on hers, the strength of his hands as he embraced her.

Inside her room she quickly undressed and washed in the basin on the table. As she toweled dry, she caught a glimpse of herself in the pier glass. She stopped, staring at her naked body in the glass. Although not unduly modest, Jemina rarely looked at herself unclothed. Such an action always struck her as narcissistic.

But now she did spend a minute looking at the image of herself—at the body she would soon offer to a man. She knew that she was very attractive: tall; high breasts with prominent nipples; wide hips, with a triangular nest of black hair at the juncture of her thighs; and long, sleek, shapely legs.

Her gaze riveted on her breasts, and at the thought of Warren's hands and lips on them, the nipples sprang erect. Shame caused her to blush deeply, and she turned away from the mirror with an exclamation of self-scorn.

Hastily then, she got into a nightgown and robe, stepped into a pair of house slippers and started toward the door. Halfway there, she stopped, appalled. What was she doing?

She turned slowly and sank down on the edge of the bed. She simply could not go through with it. It would be a betrayal of everything she believed in, and a despicable betrayal of Warren's wife. Being in a foreign country was no excuse for behaving any dif-

ferently than she would behave back home. If she
traded her self-respect for a few moments of pleasure, she would go through the agony of guilt later.
Back in the United States, she would not dream of
letting a married man make love to her.

What would Warren think, waiting for her in his
room? For a moment she thought of going down the
hall and trying to explain that she could not go
through with it; but if she did that, if she faced him,
allowed him to touch her, her will might not be strong
enough to resist. No, think of her what he would, she
was not leaving her room tonight!

IN HIS ROOM, wearing only a dressing gown, Warren
waited with mounting impatience. Minutes passed
slowly, and he began to pace—first to the window to
stare out at the empty streets below, then back to stare
at the door, willing the sound of her knock. He did
not understand what was keeping her; Jemina had
seemed as eager as he.

After close to an hour had ticked by, he knew that
she was not coming. For some reason he couldn't
fathom, she had changed her mind. He should not
have let her out of his sight; he should have brought
her immediately to his room. He ached for her; he
wanted her desperately; he felt that he could not live
out the night without her.

For a moment he was tempted to go down the hall
and bring her back. Perhaps she was just shy, unac-
customed to coming to a man's room late at night.

He actually had his hand on the doorknob, starting to turn it. Then he jerked his hand away as if the
knob was a blazing coal. No! He would not humble
himself; he would not beg. He had too much pride for

that. If she could not come to him of her own free will, so be it.

He threw himself across the bed, feeling desolate and alone.

For the rest of the night, Warren lay sleepless, staring wide-eyed at the ceiling, his ears straining for the sound of her knock. He lay until dawn seeped through the curtains.

WHEN JEMINA came downstairs the next morning and peeked into the dining room off the lobby, she saw that Warren was not there.

At that moment Madame Blanc came bustling out of the kitchen. Her eyes were bright with curiosity. "You are looking for Monsieur Barricone, yes?"

"Well . . . yes. Perhaps he is still in his room."

"*Non*. Monsieur Barricone left some time ago. He did not even return my greeting. Perhaps he is not feeling well?"

"He may be breakfasting somewhere else. It is such a fine day."

Madame Blanc's gaze rested on her speculatively. "Ah, yes, little one. A fine day indeed."

Jemina said, "I believe I shall also go out."

Leaving the pension, something drew her to the sidewalk café where Warren had found her his first day in Paris, and her instinct proved correct. He was sitting at the same table, a cup of coffee and a plate of bread and jam, untouched, before him. His head was down, and he didn't see her until she took the chair across from him.

Then he looked up. His face looked drawn and gray, and his eyes were bloodshot. He was unshaven and his clothes were badly wrinkled.

It was the first time she had ever seen him looking so unkempt, and her heart went out to him.

"Oh, Warren, I am so sorry! But I just couldn't! Can you ever forgive me?"

"There is nothing to forgive, Jemina," he said. "It was your choice to make, and if you did not want me, I wouldn't have wanted you to come to me out of pity."

She was shaking her head. "No, no, you don't understand, Warren. It had nothing to do with you personally. It just wouldn't have been right, don't you see? I would always have felt guilty about your wife."

He studied her face for a long moment, then slowly nodded. "Perhaps you are right. Perhaps I also would have experienced guilt." He managed a wan smile. "Now we will never know, will we?"

"I hope you don't think too badly of me. I wasn't playing the coquette. I just got carried away by your ardor, which I shared, until I had time to think about it."

"No, Jemina, I could never think badly of you. And I want you to know that I shall always love you."

She glanced away, vaguely embarrassed.

"And I will never give up. Our days will be full during the rest of our stay in Paris, but we still have the nights. I have shown you little of the nightlife in Paris."

She looked back at him. "No, Warren, I don't think that would be wise. It would only make matters worse. Besides, I have much work to do. I have neglected my pieces on Madame Roland and Marie Antoinette. I wish to have them ready to show Sarah when we return. Also, I will have to write about the fashion showings. No, my dear," she said gently. "It will be far better if we see each other as little as possible during the next week.''

OF COURSE, they necessarily saw each other daily, and the hours were long, as they covered the various fashion showings. Warren seemed reconciled to their situation, but he showed little of the joy he had evinced during their earlier days together, and occasionally she glimpsed the old sadness in his eyes when she caught his gaze. She was sorry about that, yet there was little she could do about it.

Besides, she was far too busy to dwell on the situation. She had never really made a study of the world of fashion. She had learned something of it during her employment on the *Lady's Book*, true, but she was a novice at the task of covering the fashion showings with an eye to doing a piece on them. Yet, despite her preconceptions, she found the next few days endlessly fascinating. Fortunately, Warren was intimately familiar with the milieu; and representing *Godey's Lady's Book* as they did gave them VIP access, not only to the official showings but to the scene backstage, which Jemina found absorbing.

The material in vogue was raw silk, of many brilliant hues. Many were made with heavy, brocaded patterns of small bouquets of bright, gay colors or with a wreathed vine running lengthwise, giving the appearance of stripes of rich ribbon. The predominant colors were crimson, yellow and blue, or yellow and green.

Jemina observed that ladies' bonnets were somewhat smaller in the brim than those of the previous season, standing open at the ears and tied at the side or close to the chin by strips of broad ribbon. The bouquets and wreaths were exquisitely natural, mostly imitation field flowers—corn poppies, harebells and dahlias. Ribbons were in the richest style, and broader than they had been in past years.

Jemina found the public showings for the buyers and the journalists rather boring after a while; but the behind-the-scenes fittings were most interesting. The one dressmaker who she found particularly intriguing was, astonishingly enough, an Englishman—always fresh and clean shaven, wearing a curled black coat, white cravat and cambric sleeves fastened at the wrist with a gold button. He affected a monocle and officiated at the fittings with all the gravity and aplomb of a diplomat.

Yet he was a genius with scissors and pins. He had the models dress and undress before him, as if they were no more or less than the wax figures Jemina had seen in a hairdresser's window.

He seemed to know exactly where the material should fit tightly and where it should flow. He appeared to understand, at a single glance, the whole context of a woman, what should be shown and what concealed. The first time they observed the Englishman at work, Warren had commented that "the Almighty seems to have created this fellow with a born knowledge of the law of crinolines and the true curve of the petticoat."

When the dressmaker was fitting a dress on a live doll, it was with the most profound contemplation that he touched, fitted, measured and marked a defective fold of the material. After a bit he would step back and, screwing the monocle tighter into his eye socket, he would judge his handiwork. Then he would resume modeling the dress to the figure—sometimes planting a flower here, a ribbon there—until he finally had the harmony he sought. And all the while the woman would stand motionless, unless ordered to move, scarcely daring to breathe lest she excite the wrath of the dressmaker.

At last, the dressmaker would back halfway across the fitting room and seat himself upon a sofa. Then he would direct his work with a long-fingered hand, like a conductor wielding a baton.

"To the right, madam!" The lady moved accordingly.

"To the left, madam!" The woman turned as directed.

"Now face me." The model looked straight at the designer.

"Now, right about-face."

Finally, perhaps after a few more tucks and snips, he would nod his approval and turn his attention to the next garment.

Jemina found other dressmakers entirely different in character and actions. Many were quite feminine in their gestures and conversation, and they loved to gossip. They always had a fund of tales about people in high places, especially the highborn ladies for whom they made dresses.

One story in particular she thought highly amusing; it concerned the mistress of Louis-Napoléon Bonaparte, who had been elected president of the Second Republic of France in December of last year.

Jemina had already been informed that Bonaparte's mistress was considered the best-dressed lady in Europe. She set the fashions for the world, employing not only modistes but artists to design and make her garments. It had been said that she owned a dress for every day of the year.

According to the tale one dressmaker told Jemina, in the center of the woman's dressing room there was a trapdoor opening into a room above, which was filled with "presses," each containing a dress, exhibited on a frame—in effect, an effigy. There was also a track in the room above, on which the effigies could be run to the trapdoor and lowered into the room below for the vain woman's inspection. If the dress pleased her, it was immediately placed upon her person. If, on the other hand, it did not please her, it was whipped back up and another lowered in its place until Bonaparte's mistress found one that suited her fancy.

Jemina repeated the story to Madame Blanc. "I wonder if the story is true? So many of the tales these dressmakers tell are simply too outrageous to be believed."

"Nothing about Bonaparte's consort is too outrageous to be believed," Madame Blanc said with an unladylike snort. "Louis-Napoléon Bonaparte himself is expecting to become emperor of France."

"But I thought royalty was no more in France," Jemina said in surprise. "I understood that the country was henceforth a republic?"

"So did we all, those of us who scorn royalty. But I prophesy that Bonaparte will be emperor of France within four years," Madame Blanc said darkly. "According to our hard-won constitution, no man may serve more than one four-year term as president. But before that time has passed, before his term has expired, Bonaparte will have seized power and made himself emperor!" Madame Blanc moved her lips in a spitting motion. "And all the blood shed, all the lives lost in our glorious revolution, will have been for naught!"

Jemina was thinking that she now had the perfect ending for her piece on Madame Roland. The words were writing themselves in her mind: "Parisians who are aware of such matters are predicting that France will return once more to a government by monarchy. If this occurs, it will mean that all of Madame Roland's efforts to free the French people from a tyrant's yoke, the sacrifice of her very life, will all have been in vain...."

She said nothing of this to Madame Blanc, of course. Instead, she said, "I can only pray that this does not come about."

FINALLY, IT WAS TIME to return to America; the fashion showings were over. Jemina had sufficient material for her article about the spring fashion scene in France, and Warren had the material for his fashion plates. Jemina's pieces on Madame Roland and Marie Antoinette were also shaping up nicely. She fully intended to finish them, ready for publication, on the ship going home—if she did not come down with the *mal de mer* again.

Warren was sailing on the same ship with her, but she did not think there would be any trouble with him. He had been careful to keep his distance since his failure to get her to come to his room, and she was confident that their relationship would continue in the same vein.

And so, on a morning in late May, they said fare-well to Madame Blanc, and to Paris, and took a carriage to Calais, where they would board their ship for New York.

Chapter Seventeen

IT WAS LATE in the afternoon, and Owen sat with his back against the trunk of a pine tree, gazing down at the sprawl of log-and-board buildings that made up the mining town that had sprung up along the old pack-mule trail. His and Riley's horses were hobbled nearby, and their bedrolls were on the ground, where they would spend the night. Riley was somewhere in the town below, probably in a saloon getting drunk. He had tried to cajole Owen into accompanying him.

"Come with me, Owen. We haven't been in a saloon in a week," Riley had said. "I sure could use a drink or two."

"Or three or four," Owen had said dryly. He had grudgingly doled out the money Carruthers had sent along to pay the artist. "But I think I'll skip this one. Probably all they'll have down there will be tarantula juice." Tarantula juice had become the popular name for the vile brand of home-brewed whiskey served in the camp saloons. "And please go easy on the money, Riley. God only knows when the mail will arrive with more."

"It's my money," Riley said sullenly.

"And you've spent it in about a tenth of the time it took you to earn it."

"You're not my guardian, Thursday!"

"That's true enough, but you, by God, need one!"

Riley had glared at him, opened his mouth, then closed it with a snap and went charging off down the hill.

Now Owen arranged his writing materials and began a new dispatch: "Hangtown, California; May 10, 1849. Until recently the gold camp now known as Hangtown was called Old Dry Diggings. But due to a particularly tragic circumstance, the name has been changed.

"Five men were caught trying to rob a local gambler. The five would-be thieves were tried by a jury of miners and sentenced to thirty-nine lashes with a bullwhip. After the lashes had been administered, further charges were raised against three of the men; they were accused of an attempt at robbery and murder the previous year on the Stanislaus River.

"Another illegal trial was held by approximately two hundred miners. None of the accused men spoke a word of English, and undoubtedly they had no understanding of the proceedings. Being too weak from the floggings to protest, the three were found guilty and sentenced to hang within less than a half hour.

"A few saner heads argued that God, humanity and justice were being outraged by such proceedings, but to no avail. Your correspondent talked with one man who protested, Tyler Howard, a former army lieutenant who had resigned his commission in the pursuit of gold. Lieutenant Howard informed me that the crowd was by this time drunk and rowdy, beyond reasoning, and threatened to also hang the protesters if they did not cease their opposition.

"Now sensing their fate, the condemned men begged for an interpreter, but their pleas were ignored. The miners were filled with liquor and blood

lust. A horse-drawn wagon was driven up; the men
were made to stand in the wagon bed; nooses tightened around their necks, and the other ends of the
ropes were tied to a tree limb. Then the wagon was
driven away.

"Thus it too often is with mining-camp justice.
And thus it was that Old Dry Diggings became
known as Hangtown. This name has wounded the
pride of the more permanent residents, and an effort
is under way to find a new name. Since much placer
mining is taking place in the area, the most popular
name so far mentioned is Placerville.

"Although this incident seems a particularly vile
miscarriage of justice, this type of thing is not un-
common in the mining camps, where there is almost
no law and rough justice prevails. To make matters
worse, the mood of euphoria has passed, as gold is
becoming harder to find. Disgruntled miners appear
to delight in taking out their disappointment on anyone handy, and someone charged with a crime is a
good target for their spleen.

"For the truth is that the tales of finding nuggets
worth thousands of dollars, or finding five thousand
dollars' worth of gold dust in a single pan, are no
longer current. Now it is a matter of back-breaking
labor, separating the gold dust from rock and sand.
In the beginning a miner's basic tool kit consisted of
a shovel and a wash pan. Now a claim is worked with
a device called a cradle or a more elaborate device
called a Long Tom.

"The cradle takes its name from a baby's cradle.
It is an oblong wooden box about three feet in length,
mounted on wooden rockers. Bars called riffles are
nailed at intervals along the bottom of the lower, open

end, and an apron of canvas is stretched over a frame placed at a slant inside the upper, closed end. A hopper with a perforated base and a side handle is fitted over this end. Rocking the cradle with the handle, the miner pours water over gravel in the hopper. The water, strained through the hopper and deflected by the apron, runs out of the rocker's lower end and leaves gold dust behind each riffle, if the gold-bearing sediment is present. Often, it is not.

"A Long Tom consists of two parts: a slanting, twelve-foot-long trough that ends in an uptilted, perforated iron sheet called a riddle; the lower end of the trough rests on a riffle box. Shovel loads of gold-bearing gravel are then washed through the riddle and into the riffle box, where the particles of gold are trapped by the wooden bars...."

Darkness had descended before Owen was aware of it, and he had to stop writing. Lights now shone in Hangtown, and raucous shouts and laughter could be heard.

Owen ate a cold supper—hardtack and jerky, washed down with cold spring water—and unrolled his blankets. He lay for a long time on his back, with his head propped on his arms, staring up at the night sky that was atwinkle with bright stars.

The old familiar restlessness was upon him again, which meant that his interest in the goldfields was flagging. Past experience had taught him that, if his interest waned, so would that of his readers. Besides, he had written some twelve articles in all, covering most aspects of the gold rush. And while he was confident that the gold camps would flourish for some years yet, the first fine frenzy had passed; there was very little new left to write about.

Also, if he was honest with himself, he was homesick for Philadelphia, a malady strange to him. Could
it be because he missed Jemina? Yes, he was forced to
admit, he would like to see her. She had not replied
to any of his letters, and he was beginning to think
that she was indeed not pining away for him.

He fell asleep with Jemina on his mind, only to be
rudely awakened sometime later by someone shaking him roughly and a voice urgently calling his
name.

"Mr. Thursday, wake up!"

Owen shook his head groggily, sitting up.
"What . . . ?" Then he recognized Tyler Howard.
"Why, Lieutenant! What is it, what's wrong?"

Lieutenant Howard squatted down before him.
"It's your friend, John Riley. He's in bad trouble,
and he's asking for you."

"Oh, Christ!" Owen rubbed a hand down across
his face, becoming more alert. "What's happened
now? Did he get beaten up again?"

"I'm afraid it's far more serious than that. Riley
killed a woman tonight, strangled her with his bare
hands."

Owen felt his mouth fall open. "Riley killed a
woman? Who, for God's sake? And why?"

"The 'who' we know; the 'why' we don't know for
sure yet. The woman was Gladys Riggens. She's a
tart; came to Hangtown about a month ago and set
up business."

"And Riley *killed* her?"

"It would appear so. Leastways he doesn't deny it.
The tart took him to her crib. Some passing miners
heard her scream for help, and they rushed into her
little shack. They found her dead, with Riley, his

breeches at half-mast, his hands still around her throat. He was pissing drunk and made little sense. We had to lock him up until we can get it all straightened out. He's sobered up enough now to ask for you.''

Owen was out of his blankets, pulling on his boots. ''Then I suppose I'd better pay him a visit,'' he said with a sigh. ''Damn and blast him, Riley is more trouble than he's worth.''

As he trudged down the hill with Howard, Owen thought that Riley was indeed in deep trouble this time. Women in the gold camps, even whores, were at such a premium that killing one was about as heinous a crime as one could commit.

John Riley was being held in a crude jailhouse, built with logs. The building had one tiny, barred window and a padlocked door. Howard let Owen in and stood just outside the door.

Riley was a mess. He stank of vomit, his clothes were filthy and torn and he was asleep on the ground on his back, snoring loudly.

Not wanting to touch him, Owen prodded the artist with his toe. ''Come on, Riley, wake up!''

Riley finally opened his eyes and sat up, his bleary gaze trying to find Owen. Then he gave a glad cry. ''Owen, am I glad to see you!''

''It looks like you've really done it this time,'' Owen said in a gritty voice.

''I don't recall too much....'' Riley shook his head as though to clear it, winced and buried his face in his hands. In a moment he looked up. ''Now I remember. Some of it, anyway. I found this woman in one of the saloons. I don't remember which one. Hell, I don't even remember her name.''

Owen said grimly, "Her name was Gladys Riggens, and she's stone-cold dead. They caught you with your hands still around her neck."

"She robbed me, Owen! She went through my pockets while I was asleep. I paid her enough as it was, a gold eagle. That's ten dollars, Owen! But she wasn't content without taking every cent I had. See?" He turned out his pockets to show that they were empty.

"That's hardly enough reason to kill her, Riley. Why didn't you just report her to the justice of the peace?"

"What good would that have done?" Riley snorted. "The law here is worthless, you know that."

"Perhaps not as worthless as you think. They just may hang you!"

Riley blanched. "Hang me? For killing a thieving whore?"

"Riley, you well know how much they value women in the camps. If she stole from you, why didn't you just take your money back? You should have been able to manage that without killing the woman, for God's sake!"

Riley hung his head and mumbled, "When I found out she had rifled my pockets, I lost my head."

"Out of your head with liquor, you mean."

Riley glanced up, his eyes alive with fear. "Surely they won't hang me, Owen?"

"The chances are good they will. Hell, you can't even prove she stole from you. There's only your word for that."

"Surely you believe me, Owen?"

"It doesn't matter what *I* believe, Riley." Owen made an impatient gesture. "All that matters is what a jury believes, and the jury will be made up of miners. The miners in Hangtown seem to delight in hangings; it's their chief entertainment.''

Riley looked down at the ground again, and a glum silence prevailed for a few minutes.

''I know a way to prove it!'' Riley said suddenly, looking up.

''How's that?''

''You remember you had to go to San Francisco to cash in those bank drafts from your newspaper?''

''Of course I remember.''

''Well, you brought back gold coins. Eagles, half eagles and quarter eagles. That's what you paid me with. And that's all I had in my pockets last night, what was left. I had three eagles, two half eagles and two quarters. Now, I gave the whore one full eagle, leaving me with two, the halves and the quarters. All together I had thirty-five dollars left. That's what she stole from me.''

Owen was frowning. ''I still don't understand...''

''Don't you see?'' In his excitement Riley got to his feet. ''Everybody in the camps pays in gold dust. Gold coins are rarer than hen's teeth, Owen. If she has those gold coins hidden around her shack, it means she had to steal them from me!''

''That strikes me as rather tenuous proof,'' Owen said dubiously. ''But I suppose it's worth a try.''

He knocked on the door. Lieutenant Howard opened it, and Owen stepped outside. ''Lieutenant, was a search made of the woman's quarters?''

''Not to my knowledge. There is a man left on guard at the door, until the woman can be buried in the morning. Why do you ask?''

Owen told him about Riley's gold coins. Howard seemed as dubious as Owen had been. "But I suppose a search is in order. If the coins are found, it would at least lend some credence to your friend's story."

Owen put his head back into the room. "Riley, we're going to look for the coins."

Riley's voice came out of the darkness. "You'll find them, Owen. My word on it."

At this moment, Owen thought sourly, Riley's word is worth damned little! He was, finally, thoroughly disillusioned with the artist, and he would have just walked away, washing his hands of the whole mess; yet Riley *was* a friend, to a degree.

Lieutenant Howard locked the door, and they walked, without speaking, the short distance to the dead woman's crib. A man moved out of the shadows, barring their way. "Who goes there?"

"It's all right, Jed," Howard said.

"Oh, it's you, lieutenant. Nobody's been about."

"That's good, Jed. We need to search the woman's effects for something. Will you step in with us? We'll need you as a witness to what we find, if anything."

A lantern burned dimly in the hut. It was a poor place, without even a chair or a table. A straw mattress was on the dirt floor, a washbasin sat on a stand in one corner and a few items of women's clothing hung on nails in the walls. After catching a glimpse of a still form wrapped in a sheet on the mattress, Owen averted his gaze.

"If there is anything belonging to your friend here," Howard said, "it shouldn't be hard to find. There are few hiding places."

"Be it something of value you're looking for, lieutenant?"

"Well, yes, Jed. Relatively speaking."

"Then I'd suggest you look in or near the mattress." Jed grinned in the dim light; he was missing most of his teeth. "Been my experience that women of her sort hide valuables within reach, even when bouncing on the mattress."

"All right, we'll look there first. Jed, will you help me move the body?"

Gingerly, the two men moved the dead woman onto the ground. Owen was grateful that her face was covered, knowing how horrible a throttled person usually looked.

In a shallow depression under the head of the mattress, they found a tattered reticule. In it was a sack holding a small amount of gold dust and several gold coins. On counting the coins, they learned that they were of the amount and exact denomination that Riley claimed he had lost.

Howard said, "Jed, you will be required to testify at John Riley's trial that we found these coins."

Owen and Lieutenant Howard left the hut together, walking back toward the jail building.

"Well, at least we have proof that the woman robbed Riley," Howard said. "Not the greatest proof, since it is actually circumstantial. But the fact remains that he killed the woman, and it is doubtful that a jury will consider his loss motive enough for a killing."

"Especially not here, where they hang men for far less," Owen said glumly.

"Mr. Thursday, I will undertake to defend your friend, if you wish. I have had some training with the law and have defended two soldiers brought up on charges while I was still in the army.''

''It's certainly all right with me. Of course, it's Riley's decision, but I don't see that he has much choice. Hell, he should be grateful. Any idea when the trial will take place?''

''I would hazard a guess that it will be tomorrow. Carl Larkin, the justice of the peace, is out of town, but he's due back in the morning. As you know, they don't waste much time bringing a man to trial in the camps.''

The trial of John Riley began shortly after noon the next day, with Carl Larkin presiding. Larkin was a cigar-smoking man of indeterminate age, bald, with a large nose crisscrossed with the purple veins of a heavy drinker. In fact, Owen was sure that he had already been at the bottle before convening the trial.

Larkin asked for volunteers, and he selected the first twelve men to step forward as members of the jury. He appointed an ex-marshal as the prosecutor, and Lieutenant Howard defended Riley. Then Larkin declared the court in session.

There was definitely a farcical air about the proceedings, Owen thought, already writing his article in his head. To begin with, the selection of the jury by such means was a farce in itself. And the courtroom was in the open, with Larkin sitting at a card table before a saloon, with an empty rum bottle for a gavel. It would seem that most of the miners had taken the day off to attend the trial. Due to its late start, many of them were already drunk and boisterous; and it was all Larkin could do to keep them quiet.

A pale, sweating Riley sat next to Owen on the ground, since no chairs were provided. A miner sat next to him, with a pistol in his lap pointed at the artist.

Riley leaned over and whispered to Owen, "You're right, they're going to hang me, sure as hell! It's not right, Owen. This trial isn't legal in any sense of the word."

"I would have to agree with you there, Riley, but it's all the trial you're going to get."

"I could make a run for it."

"Don't be more of a fool than you've already been, Riley," Owen whispered back. "In this crowd you wouldn't even get started before they shot you down."

"Better than dangling from a rope." But Riley subsided, muttering to himself.

The only two witnesses called by the prosecution were the two miners who had heard the woman scream and rushed into the hut to find her dead, with Riley's hands still around her throat. No chairs were provided for the witnesses; they stood by Larkin's table while they testified.

Lieutenant Howard called John Riley to testify, in his own behalf, to what little he knew or could remember. When Riley related that the prostitute had stolen his money, a miner stood up in the crowd. "The man's right about Gladys," he shouted. "I was down at Angel's Camp some months ago. She was caught stealing a miner's poke and was run out of town!"

Voices in the crowd called out to the miner to shut up and sit down.

Larkin banged the rum bottle on the table. "Sit down, sir, and be quiet! What the dead woman did before she came here has nothing to do with this here trial!"

Owen and the man named Jed were called to testify that they had found Riley's money in the dead
woman's reticule. Lieutenant Howard testified to the
same effect.

There were no more witnesses for either side. The
giving of the testimony had taken less than an hour.

Behind Owen a man muttered, "Looks like we'll
get to see this gent hang before sundown."

At Owen's side Riley groaned and moved uneas-
ily. Owen grabbed the artist's knee in reassurance—
something he was far from feeling.

The ex-marshal made his address to the jury; his
remarks were few. "Gents, this man here killed
Gladys Riggens. He don't even bother to deny it.
And we do not deny that she was a soiled dove, a
fallen woman, but she *was* a woman. She was of the
weaker sex, unable to defend herself against a
liquored-up man! We all know how precious few are
those of the fair sex among us. As for this man's claim
of robbery, that is no excuse for his foul deed! John
Riley must be made an example of, to show that we
will not allow such things here. When you get together to decide, there is only one thing you *can* decide. John Riley committed murder, and he must
hang for his crime!"

There was some applause from the crowd at the
end of the short speech, and Larkin did not bother to
bang his bottle.

Lieutenant Howard spoke at length. "Gentlemen
of the jury, we have proven that this unfortunate
woman robbed the defendant, robbed him of every
cent he possessed! Should we tolerate such behavior
in Hangtown? I say no! If you find the defendant

guilty, we announce to the world that we condone thievery here in Hangtown.

"I must ask you to search within yourselves. What if you, any man present, found yourself in a similar situation? What if you had labored long and hard for your few ounces of dust, and a woman, whom you had already paid well for her services, tried to steal the results of your labor? Would you not have reacted in much the same manner? I put it to you that if you search your soul you will find it in your heart to forgive the defendant.

"I put it to you that this was a case of self-defense. While it is true that perhaps the defendant's life was not in danger, his purse was, and if we cannot defend our purse, we have come to a low estate.

"The man on trial for his life is one of us, one of *you*; not from foreign soil, but a true American.

"If you sentence this man to hang, the name of Hangtown will once more be on everybody's lips. The name of Hangtown will live in infamy. We shall never be able to adopt a respectable name. We shall never be looked upon with respect by the rest of the world.

"If you search your hearts and souls, gentlemen of the jury, I am confident that you will find the defendant not guilty!"

Justice of the Peace Larkin gave no instructions, as such, to the jury. He merely thumped the bottle on the table and said, "All right, gents. Take yourselves inside the Bottle and Keg and deliberate."

The Bottle and Keg, of course, was the saloon directly behind where Larkin sat; it had been cleared of customers earlier, so that it could be used by the jury.

Owen had to wonder if free access to all the liquor in the saloon would affect the jury's deliberations.

Lieutenant Howard wandered over toward Owen. Owen got up to meet him, drawing him out of earshot of John Riley. "That was a stirring speech, Lieutenant," Owen said sardonically. "Do you think it will have any effect?"

Howard shrugged. "There is no anticipating what will bear on the minds of the jurors, and I have the feeling that the minds of this jury might have been made up, their verdict already decided, before they were ever selected."

"And that verdict is?"

"Guilty, I'm afraid," Howard said dolefully, his gaze coming to rest on Riley, who sat on the ground, head down, shoulders hunched, as though already fending off an adverse verdict.

"I must tell you, Owen," Howard continued. "Those two soldiers I defended . . . I lost both cases, and neither charge was serious. Perhaps your friend would have been better served by someone else."

"Who? There are no practicing lawyers here that I know of. You gave him a better defense than he probably deserves." Owen clapped the lieutenant on the shoulder. "And thank you for your efforts. Riley probably won't."

The jurors were inside the saloon less than half an hour, but long enough, Owen concluded, to have helped themselves to free drinks.

When they returned, Larkin bellowed, "Bring the prisoner before the bench!"

The miner guarding Riley prodded the artist up before the justice of the peace with his pistol.

Larkin said, "Well, gents? Did you decide?"

One juror, a tall man with a long beard, said solemnly, "We have decided, Your Honor."

"Well, what did you decide?"

"We found the prisoner not guilty, Your Honor."

The crowd erupted with cheers and applause, and what had struck Owen as a hostile mob now turned into a group of enthusiastic well-wishers. They surrounded an unbelieving John Riley and hoisted him up on their shoulders, heading for the saloon.

A stunned Owen could only stare; five minutes ago he would have been willing to wager every penny he had that the artist would be found guilty.

An amused voice said, "As I said, there is no predicting how a jury will turn."

Owen looked around at Lieutenant Howard. "Can you explain it, Lieutenant? I would have sworn . . ."

Howard was nodding. "So would I. How to explain it? I expect there are several factors involved. The woman *was* a whore, and I think we proved that she stole from Riley."

"Even so, as we talked about earlier, she was a woman, and females are precious in the gold camps."

"I think two other factors entered into it. First, the people living here aren't too pleased about the name and reputation the town has. Another hanging would only have worsened the situation. And the other factor is Riley is not from foreign soil. The three men they hanged before, giving Hangtown its name, were all foreigners, you know. Also, one thing I said in my remarks may have struck home, about how they might do what Riley did, should a whore rob them." Howard smiled broadly. "Especially after they got inside and had a few drinks while they, quote, 'deliberated.'"

Owen was scarcely listening. A sentence that he had written to Jemina in his last letter kept ringing in his mind. *If Etta had been a man in the same situation, he would have paid the same penalty.*

"Well, I suppose I'm glad of the way it turned out," he said slowly. "As much as I think Riley's deed was reprehensible, I'm just as happy he didn't have to hang for it. Lieutenant, will you do me a favor? I'm leaving Hangtown today, and John Riley. Would you tell him that the rest of the money owed him will eventually be left with Miranda Kent in Coloma?"

IT WAS LATE AFTERNOON when Owen rode up before Miranda's store. He dismounted and tied off his horse, then went inside. Miranda was busy waiting on two miners, but she glanced his way, her face breaking into a wide smile. "Owen! I'm happy to see you. I'll be with you as soon as I finish waiting on these gents."

The two miners paid for their purchases and departed. Miranda immediately rushed into Owen's arms. She accepted his kiss and snuggled against him. After a moment, she took her mouth away and leaned back to gaze up into his eyes, her face luminous.

"I've missed you, Owen," she whispered.

"And I've missed you, Miranda."

"Damn you, Owen Thursday!" She broke free of his grasp. "I should never have admitted that to you!"

Smiling, he said, "Why not, my dear?"

"You know why not." She cocked her head at him. "Soon you'll be gone, gone for good, not just for a few days."

Owen had been thinking of how he was going to tell her that that time was here; he had already made up his mind to leave for Philadelphia as soon as possible.

"I didn't expect you back from Hangtown so soon."

"Something happened, Miranda." He told her about John Riley.

She shook her head in commiseration. "I won't bother saying I told you so; you already know how I feel about that man. John Riley should get down on his knees and thank God he got off so easy. But I suppose he headed for the nearest saloon instead?"

He nodded. "I'm afraid so. By the way, there will be some money coming to him from the *Ledger*. I left a message for him to pick it up here."

"Oh! That reminds me." She went around behind the counter. "A mail pouch came for you."

She gave him the pouch. Owen opened it and dumped the contents onto the counter. There were the usual copies of the *Ledger* and a letter from Thomas Carruthers, with two bank drafts enclosed. Nothing from Jemina.

His disappointment must have been mirrored on his face, for Miranda said, "No letter from her?"

Startled, he glanced up. "From her?"

"You think I don't know you're in love with someone back East?"

"In love might be a little strong, but there is a woman in Philadelphia, yes, and I've been expecting a letter from her."

"Wait a minute! What you said a moment ago just struck me. You said money will be coming from your newspaper for Riley, and he's to pick it up here. That means you're leaving, doesn't it?''

"I'm afraid so, Miranda. I'm fed up with Riley, but also I've mined most of the news I can here. It's time to move on to something new. I'll be leaving in the morning, as soon as I can buy an extra horse. I'm going home the quickest way this time, overland instead of by water.''

He was moved by the stricken expression that came over her face, and for a moment he feared that she might weep.

"Miranda, I'm sorry.'' He tried to take her hand. "Please don't cry. You knew this would happen sooner or later. When a story is over, I pack up and move on.''

She snatched her hand away. "I'm not going to cry! Not over the likes of you.'' She turned away to brush away a furtive tear.

"You're right, of course. I'm not worth wasting any tears over.''

"Don't speak so of yourself, Owen,'' she said crossly. "It ill becomes you.''

She moved past him toward the door, closing and bolting it.

"What are you doing?'' he asked.

"I'm closing up. What does it look like?''

He said tentatively, "I have no right to ask anything of you, Miranda.''

"I'm the one doing the asking. Who knows when a man I'd care to bed with will come along?'' She cocked her head at him. "Now, are you going to help me close the store? It seems to me that's the least you can do.''

BOOK IV

"Arguments for the right are never so
powerful in influencing the heart to love
goodness, as examples of right conduct.
True love is best comprehended by its effect
in producing happiness; therefore happy
love must be true love."

—*Godey's Lady's Book*

Chapter Eighteen

AN EARLY SUMMER had arrived in Philadelphia on Jemina's return. After the cooler weather of France and the ocean voyage, the heat was enervating; yet she was so pleased to be home that she endured the discomfort cheerfully enough.

The long voyage across the Atlantic had been a trial. Warren didn't really bother her, and yet his mere presence created a mood not conducive to writing. Not once did he allude to what had happened in Paris, but for that very reason it was difficult to have a conversation with him. Although he generally maintained a cheerful countenance in her presence, Jemina knew that he was far from happy, and in unguarded moments she glimpsed that sorrowful expression on his face. This caused her to feel guilty and at the same time irritated her. What did *she* have to feel guilty about?

Fortunately, there was no recurrence of the seasickness she had experienced on the voyage over, not even when they encountered a spot of rough weather. But, due to Warren's inhibiting presence and the fact that it was usually quite difficult to write on board a clipper ship unless one was becalmed, she accomplished very little in the way of work. Her articles were still unfinished when they reached New York Harbor.

Aunt Hester was delighted to welcome her home. After a hug and a kiss, Hester stood back and surveyed her judiciously. "Well, let me see how the woman of the world looks! I've heard tell a trip to Paris changes a person."

Embarrassed, Jemina said, "I certainly don't feel changed, Aunt Hester."

"Well, to listen to your parents, especially your father, they fear for your very soul. Henry seemed to think you would come back a wanton, a fallen woman," Hester said dryly. "They have bombarded me with weekly letters. And when they received no communication from you . . . well!"

"I was only gone a little over two months, for heaven's sake!" Jemina said in annoyance. "What use would it have been to write? Mail delivery takes so long between here and France. I'll write them tonight, Aunt Hester."

"You have some other mail, as well," Hester said with a sly look. "You have an admirer in California, it seems."

"They'll be from Owen Thursday," she said in an offhand manner. "He's a journalist I know who works on the *Philadelphia Ledger*. He's out in California reporting on the gold strike."

A few minutes later she was behind the closed door of her bedroom, tearing open the letters from Owen with trembling fingers, opening them in sequence, by date. The first two held nothing personal, just amusing comments about the trip to California and the goldfields.

The third and last letter had been written after he received the clipping about the death of Etta Logan.

Jemina read that letter quickly, then read it a second time more slowly.

She could not deny feeling a leap of gladness upon reading that Owen had missed her, yet the general tone of the letter was disappointing. She was intrigued with the further revelations about his father; however, she found his statement that he feared marriage because he was a bastard unconvincing. In fact, on the second reading, she was so annoyed by it that she started a letter to him, going so far as to write the first paragraph. Then she put her pen down and tore up the page. It would be better to wait a few days, until her mood was better, to write a response; she might write something that she would later regret. Anyway, she thought, there was no hurry, since he would evidently be in California for two more months or so. Since he didn't know about her trip to Paris, he might be wondering why she had not written to him. Well, let him wonder a while longer—it would be good for him!

ON THE DAY OF HER RETURN to the *Book*, Jemina was closeted with Sarah Hale for most of the morning. Sarah was avid for the latest news from Paris, including the rumors and gossip. She laughed inordinately when told the story of Bonaparte's mistress and her "effigies."

Finally, Sarah leaned back and studied Jemina critically. "Well, the trip appears to have been good for you, I must say. Your health seems to be much improved, as well as your spirits."

"Oh, yes!" Jemina nodded vigorously. "I really don't know what was wrong with me last winter. But

I am fine now and have regained my old enthusiasm."

"Excellent." Sarah's stare was keen. "And how did you and Warren get along together in Paris?"

Jemina felt her face burn and hoped she wasn't blushing. "Why, we got along just fine. In fact, I would not have enjoyed myself nearly so much had Warren not shown me Paris. He knows the city intimately." She laughed lightly. "Besides, who could not get along with Warren Barricone?"

"Who, indeed?" Sarah said in her dryest voice; but she seemed satisfied with the answer. "Now tell me about the pieces you have planned for the *Book*."

Jemina told the editor about her planned articles on Madame Roland and Marie Antoinette.

Sarah nodded approvingly. "They both sound excellent. You showed good judgment. The contrast between the two women should interest our readers greatly."

"Well, I cannot take all the credit for that. It was actually Madame Blanc's suggestion."

"Do not be modest, Jemina. Any author worth her salt is not averse to accepting suggestions. The ability to judge whether or not the suggestion is good is the true test. How far along are you on the articles?"

"Not as far as I would like. I had hoped to finish them on board ship, but I have learned that it is not that easy to write on a sailing vessel. But I can have the piece on fashions ready for publication within two days at the most. I thought you would want that quickly so that our readers can learn what is fashionable this autumn."

Sarah was nodding. "That one must receive priority, of course. The others can be published later.

By the way, your article on Betsy Ross came out while you were gone and received much acclaim. A great deal of mail was generated by it, and even Louis unbent enough to speak a kind word about the article *and* you." She smiled briefly. "I would even venture to say that its reception was good enough to place you in his good graces again. He has evidently forgiven you for the Etta Logan incident."

Jemina felt herself tighten up inside. She still resented that episode, and Owen's letter had only heightened her resentment. On the other hand, now that time had distanced the incident, she could understand the publisher's position, so she kept quiet.

Sarah continued, "In respect to the Betsy Ross story and its reception by our readers, I have in mind to continue the series about important American women, but going beyond women of Philadelphia history. There are a number who were not covered in the earlier stories. Abigail Adams, for example. And there are others. We can select the appropriate ones later. You do this sort of thing very well, Jemina, so I was wondering if you would undertake the project for us?"

Jemina experienced a pulse of rebellion. She much preferred writing about living people; such pieces, it seemed to her, had more immediacy.

Evidently, something of her displeasure must have been revealed, for Sarah said quickly, "Not that you cannot do a fine job on contemporary women, but we do like to pursue a sense of history in the *Book*, and it is difficult to find an author with just the right feel for it."

"Oh, I would be happy to do the articles, Sarah," Jemina said. After all, Sarah *was* her employer. "I was just thinking about the unfinished work I have on hand.''

"Go ahead and finish what you have started, by all means, my dear. There is no rush on the new project.''

"Well, with all that before me, I suppose I had better get back to work." Jemina got to her feet, prepared to leave.

"By the way," Sarah said casually, "have you heard from Owen?''

"As a matter of fact, I have. There were three letters waiting for me on my return.''

"Three letters? Good heavens, I *am* surprised! You should feel flattered.''

"I suppose it all depends on the viewpoint," Jemina said in a tight voice.

"Owen is an excellent journalist, don't you agree?''

"Everyone says so. Actually, I haven't read much of his writing. Just the one piece about . . .''

Sarah interrupted her. "He has been sending back some colorful material from the goldfields, which the *Ledger* published in your absence.''

"I should read them.''

"I saved them for you, Jemina." Sarah was looking at her quizzically. "I thought perhaps you might wish to read them.''

"Why, thank you, Sarah. I will when I have the time.''

Jemina was thankful to make good her escape, wondering why Sarah had been so insistent about bringing up Owen.

A short way down the hall she remembered something and came to a full stop.

In the excitement of being back, she had completely forgotten about her planned articles on the disgraceful conditions of the garment workers in New York; she hadn't even remembered to ask Sarah what she had thought of the letter she had written to her from New York on the eve of her departure for France.

She turned and started back toward Sarah's office, then stopped again. It was obvious now that Sarah had deliberately avoided discussing the matter. When Jemina had started to mention reading Owen's piece about Lester Gilroy, the editor had interrupted her. That could mean only one thing—Sarah was not in favor of the project. Or else she had discussed it with Louis Godey and the publisher had vetoed it.

Jemina realized that this would not be a good time to bring up the subject with Sarah, especially if Sarah was purposely avoiding it. Her determination to do the pieces had not diminished in the slightest; but it would have to wait until she had finished the articles on Madame Roland and Marie Antoinette and the new subjects Sarah had assigned to her. When that work was done, or at least most of it, she would approach Sarah about the article on the garment workers.

WHEN WARREN RETURNED to Philadelphia, it was to find that Alice's condition had deteriorated during his absence, and an enormous guilt and depression descended upon him. Her cough had worsened and she was occasionally coughing up blood.

"I should not have gone to France and left you," he said in a voice quivering with remorse. "I should have remained by your side."

Alice smiled wanly and reached out with thin fingers to touch his cheek. "My darling, we agreed not to talk that way. I wanted you to go. You deserve time away from a sickbed and a sick wife. Besides—" she brightened "—I was fine up until a week or so ago. You know that I always feel much worse in summer, and this summer is worse than most. And what could you have done, had you been here? I was well taken care of. Now please, Warren, don't agonize so. I only feel worse when you blame yourself."

He tried to put on a more cheerful face. "Well, at least I am back now."

"And I am glad to have you back, dear Warren. Now, tell me all about Paris and the new dresses for this season."

She listened with much interest as he told her about Paris. He tried to keep Jemina in the background as much as possible, at the same time attempting to keep Jemina out of his thoughts, as well; but he felt it incumbent upon him to mention her in passing. There was always a chance, however slight, that Alice might learn of Jemina's presence in Paris and that they had been seen together.

"This girl, Jemina Benedict," Alice commented. "I don't believe you have mentioned her before."

"Haven't I? You must remember that I escorted her to one of Sarah's soirees."

"Is she nice?" Alice's gaze was intent.

"Nice?" He made a startled sound. "Well, yes, I suppose she's nice. She's certainly a talented author. Sarah thinks highly of her."

"I hope you showed her around Paris."

"Well, yes," he said cautiously. "When I could spare the time. I was quite busy, you know."

"Do you remember that week we were in Paris?" she said wistfully. "We had such a wonderful time!"

"I remember very well. I shall never forget it." He got to his feet. "And now I'll fetch your supper."

"Warren . . ." She caught his hand in a tight grip. "I want you to promise me something."

"Of course, dear. Anything within my power."

"When I am gone, I don't want you to grieve too long. You deserve a good life, with a healthy wife, someone nice, like this Jemina Benedict."

"Ah, don't, Alice!" Warren felt his heart wrench. "Don't talk like that!"

"Why not?" she said, looking at him without flinching. "It's time to face the truth. I'm not getting any better. Promise me, darling, please!"

"All right, Alice," he said gently. "I promise."

She let her breath go with a huge sigh and sank back onto the pillows, her eyes fluttering closed.

He said anxiously, "Are you all right, Alice?"

Her eyes opened slowly. "I'm fine, darling. I just feel suddenly exhausted, as though I've been running. That is something I've been wanting to say for a long time."

"Perhaps some good hot food will perk you up," he said with false cheer.

"Perhaps," she murmured.

As he went into the kitchen, Warren felt like a traitor. He had lied to her by omission, and he had felt a fierce leap of joy when Alice made him promise to consider marrying again—to someone like Jemina. Warren had often been astonished at how easily Alice could read his mind; now he felt something like awe. How could she know that Jemina was in his thoughts almost constantly?

As he prepared Alice's tray, he toyed with the thought of telling Jemina that Alice had, in effect, made him promise that he would marry again after her death and that she had mentioned Jemina as a possible spouse. Then he dismissed the idea. There was no way of prejudging how Jemina would react to such a disclosure. Better to wait until...

He stopped, appalled, a fresh wave of guilt washing over him. He was acting as if Alice was already dead!

He finished arranging the tray and hastened down the hall with it, fixing a cheerful smile upon his face.

WITH SARAH'S permission, Jemina had not been into the office for three days. She had argued that she could work better at home; with her aunt out all day, there were no interruptions. She had finished the final draft of the Marie Antoinette article, which Sarah thought should be published first.

"Then, when we publish the Madame Roland story," the editor had said, "the reader will be better able to grasp the contrast between the two women."

The first person Jemina encountered when she entered the offices of the magazine was Warren.

"Hello, Warren. I haven't seen you since we returned from Paris."

He nodded somberly. "My wife... Alice was feeling poorly on my return. I have been spending some time with her, but I had to come in today to work on the fashions for the September issue."

"Oh, Warren, I am sorry!" Instinctively, she reached out to touch his cheek. But actually all she could think of was what had happened in Paris—what had *almost* happened—and she knew that she would have felt terrible now if she had allowed Warren to make love to her. "I hope she is feeling better now."

"She does seem to have improved." He smiled palely. "I'm not sure if my return has anything to do with that."

"I'm sure it has a lot to do with it, Warren. You underestimate yourself."

He got a strange look on his face, opened his mouth as though to speak, then closed it again.

Jemina said, "I must run, Warren. Sarah is expecting me."

"Yes, I have a busy day before me, as well. Perhaps in a day or so, we could have . . ." He made a dismissive gesture. "Never mind."

He turned on his heel and strode away, leaving Jemina staring after him in puzzlement. He was acting strangely; and yet, the Warren she had seen in Paris was not the Warren she thought she knew. Did anyone, she wondered, ever really know another person? She felt compassion and a surge of affection for him and almost called after him. But to what purpose?

With a shrug she knocked on Sarah's door and entered at the editor's bidding.

"I finished the Marie Antoinette article, Sarah." She placed the manuscript on the desk.

"Excellent!"

"I'll leave you to read it. . . ."

"No, Jemina, why don't you stay while I read it? Unless it bothers you to be present," Sarah said with a faint smile.

"No, not at all." Jemina sat down and tried to compose herself. In truth, it did bother her to be there while Sarah read her material.

Sarah read a page and glanced up with a smile. "Such beautiful penmanship, my dear. Such a pleasure to read. You should see some of the manuscripts that come across my desk. It is like threading a maze of hedgerows, with thorns. But of course you have seen some of them, haven't you?"

"Yes, Sarah, I have. They are difficult to decipher sometimes, I agree."

Sarah resumed reading. A fast reader, she was soon finished. She shuffled the manuscript, arranging the pages neatly, then looked at Jemina with a nod. "Excellent craftsmanship, Jemina. Just what I have come to expect from you. However, I do have a few quibbles."

Having worked with the editor long enough now, Jemina had expected no less. "I hope it's nothing I can't fix."

"Of course you can, my dear. My chief objection is my usual one. You must cultivate more objectivity. Generally, you have done so here, but in a few instances you have allowed your dislike of the woman to show."

"In many ways, Sarah, she was not a very nice woman."

"Naturally. But show it in the writing, not in author intrusion. I very well know that most of our authors allow their prejudices to show in their work, but I am laboring to overcome that. It shows in my own work, as well, as I'm sure you are astute enough to observe." Sarah smiled wryly. "Unfortunately, I am too old and likely too set in my ways to change very much; but just the opposite is true with you, Jemina. You are just beginning. Heretofore, I have said little in this regard, wishing to wait until you had settled in.

But from this time forward, I am going to be a little more critical.'' She motioned. ''Come around to this side of the desk and allow me to be more specific.''

Jemina did as she was asked and Sarah picked up her pen.

Jemina worked on the article for the rest of the day, following Sarah's suggestions. Most of the staff had already gone for the day, including Sarah, by the time Jemina had the piece done to her satisfaction. She left the finished manuscript on Sarah's desk and went home.

The day was blistering hot, and Jemina was longing for a long, cool bath by the time she reached the apartment. She knew that Aunt Hester would already be home, yet she was surprised to hear voices coming from the flat as she paused in the foyer to get her key from her reticule.

As she entered the small parlor, she saw Aunt Hester and a man sitting side by side on the divan.

Hester turned a beaming face toward her. ''Look, Jemina! You have company!''

Jemina stopped short in astonishment as Owen Thursday got up and inclined his head in her direction. He said quietly, ''Hello, Jemina.''

Chapter Nineteen

JEMINA WAS CAUGHT unaware by the wave of relief and happiness that seized her at the sight of Owen. It left her light-headed and dizzy. It took tremendous effort not to rush headlong into his arms. Struggling to keep her voice calm, she said brightly, "Owen, this is a surprise! I thought you would remain in California through most of the summer."

His gaze was fixed upon her face. "So did I, but circumstances changed my mind. Besides, I came to the conclusion that I had just about written out the gold strike. How are you, Jemina?"

Jemina nervously began to pull off her gloves. "I am just fine, thank you."

"Your aunt tells me that you have only recently returned from Paris. That must have been a pleasant experience for you."

"Yes, it was."

Hester said brightly, "Well, I have things to do. I'll leave you young people alone."

"No, don't go, Aunt Hester!"

"Nonsense, child. I have very much enjoyed chatting with the young man, but I'm sure he didn't come here to see an old woman like me."

Hester left the room. Jemina stared after her in dismay, avoiding Owen's gaze.

"Afraid to be alone with me, Jemina?" Owen asked softly.

Reluctantly, she turned back to face him. "Of course not!"

"There's no need to be, you know. Did you get my letters? All three?"

"Yes, they were waiting for me when I returned from Europe."

"Then you know how much I missed you. What you don't know is what happened after I posted the last letter; something that caused me to change... well, if not my mind, at least my attitude toward Etta Logan. I'd like to tell you about it, but not across the room like this. Come, sit down." With his cane he motioned to the divan.

After a moment's hesitation Jemina crossed the room to take a seat on the divan. Owen sat down beside her, with a decorous distance between them, and told her about John Riley.

At the end of his tale, he said, "So you see, although I still think that Etta should have paid for her crime, I can now better understand your attitude. For, you see, I also think that John Riley should have paid for *his* crime. I well remember writing you that had Etta been a man, he would have paid. Although the parallel is not quite the same, it is certainly close enough so that I can finally see your viewpoint."

He paused, looking at her expectantly, and Jemina said, "What do you expect me to say, Owen? It's a little late for Etta."

"Jemina..." He spread his hands. "Even if I had agreed to help with Etta at the time, nothing I could have done would have changed the outcome. Surely you can see that?"

With some reluctance she said, "Yes, I suppose you are right."

He sighed. "Thank God that is settled. Now...may I invite you to supper? I know you haven't dined, just having come home from work, and neither have I."

"Oh, I can't, Owen! I need a bath and..."

"So? I'll wait," he said with a shrug.

"But Aunt Hester is preparing supper right this minute."

"No, she isn't. I've already told her you and I would be dining out."

"I see you haven't changed all that much," she said with a flash of temper. "Going around making unwarranted assumptions."

He was grinning lazily. "Did you really expect me to change?" He became serious. "My dear Jemina, we haven't seen each other in half a year. What's wrong with dining together?"

"No harm, I suppose." She studied him closely. "Just as friends?"

"But of course, just as friends," he said innocently.

"Because if you think you can just come back into my life and..." She felt herself flushing under his gaze and jumped up. "All right! But it will be a while before I'm ready."

He leaned back, crossing one elegant leg over the other. "Take all the time you need. I am in no hurry. I have been doing nothing but hurry these past weeks. I think I may have set some sort of record from California to Philadelphia. I braved storms, thirst, hunger, savage Indians and wore out two horses getting here."

She felt herself melting toward him. "All that for me, Owen?"

"What other reason could there be?"

Flustered, she started away, then turned back. "I will hurry as much as I can. Would you like something to drink while you're waiting? I don't think we have anything stronger than port."

"Port will be fine, thank you."

Jemina found her aunt in the short hallway just outside the parlor, and she had the suspicion that the older woman had been eavesdropping.

"I'm going out to supper with Mr. Thursday."

"I know," Hester said with a broad smile.

"I must bathe and change clothes. Will you serve him a bottle of port?" She added tartly, "Or did you already overhear that?"

Hester drew back, offended. "I would not do that!"

"Aunt Hester, I'm sorry!" Jemina threw her arms around her aunt and hugged her fiercely. "He behaved like a cad, and I shouldn't be happy he's back, but I am!"

Hester patted her back. "Jemina, all men behave like cads at times." She stood back. "Now, go and perform your toilet and I'll entertain your young man in your absence. If I was only thirty years younger..." Hester rolled her eyes comically.

Laughing, Jemina hastened back to her bedroom. The washbasin was already filled with hot water. Bless Aunt Hester!

She got undressed and washed. She debated for a few moments before choosing what dress to wear. She had brought back two complete outfits from Paris, but both were fall fashions. She chose one anyway, with a blithe disregard for the weather. It was a silk dress of soft green, bedecked with colorful ribbons, and she chose one of her stylish new hats to wear with it.

Finally she stood before the pier glass, turning this way and that. Satisfied that she looked her best, she gave a mocking curtsy to her image and went down the hall to the parlor.

Hester and Owen were at ease with each other, chatting away like fast friends. As Jemina entered the parlor, Owen had just finished telling a story and Hester was doubled over with laughter.

Owen saw Jemina, and his eyes widened. He got to his feet and made a graceful bow. "My dear Jemina, you are a vision, truly a vision in green."

"I hope I didn't take too long?"

"Not too long at all," he said gallantly. "And it has been well worth the wait."

He crossed the room to give Jemina his arm. Back over his shoulder, he said, "I was delighted to make your acquaintance, dear Hester. You are such a charming woman, I can easily see why Jemina has not seen fit to introduce us before this."

To Jemina's amazement her aunt actually blushed. "It was my pleasure, sir, and I am looking forward to seeing you again."

Outside, as they waited to hail a passing hackney, Jemina murmured, "I do believe you have made a conquest in Aunt Hester."

"I wasn't playing her false. Your aunt is a charming lady."

An empty hackney clattered down the street, and Owen lifted his cane to hail it.

He took her to dinner in a French restaurant—to her knowledge the only one in the city.

"I thought you might be homesick for Paris," he said with a flashing grin. "I know I was, after my one brief trip there."

The restaurant was crowded, and people were waiting for tables. With Jemina on his arm, Owen walked confidently through the crowd to the maître d'. "I don't have a reservation, André," he said in a low voice.

Jemina saw Owen extend his hand, and the light glittered off a gold coin.

The maître d' accepted the offered coin deftly and said, loud enough for those waiting to hear, "Your table is waiting, Mr. Thursday."

As they were escorted to a table halfway across the room, heads turned and conversation lapsed. The men eyed Jemina with open admiration, and the women with scarcely concealed envy. She felt light-headed to be again on Owen's arm, the cynosure of all eyes, and about to dine in a fine restaurant.

The menus were printed in French. "How is your French, Jemina?" Owen asked.

"I have a poor grasp of the language. I learned only a few phrases while I was in France."

"Well, let's see how good you are. Suppose you order for us?"

She was dubious. "Are you willing to risk it? There's no telling what you may end up eating."

"Food is of little consequence on this night," he said with an airy wave of his hand, his gaze intent on her face. "You alone are a feast for the eyes."

She laughed uncertainly. "California has done wonders for you, Owen. You are full of compliments tonight."

"Tonight you are most deserving of compliments, my dear."

Flushed, she hid her face behind the large menu and consulted it. She settled for what she thought was the safest choice and ordered fresh prawns for an appetizer, a clear soup and filet of beef with fresh vegetables.

When the waiter came, she gave the order, stumbling over a French word or two; and then Owen ordered a bottle of the best French champagne.

Jemina sat tensely waiting while it was poured, wondering what toast he would propose this time.

He raised his glass. "Here's to the reunion of old and dear friends."

"I suppose I can't object to that." After the toast was drunk, she said, "Tell me about California, Owen. From what I gleaned from your letters, it must have been very interesting. Sarah saved me the copies of the *Ledger* with your pieces, but I haven't gotten around to reading them yet."

All through dinner he regaled her with tales of what he had seen and experienced. He was at his wittiest, and she laughed through most of the meal.

As they ate their dessert—fresh berries in heavy cream—she said wistfully, "It all sounds so interesting. How I wish I could have been there to share it with you."

He was shaking his head. "You wouldn't have enjoyed it, Jemina. The conditions are miserable, the food is poor and the few hotels are expensive and poor in quality. And ninety percent of the women are strumpets."

"I'm not all that delicate, Owen," she retorted. "It may take time, but someday there will be women field correspondents."

He smiled tolerantly. "I much doubt that either of us will live to see that day. Perhaps when the country is more civilized. Most women would not even dream of taking on such an assignment."

"I am not most women! You should know that by now."

"Oh, I know that. How well I know that! In fact, I have decided that is your greatest charm, my dear."

His remark left her at a loss for words, and then they were out of the restaurant and in a hired carriage. As the carriage got underway, Owen turned to her and said diffidently, "I know I promised that tonight was just an engagement between old friends, but I was wondering . . . Do you wish to go directly home, or would you like to stop off at my apartment first?"

Perhaps he *had* changed for the better, she mused; the old Owen would never have shown such hesitancy.

To her surprise, she heard herself saying, "I suppose I could stop there for a short while. Sarah has given me some new assignments, more stories on women who figured prominently in American history. I could make use of your library."

He did not try to kiss her but simply took her hand and pressed it gently. Jemina felt the old familiar weakness steal over her, and she knew that she was lost.

Owen rapped on the roof of the carriage with his cane, and when the driver peered down at them, he changed their destination.

Leaning back, Owen said, "You're welcome to use my library anytime. You may work there as you did before, if you like."

"What will your next assignment be, Owen?"

"I haven't the least idea. I may not even have a job." In the light of a passing street lamp Jemina saw that he was smiling slightly. "I came back on my own initiative, and I haven't even seen Carruthers yet. I just returned last night, and I slept most of today. When he learns that I *am* back, without authorization from him, he may boot me off the paper."

"But surely you're too valuable to be discharged?"

He laughed. "Jemina, in time you will learn that journalists are never too valuable. At least, not in the opinion of editors and publishers. But I'm not unduly concerned. I can always find employment. I've often thought of trying for a job on Horace Greeley's paper."

"In New York?"

"Yes, but in case you're worried," he said with a soft laugh, "I doubt that Carruthers will discharge me. I've done this before, and he roars and grumbles, but it's soon forgotten."

The carriage drew up before Owen's building. As he helped her out and paid the driver, Jemina looked at the downstairs apartment. There were no lights showing, and the curtains were drawn across the windows.

Turning away from the driver, Owen noted the direction of her glance. He said, "It's standing empty, I believe. At least, I've seen no signs of life."

Jemina hugged herself, despite the heat of the night; in her imagination the ghost of Etta Logan lingered inside the downstairs apartment. "What will happen to the building now?"

He shrugged. "I have no idea. It's my understanding that Etta had no kin. I suppose it will revert to the state and in the end will be sold."

He gave her his arm, and they mounted the stoop. As they went inside, her glance went to the closed door.

"It has crossed my mind to buy the place."

"Don't, Owen!" She shivered. "I know there are no such things as ghosts, but in my mind Etta's place will always be haunted."

He squeezed her hand. "I never really considered it seriously. I have no use for property. Who would take care of it during my long absences?"

Although Jemina was happy to be back in the familiar surroundings, she couldn't help but notice that the rooms had a stale, musty smell.

Owen grunted. "The place needs airing. I was in and out so quickly last night I only opened the bedroom window."

He quickly made the rounds, opening all the windows to let in fresh air. When he came back, she was still standing in the middle of the room where he had left her. He lit a lamp on the mantelpiece and crossed to her.

"You know, Jemina, something strange happened to me last night." He tipped her face up to his with his fingers under her chin. "When I walked in here, I felt a loneliness I've never experienced before. I've always considered myself a self-contained man, perfectly content to be alone. You've changed all that. Now..." His smile was lopsided. "Now the loneliness is gone, with you here."

A warmth spread through her, and a trembling set up deep inside. With a teasing smile, she said, "No woman in California, then?"

His gaze did not waver. "I will not lie to you. There was one woman, yes."

"Was she pretty?" Jemina asked despite herself.

"Yes, quite pretty, but not nearly as pretty as you. And she was *not* you, my dear." His voice was husky with a powerful emotion.

He swept her into his arms then, and she did not resist when his mouth descended on hers. Hunger fed on hunger, and all else was blotted from Jemina's mind. Somehow, they were in the bedroom, tearing at restricting clothes.

They tumbled onto the bed, locked together, and then they were one; and Jemina knew again the ecstasy she had missed so desperately over the long months.

The storm passed, leaving them spent and happy. Jemina's head was cradled on Owen's shoulder while he caressed her hair in long, tender strokes.

He said quietly, "Riding across the country, I reached a decision, Jemina. I want to marry you."

Her breath caught, and then she lay silent, her thoughts racing.

"Jemina? Did you hear me?"

"Yes, Owen, I heard you." Her voice was muted. "This is rather sudden, isn't it?"

"Is it? As I recall, we talked of it before I left for California."

"I know, but I'm not sure that I'm ready for marriage."

"But you said . . ."

"I never said I wanted to get married right away. I said I probably would want to at some time in the future, and then where would I be, since you seemed so set against it?"

"Damnation!" He sat up, dumping her head off his shoulder. "You are the most aggravating woman!"

She laughed softly. "You haven't really changed, have you, my love? Now that you've suddenly decided you're ready to get married, you think I should agree without a quibble."

"You don't seem to realize how much soul-searching I went through to reach that decision." His voice was tight with anger.

"I think I do.... Owen, don't let's quarrel about it. There are a great many problems to work out."

"I am well aware of the problems, but I'm willing to take a chance on their working out."

"Even if our son should someday find out that his father is a bastard?"

"I've thought long and hard about that, and I finally decided that if I came to terms with it, so can any child we have."

She was quiet for a bit, before she said, "We don't have to make a decision this minute, do we?"

"I suppose not," he said dourly.

"Owen, do you love me?"

"Damn it, of course I love you!"

"You have never told me, not in so many words."

"I didn't think I had to tell you."

Unbidden, the thought of Warren Barricone intruded into her mind. She vividly recalled that evening in Paris and his heartfelt declaration of love—no hesitation, no holding back.

EARLY THE NEXT morning Owen strolled unannounced into Thomas Carruthers's office, carrying several manuscript pages under his arm.

At the sound of his footsteps on the hard floor, Carruthers glanced up, squinting through a thick cloud of cigar smoke. He reared back. "Thursday! What in the name of all that's holy are you doing here? You're supposed to be in California."

Owen perched on the corner of the editor's desk. "I decided it was time to come home."

"*You* decided! How many times do I have to tell you that I'm the one to tell you when an assignment is over?"

"It's over, Thomas, believe me. I have reported every aspect of the goldfields. Here are four more dispatches I brought back with me, since I knew I would arrive before the post would." He placed the manuscript pages on the desk.

Carruthers scowled down at them, poking at them with a thick forefinger. "That may all be true, but someday you're going to go too far, Thursday. It's a good thing I'm in a good mood, or I would discharge you."

"In a good mood? You!" Owen threw his hands up. "When that day comes, grass will grow on a snowbank."

Carruthers ignored the comment, blowing smoke. "Well, I suppose it's just as well you came back now."

Owen stared at him suspiciously. "And why is that?"

"You're probably right, our readers may be getting sated with stories about the gold camps. And there's a story developing here that I need you for."

"Here? In Philadelphia?"

"Well, not exactly here, but in this part of the country. I don't suppose you heard about a caucus of sixty-nine Southern members of Congress held back in December last year, shortly after you left?"

"News is slow in reaching California, and I don't recall reading about it in any of the issues of the *Ledger* you sent along."

"I probably didn't send it."

"What was the purpose of the caucus?"

"There is legislation being proposed to prohibit slave trade in the District of Columbia. The spokesman for the caucus was Senator John C. Calhoun. Calhoun made much of what he called 'acts of aggression' by the North against Southern rights, such matters as the exclusion of slaveholding territories, impediments to the return of fugitive slaves to their masters and the like."

"And what was the result of this caucus?"

"Not a great deal. They held two more in January of this year, but in the end only forty members signed the protest statement."

Owen shrugged. "The usual windiness of politicians."

Carruthers shook his head. "There, I disagree. There may have been little more than wind expended this time, but I think it could turn out to be an ill wind for the country."

"How do you figure that?"

Carruthers leaned back, looking solemn. "The slavery issue is becoming serious, Thursday. In my estimation it is going to split the country asunder, perhaps even bringing about a war between North and South."

Owen stared. "Isn't that a rather drastic view, Thomas?"

"I don't happen to think so, and others agree with me. You're away much of the time, and don't keep up with what is taking place back here."

"That's true enough," Owen said slowly. "But a civil war? I find that hard to believe."

"I hope you're right, but I am convinced it's going to happen," Carruthers said glumly. "It may be five, ten years before it happens, but eventually some hot-blood is going to do something drastic, and it will explode. When it does, it will be a sorry day for the country. And we, here in Pennsylvania, will be in the thick of it. Do you realize that we border on Maryland and are not far from Virginia, both slaveholding states? Any war will likely be fought, in part, in our own state."

Owen was sobered by Carruthers's comments. Although he might often disagree with the editor, Owen had learned to respect his sense of current events. "Conceding that you are right, what do you have in mind for me?"

"Two things, Thursday. First, the Underground Railroad that is used to smuggle slaves out of the South and often up into Canada. It is very active in Pennsylvania. I want you to dig around, see what you can learn about it."

Owen arched an eyebrow. "But if we publish the story on the Underground Railroad, won't it cause trouble for the people operating it?"

"Oh, I have no intention of publishing any names or anything that will give anyone away. I just want the general story."

Owen grinned. "Why, Thomas! I didn't think you would let such scruples interfere with a good story. For that matter, I wasn't aware that you had *any* scruples."

"I am as opposed to slavery as any Northerner, Thursday," Carruthers growled. "I just want a piece on the Underground Railroad as a background for the other material I want from you."

"Which is?"

"The second thing I want is a feel of how people are thinking in the South. Take a few weeks or so, however long it takes, and journey through the South. Talk to slave owners, plantation owners and slaves, as well. Find out how deep the animosity toward the abolitionists runs. But I would advise you not to reveal yourself as a newspaper correspondent. Pose as someone else. If it's found out that you're a journalist with a Northern newspaper, your life could be in danger."

"Oh, now I really think you're exaggerating, Thomas! I've been through the South, and I've known a great many Southerners. They're not a violent people. They're warm, friendly, very hospitable."

"In general, that's true. But there are always a few hotheads, and it only takes one to blow your head off. I don't think you fully realize how deeply the slaveholders feel about this issue."

"Well, you needn't worry." Owen stood up. "If nothing else, I have learned how to protect myself, and I've been in a few tight spots. I'm very protective of my hide."

IN OWEN'S APARTMENT Jemina was humming happily to herself as she worked on her Madame Roland article; to her surprise she had discovered new material on the woman in two of Owen's books. After the passionate reunion last night she had every reason to be happy. Owen really loved her! And she found it hard to believe that he had gone so far as to propose marriage.

She stopped writing as footsteps clattered on the stairs. It was Owen coming home. Getting up from his writing desk, she took a quick look at herself in the glass above the fireplace, patted a few stray hairs into place, tugged here and there at her clothing and was waiting with a smile on her face as he came in. He was carrying a bottle of wine by the neck and was also smiling broadly.

"Well!" Jemina said. "I assume you're still employed, by the look of you."

"Not only that, but I already have a new assignment."

She felt a lurch of dismay. "Oh, no! You're not off again!"

"This one is closer to home, my love. Not in Philadelphia, but I will only be away a few weeks at a time." He held up the bottle. "I brought some wine home to celebrate. While we drink it, I'll tell you all about it."

He went into the kitchen and came back with two wineglasses. He poured the wine, and while they sat side by side on the divan, he told her about his new assignment.

Jemina said, "You know, when I was up near Allentown, doing the research for my articles on farm wives, the wife of the family I was staying with talked of the Underground Railroad. One town involved is Quakertown, not far from where they lived.''

Owen nodded. ''Yes, I know. That's one place I'll go.''

''I should think they would be reluctant to discuss it, fearing disclosure might disrupt their operation.''

''It's not going to be that easy, but then, the best assignments never are. I'll just have to be circumspect about my nosing around. And no names will be published, no one identified. Carruthers gave me his word on that. He wants the articles to show both sides of the question, that of the slaveholders and that of the abolitionists.''

''It all sounds very exciting,'' Jemina said, faintly wistful. ''Much more exciting than writing about dead people. . . .''

She broke off as Owen got up to light the lamp on the mantelpiece; it had gotten dark while he talked. ''Good heavens!'' she exclaimed. ''I didn't realize it was so late. Aunt Hester is expecting me home. If I stay out late again, I don't know what she will think.''

Owen crossed to her quickly as she got to her feet. ''I think your aunt has more understanding than you give her credit for. You don't have to go just yet.''

He folded her into his arms, and at the first touch of his lips on hers any resistance she might have mustered melted away. He led her into the dark bedroom; and soon they were together in love, breast to breast, thigh to thigh.

After their lovemaking, they lay close together in the warm darkness, in companionable silence.

Jemina was the first to speak. ''Your new assignment, the issue of slavery, reminds me of a project that I have in mind. Do you remember the garment manufacturer, Lester Gilroy?''

''Very well indeed!'' Owen said with a chuckle. ''I'm proud to think that my article was instrumental in sending him out of Philadelphia.''

''Well, by the strangest coincidence, I ran into him in New York while I was waiting to sail to France.''

She felt him go tense. ''You did? I hope he didn't recognize you. It's my feeling he can be a very dangerous enemy.''

''Oh, I didn't actually meet him face-to-face, but I did see him.'' She told him then about her experience in New York and the woman garment worker she talked with at length.

''You know, Owen, what she told me is appalling. The conditions those poor women and children work under is terrible.''

''Yes, Gilroy is a proper bastard, right enough.''

''Well, something should be done about men like him. I understand from what Marigold told me that other garment makers are just as bad.''

''That is probably true.'' A note of amusement crept into his voice. ''Do I detect the start of another Jemina Benedict crusade, my dear?''

''I think these slop shops should be exposed to the public, and I fully intend to write a series of articles about it!'' She rose up, staring at the smile on his face. ''What it comes down to is that these poor garment workers are suffering a form of slavery! They're trapped in a cycle from which they can never escape.''

''I cannot argue with that. But these pieces you intend to write, what do you intend to do with them?''

''Why, publish them, of course.''

"Where?"

"In the *Lady's Book*."

Owen laughed shortly. "Jemina, you're dreaming! The *Book* won't touch such a subject."

"But the *Ledger* is publishing your article about slavery, which is a much more controversial subject."

"The *Ledger* is a newspaper. *Godey's Lady's Book* is a magazine, and you should know by now that Louis Godey, in general, avoids controversy. Have you noticed the *Lady's Book* taking a position on slavery, pro or con? No, and Godey never will, not even if we come to the civil war that Thomas Carruthers predicts. The *Lady's Book* has both abolitionists and slave owners as readers, and to take sides would offend one or the other."

"I know from what I've read that Sarah did battle with the garment makers in Boston while she was the editor of the *Ladies' Magazine* there. I'm sure she will sympathize with the workers' plight."

"She may very well sympathize, but that will be the extent of it. She will never sway Louis Godey."

"I am going to try, anyway."

"Oh, I'm sure you will," he said, laughing. "I've learned that once that mind of yours is made up, nothing will dissuade you. You know what you are, my dear Jemina?" He pulled her against him. "You are a female Don Quixote, a tilter at windmills."

"Is that bad?"

"In some respects, perhaps not. On the other hand, it could get you into trouble, perhaps even place you in jeopardy. Especially with this Gilroy man. I have the feeling that he could be as dangerous as a poisonous snake, should you step on his tail."

"He wouldn't harm a woman, Owen!"

"I wouldn't be too sure about that. You told me that he threw his employee bodily out of his shop, and she is a woman, isn't she?"

Jemina was thinking about something else and responded absently, "He didn't actually do harm to her."

"But he might, if provoked enough."

"This new assignment of yours, Owen...when are you going?"

"I'm leaving for Quakertown early in the morning."

"May I continue to use your apartment to work in while you're away?"

"Use it and welcome. In fact, it will comfort me to know that you're here while I'm away. And since I *am* going to be away for ten days or more, we must make up for my absence now." He pulled her close.

Laughing, she protested, "Owen, I must get home."

Her protests were soon smothered under his kisses.

DURING THE NEXT WEEK, Jemina worked harder than she had at any time during her stint on the *Lady's Book*. She had determined her future course of action, and she wished to finish the articles on Madame Roland and Abigail Adams. Fortunately, Owen had ample material in his library for the piece on Abigail Adams.

She finished the Madame Roland article in three days and then began the Adams piece: "Abigail Adams was a great lady, certainly most fitted to be the wife of one of our greatest presidents, John Adams, who, as our readers are well aware, was one of the framers of the Declaration of Independence and one of the document's signers...."

BY FRIDAY of the first week of Owen's absence, she had the final draft done to her satisfaction. Carrying the manuscripts under her arm, she knocked on Sarah's door early in the morning.

When Sarah called out, Jemina entered the office, then stopped short just inside the door. Sarah wasn't alone; a woman sat across the desk from her. The woman faced around, and Jemina recognized her.

"Miss Blackwell!" she exclaimed.

"It is now Dr. Blackwell," Sarah said with obvious pride. "The first woman in the United States to receive a medical degree. Not only that, Elizabeth graduated at the top of her class."

Jemina advanced into the room. "Congratulations, Dr. Blackwell."

"Thank you, Miss Benedict." Dr. Blackwell inclined her head graciously and looked across the desk at Sarah. "But without Sarah's generous help I doubt that it would ever have happened. I shall be eternally grateful." She looked back at Jemina. "Also, I wish to thank you for your article, Miss Benedict. It was beautifully written, striking just the right tone."

Jemina flushed slightly. "I'm happy you liked it. Are you going to set up a practice here in Philadelphia?"

The doctor's face fell. "I fear not. I need two or three years of medical experience in a hospital, but no hospital in this country will accept me. I have no alternative but to go to Paris, where they do accept women. I am sailing next week, but I wanted to come to Philadelphia to say farewell to people I know, most especially Sarah.''

A sudden thought came to Jemina. She said excitedly, ''I know someone here, in Philadelphia, who I am sure would be most happy to have you examine her.''

Dr. Blackwell shook her head. ''I am afraid that I could not do that, Miss Benedict. I lack experience, and I have yet to treat my first patient.''

''But this is a woman, and you said that one reason you became a doctor was that your dying friend said she would have been much happier to have been examined and treated by a woman doctor.'' Jemina looked over at Sarah. ''I'm thinking of Warren's wife. Other doctors haven't been able to help her. They don't even know what is wrong with her.''

Sarah's look was penetrating; then she nodded slowly. ''It certainly cannot do any harm, Elizabeth. The poor woman is in a bad way, I understand. As I am always telling Jemina...'' She smiled briefly. ''You will at least come to her with a fresh viewpoint.''

''Well, I suppose it cannot do any real harm,'' Dr. Blackwell said uncertainly. ''So long as everyone understands that I may not be able to offer any hope.''

Jemina said, ''Come along. Her husband works on the *Book*. I will introduce you to him.''

She led Dr. Blackwell out of Sarah's office. It wasn't until she was in the hall that Jemina realized she had forgotten to discuss the manuscripts she carried under her arm. Well, the matter before her was more urgent.

Warren was alone in his office. Jemina knocked on the open door. ''Warren, I would like you to meet

Elizabeth Blackwell. *Doctor* Blackwell,'' she said meaningfully. ''She is willing to examine your wife, if you have no objections.''

Chapter Twenty

IT WAS NOT DIFFICULT to persuade Warren to allow Dr. Blackwell to examine his ailing wife. "I am willing to seize on any chance," he said. "Any chance at all!"

"So long as it is understood that I may be able to do nothing," Dr. Blackwell said.

"I understand." Warren's glance went to Jemina. "Please come along, Jemina. I'm sure Sarah won't mind. Alice would very much like to meet you."

Jemina wavered. She had keyed herself up for the confrontation with Sarah, but she had let that moment slip by; and she *was* curious about Alice Barricone.

After informing Sarah of what they were going to do and receiving her blessing, Warren, Dr. Blackwell and Jemina caught a hackney on Chestnut Street and rode out to the Barricone residence. On the way Dr. Blackwell questioned Warren closely about his wife's illness, and he answered as best he could.

Dr. Blackwell asked the hackney driver to detour by the hotel where she was staying. She went into the hotel and was back within a short time with a small black bag. Getting into the hackney, she said, "My instruments. This will be my first real opportunity to use them."

As Warren ushered Jemina and Dr. Blackwell into his house, a middle-aged woman came from the back.

"Why, Mr. Barricone, whatever are you doing at home in the middle of the day? Is anything the matter?"

"No, Mrs. Wright. This is Jemina Benedict and Dr. Blackwell. Dr. Blackwell is going to examine Alice."

The woman's heavy eyebrows rose. "A woman doctor, is it? Well, I never!"

Warren led Jemina and the doctor down the hall to a back bedroom. A thin, once-pretty woman was sitting up in bed, reading; Jemina was pleased to note that she was reading *Godey's Lady's Book*. The woman's hair was a drab brown, and she had huge brown eyes, sunken into a face so gaunt that the bones seemed about to pierce the flesh.

"Alice," Warren said, "I'd like you to meet Jemina Benedict. I've told you about her."

"Oh, yes," Alice Barricone said with a sweet smile. "I have read your stories in the *Lady's Book*, Miss Benedict. You are a fine writer."

"Why, thank you, Mrs. Barricone."

Warren said, "And this is Dr. Elizabeth Blackwell. She is here to see if she can help you."

Alice frowned. "Warren, I thought we had agreed, no more doctors?" Then she blinked in astonishment. "A *woman* doctor? I didn't know there were any."

Dr. Blackwell smiled. "I'm the first, Mrs. Barricone."

Alice started to speak, then was suddenly taken with a spasm of coughing. She turned her face aside, a white handkerchief held to her mouth, until the coughing eased. She started to hide the handkerchief, but Dr. Blackwell was too quick for her; the doctor caught her hand and took the handkerchief away.

As the doctor studied the piece of white cloth, Jemina saw a splash of bright red and realized that it was blood.

Dr. Blackwell made no comment; instead, she opened her bag and took out a few items. One Jemina recognized as a wooden stethoscope, an instrument she knew had been recently developed to enable doctors to listen to the heart and lungs.

Dr. Blackwell started to unbutton Alice's blouse, then paused to look around. "Would you leave us, please? I prefer privacy when I examine a patient."

As Jemina left the room with Warren, she heard the woman on the bed say brightly, "I have never been examined by a woman before. It should be far less embarrassing...."

In the hall Warren said, "It's about time for lunch, Jemina. Are you hungry? Mrs. Wright can fix us something."

A short time later they were seated across from each other in the small dining room, with glasses of cold lemonade, thick slices of ham and a potato salad.

Gazing down at his plate, Warren said, "I wish to thank you for your thoughtfulness, Jemina. I don't know if Dr. Blackwell can help Alice at all, but at least it is a chance."

Jemina smiled uncertainly. "Well, Warren, I thought it was worth a try. As you have told me, the other doctors certainly have been able to do little."

"And I am glad that what happened between us in Paris went no further than it did." He looked up now, his eyes mournful. "If it had, I doubt that I could live with myself now. But I also want you to know that I love you still. . . ."

"Warren, please!" she said, dismayed. "Don't speak so!"

He plowed on. "When I returned and told Alice about your being in Paris with me and what a nice, talented person you are, she extracted a promise from me. I know this isn't the time or the place, but I must tell you. She made me promise that if anything happened to her, I would get married again, to someone like you."

"Warren, this conversation is distressing," Jemina said in a low voice, fearful that Mrs. Wright would overhear.

"You are right, of course. It is wrong of me." He lowered his gaze to his plate again. "But I simply had to tell you."

They ate in awkward silence now. Jemina was tempted to get up and leave—she could not remember when she had been so uncomfortable—but she had no wish to hurt Warren. She was saved the decision by Dr. Blackwell's appearance; the doctor seemed unduly grave.

"Well, doctor?" Warren said eagerly.

"Your wife is very sick, Mr. Barricone." Dr. Blackwell sat down at the table with a sigh. "How long has she been coughing up blood?"

"To the best of my knowledge, not too long. Within the past two weeks. Unless she has been hiding it from me, which she is perfectly capable of doing."

"Yes, two weeks is what she told me." Dr. Blackwell shook her head, sighing again. "There is so terribly much we don't know about illness. And the

medical profession is almost totally ignorant of diseases of the lung. Your wife has some form of lung
disease; that is clearly evident. Her lungs are badly
congested, and blood in the sputum is a bad symp-
tom. Some medical research is being done in the
field, finally, but we still know so little.

"It is known that miners working long hours in the
dampness of the bowels of the earth often get lung
disease, but others, like your wife, also contract some
form of it. A wet climate, even a humid climate, is
also known to aggravate the condition, if not bring it
on."

Warren looked stricken. "There is nothing you can
do, then?"

"There is no medication presently known to medical science that can help her. The medication she is
already taking is as good as any, since we are at a loss
as to the precise nature of her ailment."

Warren sat with his head lowered, his shoulders
slumped in dejection.

"There is one thing, Mr. Barricone. I have read in
medical literature that some doctors are recommending a change in climate in such cases, and the results
have been encouraging. At least, it appears to slow
the onslaught of the disease."

Warren's head came up. "A change of climate?
I'm not sure I understand."

"Along the eastern half of the United States, the
climate is very wet in winter and humid in summer.
This causes the lungs to work unduly. The patients I
have read about were advised to live in dry places, hot
areas that lack the humidity. The New Mexico and
Arizona territories, for example. In what they call the
high desert."

Jemina gasped. "But that is all the way across the country!"

"That would mean I would have to give up my position with the *Lady's Book*, our home and everything," Warren said. "I certainly couldn't send Alice off alone."

Dr. Blackwell inclined her head. "I fully realize that, Mr. Barricone. It would involve a great many sacrifices on your part. On the other hand, if your wife remains here, there is no hope. She cannot live much longer."

"I just don't know. This is so sudden." Warren shot a quick look at Jemina. "It gives me a lot to think about."

Dr. Blackwell stood up. "I am sorry, Mr. Barricone, but I did warn you that I might not be able to help. You have my deepest sympathy. Now, you must excuse me. I am leaving Philadelphia in the morning, and I have much to do."

Jemina also got to her feet. "I will go with you, doctor." Turning to Warren she said, "Why don't you stay home for the rest of the day? I'm sure Sarah will understand."

Warren simply nodded without looking at her. But as they started out of the dining room, he said, "I apologize for my manners, Dr. Blackwell. In the shock I forgot myself. I wish to thank you for coming. And what do I owe you?"

"You owe me nothing, Mr. Barricone," she said with a wave of her hand. "I am not officially practicing medicine yet."

In the hackney they were finally able to hail, Dr. Blackwell said heavily, "I feel so inadequate, so helpless. I feel that I have somehow failed that poor woman and her husband.''

Jemina placed her hand on the doctor's arm. ''I don't think you should feel you have failed. I should think the fault, if any, lies with medicine.''

''Perhaps so, but I am a representative of the medical profession, and unfortunately people look to us for miracles. My instructors at Geneva College said over and over that we are on the threshold of tremendous breakthroughs in medicine, that eventually we will be able to cure most diseases. I can't help but think about how many people will die needlessly before that great day arrives. I asked one instructor when he thought that day would finally come, and he said perhaps in a hundred years.'' She laughed bitterly. ''A hundred years! Dear God!''

''At least now that you have succeeded in becoming a doctor, you have a chance to do some good.''

''Hopefully that is true. But that is why I must have some hospital experience and why I must go to Paris.''

''Have you been there before?''

''No, only to England. I was born there, you know.''

''I only recently returned from Paris.''

Until they reached the hotel where Dr. Blackwell was staying, Jemina regaled her with the wonders of Paris.

As she got out before her hotel, Dr. Blackwell said, ''I wish to thank you, Jemina, for your strong support.''

''Write me in detail of your hospital experiences in Paris, when you have the time. Perhaps I can gather enough material for an article, which in the end might possibly open the way for other women to gain hospital experience in this country."

"I shall certainly do so."

The next morning Jemina, full of new resolve, once again knocked on Sarah's door, the completed manuscripts under her arm.

But before she could speak, Sarah immediately got onto another subject, as if she sensed what Jemina had on her mind. "What happened with Elizabeth and Warren's wife yesterday? I suppose Warren came into work this morning, but I have been quite busy."

Jemina told her in detail what had taken place.

Sarah looked distressed. "Poor Warren! And his poor wife. We would hate to lose Warren; he is very valuable to us. But I suppose he must do what he thinks best."

"I really don't know what he is considering. He said he would have to think it over."

"Sad, sad! Well." Sarah gave her head a hard shake. "You have a manuscript for me, Jemina?"

"I have two. Madame Roland and Abigail Adams." Jemina placed the pages on the desk.

"Well, that was quick, I must say."

"I had a reason. I worked long hours to finish them." Jemina sat back, looking at Sarah intently. "Sarah, do you recall the letter I sent to you just before I left New York for Paris? You *did* get it?"

Sarah sighed, folding her hands on the desk. "Yes, my dear, I received the letter."

"You haven't mentioned it since I returned, so I wasn't sure."

"I did not mention it, hoping that you might have changed your mind once your passion had cooled.

But of course I knew that the chances of that occurring were poor, very poor indeed.''

"Sarah, this is an evil that should be exposed. It *must* be exposed. I can get employment in one of Lester Gilroy's factories and gather the material for a number of articles.''

"I fully agree that it is evil, I fully agree that it should be exposed to public scrutiny, but the *Lady's Book* is not the place to do it, Jemina.''

"Why not?''

Sarah shook her head, her expression showing her exasperation. "Jemina, we have been over all this! The *Lady's Book* is a family publication. More specifically, it is a book for women. The pieces you are proposing are sensational and controversial. We do not deal in sensation and controversy. We have discussed this again and again! Our readers would cancel their subscriptions by the thousands.''

"Did you ever consider that by publishing stronger material, instead of all these sweet and light stories, you might gain new readers?''

Sarah's brows knitted in a dark scowl. "I have made excuses for your youth and inexperience before, Jemina,'' she said severely. "But my patience is stretching quite thin. Louis Godey and I have been in the publishing business for a good many years, and I believe we have a good grasp of the sort of material our readers demand.''

"You told me that you were hoping for more realism in the *Book*!'' Jemina cried.

"What I am looking for is more objectivity from my authors, not realism as such. And certainly not sordid pieces, which is what you are proposing.''

"I have been doing some research since returning from Paris, and I found that the *Ledger*, Owen's paper here in Philadelphia, published something about garment manufacturers as far back as 1836. I can quote one paragraph verbatim. 'A common stock, the material of which costs about twenty-five cents, and for making which a female receives about as much more, is sold by a merchant tailor for three dollars, or a five-hundred percent advance.' The article went on to state that those who employed female labor are deriving from it immense fortunes."

"The *Ledger* is a newspaper, and we publish a magazine," Sarah pointed out. "The *Ledger*'s readers are not our readers, Jemina."

"Also, I have learned that you, as editor of the *Ladies' Magazine* in Boston, fought the shoddy practices of the garment makers there, the 'slop shops,' as they were called. And you won the fight!"

"You have been doing thorough research, I see," Sarah said with a wintry smile. "And what you say is quite true. I did not, however, use the *Ladies' Magazine* as a forum from which to conduct my fight. All of my activity in that regard was conducted outside of the magazine."

Jemina slumped back in her chair, defeated. "Then nothing I can say will change your mind?"

"Nothing, my dear Jemina. As much as I sympathize with your compassion for the downtrodden, your fire and zeal, I would offer you a word of caution. Leave the authorship of this sort of material to the men. It is the sort of journalism they revel in and do so well. It is not a field of endeavor for women. Certainly not now, and I seriously doubt that it ever will be."

Jemina leaned forward, catching fire again. "But that is wrong! Women should have the opportunity, at least. This from you, Sarah, who have always advocated freedom of opportunity for women."

Sarah was shaking her head. "You have misread me, I fear. I do not advocate the right of women to be granted the opportunity to deal with sordid, sensational matters. That is for the likes of Elizabeth Cady Stanton and her forthright support of equality for women. I have never shared their views. In my opinion, such strong advocacy lessens a woman's femininity. I penned an editorial not too long ago, citing the influence that *Godey's Lady's Book* has had on public opinion as regards woman's sphere."

Sarah frowned severely. "Along with my advice, I would like to add a word of caution. Since the Etta Logan episode, you are on sufferance with Mr. Godey. If one word of what you have in mind reaches Louis, nothing I can do or say will save you from being severed from the *Book*."

Jemina's thoughts were bitter. Owen had been right once again, as much as it galled her to have to admit it. Yet, if Sarah would agree to let her write the articles, Jemina was convinced there was a good chance, if she did a good job, that the editor would do battle with Mr. Godey over publishing them. But Jemina now realized that Sarah would never agree to her undertaking such an assignment.

Sarah was speaking again, Jemina realized with a start. She said, "I beg your pardon?"

"I said that I trust we have heard the last of this matter."

"Yes, Sarah," Jemina said dully.

"Excellent!" Sarah picked up the manuscripts. "I am looking forward to reading these."

Jemina got up and started for the door.

"Jemina?"

She stopped to turn back.

"I know exactly how you feel, and I am sorry. As you grow older and wiser, you will realize that life is filled with disappointments, large and small. We must accept it as God's will and bear up."

Jemina's anger began to build again as she left the office, and her mind was occupied with what she intended doing, what she realized she had been subconsciously considering all along.

So preoccupied was she that she collided with someone coming down the corridor and might have fallen if she had not been caught by a pair of strong hands.

"Jemina, I am sorry," Warren Barricone said. "I almost knocked you down."

"It was my fault, Warren. I'm afraid I wasn't looking where I was going."

He stared at her gravely. "I was just going to Mr. Godey's office. Last night, Alice and I talked it all out, and I have made a decision."

Jemina tried to show some interest. "What decision is that, Warren?"

"I am going to follow Dr. Blackwell's advice. I am resigning my position here and taking Alice to New Mexico. We have some money saved. Not a great amount, but enough to start a small newspaper in whichever town we finally settle. It may not help Alice, but I feel honor bound to take the chance that it will."

"Oh, I feel sure that it will, Warren." She smiled at him. "But we shall all miss you."

"Will you miss me, Jemina?"

"Of course, Warren," she said, realizing with a pang how much she meant it.

"I know that I shall miss you. I shall never forget you, Jemina. We will keep in touch?"

"Naturally. Write to me when you get settled, and we will correspond regularly. I will be very much interested in how matters go with you and how your wife fares."

Warren seemed on the point of saying something else. Then he shook his head slightly and said merely, "I'll not say goodbye now, since it will be several days yet before I leave."

WHEN HESTER got home from work, she found Jemina packing a traveling bag.

"Where are you going, Jemina?"

"I'm going to New York, on a new assignment for the *Book*," Jemina lied, looking her aunt directly in the eye, praying that the older woman would not question her.

Hester smiled. "You certainly are becoming a well-traveled woman, Jemina. Here, let me help you. You never were very good at packing to travel."

Chapter Twenty-One

NEW YORK WAS VITAL and full of life; Jemina felt a charge of energy just being there. She took a hotel room the first night in the city.

She needed some advice and help if she was to carry out her plan. She had Marigold Tyler's address, and after supper that evening she took a horse-car to Marigold's lodging house. Jemina could only hope that the woman was still living there.

The address was located in a district of lodging houses, within walking distance of Hester Street. The building was in sorry condition; the inside stank of years of cooking, and there were various other odors that Jemina didn't care to identify. It was dark and gloomy, and Jemina's confidence began to ebb as she made her way down the dreary hall.

Marigold's room was on the third floor, and Jemina had to feel her way carefully up the dark stairs, stumbling once and falling to her knees. It took considerable courage for her to get to her feet and continue.

At last, after what seemed an interminable time, she found the door she was seeking. She had to knock twice before she heard dragging footsteps beyond the door; then the door was cracked open to reveal the tired face of Marigold Tyler. She peered at Jemina without recognition. In the room behind her, a child began to wail.

"Mrs. Tyler?" Jemina said urgently. "Do you remember me, Jemina Benedict?"

"Who?" Then the woman's haggard face brightened. "Oh, yes! You are the lady who was so nice to me when Mr. Gilroy threw me out of his shop."

"May I come in?"

Marigold hesitated briefly, then stepped back, holding the door open, and Jemina entered. There was only one room, furnished with scraps and pieces of furniture. A small, coal-burning stove, serving both for heating and for cooking, stood in one corner. There was one bed, with two small forms on it. As Jemina glanced at it, a small, tousled head raised up and frightened eyes peeped at her.

Marigold gestured helplessly. "I am sorry for the mess, but I just got home from work a bit ago, and one of the wee ones is ailing again."

"Don't apologize, for heaven's sake. I don't know how you manage at all." Privately, Jemina was appalled at the squalor and the meanness of the lodgings. The room was begrimed with the dirt of years. It would be impossible to keep clean, even if one had time and money to spend on it.

Marigold cleared some clothes from a hard chair and motioned for Jemina to sit down. "I have a pot of tea, if you would like some, Miss Benedict. It's poor stuff, very weak, but the best I can afford."

"Call me Jemina, please, Marigold. And I would like some tea, thank you."

A few minutes later they sat facing each other, each with a cup of tea, which was weak indeed.

Jemina said, "You say you are working? Not for Lester Gilroy, surely?"

Marigold shook her head. "Oh, no. But the man I am working for is near as bad. The piecework wages are the same, but at least our overseer is not so mean as Bert Conroe."

Jemina took a sip of tea. "Marigold, may I depend on you to keep in confidence what I am about to tell you?"

"Of course, Miss . . . Jemina. Nobody has been as nice to me as you were, not ever."

"I believe that I told you I am a journalist. Well, I am here to help you. Oh, perhaps not right away, but I intend to write a number of articles exposing the terrible conditions garment workers suffer. When they are published, I am confident there will be such a hue and cry that the public will demand that changes be made."

Marigold was staring at her dubiously, and Jemina rushed on, "But to accomplish my purpose, I need your trust and your help."

Marigold looked confused. "I would be happy to help, but what can *I* do?"

"First, I need to have a few sewing lessons." Jemina smiled. "I learned some sewing at home, but nothing that would enable me to hold down a job as a garment worker for however long it takes to gather my material."

Horror dawned on the other woman's face. "You are not thinking of becoming a seamstress! A fine lady such as yourself?"

"There you can help me, as well. You can teach me things I must know, so that I may be no different from the rest of you." Jemina had considered her options carefully. She could probably write her articles through interviews with women and children working in the task shops; but to really get down to the bone, to paint the vivid word pictures she desired, she had to live and work among them. Besides, she had to admit to herself that there was an excitement about the prospect that she had never experienced before. Now she could more readily understand the satisfaction Owen received as a field correspondent.

She continued, "When I ask Lester Gilroy for a job, I want him to look upon me as just another unfortunate woman like yourself, Marigold."

"Mr. Gilroy?" Marigold shrank back in shock. "No, Jemina, no, I pray you! That man is dangerous. If he learns what you are up to, he might do anything. Others along Hester Street might not like it should they find out what you're doing, but they wouldn't be as likely to harm you."

"Oh, I think it unlikely that he would do me any physical harm. Besides, I don't intend for him to find out. I'll just be another garment worker to him. And hopefully I will only be there two weeks at the most."

Marigold was staring at Jemina's clothes. "He would never take you for a seamstress, dressed in such fine clothes."

"Naturally, I won't be wearing these clothes. I shall depend on you to show me how to dress so I'll go unnoticed." She leaned forward. "So, will you help me, Marigold? I know your time is limited, but if you can spare me a few evenings and perhaps a Sunday... I don't expect to become a good enough seamstress to earn my livelihood, just good enough so that I can get by for a time. Oh...and I don't expect you to do this for nothing. I shall pay for your time, and well."

At the mention of money, Marigold's face lit up. "Could I have money now so that I can get a doctor for little Molly?"

"Of course." Jemina opened her reticule and handed Marigold some money, which the other woman accepted unashamedly.

"Oh, thank you, Jemina! Your coming here like this tonight is a godsend. I don't know how to thank you."

Jemina smiled and patted the other woman's hand. "You can thank me by helping me as I asked. Now, I am staying at a hotel for tonight, but I must have a place like this for the duration of my stay. Do you know if there is a vacancy here?"

"Yes, there is an empty room right next to mine. It rents for a dollar a week. But are you sure you want to stay *here*? It's such a poor place for a fine lady such as yourself."

"Marigold, you must stop thinking of me as a 'fine lady,' " Jemina said with an edge to her voice. "For the next three weeks, at least, I am one of you, and you must think of me as such. If I cannot practice such a deception successfully, I have failed before I even get started."

JEMINA RENTED A ROOM next to Marigold's and moved in. She did not make the mistake of approaching the owner of the building as a 'fine lady'; it would certainly arouse suspicion. With Marigold's help she bought two changes of clothing at a second-hand shop—cheap garments, worn and patched, such as the garment workers habitually wore.

The room she rented was indeed sorry. It was sparsely furnished, with a most uncomfortable bed, and was infested with cockroaches and fleas. There was only one small window, which provided very little ventilation, and the room was as hot as an oven even when the window was open.

The first night she occupied the room she didn't sleep at all; it was stifling, and she constantly imagined things crawling on her. She almost gave up the project the next morning—at least the role she was girding herself to play. Then she thought of the thousands of women and children who not only lived in such quarters but worked twelve or more hours a day under conditions much worse. If they could endure such hardships day after day, surely she could bear up for two or three weeks. If she gave up now, Jemina knew that she would have to live with her failure for the rest of her life.

She spent the days during the next week with Marigold's children, watching over them while their mother was at work. Jemina had offered to pay Marigold to stay home during the week, for more than she would earn at work; but the other woman was horrified at the suggestion.

"If I do not show up for work for a week, I will lose my job," she had said. "Then what would I do when you are gone, Jemina?"

So Marigold continued to go to work each day, and Jemina grew acquainted with her two children. Robert was the older one at seven—named after his father, Marigold had said with shy pride—and Molly was five. Jemina's money had paid for several doctor's visits, and the little girl was well now; but both children were undernourished and pale from being indoors so much. Jemina took them out during the day, let them play in the nearby park and bought them treats. She became quite fond of them and thought with despair of what would happen to them later in life. If they survived childhood, would they eventually end up working in a garment factory like their mother?

There was not much she could do to help them. When she left New York she could give Marigold some more money, but that would ease their problems only temporarily. The best thing she could do for them was to write such scorching articles that the public's sense of decency would be outraged and an uproar would be raised, demanding that the garment workers be paid a decent wage and be provided with better working conditions. If that happened, the futures of Robert and Molly might be less bleak.

Being with children every day caused Jemina's thoughts to turn to motherhood. She had never given much thought to bearing children; naturally, she expected to have a family in the future, yet there had never been any immediacy to her feelings. Now she discovered within herself a wellspring of love for children, heretofore unsuspected.

This thought, of course, led to the next logical question. What were Owen's thoughts concerning children? He had mentioned his fear that any son of his might someday learn his father was a bastard, but that was the extent of it.

Jemina spent the evenings in Marigold's room. They shared meals together, with Jemina purchasing the food—food that was superior to what the Tyler family was accustomed to. Then, after the children were put to bed, Marigold gave Jemina sewing lessons, showing her how to make the shirts that Lester Gilroy produced.

Jemina soon discovered it was tedious, difficult work, much different from repairing a ripped garment or replacing a button. Her fingers quickly became sore and stiff, pricked many times by the needles. Yet she kept at it; and since she was a quick learner she became, if not a skilled seamstress, at least a capable one before the week was out.

Finally, both women decided that Jemina was as ready as she ever would be; and on the Monday morning of her second week in New York, she set out to seek employment in Lester Gilroy's establishment. Despite her brave reassurances to Marigold—and to herself—she was frightened. Could she carry off the masquerade? Was there a chance that Gilroy would recognize her?

Fortunately, she did not have to confront Gilroy—he wasn't in the task shop when she arrived. Instead, Jemina found herself facing Bert Conroe. Conroe was a short, burly man with unkempt sideburns, a hacking cough and a perpetual scowl.

It was only a little after six in the morning and the women were already bent over their sewing tables, their fingers flying nimbly. The air was close and stifling in the room, and Jemina felt herself beginning to perspire. She wondered if she would be able to endure these conditions for the time it took her to gather her material.

Stiffening her resolve, she said, "Kind sir, I am seeking employment. I badly need a job."

Conroe studied her for a moment in silence, his brown eyes shrewd. With Marigold's help Jemina had made herself as unattractive as possible. Her hair was completely covered with a scarf, and the shabby dress she wore was voluminous enough to conceal the lines of her figure. Marigold had warned her that Conroe always hovered around the comelier girls, fondling and pinching them—an indignity the girls had to suffer or risk getting discharged.

Finally, Conroe spoke, his voice rough. "You had any experience making men's shirts, girl?"

"No, sir," Jemina said timidly. Marigold had explained to her that Gilroy liked to hire women inexperienced in the trade. That way, he could pay an even lower price for each shirt; and if a new employee's production wasn't up to standard, he could easily get rid of her. "But I learned sewing from my mother back in Boston."

"Well, this ain't sewing for your mother," Conroe said, coughing into her face. "It's hard work, girl, and if we find you ain't good enough, you're out in the street within the week. We have no room for idlers here."

"I'm a hard worker, sir," Jemina said, putting a pleading note in her voice, although she longed to lash out at this ruffian. "I do need the work. Please, sir."

"You understand that we pay piecework here. If you don't produce the work, you don't earn much." He coughed. "For a learner we pay ten cents the shirt."

Jemina felt rage boil up inside her. She knew that Conroe was taking advantage of what he thought to be her inexperience; the going rate in even the worst task shops was twenty-five cents a shirt, which was certainly poor pay enough. She tried to keep her feelings from showing.

"Is that satisfactory, girl?"

Jemina swallowed bile. "Yes, sir."

"What's your name?"

"Ida Morgan, sir."

"All right, Ida. We just happen to have an empty table. Did you bring your scissors and thimble?"

"No, sir. I didn't know . . ."

"All our seamstresses are supposed to supply their own," he said in a grumbling voice. "I can probably dig some up for you, but you have to pay for them out of your wages. So, come along, Ida."

He led her over to an empty table. Jemina had to squeeze in between two other women who were working, elbow to elbow, at the next table. None of the women in the room had raised their heads to look at Jemina since she had entered the shop. The narrow chair assigned to her was hard, and the laddered back was straight as a ruler.

In a moment Conroe returned with a stack of shirt goods already cut to a pattern. Along with that he had a pair of scissors, a thimble and two needles and thread.

"We furnish the needles, Ida, but if you break one it comes out of your pay. All you have to do is sew the shirts together. Someone else sews on the buttons."

It was only after Conroe had gone away that one of the women spoke to her, the one on Jemina's left. She spoke without looking up from her work or turning her head. "The reason they don't make us supply our own needles is because theirs break so easily."

Jemina glanced over at her. The woman was middle-aged, with a weary, sagging face, but her slender fingers wielded the needle and thread deftly.

"Don't look at me, dearie," the woman said in the same low voice. "Should Bully Conroe see you, he'll likely throw you out before you get started. The rule here is look at your work, nowhere else. He don't mind talking so much, long as it don't interfere with the work. You'll soon get the hang of it, so you can talk and sew at the same time. My name's May Carter."

"I'm Ida Morgan." Jemina had picked up needle and thread, beginning work on a shirt.

"Well, I'm sorry for you, Ida, having to come to work in such a pesthole as this one."

"How long have you worked here?"

"Two years now."

Tentatively, Jemina began making stitches in the shirt. "If it's so bad, why do you work here, then?"

"That's a silly question, dearie." The woman's flying fingers never paused—she pushed the needle through, made a stitch, then pushed it through again. "I have a bedridden husband to support."

"I mean, why here, if it's so terrible? There are a great many other task shops."

"Most around here pay straight wages, by the week or the day. I like piecework. I'm the fastest shirt maker on Hester Street," May Carter said with a coloring of pride. "Gilroy knows this, so he pays me ten cents more the shirt than any others here. He knows I'd go to work for another shop, without the extra. It's only them that can't make very many shirts a day that are in a bad way in a piecework shop. Sure, this place is a pesthole, but the other shops ain't all that much better.

"And since Gilroy don't want to lose me, Bully Conroe don't bother me. You have to watch out for Bully. The pretty ones he likes to get his hands on."

"I shouldn't think that would increase production very much."

May laughed softly. "He only does it when Gilroy ain't around."

"Gilroy? That's the owner?"

"Lester Gilroy, yes. He's got several task shops along the street, and he comes and goes. He don't bother us much, unless he thinks a woman ain't doing enough work to suit him. Then he's apt to throw you out arse over teakettle. Mean ones, both him and Bully."

Jemina had used all the thread in one needle and started to rethread it.

"No, we don't waste time doing that, dearie." May raised her voice. "Billy, needle!"

In a moment a boy not much more than seven or eight was at Jemina's table. He was thin as a rail, and he had enormous blue eyes in a pale, gaunt face. He picked up the needle Jemina had placed down and adroitly threaded it.

After he left Jemina said, "Poor little tyke. He looks half-starved."

May shrugged indifferently. "Probably is. Better that than full starved. At least working here the lad earns enough to live, if barely. Otherwise, he would be found dead in some doorway one fine morning."

Jemina looked furtively around the shop. "What happens when a person has to relieve herself?"

"There is a privy in the alley out back."

"I haven't seen a soul leave their worktable since I sat down."

"They don't dare ask Bully for permission," May said with a short laugh. "They wait until it's time for lunch."

"But that's terrible!" Jemina exclaimed. "That must be hard, especially on the older women."

"It is. Seamstresses ruin their kidneys."

They fell silent then, as Jemina digested this bit of information, wondering if she could include it in her articles. It took her an hour to finish the shirt, and she noticed that May had completed two in that time.

She finally put the shirt aside with a sigh. "One finished, finally."

She started to sort out the pieces for the next shirt, when May spoke, "No, Ida. You'll have to call Bully over to inspect it before you start another. You may have to do that one over."

Jemina called, "Mr. Conroe, I've finished a shirt."

Conroe ambled over. "It's high time." He picked up the shirt, tugged at the sleeves and the sides and finally grunted. He said grudgingly, "I reckon it will do. But you'd better pick up the pace, girl, or you won't earn enough by day's end to pay for the scissors and thimble."

After he wandered off, Jemina said, "I notice he didn't inspect any of your shirts, May."

"No need to. He knows it's a waste of time to try to tear out my stitches."

Jemina's fingers soon pained her from needle pricks, and her back and legs ached from sitting so long and bending over the table. The only light came in through the narrow basement windows, and it was so dim that it was difficult to see. Her eyes became dry and burning, and more than once her vision blurred.

As the day moved toward noon, the heat grew almost unbearable, even with the two windows open. Tiny pieces of the shirting material floated in the still air, getting into her eyes and nose and sifting down her neck and under her clothing, setting up an itch. Along with the other discomforts, no one could escape the odors generated by the perspiring bodies of twenty people in such close quarters.

Perspiration formed on Jemina's forehead and ran down into her eyes, obscuring her vision. She pricked a finger and muttered in exasperation.

In an aside to May, she asked, "Can't they provide more light to sew by?"

"Lamp oil costs money, dearie. Bully says if you can't see to sew by the light God provides, you should do something else for a living. Oh, on dark, winter days he'll light a lamp or two."

"I should think that sewing day after day in this light would harm a person's eyesight."

"It does, dearie. That's what happened to the woman who had your table. Her eyes got so bad she could no longer see to use a needle."

"What will happen to her?"

"Poorhouse, I'd reckon," May said with a shrug. "If she can find one to take her."

Before Jemina could respond, a cowbell rang. With a start she glanced around and saw Bert Conroe ringing the bell. She said, "Is there a fire?"

"No." May straightened up from the table. "Time for the noon meal. We're allowed twenty minutes."

"Where do you eat?"

"We all bring something. We don't have the money for restaurants. Did you bring a lunch?"

"No, I didn't think of it. I couldn't eat anyway, not after all this heat and the smells." She saw the other seamstresses getting up. "Surely you don't eat in here?"

May laughed. "On warm days such as this we usually eat on the steps outside. Wintertime, we eat in here. As for the heat and the smell, you'll get used to all that in time."

Jemina noticed that most of the women were going out back, where they formed a line to use the privy. Jemina and May decided to wait until the rush was over and went outside to the front steps. As Jemina sat down beside May, she noticed Bert Conroe heading up the street.

"Where is Mr. Conroe going?" she asked.

"Oh, he wouldn't eat with the likes of us. He eats in a nice restaurant up the street," May replied. "But be thankful, Ida. These twenty minutes are the only time we ain't under his eye all the livelong day."

Jemina soon found out that the women took advantage of Conroe's absence. They chatted among themselves, a litany of complaints against Lester Gilroy and Bully Conroe. Jemina listened as closely as she could without being too obvious. How she longed for paper and pen! She tried to store everything in her memory, hoping she wouldn't forget anything. Their complaints ranged from the amount of money Gilroy paid and the sorry working conditions to Conroe's penchant for fondling the younger women.

Shortly before their twenty minutes had expired, Jemina whispered to May, "From what I hear, you all have many things to complain about. Why don't you complain to someone else, instead of just among yourselves?"

May gave her an incredulous look. "Complain to who? Bully or Gilroy? Some have tried that, and they were out the door before they got all the words out."

"Well, to the authorities, then?"

"Some have tried that, too. Word always gets back to Gilroy." May laughed harshly. "The authorities don't care a hoot what goes on along Hester Street. Gilroy makes garments for the fine gents and ladies uptown. If things were made better for us here the dandies and their ladies would have to pay more for their clothes. You think they want that to happen?"

They were interrupted by the reappearance of Bert Conroe. He towered over them from the top step; his shadow falling across Jemina gave her a sudden chill in spite of the heat.

Conroe clapped his hands together sharply. "Time to get back to work, ladies! You've idled away enough time."

As she trudged to the lodging house after dark that evening, Jemina could not remember when she had been so exhausted. It took an effort of will to drag one foot after the other; and at the lodging house the three flights of stairs seemed endless.

She went to her room first, washed in cold water and changed into fresh clothing. Then she went next door. Marigold was already home and was preparing supper for them.

The children ran to Jemina, clamoring for attention; and Marigold came toward her, wiping her hands on the apron tied around her waist. For the first time Jemina realized that Marigold and her children had bloomed in just the one short week she had been with them. The good, healthy food had added a little weight and put new color in their faces. It made everything she had gone through worthwhile, Jemina concluded.

"How did it go, Jemina?" Marigold asked.

With a sigh Jemina sank into the nearest chair, a child at each knee. "It was awful, Marigold! I honestly don't know how any of you manage to endure."

Marigold made a clucking sound. "I was fearful it would be bad for you. I well remember my first few days in a task shop."

"Does it ever get any easier?"

"Some, but not much. Some things you do grow accustomed to, but others you do not. Well..." Marigold turned away. "Supper is about ready. A good hot meal will make you feel better, and then to bed with you."

JEMINA COULDN'T GO TO BED immediately after supper, as much as she wanted to. She sat up until midnight, until her eyes burned so badly she could scarcely see, writing down all that she had seen and heard that day. She did not dare postpone the note taking for fear she might forget something of importance.

Consequently, when she crawled out of bed at five the next morning to go to work, she was exhausted.

Thus the pattern was set—bent over the sewing table twelve hours a day until her fingers bled, coming home at night to write until she fell asleep—a cycle that could have been conceived by demons of hell.

Yet, a sense of growing excitement kept her going. As the first article began to take shape in her mind, Jemina knew that it was going to be powerful, by far the best thing she had ever written; and if the articles had the effect she hoped for, it would be worth all the torture, all the risks she was taking.

Several times during the next few days, Lester Gilroy came into the shop, but as far as Jemina could tell he paid little heed to her; and she tried not to call attention to herself, hoping that he could not feel the hate and loathing for him that burned deep within her.

During their brief lunch periods she managed to casually discuss the plight of the garment workers with all of the women; they seemed to suspect nothing and talked freely. In fact, they appeared grateful for a willing ear. Jemina heard horror story after horror story, not only about Gilroy's operations but about others almost as bad. Unlike May Carter, few of the women remained very long in one place. They were constantly seeking employment elsewhere, hoping for better wages and better working conditions and rarely finding them.

All of this was raw material for her articles, and she could look forward to an end to her agony. At the end of the first week she calculated that in one more week, she would have collected more than enough material for her pieces.

And then came that fateful day when Lester Gilroy recognized her.

"You're here under false pretenses, girl, and I aim to find out the reason why," Gilroy bellowed as he gestured for Jemina to get up from her chair. "You come along with me. Now!"

Chapter Twenty-Two

BRACKETED BY GILROY AND CONROE, Jemina was escorted to the staircase at the rear of the basement. The stairs led to the ground floor.

By the time they had reached the steps, some of the shock had worn off, and acutely aware of the danger she was in, Jemina found her voice. "Where are you taking me? You have no right to do this!"

"This is my shop, and I have any right that I say I have," Gilroy said in a grating voice. "Now, come along, and don't make a fuss."

"No, I won't do it!"

She started to whirl about, and Gilroy called a warning. "Bert!"

Bully Conroe seized Jemina around the waist in a powerful grip. "Now, girl, don't make a fuss. Either come along nice or I'll drag you."

Jemina shot one despairing glance around the room. With one exception the women were all bent over their worktables. The one exception was May Carter, who had turned around and was staring at her.

"May!" Jemina cried. "Help me!"

Conroe clamped a sweaty hand over her mouth and began to drag her bodily up the stairs. Jemina fought hard, but Conroe was too strong for her. There was a sour, unwashed odor about him that was nauseating, and Jemina was close to fainting by the time they reached the top of the stairs.

Gilroy opened the door and stood back while Conroe wrestled Jemina through. Then he closed and bolted the door. "Take her into my office, Bert."

Jemina had been told that Gilroy used the ground floor for his office and for goods storage.

Conroe hauled her down the short corridor and flung her headlong into a small room. Off balance, she fell and skidded across the floor. Her head struck the far wall and for a moment she lost consciousness.

She came to as she was being pulled to her feet. Conroe sat her in a hardback chair and gripped her shoulders painfully. The room held little in the way of furniture—a rolltop desk and two chairs.

Gilroy took up a position before her, his feet planted wide apart, towering over her menacingly. "Now, girl, suppose you tell me what this is about. Why are you here?"

"I am trying to make a living, like the others."

"Do you take me for a fool?" he said in a snarling voice. "You are a lady, not a seamstress."

"I have fallen on hard times. Ask Mr. Conroe. I do good work."

"The quality of your work has nothing to do with it. You are here for some other purpose. I thought you looked familiar the first time I laid eyes on you. Then I remembered. I saw you in Philadelphia, dressed to the nines. That newspaper fellow, Owen Thursday—do you have something to do with him? Are you nosing around here for him, trying to gather information to do me harm in the newspapers?"

"This has nothing to do with Mr. Thursday," she said defiantly. "He knows nothing about my being..." She quickly clamped her lips shut.

Gilroy smiled unpleasantly. "Who *does* know about you being here then?"

"A number of people know. So if you try to harm me, they will..."

"You're lying! Whatever the reason you're here, nobody knows about it." He whipped his hand around, striking her across the face with the back of his hand. Jemina felt her lip split, and the brassy taste of blood filled her mouth.

Gilroy leaned closer. "Tell me! What are you doing in my shop?"

Jemina kept her lips stubbornly shut; she could feel the blood trickling down her chin.

"Damn you, girl, answer me!"

When Jemina still said nothing, Gilroy started to bring his arm around again. In a desperate lunge, Jemina tore out of Conroe's grip; and bringing both hands up, she caught Gilroy's right arm just above the elbow. Digging her fingers into the material of his shirt, she hung on. With a roar of rage Gilroy jerked his arm free. The shirt ripped from her fingers, tearing all the way up to his shoulder.

Conroe managed to capture Jemina's shoulders again and slammed her back down onto the chair, but she scarcely noticed. She was staring at Gilroy's bared arm in disbelief. There, on his right biceps, was the tattoo of a ship, exactly as Owen had described it. Could it be? But there must be hundreds of men with similar tattoos....

"What are you staring at, girl?" Gilroy snarled. "Haven't you ever seen a tattoo before?" He rubbed at his arm. "You have ruined a perfectly good shirt!"

Jemina looked up into his face. He was about the right age to be Owen's father, and now that she looked closely, there was a vague resemblance. This man's features were coarse, and he had none of Owen's grace and charm; yet the rather prominent nose was the same shape. And the full lips, while they had a brutal cast and looked as if they never smiled, were very similar to Owen's.

"You're staring at my face!" Gilroy leaned so close to her that she could feel his hot breath. "There, take a good look, so you'll know it again, if you ever get the chance." He straightened up. "Are you going to tell me what you're doing in my shop?"

For a dangerous moment Jemina was on the verge of blurting out the truth. Just in time she realized that would be a fatal mistake, compounding the one she had already made in coming here against all advice. Now, when it was too late, she fully recognized that Gilroy was a dangerous man, fully capable of harming her, even killing her.

"I have already told you," she said in a voice that trembled slightly in spite of all her efforts to keep it steady. "I am here to earn my livelihood."

Gilroy's face grew taut in anger, and he raised his hand to strike her again, then let it drop.

Conroe tightened his fingers cruelly on Jemina's shoulders and said eagerly, "Could be I should rough her up a little, Mr. Gilroy. Time I'm through with her, she'll be begging to talk to us."

Lester Gilroy looked thoughtful for a moment, fingers caressing the tattoo. Finally, he shook his head. "Not yet. I remember her as real pretty under them dingy clothes she's wearing. Hate to have her all roughed up just yet. Could be I'll be wanting to see how she looks without any clothes, before I'm done with her."

A hot spark began to glow in his deep-set eyes as his gaze roamed over her. Jemina shuddered and tried to withdraw within herself.

Gilroy nodded in agreement. "For the time being we'll lock her in that storage room in the back. Leave her alone in there overnight to think a bit. She'll probably be ready to tell us the truth come morning. Meanwhile, Bert—" Gilroy gestured "—ask around among those women downstairs. See what they can tell you about what pretty here has been up to since she's been here. See if she's been asking questions she shouldn't."

Conroe said, "What do I tell them has happened to her?"

"Tell them nothing," Gilroy growled. "It's none of their damn business."

"They might wonder when she doesn't come back."

"All right, just tell them we discharged her." Gilroy grinned wolfishly. "They should be used to that by now."

"All right, Mr. Gilroy. Come along, girlie."

Conroe picked Jemina up from the chair by her arms and gave her a shove toward the door, then caught her arm again in a tight grip and marched her down the corridor to the very end, stopping before the last door. Conroe unlocked it, pushed it open just enough to shove Jemina inside. She heard the key turn as he relocked the door.

With a growing sense of despair, Jemina glanced around her small prison. There was one tiny window, round and about the size of the porthole of a ship, set high on the outside wall. The glass was long unwashed, letting in just enough light for Jemina to see how confined she was. The room was filled almost to overflowing with bolts of dress goods stacked to the ceiling, leaving a narrow aisle down the center.

She looked again at the window. She could see that it wasn't large enough for her to squeeze through. Perhaps she could stack the bolts of cloth high enough to stand on so she could break the window and scream for help. . . .

She whirled at the sound of a key in the lock, her heart thudding with fear, remembering the lecherous look Gilroy had given her.

Bully Conroe's grinning face appeared in the doorway. "Thought you might need this before the night's over." With his toe he nudged a chamber pot into the room. "We like to keep things neat and tidy." His glance went to the window. "Be you thinking of smashing that window and yelling for help, girlie, forget it. That window opens onto an alley. Ain't a soul back there to hear you."

As he started to close the door, she said quickly, "Wait!"

He hesitated, staring at her silently.

"If I'm to be locked up in here all night, I'll need food and water."

"Need, is it?" he said with his hacking cough. "You'll be needing nothing Mr. Gilroy don't give you. He said nothing about food and water, and he won't be back till morning." He laughed coarsely.

"Sleep tight, girlie. By morning, you'll be ready to tell Mr. Gilroy what he wants to know, or it'll be the worse for you."

He shut the door, and the key turned in the lock with a sound of finality.

Jemina stared at the door in despair for several moments. Then she gave her head a shake, realizing just how close and hot it was in this small room; she was already sheathed in perspiration.

At least she wouldn't have to sleep on the hard floor. She moved a few bolts of cloth, arranging them to make a bed. Exhausted from the heat and the tension, she sat down. She removed her shoes, unbuttoned her shirtwaist and started removing the rest of her clothing, seeking some relief from the heat. Then she paused, remembering again that look in Gilroy's eyes. What if he should decide to come back? If he found her with most of her clothes removed, it might just be enough to cause him to take her forcibly.

The light through the grimy window was already fading. She lay down on the bolts of cloth, making herself as comfortable as possible. But try as she might, she could not calm her racing thoughts as she contemplated how rash, how foolish, she had been.

She had placed herself at the mercy of Lester Gilroy. She could see no hope of rescue. The seamstresses in the shop would be told that she had been discharged. Why shouldn't they believe Conroe's lie? They saw women discharged every day for little reason; and if they never saw her again, they would think very little of it.

And nobody back in Philadelphia had any clear idea where she was or what she was doing. She had rushed headlong into this situation, without a single glance behind her, without even a thought of leaving word of where she was going. Aunt Hester, believing the lie that *Godey's Lady's Book* was sending her to New York on an assignment, would not begin to be concerned until after some time had passed. And Sarah Hale would undoubtedly be furious and wash her hands of Jemina Benedict. And why should she not? She would simply think Jemina a headstrong girl who had rushed off on an unauthorized assignment.

And the stark truth was, Jemina thought drearily, there had never been any hope that the *Lady's Book* would publish the articles, no matter how brilliant the pieces were. Jemina had known this, deep down, all along, and had simply ignored it. Even if, by some miracle, she should escape Gilroy's clutches, it would all be for nothing.

And now here she was, hopelessly trapped and soon to pay the penalty for her foolhardiness.

Long after dark, thirsty, her stomach growling with hunger, she finally fell into an uneasy sleep. Nightmares haunted her slumber. She was cornered in a cul-de-sac, and a coughing Bully Conroe was stalking her with a gigantic pair of scissors, which he clicked open and shut like cruel jaws as he advanced on her.

And then she was in an endless ocean, swimming desperately for her life, pursued relentlessly by a sailing vessel. In the time warp of dreams, the ship became Lester Gilroy, striding the water like a leviathan, bulky body naked and covered with the tattoos of ships, which moved as his muscles flexed. Gilroy roared obscene laughter, his gargantuan strides closing the distance between them. . . .

She awoke with a scream dying in her throat. Gray daylight seeped in through the window. She felt grimy and itchy, and her mouth was parched.

She went still as she heard the sound of a door slamming and then heavy footsteps, causing the floor to vibrate ever so slightly. They were coming for her!

Hastily, she buttoned on her shoes, then her shirt-waist and was on her feet, head unbowed, when the door flew open, crashing back against the wall.

Gilroy loomed in the doorway, leering at her. He stepped into the room and she saw that he was alone.

"Well, pretty, did you sleep well?"

"I slept well enough," she said steadily.

"Are you ready to tell me what you were doing sneaking around in my shop?"

"I have already told you everything there is to tell. When are you going to let me go? My friends will be wondering what has happened to me."

"Friends?" he said jeeringly. "Those women downstairs? They're not your friends."

She looked straight into his eyes. "I have friends back in Philadelphia."

He shook his head, and what passed for a mocking smile touched his lips. "If what you say is true, if you're here earning your living, you have no friends. Otherwise, they would see that you didn't have to work here. And if you *do* have friends, that means you're lying as to why you're here." He took a menacing step toward her. "I want the truth, girl. I am weary of toying with you."

"I have told you the truth. There is nothing else I can tell you, so you might as well let me go."

"You'll go when I decide. I can turn you over to Conroe; he has ways of making people talk. His name, Bully, is well earned.'' He looked at her in speculation, that spark beginning to glow in his eyes. ''But after he finishes with you, you won't be so pretty. Before he spoils that beauty, I have something else in mind for you. I've laid awake half the night thinking of you here all alone, pretty.''

Without taking his gaze from her, he backed up, closed the door and then began to advance upon her again.

Jemina felt tight with fear, and she began to retreat before him, determined to fight as hard as she could. Then, with two quick steps he was upon her.

She screamed and backed away again. Her feet struck one of the bolts of cloth she had used for a bed, and she fell back on them. Gilroy stood over her, his eyes glittering. In falling, her skirt had rucked up, and she hastily pulled it down.

''Why bother to cover up, pretty? I'm going to see it all in just a minute.''

Frantically, she cast about for a way to escape him. The door—he had closed it but hadn't locked it! If she could manage to get past him . . .

Looking between his spread legs, she saw the door slowly opening and her heart sank. It had to be Bully Conroe!

Then Gilroy grunted sharply in pain and straightened up, spinning around and to one side.

Jemina gasped, for it was Owen, who stood there with his cane still raised. Never taking his gaze from Gilroy, he said, ''Are you all right, Jemina?''

Feeling weak with relief, Jemina sat up and moved back against the wall for support. ''Yes. But thank God you came when you did.''

Gilroy drew in his breath sharply. "You! I know you. You're that newspaper snoop who sullied my name in your paper!"

"I wrote about you in the *Ledger*, true, but I scarcely think I sullied your name. That would be impossible to do."

"This girl—that's why she's here. You're working together."

"That's right, Gilroy, and for what you've just tried to do to her, I'm going to give you the thrashing of your life, you proper bastard!"

Jemina's glance had been darting from one man to the other, and she was more and more convinced that they were father and son, as impossible as that seemed. Someone not looking for the resemblance might have missed it, but Jemina could see it. Flesh out Gilroy's bony face, soften the mouth, and the resemblance was quite noticeable.

Gilroy had backed up a step, his eyes flashing. "I warn you! Do not lay a hand on me!"

"Oh, I wouldn't dirty my hands with the likes of you, Gilroy. I intend to use this." Owen brandished his cane. "The blow I just delivered was nothing to what you'll feel before I'm finished with you."

Gilroy bent slightly, his right hand flashing down to his boot. When his hand came up again, light glittered off the wicked-looking knife in his grip.

"Ha!" Owen whistled softly between his teeth. "The fangs are shown at last."

He pressed the handle of his cane, and with a snicking sound, a narrow blade slid out of the end.

Jemina watched, scarcely daring to breath, as the two men circled each other warily, two unlikely swordsmen locked in a deadly duel.

Gilroy was clearly familiar with the use of a knife, and he charged fearlessly, slashing at Owen, who moved in and out with a dancer's grace. Each time the knife missed him, he laughed in Gilroy's face, until the other man was beside himself with rage.

Finally, with a roar of fury, he charged at Owen, bringing the knife flashing up toward Owen's belly. Jemina stifled a scream. At the last instant Owen slipped aside and Gilroy stumbled past him, fetching up against the wall beneath the window.

He wheeled instantly, just in time to face Owen, who had moved lithely up behind him. Slightly off balance from his lunge, Gilroy desperately tried to swing the knife around to meet Owen's charge. Owen brought his cane slashing down across the garment maker's wrist, and the knife flew out of Gilroy's hand.

"Well, now, friend, your fangs are out," Owen said with a taunting laugh. He brought the sword cane up, the tip against Gilroy's throat. "If you have a God, Gilroy, you had better say your prayers to him, for I am going to run you through."

"No!" Jemina cried. She stepped between them, placing her hand on the cane.

Owen scowled at her. "Get out of the way, Jemina."

"No, Owen, don't kill him. He's..." It was on the tip of her tongue to tell Owen that Gilroy was his father, but she stopped herself in time. If Owen were to discover that his father, whom he had thought lost at sea years ago, was still alive, it might destroy him.

"I don't understand," Owen said in puzzlement. "If I hadn't come along when I did, he might have killed you. And you want me to let him go?"

"I shall get even with him," she said grimly. "I have gathered all the material I need. When he is exposed for the scoundrel that he is, that will be punishment enough."

Owen's killing rage had run its course now. With a shrug he said, "Whatever you say, my dear. You're the one who had to go through the unpleasantness." Still holding the tip of the sword cane at Gilroy's throat, Owen reached out to draw Jemina against him and began to back out of the room with her. "We're going now, Gilroy. You stay here until we're gone. If you're hoping your henchman, the gent downstairs, will come charging up here, disabuse yourself." Owen grinned mirthlessly. "I've already encountered him, and he's sleeping for a bit."

Gilroy glared at them in frustrated fury while they backed out of the room. As he closed the door, Owen noticed that the key was in the lock.

With a laugh he turned the key. "That should hold him for a bit."

Owen took Jemina's arm. "Come on, let's go!"

As they hurried down the hall, Jemina said, "I'm glad you came when you did, Owen. I've always thought I could take care of myself, but that man back there is a monster!"

"I warned you about him, didn't I?" he growled. "You never listen."

"You were right, I was foolish," she said meekly, then brightened. "But I got the material I wanted, Owen. It's enough to put him out of business. How did you know I was being held up there?"

"A woman downstairs told me they took you up there yesterday. The others wouldn't talk, wouldn't even look at me, but this one spoke right up."

"That must be May Carter."

They were through the door now and going downstairs. Jemina saw Bully Conroe lying on the floor, unmoving.

At the bottom of the stairs Jemina headed toward May's table; all of the seamstresses were bent industriously over their worktables, as though nothing untoward had occurred. May, hearing them coming, stopped work and faced around.

She began to smile. "Well, Mr. Thursday, I see you found her."

"Thank you, May," Jemina said fervently. "You may very well have saved my life."

"Well, when you didn't come back yesterday, I thought of reporting you missing to the police, but I half believed Bully when he said you'd been discharged, since it's happened so many times before."

"There is one thing that will likely happen. You will probably be discharged, because of me."

May shrugged. "Don't fret about it, dearie. Like I told you, I'm the best shirtmaker on Hester Street. I can always find employment."

"And I have a confession to make, May. My name isn't Ida Morgan. It's Jemina Benedict, and I am a contributing editor for *Godey's Lady's Book*. The reason I took a job here was to investigate the terrible conditions you all work under. I will be writing several articles about this. To do them right I had to actually experience the conditions personally. When they are published, I am confident that things will improve in all the task shops."

May looked skeptical. "I'm not about to hold my breath, dearie. Things have been published before."

"I'm sure those pieces weren't as strong as what I will be writing."

"Well, whatever happens, we all appreciate your trying." May peered at her slyly. "You didn't fool me for a minute. I knew all along you were up to something. The way you sew, you would starve to death trying to earn your living."

Jemina had to laugh; then she bent down and planted a kiss on the other woman's cheek. "It was nice knowing you, May. We must go now, but I will try to see you again."

Just outside the door, Owen said dourly, "Jemina, the eternal optimist! Someday a windmill is going to come crashing down on your head. It came damn close this time, you know."

"I know, but it didn't. Owen, I have collected some marvelous material on this rotten business!" she cried exuberantly. "You are going to be proud of me!"

A quick glance about told her that they were unobserved. She threw her arms around him, hugging him fiercely. "I love you, darling, and I am glad to see you!" She pressed her mouth to his.

He returned the kiss with passion, and they stood locked together for a few moments. Then Owen pulled back slightly. "This is hardly the time or the place. Any minute now your Mr. Gilroy may break out of that room. We haven't pulled his fangs, remember, just blunted them for the moment. He might shoot us both, should he find us out here like this."

"He wouldn't dare, not after all that has happened."

"With you letting him know in there that you're hoping to expose his operation in print? Don't wager on it, my dear. He just might be desperate enough. Anyway, no need to take any chances."

With his arm around her, Owen hustled her up the steps and to the street. "Perhaps we should go directly to the train station...."

"No! I have to pick up my notes at the lodging house, and I must say goodbye to Marigold Tyler. Without her assistance, I could not have carried off the masquerade as long as I did."

As they started walking along the busy street, Jemina said, "You have yet to tell me how you found me."

"It wasn't all that difficult. When I came home two days ago, I went to call on you. Your aunt told me you'd been sent to New York on assignment for the *Lady's Book*. That didn't sound right to me, so I paid Sarah a visit, and she told me about her last meeting with you, how you had tried to convince her to let you do the garment workers' story. Then I recalled our conversation about Lester Gilroy.

"So, I took the train here last night. I was at Gilroy's shop early this morning. I went in asking about you, had a brief set-to with the foreman, and then May Carter told me how they had hustled you upstairs yesterday. I ran up just as you screamed. The rest you know."

Jemina said, "I suppose Sarah is angry with me?"

"Well, she isn't pleased with you, you can be sure," he said with a short laugh. "She feels that you have betrayed her confidence in you, that you acted irresponsibly."

Jemina sighed. "She's right, of course." Then she burst out, "But this is something I had to do, Owen! As for my acting irresponsibly, I can understand how she might feel that way, and I am sorry. Sarah has been good to me, and I have no wish to hurt her. Yet I felt that it is also my responsibility as a journalist to help people like Marigold Tyler and the other garment workers, if it is in my power to do so."

Owen glanced at her sidelong. "Surely you're not still thinking that Louis Godey will consent to publish your articles?"

"No," she said dejectedly. "Locked up in that room last night, I had some time to think, and I realized that he will never agree."

"Then it looks as though you went through all of this for nothing."

"Not so. I will get them published somewhere."

"Always the optimist. Where, for hell's sake?"

"Well, I was thinking about that, too," she said slowly. "I thought you could help me there. Perhaps you could talk to your editor at the *Ledger*...."

He stopped short, staring at her. "In the *Ledger*? Jemina, you are truly unbelievable!"

They stood in the midst of the heavy pedestrian traffic, which had to divide and go around them.

"Why not? I am a good writer, Owen. You have said so yourself. Sarah told me that it was the type of material that a newspaper would publish. And the *Ledger* did publish a story about the plight of the garment workers some years ago. I told you about that."

He was silent for a long moment, still staring at her. "I suppose that if I don't agree, you will keep at me until I do."

"I certainly don't intend to just give up. If you won't help me, I'll try other newspapers, the ones here in New York. Perhaps the man you talked about, Horace Greeley." She smiled suddenly. "Think of how your editor would feel if Mr. Greeley did publish the articles and they received the attention they deserve."

Owen threw back his head and laughed heartily. "You believe they will be that good?"

"I do, I really do," she said firmly.

"All right." He threw up his hands. "I'll do my best for you, Jemina. I may be able to sell Thomas on the idea. I happen to know that he hates Lester Gilroy and his ilk with a passion."

They resumed walking, Owen holding her hand now. Jemina's spirits soared. Perhaps it had not been all for nothing, after all!

In an offhand manner Owen said, "Sarah told me something else that might interest you. She has yet to tell Louis Godey of your perfidy. She likes you, Jemina; she likes your work. I think she was trying to tell me that you might still have your job if you want it."

"That is nice of her. Sarah is a dear person."

"So?" He glanced at her. "Will you go back to the *Lady's Book*?"

"I'll have to think about it. If only they would publish something besides those sweet and light pieces!"

"It will never happen, Jemina."

"I love working on the *Book*, so I suppose I will go back. If only newspapers would hire woman journalists!" she added in a burst of passion.

"Once I would have said that would never happen, but now that I've come to know you, my dear, I wouldn't wager against it."

"It would be nice if we both had positions on the same newspaper," she said, a wistful note in her voice, "so we could work together."

He gave her a sharp look, then put an arm around her shoulders, pulling her against him. He said softly, "That *would* be nice, Jemina. Who knows? It might happen in the future."

They were in front of the lodging house now. As they went up the steep stairs to the third floor, Owen said, "What a depressing place! How could you stand it here?"

"I felt that I had to live in the same surroundings as the garment workers. Otherwise, how could I truly understand their situation?"

At Marigold's door Jemina held Owen back. "Marigold won't be home yet, but I want you to meet someone."

She knocked. After a moment there was the sound of running feet inside, and the door was flung wide.

Robert and Molly shouted in delight at the sight of Jemina and ran to her. She knelt and pulled them close.

Looking over their heads at Owen, she said, "These are Marigold's two children. Aren't they adorable?" Her gaze grew intent. "How do you feel about having children, Owen?"

EPILOGUE

AFTER FIFTY YEARS as an editor, Sarah Josepha Hale retired in 1877 and died two years later, at the age of ninety.

Louis Godey died in 1878.

Lester Gilroy was forced out of business due to Jemina's searing series of articles, published in the *Philadelphia Ledger*. He spent five years in prison after being convicted of assault upon a business associate.

Marigold Tyler, with encouragement and financial aid from Jemina, became the first woman foreman in a task shop and later married a greengrocer. Her son, Robert, went into his stepfather's business, and her daughter, Molly, eventually became a well-known novelist of women's books.

Warren Barricone and his wife, Alice, moved to a small town in New Mexico Territory, where Warren started a successful newspaper and his wife slowly regained her health.

And in the *Philadelphia Ledger*, in 1851, the following item appeared in the social column: "The *Philadelphia Ledger* would like to take this occasion to congratulate Mr. and Mrs. Owen Thursday upon the birth of twins, a boy and a girl, last evening at 7:00 p.m.

"Regular readers of this paper know Owen Thursday through his popular column and for his book, *The Goldfields of California*; and readers will be aware of Mrs. Thursday, writing under the name Jemina Benedict, for her powerful series of articles exposing the many injustices perpetrated by the task-shop operators in the garment industry. The Thursdays are also known for their very popular Sunday-afternoon soirees, where the literary lights of our fair city come to gather. All of us here at the *Philadelphia Ledger*, as well as their countless admirers, join in wishing them the greatest happiness and success upon this, the beginning of their new family.''

Dear Friends and Readers:

I have had many requests from my readers for another contemporary romantic suspense novel like *Midnight Whispers*, or *Midnight Lavender*, and so my next novel for Worldwide Library, *Mirrors*, coming out in May 1988, will be such a book.

Mirrors is the story of Julie Malone, a young woman who knows nothing of her origin or family background until she turns sixteen, but who has found happiness and security with her adopted parents and her peaceful life in a small Eastern town in Connecticut.

At twenty-four, content with her family, her job and Ken Dawson, the man she intends to marry, she receives a letter that changes her life; a letter that informs her she is, in all likelihood, the last surviving child of an old and wealthy Key West family, the Devereaux. As such, she is heir to an extremely large trust fund. Her grandmother—if Julie is indeed Suellen Devereaux, the missing girl—wishes Julie to come to Key West so that her identity may be proven.

Reluctantly Julie makes the journey and enters a lush and strange new world, where she meets the few remaining members of a family very different from her conservative foster parents: a dying grandmother, a stern great-aunt and her father's eccentric sister.

She also meets Sheldon Phipps, of Henderson, Caldicott and Phipps, the firm that handles the Devereaux's affairs. Sheldon is a pleasantly attractive man who becomes her one anchor in this sea of new and startling information and experience. The lush beauty of the Keys, the awakening knowledge that her past conceals a dreadful secret, and the unexpected dangers she finds surrounding her, make Julie feel she is living an exotic dream—a dream that threatens her sanity and, very possibly, may destroy her.

I hope you will join Julie/Suellen in beautiful Key West and be with her as she struggles to make sense of the three separate phases of her existence, and the threats to her life and sanity that send her fleeing alone and frightened across the country.

Love,

Patricia Matthews

The passionate saga
that began with SARAH continues in the compelling,
unforgettable story of

Elizabeth

MAURA SEGER

In the aftermath of the Civil War, a divided nation—and two
tempestuous hearts—struggle to become one.

A soaring novel of passion and destiny
as magnificent as the mighty redwoods.

REDWOOD EMPIRE

A.E. MAXWELL

He could offer her the priceless gift of security but could not erase the
sweet agony of desire that ruled her days and tormented her nights.